"You're lying. . . ."

Kit took advantage of Aurelia's gasp to steal another kiss and began to mount the stairs. She wanted to slap his face but her arms around his neck only tightened her hold on him, defying her own conscious wishes. And somewhere deep inside her that incendiary spark of secret desire blossomed again.

At the top of the stairs, Kit stopped and once again released her mouth, this time leaving her breathless with a different kind of outrage.

"I want you, Aurelia. I know you want me." He kept his voice to a harsh whisper and carried her into one of the cold, dark bedrooms. "I can feel your wanting, I can smell it, I can taste it."

She licked her lips at the suggestive image.

"You cannot lie to me, Aurelia; do not lie to yourself."

Books by Linda Hilton

Moonsilver
Touchstone

Published by POCKET BOOKS

LINDA HILTON

TOUCHSTONE

POCKET BOOKS
New York London Toronto Sydney Tokyo Singapore

An *Original* Publication of POCKET BOOKS

POCKET BOOKS, a division of Simon & Schuster Inc.
1230 Avenue of the Americas, New York, NY 10020

ISBN: 978-1-4516-7764-5

First Pocket Books printing March 1996

10 9 8 7 6 5 4 3 2 1

POCKET and colophon are registered trademarks of Simon & Schuster Inc.

Front cover illustration by Danilo Ducak

Printed in the U.S.A.

For three friends who should never have had to wait so long for this completely inadequate but nonetheless heartfelt thanks for their support and encouragement throughout the years: Mary Brockway, Mary Burkhardt, and Cheryl Rothwell. For Doug, who has done so much more than put up with me; for Rachel and Kevin, even if they aren't impressed; and for Cindy, Falstaff, Pixie, Gina, Cindy, Dingo, Rochester, and Gibson.

TOUCHSTONE

1

Nethergate Hall
The North of England—November 1819

ONCE AGAIN, THE THUD OF IRON AGAINST ANCIENT OAK ECHOED through Nethergate. Three times the knocker fell, with an eerie persistence that shattered the afternoon quiet.

"No one calls here uninvited," Aurelia Phillips murmured to the maid who hurried beside her down a chilly, gloomy corridor. "And all who have been invited are already here."

"Yes, miss," the maid replied breathlessly. "That's why I come to get you before I opened the door. No tellin' who might be out there, day like this."

Aurelia did not need any reminder of the miserable weather that had confined her and the other occupants of Nethergate indoors. Never warm even under the most sunny skies, the ancient seat of the dukes of Winterburn became cold and cheerless as a tomb on stormy days. She pulled the edge of her shawl closer around her neck and stepped up her pace almost to a run, in a hurry to dispatch whoever knocked on the door and then return to the comfort of a small, cozy drawing room with a roaring fire.

She and the maid had just reached the entrance hall when the great iron knocker fell again, with the same triple rap that seemed to say the caller had no intention of departing until someone answered the summons. Almost as an echo, a shiver rippled through Aurelia.

The maid jumped forward to turn the old key and lift the latch at Aurelia's signal. Bracing herself against the onslaught of the storm, Aurelia nodded. The maid pulled the door open with barely a sigh of well-oiled hinges.

A gust of frigid wind swirled into the hall, nearly enough to extinguish the taper Aurelia held. She had to let go of her shawl to cup her free hand around the fragile flame.

At first she saw only two silhouettes against the backdrop of fog and storm-driven sleet. They stood in the shelter of the doorway arch cut into a stone wall a mere six feet thick, protected from the worst of the icy rain though the wind whipped their greatcoats around their legs. Behind them waited a pair of obviously miserable horses, heads down, tails to the elements.

Without a word to the two men, Aurelia turned to the maid and snapped, "Send word to the stables at once that the horses must be seen to immediately. Blankets and warm gruel for the poor beasts. And no dawdling, do you understand?"

The girl bobbed her head and scurried off, skirts raised. Aurelia was tempted to follow her, to make sure her orders were carried out, when a masculine sniffle and a deep-throated cough returned her attention to the shadowy figures still waiting on the doorstep.

"Perhaps we'd be better off going with the horses, Emil," the taller of the two remarked.

Taller by a head, Aurelia realized in the second it took her to recover from a furious blush and find her voice again. And broad-shouldered beneath his caped greatcoat that dripped frozen rain and sleet onto the stones at his feet.

"Please, forgive me," she stammered. "Come in, come in out of the storm."

When they had stepped past her and she had closed and bolted the heavy door, she allowed herself another moment to study the men who now seemed to take up an enormous amount of space in the cavernous gloom of Nethergate's entrance hall.

To judge by their clothes, they were a gentleman and his servant, but Aurelia had noted the unmistakable colonial accent of the speaker. She suddenly wished, as she walked around to face them, that she had not dismissed Katy so quickly. Being alone with these two left her uneasy. Perhaps it was the fact that they had brought their luggage with them, giving the impression they fully expected to be invited to stay.

And having welcomed them inside and ordered their horses stabled, she could hardly now turn them away.

The American did not in any case give her the chance to.

"I've come to see the Duke of Winterburn," he told her, as though her own lack of greeting negated any need for politeness on his part. He removed one of his ice-coated gloves and reached into an inner pocket to retrieve a silver case from which he extracted a card. "Mr. Christopher Ballantyne, of Charleston, South Carolina."

He seemed inordinately proud of his oh-so-ordinary title, having put the barest emphasis on it. Familiar with that colonial snobbery, Aurelia had no difficulty giving him a reply he was sure to find not to his liking.

"His Grace is not receiving visitors, Mr. Ballantyne."

She did not doubt for one second that he could have brushed her aside with one hand and gone in search of the duke himself. The way he looked at her told her he, too, was well aware of his strength and stature, but he merely reached once more into his pocket and this time produced a sealed envelope.

"Then I should like this delivered to him and I will await his reply."

Aurelia had once again clasped her shawl more tightly around her against the pervasive chill. She hesitated to take the proffered message, as though that would validate the stranger's presence in Nethergate, but the sound of approaching voices told her the question of his staying the night had already been determined. Releasing her grip on the woolen wrap, she took the envelope from Ballantyne's outstretched hand and tucked it into her own pocket just as a very noisy group of people entered the quiet of the entrance hall.

The woman who led them glided to a halt, then waited until her entourage had fanned out around her.

"Why, Aurelia, you did not tell us you had invited guests of your own!"

Aurelia stepped back, not certain whether it was more interesting to watch the stranger's reaction to the woman who blatantly assessed him with appreciative eyes or to watch the woman herself.

Her voice was equally appreciative, low, seductive, as she asked, "And who is *this* fine gentleman?"

Aurelia cooled her rising temper. "Aunt Serena, may I present Mr. Christopher Ballantyne, of—"

"Of Charleston, South Carolina," Ballantyne finished for her.

Aurelia felt a chill go down her spine at the smile that blossomed on Serena's face, but she continued with the formality of introductions. "Mr. Ballantyne, Mrs. Serena MacKinnon."

She expected him to lift Serena's extended hand to his lips, but he merely nodded in acknowledgment. No answering smile altered his expression, though Aurelia thought she detected the slightest curl of an incipient sneer.

The first of Serena's companions stepped forward, both interrupting the minute drama being played out and demanding his own introduction.

"And Mr. Joshua MacKinnon," Aurelia went on.

They were of an age, she decided, Ballantyne perhaps a year or two older than Joshua's twenty-eight, but any resemblance stopped there. She gauged Ballantyne's height at more than an inch or two over six feet; at least half a foot shorter, Joshua carried the soft weight of easy living, whereas the harsh planes of Ballantyne's facial features hinted at a lifetime of hard work.

Those features revealed no emotions, she discovered, as she introduced him to the others of Serena's coterie, Adam Braisthwaite and Freddie Denholm. He nodded at each name, but the expressionless depth of his dark eyes never changed, his cleanly sculpted lips never smiled. And if Ballantyne was surprised to see a woman surrounded by three men at least ten years her junior, he indicated nothing.

"You *are* spending the night, are you not, Mr. Ballantyne?" Serena asked when at last the introductions had been accomplished.

"I'm not sure," he answered. His voice was a cool, casual growl to her warm purr. "The horses we rode from the village have been, I believe, taken to the stables at this young lady's orders, but we've not yet been invited to stay."

He never looked at Serena, Aurelia noticed, only at her. And though she expected, and indeed deserved, a certain amount of insulting mockery in his tone, she detected none.

In Serena's answer, the accusation and gloating were quite obvious.

"Mr. Ballantyne, you must forgive my niece. I'm afraid she is not accustomed to visitors and sometimes forgets her manners." She paused, smoothing her hand down the skirt of her wine-red velvet dress, as though in an attempt to attract his attention. When that failed, she addressed Aurelia directly without ever taking her eyes from the tall stranger. "My dear, show Mr. Ballantyne and his man to suitable quarters and then have them join us for dinner. This is not London, where a hostess can turn away a caller who comes without the proper credentials and expect him to find shelter at a nearby tavern. I do hope you'll have a pleasant stay at Nethergate, Mr. Ballantyne."

* * *

Kit Ballantyne did not watch Serena MacKinnon depart, her trio of admirers clustered around her like bees around a honeycomb. He had seen her sisters in Charleston and Baltimore, wives and widows enamored of their own power to attract younger men, and he had long ago become immune. Besides, he found the other woman, identified only as Aurelia, far more interesting—and therefore more attractive.

She said nothing to him, merely turned with almost military precision and beckoned him to follow. He had time only to glance at poor Emil to make sure he had caught the signal, too, and then it was a matter of trying to keep up with her, for though she had to take two strides to each of his, she was quickly outdistancing him.

She was not, as her name implied, at all golden. That description applied to Serena MacKinnon, identified as Aurelia's aunt. Where Serena was fair, with blond ringlets tumbling from a carefully casual coiffure, Aurelia was dark. Her hair was lustrous black as a raven's wing and, to judge by the thick braids coiled around her head, long and abundant. The few wisps that escaped hinted at curls, too, but Kit doubted she was one to allow even her hair to give in to such untamed enjoyment. Her skin, especially at the nape of her neck, was the soft cream of ivory, easily showing the slightest blush, which Kit noticed she had done when Serena confronted her.

But her eyes had captivated him beyond anything else, and even now that she walked—or marched, for she had the purposeful stride of a soldier at drill—ahead of him, he remembered their deep, sultry green, like sunlight through a summer forest after rain. She had met his own gaze directly, with no shyness, no coy flirting. Neither did he detect any innocence—only an almost savage honesty.

"Nethergate is not a public inn," she told him over her shoulder as she mounted a long staircase at the end of a longer hallway. "We do not keep rooms readied for chance travelers."

She had led them in the opposite direction from that taken by Serena, and Kit had the distinct impression that they were entering an older, less frequented part of the manor house. The comparatively well lit elegance of the entrance hall had given way to dark corridors and darker stairways. Not having a clear impression of Nethergate from their approach in the storm, Kit soon found himself disoriented by the twists and turns and the girl's hectic pace. Only the sound of Emil's footsteps and gasping breath behind him assured him he had not lost his erstwhile valet, for he dared not take even a second to glance over his shoulder. Aurelia might slip out of his sight if he did.

She halted outside the last door but one in this particular wing. Kit estimated they were on the third and highest floor, if he had counted the flights of stairs correctly, but whether east or west of their entry, he had no idea.

He was not in the least surprised when she opened the door and marched in ahead of him.

She had the only light and went directly to the fireplace, where a stub of candle sat in a pewter stand on the mantel. When she took it down and held the flame to the dusty wick, he noted that her hand trembled. She was shivering in this unheated room, and nearly dropped the taper before the second light gained enough strength to burn on its own.

The light spread rapidly, illuminating a small but adequately furnished room, the kind an upper servant might once have occupied. Any such occupancy must have ended long ago, for every item in sight was covered with a fine layer of dust. Cobwebs, vacated by spiders this time of year, festooned the fireplace and mantel where she set the stub down. But the room was dry, with no leaks in the roof, and with a merry fire crackling in the grate and a bit of supper, Kit supposed they would be as cozy as anywhere on a day like this. He had seen nowhere else to shelter on their way from the village, and nightfall would come all too soon in this weather.

"It will do quite nicely," he said.

She jumped, and again the tall column of wax slipped from her fingers.

"Though I would have preferred something a bit more isolated, further from the rest of the household."

She spun to face him. "But I've put you as far from everyone else as I possibly—"

His laughter was her undoing. She dropped the taper to the floor, splattering molten wax onto the hem of her dress. Kit dropped the sleet-encrusted carpetbag with a thud and grabbed her by the shoulders to pull her away from the danger of her clothes igniting, but the candle snuffed itself out and broke into a dozen pieces.

She seemed to dismiss his concern. Easing her shoulders out of his grasp and turning to gather up the bits of candle from the floor, she said, "Mr. Ballantyne, I am only doing what is necessary to protect my family. You could be a thief and murderer come to kill us in our beds and—"

"—And so you've tucked me safely away in some godforsaken corner of this stone pile. Believe me, Miss Aurelia Whatever-Your-Name-Is, I understand. Truly, after the ride from the inn, this room is a welcome sight."

He knelt beside her, aware now that the cold and rain had seeped through to his skin and he was on the point of shivering. If he did not get into something dry soon and warm himself, he'd likely catch his death without ever seeing the man for whom he had come all the way from Charleston.

She surprised him by refusing to meet his gaze this time. He even tried to touch her, handing her a piece of the candle, but she snatched it from him before there was any contact.

"My behavior was uncalled for," she said as she got to her feet. Hers was an odd apology, unlooked for and given with that same cold honesty he had noted earlier. "This room has not been used for a long time, and I cannot in good conscience allow you and your man to stay here. The linens have not been changed in months, and there could be mice in the pillows. Or they might have gnawed the ropes."

"Afraid the bed will fall?"

"It might."

"Are you always so honest?"

"Yes."

Again he laughed, and this time drew her gaze.

"And what, may I ask, is so funny? Is no one in Charleston, South Carolina, honest?"

"Damn few, Miss—"

Aurelia did not know if he paused because of his language or because he did not know her name. Since she could do nothing about the words he had already spoken or whatever dishonesty the citizens of Charleston had perpetrated against him, she chose to deal with the one problem whose solution was in her power.

"Phillips," she said. "Aurelia Phillips."

"Well, then, Miss Aurelia Phillips," he replied, stepping away from her with military precision that she realized mimicked her own, "we will simply have to test the bed."

His wink told her he fully intended to shock her with his comment, and also that he was only teasing. Still, she could not react quickly enough to stifle her gasp, and nothing stopped the rosy flush that she hoped he could not see in the fragile light.

Nor could anything stop her imagination from bringing into her mind's eye a frighteningly clear picture of herself wrapped in Christopher Ballantyne's arms as he fell backward onto the bed.

She winced at the image and tried to dismiss it, but it refused to leave and she had no idea why. Was it because she had become accustomed to every man ignoring her in favor of Serena, and now she had found one who did not? Or because he was different in so many other ways from anyone she had ever met?

He even laughed at her admission, when most men of her

acquaintance sneered or found it impossible to remain in her company. Perhaps, she thought, he would not treat her confession so lightly if he knew how true it was.

But whatever Christopher Ballantyne thought of her, he did not risk his life and limb on the chancy piece of furniture. Instead he picked up his own valise and the one his unobtrusive servant had carried. Though Aurelia doubted the two pieces of luggage together totaled but half the smaller man's weight, she jumped when Ballantyne hefted them shoulder-high and let them fall to the center of the bed.

The ropes gave a timid squeak, but the bed did not collapse. Dust rose from the faded quilt, and when Aurelia tried to fan the air clear she succeeded only in stirring up more dust and nearly extinguishing their only light.

"That was not a very wise thing to do, Mr. Ballantyne," Aurelia scolded. She stifled one sneeze, but another was building. To forestall it, she lit the longest piece of her broken candle from the one on the mantel. "However, if you are determined this room is satisfactory, I shall see that you are provided with a fire and something to eat and drink."

"And you'll deliver my letter to the duke."

His tone was light, as though laughter still lurked, but she knew he meant exactly what he said—and that he was challenging her boast. He said nothing about Serena's invitation to dinner.

"I will deliver your letter," she promised. "Now, if you will excuse me."

Hoping to maintain some shred of dignity, she hurried to escape before that second sneeze exploded from her—and before Christopher Ballantyne could stop her. She might have succeeded had her brash guest not called after her, "Best give in to it, Miss Phillips, else you're likely to have it sneak up on you and blow out that light. I'd hate for you to have to find your way in the dark."

Standing in the doorway, she contemplated either ignoring him completely or telling him to keep his precious colonial advice to himself. She had almost decided upon the latter when her nose refused to harbor that dust and musty smell any longer.

She sneezed not once but twice, with no delicacy at all. Thanks to Ballantyne's warning, she shielded her candle and then, with his laughter and his poor valet's coughing echoing off Nethergate's walls, Aurelia followed her first inclination and left them both behind her. She wished she could as easily dismiss the feelings of outrage and mortification, but they tagged along at her heels, as faithful as a puppy—or as tenacious as a hungry wolf.

2

EVERY INSTINCT IN AURELIA'S BODY SCREAMED AT HER TO RUN, not walk, to put as much distance as possible between herself and Christopher Ballantyne. His laughter lingered in her ears, not for its cruelty, for she had discerned none, but for the unexpectedly sensual intimacy of its unabashed delight. She could still feel the cold that emanated from his fingers when he handed her the fragment of broken candle. He must have been chilled to the bone and every bit as miserable as the horses she had taken pity on, yet he offered no reproof or complaint when she lodged him in a mean little room with neither fire nor clean linens.

And though he must have known or at least suspected that she would immediately report his arrival to the very person he had crossed an ocean to see, Aurelia somehow did not fear Christopher Ballantyne would follow her.

Why? she wondered as she forced herself to a steady but unhurried pace through the older part of Nethergate to the newer, more elegantly appointed wings. Why had he traveled so far? Surely not to deliver the letter now tucked into her pocket. He could easily have posted it from America, since obviously he did not care whether he himself or someone else actually gave the letter to its intended recipient, else he would not have entrusted it to her.

And why, she asked above all other questions, did Christopher Ballantyne trust her?

That he did made her decidedly uneasy. Or perhaps she felt guilty because of her treatment of him, treatment Serena herself had criticized, to Aurelia's mortification. She determined the best way to assuage her guilt was to see that Ballantyne and his valet were made comfortable. Accosting the first servant she encountered, she gave him explicit instructions designed to make at least some amends for her earlier lack of hospitality.

"Colin, wait," she called to a liveried footman just emerging from a room some ways ahead of her down the long corridor.

When he turned at the sound of his name, there was a weariness to his expression that sent more guilt spiraling through her. The Nethergate staff were unaccustomed to the ways of London society, which the recent influx of visitors had brought with them.

"Two more guests have arrived, Colin," she said as she approached him, keeping her voice low. "I've put them in the old east wing, the last room but one one the third floor."

He raised a graying eyebrow but said nothing.

"I know it's not the most luxurious accommodation, but I had my reasons."

"Certainly, Miss Phillips. I didn't mean—"

She waved off his apology and continued, "I want you to see Mr. Ballantyne is accorded every courtesy. The bed linens must be changed, the room cleaned, and water provided for his bath, and have a hot meal taken to him at once."

When she paused but did not dismiss him, the servant asked, "Will there be anything else?"

"No, no, I think not." The role of gracious hostess was

not one she played well, especially when Serena was so much more adept at the part.

Colin nodded then and went on his way to carry out her orders, and Aurelia resumed her trek, complete with more self-recriminations. She slowed her pace further as she neared the duke's suite, seeking a few extra moments to compose her thoughts and her emotions before facing him.

For all the animosity between them, Aurelia could not deny that Serena had succeeded where she herself had failed. And the person most disappointed by that failure was the same person Aurelia most desperately wanted to please. She dreaded the upcoming encounter, for once again she must report little progress in the task he had set her—and at the same time acknowledge Serena's triumph.

With assistance from the guests she had invited to Nethergate for precisely that purpose, Serena had smoothed the rough edges from the Joshua MacKinnon who had arrived from St. Gregory's Island a few short weeks ago. He was well on his way to becoming a proper English aristocrat instead of a colonial planter.

In stark contrast, Aurelia had not so far succeeded in stirring Joshua's interest in learning the responsibilities that accompanied his new social position.

Aurelia was not, however, one to excuse or minimize her own shortcomings. Denying them would not make them disappear. If the elimination of problems were that simple, she would have denied Serena's existence years ago, denied the loss of her parents—and denied Christopher Ballantyne entrance to Nethergate. Denial of that kind was only another form of lying, and Aurelia Phillips did not lie, no matter the cost.

When she lifted her hand to knock on the door, it abruptly opened, and a tall, middle-aged man in somber-hued clothes emerged, shaking his head in a familiar gesture of resigned frustration.

"Ah, Miss Phillips!" Dr. Arvin Ward exclaimed, narrowly

missing a collision with her. "His Grace was asking after you."

The physician's smile did not reach his eyes, which seemed incapable of fixing themselves on any one object.

Aurelia made no effort to disguise her dislike of the man, though she doubted he noticed or cared. Dr. Ward might be twenty years or more older than Serena's other admirers, but like them, he had eyes for no one else, even when she was out of sight.

"I was unavoidably detained."

He nodded as if he understood, but Aurelia knew he was probably trying to think of a reason to extricate himself from her usual questions about the duke's health.

Out of impatience rather than compassion, she was inclined to release him, to let him scurry back to the company of the woman who had brought him from London to the wilderness of Northumberland and Nethergate Hall. If he wished to make a fool of himself at Serena's feet, who was Aurelia Phillips to try to stop him? But neither impatience nor compassion was sufficient reason to neglect her duty, and so she refused to excuse him.

"Has there been any change?" she asked, careful to avoid sounding either too hopeful or too hopeless.

Dr. Ward sighed. "Alas, none. While His Grace shows no sign of improvement since recovering from the lung fever, neither has his condition worsened. And he is a most stubborn individual."

She would have probed further, but the rasp of a frail, hoarse voice calling her name from the other side of the door cut short her interrogation.

"Aurelia, is that you? Come in here at once!"

Dr. Ward made good his escape this time, fairly scampering in the direction of the drawing room where Serena held afternoon court.

Aurelia shook the image from her mind. She was not in the habit of dwelling on Serena so obsessively and gave half a thought as to why their antipathy seemed so important today, but the prospect ahead of her was too daunting as well as too inviting to let anything else interfere. She opened the door and entered the duke of Winterburn's sanctum sanctorum.

"You're late," he barked from his chair by the fire. As usual, the room was overly warm, the air stale with the smell of illness and age. But the eyes gleaming up at her were bright with life and welcome. "Where in Hades have you been?"

"More guests arrived, Grandfather. I had to see them settled."

"More parasites, don't you mean?" He attempted to laugh at his own humor, but the laugh became a series of raspy coughs. When the spasm passed he asked, "And just how many more of these vultures have come to avail themselves of my generous hospitality while they wait for me to die?"

She walked to him and leaned down to kiss the dry, leathery cheek while he flung a bony arm around her shoulders for an affectionate hug. At that moment, she could almost imagine twenty years had not passed since the day she first saw him, and he was once again the silver-haired gentleman who had so terrified an already confused five-year-old girl and just as quickly dispelled her fears upon her arrival at Nethergate. But when he freed her from that embrace, she knew the years had indeed gone by, and if Charles MacKinnon, twelfth duke of Winterburn, had cheated death another day, he knew, as did she, that the game was nearly up.

"Four more," she answered with a smile. Perhaps, this once, she could persuade him to remain here and share a private supper with her rather than make the nightly pilgrimage to the dining room. They had had so little time alone together since the first of the guests arrived over a month ago, and she feared there was little time left.

"So who are these latest beggars?" he asked, as if he had

read her thoughts and wished to change the subject. His voice was stronger, she thought: a good sign. "Anyone I might consider a prospective husband for you?"

"Grandfather!"

His wit never weakened, nor his unflagging concern for her future.

At least he had not immediately brought up the subject of Joshua. For that she allowed herself a small sigh of relief.

"The dowager marchioness of Whiston and her great-nephew, Mr. Frederick Denholm, arrived this morning from London."

The old man chuckled.

"Ah, yes, I remember Lady Whiston when she was Gwendolyn Graham. Loved men in uniforms, she did. Her father married her to Whiston when she was no more'n fifteen, I believe, so she wouldn't elope with the first brass-buttoned rapscallion who'd have her." The years had not dimmed his memory. "Freddie, he'd be Whiston's brother's grandson and heir. I take it you don't find him to your liking."

"No, the Honorable Mr. Denholm is not to my liking, Grandfather. He is insufferable."

"And I have no doubt you told him so."

"Twice."

He laughed again, and this time did not dissolve into the wracking coughs that had plagued him for weeks.

"Gwen was always a good sort, and I'm sure she's got poor Freddie on a short lead. He damn near grew up at court, you know, so he'll be of much use to Joshua before the boy takes his seat in Parliament. Serena chose wisely."

Aurelia groped for words to fill the silence that followed. She could pull up a chair to sit down beside the old man, but she could not reach into herself for a simple lie to give his mind ease. No matter how hard she tried, no matter what falsehoods came into her head, she could not utter any words but the true ones.

So she said nothing. The very idea of Joshua MacKinnon

serving in government made her shiver; the thought of Joshua MacKinnon becoming duke of Winterburn made her ill.

Yet it was her task to see that he did exactly that.

"You said there were four arrived today," the duke reminded her, bringing her out of a morose reverie. "Who were the others? I did not know Serena had invited anyone else."

Aurelia slipped her hand into her pocket but did not at once retrieve the letter.

"Serena did not invite them, Grandfather. They are strangers. Americans."

"What could bring a couple of colonials to this corner of England?" the duke snorted, then added with a note of apprehension in his voice, "They're not friends of Joshua's, are they?"

She recalled the instant Ballantyne and Joshua had been introduced to each other. If she had perceived an unspoken enmity, there had surely been no sign of recognition between the heir to Winterburn and the stranger from the storm.

"No, not friends," she said, knowing she spoke the truth. "They are from Charleston, not the Caribbean."

Running her thumb lightly over the uneven blob of wax that sealed the envelope, she wondered what device a man like Christopher Ballantyne had chosen to impress into it. She had not looked when he gave her the letter, and now she tried to make out the details of the design through the tip of her finger.

The duke leaned back in his chair with a satisfied sigh. "Good, for I want no ties to the boy's past to influence him here. He has enough bad habits as it is."

Aurelia braced herself for the inquisition. The brief discussion of Ballantyne's arrival had only delayed the inevitable. Today's recounting of Joshua's progress would be more difficult than most, for try as she might, Aurelia could find no fault in her own behavior. She had done her best to impress upon him the importance of his position as heir to Winterburn, the title as well as the extensive properties. The simple truth was that Joshua MacKinnon, sole male descendant of the ancient line, did not give a fig about his responsibilities; he wanted only to enjoy the entertainments and luxuries his newfound status—and his grandfather's deep pockets—afforded him.

A simple truth, but one Aurelia could not reveal to the man whose fondest dreams rested on his only grandson.

"Then if they did not come to see Joshua and assist with his education, what *are* they doing here?"

Charles MacKinnon might be well into his eighty-third year, with fading eyesight and frail health, but he demonstrated time and again that his mind remained sharp as ever.

Aurelia stroked her thumb one more time across the seal of Ballantyne's letter, then slowly she drew it from her pocket.

"They came to see you, Grandfather," she said. "Or at least that is what Mr. Ballantyne told me."

"Ballantyne? I don't know anyone named Ballantyne. A Scot, is he?"

"I have no idea." Unprepared for these questions, she blurted the first thing that came to her mind. "He's dark as a red Indian, and very tall." Then she blushed, fiercely. What difference did it make what Christopher Ballantyne looked like? "I told him you weren't receiving visitors, and he gave me this letter."

She did not expect the sudden reluctance to turn over Ballantyne's missive. In such a short time she had developed an odd possessiveness about it. Shaking off the silly feeling, she leaned forward and handed it to the elderly duke without further hesitation.

He took it but said nothing. He was so silent that Aurelia felt another quiver of disquiet, though she tried to tell herself there was no reason. His eyesight had deteriorated over the years, forcing him to rely on others to do his reading for him. She waited for him to return the envelope so she could break the seal and read whatever message the mysterious Mr. Ballantyne had penned.

But the duke did not give it to her. Instead, he turned the folded bit of paper over and over in his hands. The motion made her aware of the skeletal frailty of his long fingers, the skin stretched taut over old bones and knuckles so the veins protruded. Even when half-frozen, Ballantyne's fingers were strong and steady.

Despite the blaze of the fire, Aurelia shivered with an eerie foreboding. Until an hour ago, nothing in her life had affected her so intensely. Not the death of her father, the Reverend Titus Phillips whom she barely remembered, for he succumbed to consumption when she was only four. Not even her mother's remarriage to the handsome, dashing youngest son of the duke of Winterburn, though that marriage had brought Aurelia to Nethergate and a life far different from what she would have known as the daughter of a country parson.

And when her mother and Robert MacKinnon died, Aurelia had accepted the tragedy, the loss, and the blame, then she had gone on with her life. There was nothing left to fear, for the worst had already happened.

Now it was the future she feared, the unknown. She had no idea what might happen, what Christopher Ballantyne might *make* happen.

"Shall I read you Mr. Ballantyne's letter?" she asked. Perhaps there was an explanation on that sheet of paper that would relieve this formless apprehension growing within her.

But the echo of her words faded, and only the crackle of the fire and the rustle of paper in the duke's hands remained to break the silence that deepened around them.

Would he destroy the letter unopened and unread? she

wondered. He had but to lean forward and with a flick of his wrist consign the envelope and its unknown contents to the flames. Aurelia felt her nerves tense as he continued to stare out of eyes grown glazed and unseeing. She admitted she was afraid of what she might do if he did indeed toss the letter into the fire.

Unable to bear his silence longer, she offered, "Mr. Ballantyne is here, Grandfather, if you would prefer to meet with him privately. Aunt Serena invited him to join us for dinner, but I did not think that appropriate. I ordered a meal sent to him instead."

She bit her tongue to stop the rambling flow of words. Once started, they threatened to go on forever, but the expression on Charles MacKinnon's ancient face hinted that he heard little or nothing of her prattle anyway. If not for his incessant turning of the envelope, she could have imagined he had suffered an apoplexy. Behind the blind gaze, there lurked a fevered intelligence, as though he were trying desperately to find something in the vast storehouse of his memory.

"Perhaps it would be better if we did not join the others tonight," she suggested, her voice lower and more soothing even to her own ears. "It's really quite dreadful outside and the dining room is bound to be cold—"

"I want him gone tomorrow," the duke interrupted. "He may stay the night, but he is to leave my house come morning. Do you understand?"

Startled by the vehemence of his reply, she answered instinctively, "Yes, of course, Grandfather. I shall send word to him at once."

A trembling sigh escaped him. The unexpected anger had disappeared, the gentleness returned.

"Go, child, enjoy your dinner." His voice weakened, as though what he had looked for was hope and he had found none. "Tell our guests I shall join them tomorrow, that I prefer the comfort of my own hearth this 'dreadful' night."

Though he smiled at his reiteration of her own descriptive phrase, he never looked at her, never stopped the rhythmic fingering of the sealed envelope.

Aurelia had no choice but to do as he ordered. If she did not for a moment consider disobeying, neither did she wish to leave until she knew the contents of Ballantyne's letter—or at least knew the missive would not be destroyed.

"Shall I send in Mr. Sullivan?" she asked.

"Whatever for? I've no use for a secretary this time of the day, and besides, he's no doubt at his own supper."

"I don't like leaving you alone, Grandfather."

Finally, he turned and fastened his old gray eyes on her. His fingers fell still and silent.

"If I die, I die," he said with a feeble shrug of his shoulders. Then, releasing the letter to settle on his lap, he patted her knee and added, "Go now, child, dress yourself in something lovely and enjoy your dinner. Let an old man be alone with his memories for an evening. And give poor Freddie another chance. Gwen wasn't overfond of her marquess at first, but she did all right with him in the end."

His smile was a ghost of the one that had banished her fears twenty years ago. Aurelia recognized, as she got to her feet and leaned down to kiss the cool, dry cheek once more, the same uneasiness that had assailed her that first day at Nethergate. She had faced an unknowable future then, so different from her past that she could not begin to imagine it. Her new grandfather, with his silver hair and twinkling gray eyes and ready smile, dispersed her childish fear and made the great old house instantly feel as much like home as the cottage where she and her mother had lived after her father's passing.

Now, as she left the very room where the duke of Winterburn had welcomed a frightened child, she realized she would have to deal with this new future on her own.

She closed the door behind her and could not tell if the sound that reached her ears a tiny instant before the click of the latch was a pop from the fire or the tearing of a piece of paper.

She tightened her shawl around her shoulders, for the corridor was cold after the warmth of the duke's chamber, and muttered, "I don't *need* to read the blessed thing."

Stepping up her pace, she headed for her own rooms. She had only enough time until dinner to change her clothes and then pay a call upon the man who had written the letter.

Kit shoved his feet into a dry pair of boots, then slipped his arms into the sleeves of his still-damp coat. Two hours in front of a roaring fire was not long enough to dry the fabric after half a day in the wind and sleet, but at least it no longer dripped.

"Where do ye think ye're goin', sir?" Emil Drew asked around a mouthful of mutton.

"To find His Grace the Duke of Winterburn. Did you think I came all this way to be denied meeting the man face-to-face? I'll not sit here and wait for him to come to me."

"But what about yer letter?"

Kit let out a short bark of laughter before saying, "I doubt he'll even open it, much less read it. He probably tossed it into the fire as soon as Miss Honesty Phillips told him who wrote it."

He ran his fingers through his hair in an attempt to bring some veneer of civilization to his appearance. The shabby room contained no mirror, though Winterburn's servants had brought water for washing as well as clean linens for the bed, a goodly stack of firewood, two lamps, and a hearty meal of stew and bread fresh enough to have been baked that morning. Emil, who insisted on acting the part of valet, had taken care of Kit's wet clothing the best he could and now helped himself to a well-earned meal. Perhaps, Kit thought, it was the comfort of being warm inside and out that made Emil encourage his erstwhile employer to enjoy the same.

But Kit was determined, as he had been from the start.

"I learned a hard lesson at the hands of William Cooke. I waited and waited, *expecting* my reward for fifteen years of service, but never taking action to ensure my investment."

The bitterness was still fresh, still raw, which he found somewhat surprising. The wound should have healed long ago, unless today's setback opened it.

Some wounds, he knew only too well, never healed. He still felt the pain of his father's ignominious death, a debt-ridden suicide that had sent a fifteen-year-old Kit to abandon his dreams of a university education. Forced to rely on what schooling and skills he had, he had found work with Cooke, a shipbuilder, first as a clerk and then gradually working his way up to overseer of the entire operation. Though there was never a formal agreement between them, the unmarried, childless Cooke always hinted his industrious employee would be rewarded for his loyalty and hard work. For fifteen years Kit worked twelve- and fourteen-hour days, and received most of his wages in the form of vague promises and hopes encouraged.

Then Cooke, as deep in debt as Malcolm Ballantyne had been, sold out to a competitor—who had no need for an industrious overseer. In the space of fifteen minutes, Kit learned of the destruction of fifteen years' worth of work.

"I won't wait this time."

He walked to the valise that sat open on the bed and extracted a square wooden box, no larger than the palm of his hand and no more than an inch deep. A silver hasp but no lock secured it. Without examining the contents, Kit dropped the box into his pocket.

"If he read the letter, he knows I pose no threat to him or his heir."

Emil shook his head vehemently.

"Ye're a threat, no matter what ye do, sir," the wiry sailor insisted. "If he did what ye said, he won't sleep easy 'til ye're gone."

"Then he need only acknowledge who I am and what he did, and I'll leave him in peace. That's all I came for."

Again Emil shook his head, but more slowly, with a quiet sense of steady denial.

"I'll not say ye're lyin' or that ye don't know yer own mind, Mr. Ballantyne, but I find it hard t'believe a man'd come all the way from Charleston to this miserable cold place just to have an old man pat ye on the head and say, 'Aye, ye're my brother's grandson and rightful heir to what I stole' and then walk away from it all."

Kit felt the cold from his coat seep through his dry clothes.

"And I've told you a hundred times, Emil, and your Captain Trethevy, too. Even if it's true, which I doubt, I'd not be Winterburn's heir. My Uncle Jeremiah is, and I want none of it anyway. I want to lay the lies to rest—or learn the truth, which may be a very different thing—and nothing more."

He took a deep breath to steady his temper. This argument, spawned by his mother's insistence and then supported by his uncle's tales, was five years old or more. The story of an English lord wounded fighting the French, who more than fifty years ago settled in the backwoods of Pennsylvania while it was a British colony, strained credibility. Kit considered it a fanciful tale, accepted as truth by his mother and uncle out of respect for a father they loved and honored. Kit, who had never met David MacKinnon, held no such prejudices.

Presented with the opportunity to resolve the debate, he had left Charleston to end it. Now that at least part of the tale was proven true with the discovery that Nethergate existed and was ruled by the same Charles MacKinnon, duke of Winterburn, Kit had been told he would find, was it simple impatience that drove him to want to explore the labyrinth in search of the man with the answers? Or could it be something else, something he was unprepared at this point to acknowledge? Did he, upon seeing Nethergate itself, believe it might *all* be true?

He ran the back of his hand under his chin. He needed a shave, his coat smelled like a wet sheep, and without a mirror he could only guess how tidy his overlong hair was. Not the appearance he had planned to present, but he suddenly did not care. He was no English courtier, no snuff-taking, satin-waistcoated fop living on inherited wealth earned by others, nor had he any wish to become one. He was a hard-working businessman who had made but one mistake in his life. He would not make the same mistake again.

Without another word, Kit strode out of the room. The door had neither lock nor bar, so that if Miss Phillips intended to keep him prisoner, she had made a poor choice of gaol.

He took closer note of the details of his surroundings, partly so he would be able to find his way back but also partly from sheer curiosity.

The windowless room in which he and Emil had been quartered was in fact built into what he suspected was the curtain wall of Nethergate's medieval precursor. If the Winterburn title was as old as he had been told, the present ducal seat could easily be constructed upon the remains of a castle fortress and have taken its name from the lower entrance to the original bailey.

Or it might be considered the entrance to hell.

He shook his head to chase away such a fanciful thought and made his way confidently down the long corridor to a short flight of stairs that led to a door and the manor house proper. While he paused before descending, raking his fingers once more into his hair, the door opened and Aurelia Phillips walked through.

3

SHE SAW HIM STANDING AT THE TOP OF THE STEPS AND STOPPED at once, midstride, affording him ample time to study—and enjoy—the picture she presented.

Gone was the drab gray dress, the prim apron, the functional woolen shawl, replaced by a gown of green velvet trimmed with ivory lace. Only the tight coronet of dark braids remained of the chatelaine of Nethergate.

He might have dismissed the impression of jewel-like beauty as nothing more than a contrast to the housekeeper image she had created at their first meeting, but Kit quickly recognized a resurgence of his earlier attraction to her. And just as quickly dampened it.

Her fine features had not changed with her dress, but the deep emerald fabric intensified the green of her eyes. As though coming slowly aware of his scrutiny—and of her own extended silence—she blushed, her cool English complexion brightening to rose as the flush crept up her throat to her cheeks. Kit could not stop a slight smile at her discomfiture, nor keep his stare from wandering a bit lower, to where a lacy insert modestly covered the curves that would have been revealed by the gown's decolletage. Lace, however, failed to conceal the warm, tempting shadow between breasts that rose with her quickened breath.

If she could not find words, he had no such difficulty.

"Have you come to escort me to dinner, Miss Phillips? I'm so sorry to disappoint you, but I've already eaten."

The rosebuds in her cheeks blossomed; he knew as well as she that her intention was to see him stay in his isolated room.

"Then where are you going, Mr. Ballantyne? Did the servants not bring you everything for your comfort?"

Her retort, after her blush, took him by surprise, for he expected at best a stammered apology. Apparently Aurelia Phillips, whatever position she occupied in this odd household, was no cowering servant herself.

Nor, once she had addressed him, did she appear the least affected by him, not even intimidated by his advantage of height, which forced her to tilt her chin up. He wondered if she would have been so calm had she known how the pose accentuated the graceful line of her neck and throat, even to exposing the beat of her pulse in the intimate hollow above her collarbones.

"Miss Phillips, I made no secret that I came here to see Winterburn," he answered with frankness to match hers. "As I was not locked in my room or ordered like a trained dog to stay, I decided to seek him out."

"He does not wish to see you, Mr. Ballantyne. He sent me to tell you he wishes you to leave Nethergate as soon as possible in the morning."

Aurelia noted the raising of the American's eyebrow. She had surprised him, and she liked the sense of triumph it gave her. He wore his confidence too comfortably, his boldness too easily, when she was more accustomed to dealing with the likes of Freddie Denholm and Adam Braisthwaite with their shallow conceit. They were like spoiled children who expected to be given whatever they wished, whether it was a new coat of the most fashionable cut or a woman's favors, and even to have their wishes anticipated. Thwarted, as when she rebuffed their unwelcomed advances, they tended to pout, and simply believed eventually they would get what they wanted.

Ballantyne, she understood, would go after what he wanted, not wait for it.

Her advantage was short-lived.

The raised brow settled into a scowl as he descended the five stone steps to stand immediately in front of her. He could have made her feel trapped and vulnerable, alone here away from any aid, but she felt no fear, only a powerlessness to stop his determination.

"I mean to see him before I leave. One way or another."

"Are you threatening me, Mr. Ballantyne?"

"Not you, Miss Phillips, unless you leave me no other choice."

Her nose twitched involuntarily. He smelled of wet wool and wood smoke and of some indescribable essence that communicated his sheer masculinity to all her senses. Denying herself the urge to retreat from her mission, Aurelia resorted to her most faithful weapon—and most dangerous enemy.

"What do you want from my grandfather?" she asked with undisguised honesty. When he hesitated to reply to her frontal assault, she continued, "I did not read your letter, if that is what you're wondering, nor did my grandfather request that I read it to him, though I asked him if he wished me to."

This time he showed no surprise, but she suspected he merely masked his reaction, and before he recovered she plunged onward.

"He is an old man, in failing health. He has suffered a great many losses, and it is my intention to see that he spends whatever time God permits him in peace."

"What makes you so certain I intend anything different?"

She had no answer. Even in her own mind, she could not find a rational explanation for her anxiety.

"I don't know," she admitted.

"Then why not give me the chance to—"

He was interrupted by the opening of the door behind Aurelia, and the brittle music of Serena MacKinnon's laughter.

"Well, this is surely cause for celebration," she said, sweeping in to circle both Aurelia and the man whose request hung unfinished on the air. "Twice today I've found you alone in Mr. Ballantyne's company, Aurelia. An assignation, perhaps, with our handsome American guest?"

Though spoken lightly and tinged with silvery laughter, the words stung exactly as Aurelia knew they were intended to. No matter which truth she used to exonerate herself, she would still look a fool, a clumsy child lacking all grace, an outcast with an insurmountable flaw that kept her forever beyond the pale.

"Quite the contrary, Mrs. MacKinnon."

The wounded innocence in Ballantyne's deliberate reply brought Aurelia's eyes to meet his. She did not expect anyone else to champion her cause.

"Miss Phillips came to escort me to the dinner to which *you*"—how slight, but how telling was his emphasis—"invited me. I've been making my excuses and suggesting instead she send a hot meal to the room for my servant and me."

"Oh?" Now it was Serena who arched a brow, but before she could question his lie or his obsequiousness, he elaborated on the falsehood with disturbing facility.

"I did not know if I was to find my own way and so set out in search of someone to ask. It was my good fortune to encounter Miss Phillips before I lost my sense of direction."

Aurelia had never seen Serena so unsettled in the presence of a man. She seemed to fumble for words, and her smile became more fixed and artificial than ever. She touched the strand of pearls clasped around her throat but did not stroke the iridescent beads the way she usually did.

"An easy enough thing to do," Serena agreed. "Nethergate is a veritable web of wings and corridors. How fortunate indeed that you happened upon my niece."

Liars! Aurelia wanted to scream at both of them, but some unknown force held the word frozen in her throat. Serena had tried to insinuate herself between Aurelia and the American, but Ballantyne maneuvered away from her, to stand behind Aurelia's right shoulder. She wanted to see him, to hurl the most damning accusation she knew in his face, and yet to do so would put her squarely in Serena's camp—and power.

"You must forgive me for declining your invitation, Mrs. MacKinnon," he replied in that same fawning, unnatural voice. It curdled something in Aurelia's stomach. "You have already shown me more hospitality than a stranger has a right to expect, and I could not intrude further."

Aurelia felt his presence very close behind her, close enough almost to be a warmth, a subtle cocoon of protection, as a boulder on a windy hilltop provides shelter from the gale. Guilt coursed through her for her silent complicity.

Unable to see his face, she struggled to read him via Serena's reactions. That dreaded unknown was unfolding before her, forcing her to deeds and measures unfamiliar. The blue eyes narrowed and Serena's smile tightened further to a grimace. She who was so accustomed to her own lies both great and small seemed at as great a loss to deal with this as Aurelia. Did Serena believe Ballantyne? Or did she simply not want to expose him, though in doing so she also denied herself the pleasure of exposing Aurelia?

Now her slender fingers began to caress the pearls, in a gesture Aurelia recognized with no little dismay. Exactly so might a hunter caress an arrow before nocking it to his bow.

"I assure you, Mr. Ballantyne, your presence would be no intrusion," Serena purred. "But a hostess does not impose upon her guests."

Her voice and the action of her hand belied her words. There was more than a hint of seduction in the way her thumb and middle finger spread wide to frame her throat, then stroked downward to meet at the center of the strand of pearls. Her slim, unadorned wrist concealed but did not hide the valley between her breasts.

But suddenly she moved her hand from the necklace, as if aware for the first time of what she had done. She even looked away, though Aurelia saw the barest flush of pink tingeing Serena's throat. Did such a reaction indicate Ballantyne resisted the obvious enticement? Again Aurelia desperately wanted to face him, to read what she could from his own expression.

She had to be satisfied with Serena's response. The older woman looked at her, any trace of embarrassment gone.

"You'll have a decent meal provided for our guest?" Serena snapped.

For a heartbeat, Aurelia froze. Her mouth went dry, her tongue paralyzed. She knew the words; they echoed screaming in her head in their effort to escape, to be heard, but her lips refused to shape them. No matter what befell her, she could not lie, not even when she wanted to.

"Consider it done," she finally whispered, lowering her eyes as Serena spun and stormed out the door in a flurry of red velvet and shimmering pearls.

The corridor felt colder after Serena's departure. Aurelia released the rest of the breath she had held after making her brief statement. It was not a lie, she told herself sternly, no matter that Serena would not take it at its true meaning.

"What will you do now?"

His voice, so close behind her, was soft, intimate, and Aurelia realized she was indeed alone with Christopher Ballantyne—again.

"I shall go to my grandfather and inform him what has happened."

She stepped away from him before turning, afraid that his nearness might affect her thinking. He had changed again, from fawning to mysterious, and when she faced him at last, she found him frowning at her.

"Does my honesty anger you?" she asked. "I make no apology for it."

"I am far from angry. Perplexed, yes. And curious, too. But angry? Not with you, Miss Phillips."

A little quiver sped along her nerves. She blamed it on the chill of the old stone walls finally penetrating the heavy fabric of her gown, not on the loss of Christopher Ballantyne's nearness. And it certainly had nothing to do with the way his dark eyes stared at her, as if he were trying to see beyond the surface into her soul. She had only to step through the door into the main part of Nethergate to escape the cold, but could she as easily escape him? Even if he did not physically follow her, as she suspected he would, would she be able to forget those eyes, the way he had lied for her?

"It was not necessary for you to say what you did." She was not sure if he knew what she meant and was about to explain herself when he replied, letting her know he understood perfectly.

"I saved you from having to explain to your aunt that you reneged on her invitation, and kept her from thinking something that might have resulted in my being asked to leave Nethergate even before His Grace the duke has ordered me."

"I'm not afraid to tell her the truth," Aurelia insisted. "She is not mistress here, nor is she ever likely to be. My grandfather, on the other hand—"

"And that is precisely what perplexes me."

She could resist the cold no longer. A sharp shiver rippled through her, so strong she almost lost her grip on the candle she held. In an instant, Ballantyne had his coat off and draped it over her shoulders, then took the taper from her. She had no chance to protest before he placed a large hand firmly on her waist and gently propelled her up the steps and down the dim corridor.

Not into the brightness and warmth that waited on the

other side of the door. Not in the direction where Serena had gone. But toward the isolated room where she had lodged him.

"They'll expect you to spend some time ordering my supper," he told her, providing another lie to cover her actions. "In fact, they'd be more suspicious if you show up too soon."

His legs were long and his strides hurried, forcing Aurelia to a half-trot to keep up with him. She complied, unable to speak because of the rapid pace he set but also startled and disoriented by her own reaction to the sensation of having his coat, still warm from his body, touching her skin.

"Your explanations won't mean a thing," he went on, keeping up a steady stream of conversation as he guided her down the corridor. "She'll believe what she wants to. You think I don't know she came for me, not you? She was not pleased to find you had got here first."

"You make a very rash judgment, Mr. Ballantyne," she managed to tell him, "and a very wrong one."

She tried to draw away from him, and short of grabbing her with both hands, Kit knew he could not stop her if she truly wished to escape. Still, he chanced snaking his arm more securely around her waist and silently admitted she was quite right about the rashness of his reasoning.

"Serena will believe exactly what I tell her because she knows I do not lie. Ever."

With a deftness that left him too surprised to react, she slipped her shoulders out of his coat in such a way that the heavy garment fell over his arm. Before he realized how clever she had been—and how very confident of her own cleverness she was—she had extricated herself completely and stood several feet away from him. Except for the candle he held in his hand, there was no light in the corridor; she was probably familiar enough with the winding ruin to find her way in the dark at a dead run, but he would be left to follow at a more cautious pace. And at the moment, both of his hands were full. He could not even grab her to stop her if she decided to flee. She seemed well aware of that, too.

She appeared unaware, however, that when she shrugged off his coat, her dress slipped, baring a few extra inches of the curve of one shoulder. Kit felt a temptation to pull the garment up, to protect her as he had done earlier, but he feared the consequences of touching her before he knew exactly who she was.

"You may not have lied to your aunt, Miss Phillips, but neither did you correct my own lie when you had the opportunity," he pointed out.

His accusation had the desired effect. Utterly appalled at her own actions, she was too speechless to argue with him, at least for the moment or two he needed.

"I ask five minutes, Miss Phillips. You'll need that much time to verify the servant followed your orders, and I will neither require nor suggest that you lie any further."

She was cold again. The silken skin of her shoulder and throat and even the swell of breast above the lacy insert roughened with goose bumps. She wrapped her arms around herself against the chill, and the velvet of her sleeve dipped lower. She must have felt it, for she reached to pull the garment into position, and in doing so revealed what he had not seen before.

Two long, livid welts marred the perfection of her flesh. They appeared freshly made, the skin abraded and rough at the center of the angry swelling. Now the protective instinct Kit had resisted earlier would not be denied.

"You've been hurt," he said, closing the gap between them to shed brighter light on the injury.

She tugged the dress up over the marks.

"It's nothing," she insisted, backing another step away from him. "I forgot that Galahad had been shut indoors all day and would be enthusiastic in his greeting. He scratched me."

"Galahad?"

"My dog."

So she had a protective streak in her, too, though he found it difficult to imagine the proud Aurelia Phillips on her knees beside some mongrel pup, her arms around its neck, defending the mutt as passionately as a lioness her cub.

Something told him she had not been on her knees when Galahad greeted her.

"A good-sized animal he must be, to leave marks on your shoulder."

Pride and affection animated her, bringing her eyes to brilliant life and a smile to her lips that invited laughter and kisses. The porcelain doll came alive, and so did the half-forbidden, half-delightful desire Kit felt for her.

"I daresay he could do the same to you, Mr. Ballantyne. Deerhounds are, as the Scots themselves say, braw beasties, and Galahad may have been the runt of his litter, but he's outgrown all his mates."

But as swiftly as that vivacity came, it disappeared, and the cool aloofness reasserted itself.

"I'll give you your five minutes, Mr. Ballantyne," she said, again pulling at the green velvet to make certain nothing of the red scratches remained visible, and lifting her chin a hair's breadth to let him know her pride was once more intact. "Do not waste them with idle chatter."

There were a hundred questions he knew he should ask her. About the old man who refused to see him or to reply to his letters. About Joshua MacKinnon, the heir to Winterburn. About Serena MacKinnon, who would seduce a stranger. But he wanted to know more about this intriguing creature before him, this unexpected granddaughter of the duke of Winterburn, with the green eyes and alabaster skin.

He could choose his words carefully or he could be blunt. If it were true that Aurelia Phillips did not lie, no subterfuge was necessary.

"Charles MacKinnon inherited his title after his elder

brother David was reported killed fighting the French in the American colonies nearly sixty years ago. Married twice, Charles sired three sons," he said, not to inform her of facts with which she must be intimately familiar but to let her know he was not entirely ignorant himself. "The eldest, Henry, married late and produced no heir before he committed suicide ten years ago."

He thought she flinched at the bald statement, but perhaps she merely shivered. He walked behind her and again wrapped her in his coat, slipping his hand into the pocket to retrieve the small wooden box as he came around to face her once more. Her features never altered. She did, however, apparently welcome the respite from the penetrating cold of Nethergate. Kit refused to let his mind dwell on the warmth they could have enjoyed in the room where Emil waited for him, and returned to his quest for information. He might never have such an opportunity again.

"Serena, I presume, then, is Henry's widow."

She nodded, but in no other way gave the slightest indication to her thoughts.

"The second son, Michael, exiled himself to a Caribbean plantation and incurred his father's wrath for it. He died disinherited, but left a son, the same Joshua to whom I was introduced this afternoon."

Though he had not asked for confirmation, Aurelia nodded again. She also lowered her eyes for a fleeting instant, but so brief was the gesture he almost dismissed it. Almost.

"Joshua was welcomed back into the fold and proclaimed the heir only because the third son, Robert, who was his father's delight, also died childless. The present duke has no legitimate grandchildren."

Now there was no mistaking the shudder that made Aurelia's arms tighten around her beneath the enveloping bulk of Kit's coat. These naked truths had touched some chord within her, a harsh note that reverberated its dissonance painfully along the strings of her nerves. She winced, but another lifting of her chin told him she would answer the oblique question about her own position in the MacKinnon family. He waited, not prodding, not pushing.

"My own father died when I was four, Mr. Ballantyne. A year later, my mother married Robert MacKinnon."

Her lower lip trembled. She caught it between her teeth and drew a deep breath before she could continue. Still he waited, silent even to holding his own sigh of relief until she had finished.

"I loved him as a father, for I knew no other, and if I am not of Charles MacKinnon's blood, I remain his granddaughter in both my heart and his."

When a single tear hovered at the edge of her eye, she tried to blink it away, but that only made it fall to her cheek. Kit reached out to brush away the glittering drop, more lovely and precious than all of Serena's pearls.

Whether or not he was in truth David MacKinnon's grandson, at least Kit knew Aurelia Phillips was in no way related to him. She was neither Charles's illegitimate daughter nor a by-blow of one of his sons.

Giving in to a desire he had hoped was not forbidden, he whispered, "Thank God," then slipped his hand under her chin and tipped her face up to kiss her.

4

AT THE FIRST TOUCH OF HIS LIPS ON HERS, AURELIA FELT SUCH A surge of heat through her body that her very bones seemed to liquefy. Suspended like a puppet, with only Christopher Ballantyne's finger beneath her chin to hold her upright, she knew she must not allow the kiss to continue. To move, however, even to turn her head the scant inch or two needed to sever the connection, required strength she no longer possessed.

Out of the warmth, a slender thread began to spin, fine and soft as spider's silk. Aurelia struggled against its entrapment, and then suddenly it snapped as if of its own accord when Ballantyne withdrew as calmly and deliberately as he had begun.

She stumbled backward, first one step, then another. Breathless, frightened, she hiked her skirts and ran, heedless of the cold as Ballantyne's coat once more fell from her shoulders. She did not hesitate but ran blindly, and did not turn to see if he followed until she had reached the safety on the other side of the door, where light reigned instead of darkness and shadow.

Sensibility slowly returned. Before she reached the dining room, Aurelia had her breathing under control and took a moment or two to check her gown and hair for any signs of disarray. She wanted no evidence of her wild flight to stir curiosity. Any blush to her cheeks could be blamed on the pervasive chill, and with that explanation ready she entered the noisy dining room.

For the first time since the arrival of Joshua MacKinnon and the guests gathered to welcome the estranged heir into Nethergate's fold, Aurelia found herself relieved, if not glad, to be surrounded by people. She might not be particularly fond of any of them, but she did not worry that they held secrets or that their lies stemmed from anything other than superficial conceit.

Her relief, however, did not last long.

"Were you unable to persuade Mr. Ballantyne to join us after all?" Serena baited from her place at the head of the long, lavishly set table. Though a vacant chair beside her indicated the duke's absence, Charles would not have shared his position of authority with anyone, and certainly not with Serena. She was taking pointed advantage of the situation.

If Serena was inclined to pursue the matter of their uninvited guest, Aurelia was not, but neither did she wish to give any cause for suspicion.

"He said he was perfectly comfortable," she insisted, as she took the chair held for her by one of the footmen. The first course was already being served.

James Braisthwaite, Viscount Moresby, seated directly across from Aurelia, set down his wine long enough to ask, "Who is this Ballantyne fellow anyway? Anyone we ought to know?"

His glance at the pale young woman to his left told Aurelia the portly Lord Moresby was fishing again. His daughter Charlotte, who obviously understood the meaning behind her father's question, blushed furiously and unbecomingly. The splotchy redness intensified her sallow complexion, and the apple green dress someone had chosen for her made the effect even more unflattering. Aurelia felt a sympathetic twinge as Charlotte stole a peek from beneath lowered lashes at Freddie Denholm, who sat beside Aurelia. The poor girl looked as if she would burst into humiliated tears at any moment.

"Ballantyne's a bloody American, an uncouth backwoodsman," Charlotte's brother Adam interjected, his mouth full of food. He had been granted the place of honor at Serena's right hand tonight, but he seemed more interested, at least for the present, in whatever delicacy filled his plate.

Adam, Aurelia decided, would end up more obese than his father.

Frederick Denholm, the object of Charlotte's undisguised devotion, was not nearly so handsome as Adam, but he would undoubtedly hold his looks longer.

"There are fortunes to be made in those backwoods," he pointed out, and this time it was Adam's face that turned splotchy.

Aurelia tried to stifle an angry sigh. There was nothing she could do but endure what she had come to think of as The Ordeal—dinner at Nethergate. If tonight's performance was to be Baiting and Bickering instead of The Braggarts, she still found it as distressing as the most morbid Greek tragedy.

More than two hours passed before she was able to effect her escape in the middle of a heated discourse on the inclement weather and how miserable it made the prospects for hunting on the morrow. Freddie Denholm was obviously eager to show himself Adam's superior in the sport and bemoaned the possible loss of the opportunity to do so without further ado. Disgusted by such bloodthirsty competitiveness, Aurelia excused herself with no explanation. When the debate continued without interruption, she was certain no one, save perhaps Serena, even noticed her departure.

She went first to her grandfather's room, but the servant posted outside the door informed her the duke was sleeping and wished not to be disturbed. Though she would have enjoyed a quiet evening with him, Aurelia was glad he would get some rest this night. And, she realized as she made her way to her own room in an adjacent wing, she had neglected Galahad nearly the entire day.

Unlike on her earlier, slightly distracted entrance to her room, she was prepared this time for the dog's boisterous welcome. As soon as she was halfway through the door, the gangly beast launched himself at her, a mass of shaggy, long-legged excitement. A sharp tap to his nose brought him up short.

"Down, Galahad," she admonished sternly, her hand raised to deliver another smack if needed. He sat, an expectant grin on his face, and raised a paw to scratch at her skirt. "Grant me ten minutes," she told him, remembering that Ballantyne had asked only for five. "Long enough to change my clothes, and we'll go for a walk. It's bitter cold and windy out of doors, but the rain has stopped."

Aurelia walked past the dog, her fingers already busy with the buttons down her back. She could have rung for a maid but decided in favor of undressing herself despite the difficulty of reaching behind her. Galahad was prancing in circles around her, panting and whining impatiently. His long tail wagged constantly, and half his body along with it.

After stepping out of the green velvet gown and laying it carefully over the chair, Aurelia pulled on the same gray wool she had worn that afternoon. The front buttons fastened more easily, and the sturdy fabric offered additional warmth. It also irritated that long scratch on her shoulder, a reminder not so much of Galahad's roughness but of Christopher Ballantyne's attention.

Vowing that it should also serve to remind her to be wary of the man until he had safely departed Nethergate, she exchanged her dainty slippers for sturdy boots, then took a hooded, fur-lined cloak from the wardrobe and wrapped herself in it.

When she collected Galahad's lead from its peg by the fireplace, he barked once, a deep-throated *woof* that normally earned him a pat on the head and two or three scratches behind his ears. This time, however, all Aurelia did was jump, startled from an uncomfortable reverie. The lining of her cloak was cool, unlike the warmth of Ballantyne's coat.

"Come, Galahad," she ordered, but the dog needed no further encouragement. She fastened the leather strap to his collar, then strode to the door while she slipped her hands into a pair of gloves.

He trotted eagerly, with a minimum of straining at the leash, and they made their way down a stairway to one of the seldom-used servants' entrances in an older part of Nethergate. The door opened with a creak.

During the long dinner, Aurelia had frequently glanced out the single window whose curtains were not drawn—Freddie and Adam being more concerned with the weather than with the cold that emanated from the expanse of exposed glass—and knew that the rain and sleet had given way to a clear, star-sprinkled night. The shock of that icy air came as no surprise, though her lungs gasped at the first intake of breath.

She pulled the door closed behind her and crossed the flagged courtyard formed by one of Nethergate's most ancient wings and a high stone wall built to screen the near-ruin from the formal gardens. Three torches brightened the narrow space, their welcome light glittering on the ice-rimmed puddles. The guests would never use this walkway, but the servants often did, for it was the shortest way from the shelter of the great house to the stables. And it made a convenient area for an energetic dog to run.

Aurelia tugged on Galahad's lead and brought the dog to heel. When he promptly sat at her command, she slipped the lead to allow him his nightly romp. In an instant, he had streaked off, a blue-black specter disappearing into the darkness.

The high walls broke the bitter wind that had chased the rain, but the air remained frosty. A steady pace and the heavy cloak kept Aurelia from feeling the full bite of the cold, but nonetheless she hurried toward the long, low building where, at this hour, the grooms and stable boys would be settling the horses for the night. She could wait there, using the opportunity to see if any of the animals required special care, while Galahad made his rounds.

She could also see that instructions were given for Ballantyne's horse and his servant's to be readied first thing in the morning.

A sudden sound from the stable halted her in her tracks. At first she thought it a shout or even a cry, but almost immediately identified it as a burst of masculine laughter, of which she had heard too little lately.

The duke kept a respectable stable, with the usual complement of riding, carriage, and draft horses, as well as the necessary vehicles and pertinent equipment. The men and boys charged with the care of those animals had, over the past few weeks, found themselves suddenly burdened with more work than they could handle. Despite the relatives who had been enlisted from the farms and villages around Nethergate, Aurelia knew the men needed more help.

At least tonight they had found something to laugh at.

Not wishing to intrude, she waited beyond the half-door until the voices returned to normal. When the murmur of conversation resumed, she ducked under the low overhang of the roof and approached the entrance.

The sight that met her eyes left her speechless.

In the open area between two rows of stalls, four young boys sat on wooden boxes or cross-legged on piles of straw. Each was busy at some handwork, polishing brass or oiling leather or mending a piece of broken harness. The older grooms and coachmen leaned against wooden partitions or stood with feet planted wide, arms across their chests, while one of their number brushed an unprepossessing bay gelding.

Though the man had his back to the door where Aurelia stood, she sensed his identity before she truly recognized him. He had removed his coat, so that his loose-fitting white shirt and unadorned black waistcoat emphasized the width of his shoulders and the narrowness of his waist. With each stroke of the brush down the horse's flanks, Aurelia marveled at the smooth power and grace of his movements. She was nearly mesmerized by the rhythmic brushing when, as if he, too, intuited her presence without his physical senses being aware, he glanced over his shoulder with a smile that contained a question as well as a greeting.

"I did not expect to find *you* here, Mr. Ballantyne," she said.

Something glittered in his eyes. She felt another blush creeping up her throat, for she had once again blurted out the truth without thinking.

"If I'm to leave early in the morning, I wanted to be sure my horse would be ready."

He was lying again, she was certain. Neither the directness of his gaze nor the ease of his answer dispelled her suspicions.

"There are grooms to see to the horses. And do you not have a servant?"

Quickly suppressed boyish giggles mixed with adult coughs and snickers. Ballantyne only grinned, but he began to walk from the bay horse and toward Aurelia. She wanted to melt into the night shadows and then run for the safety of Nethergate, but he seemed to hold her against her will.

To break the spell, she asked of him as well as of the assembled stable hands, "And what, pray tell, is so amusing?"

His smile was too open, his eyes too honest. When he

reached for the latch and opened the half-door to allow Aurelia into the stable, she did not know whether to slap his face or stride haughtily past him.

"Forgive us all," he said, cupping her elbow to guide her into the lantern light and relative warmth. He must have known her desire was to do otherwise, for he held her tightly enough that to withdraw would have caused a scene. "I've been explaining that Emil is a seaman, pressed into service as my most reluctant valet. He does not like horses and is in fact rather terrified of them, which has led to some amusing incidents along our travels."

He steered her toward one of the wooden chests where brushes and combs and other grooming tools were stored. The boy who had been sitting there tugged on a red forelock as he vacated the spot and, with a swipe of his sleeve, brushed the dust from the chest.

"'Twere right funny, Miss Phillips," he chuckled. "Wish I'd've been there t'see it."

She was about to lecture against making fun of another's misfortune but she was unsure that was what had the boy laughing. Besides, Ballantyne allowed her no opportunity.

"And I thought an extra hand in the stables might not be unwelcome."

He maneuvered her with the skill of a dancing master, even putting a swirl to her cloak as she sat down. Yet grace and gallantry provided no disguise for this latest of his lies. He had no way to know how overworked the Nethergate staff was.

Or did he?

He could have talked to the servant who brought his meal or even to the men he helped right now. She cautioned herself against jumping to conclusions based on nothing more than her distrust of this man.

A sudden flurry of activity around her broke into her thoughts. The boys were scrambling to their feet, as though someone had chased them back to their work. Guthrie, the head groom, growled orders almost unintelligible for the pipe clamped between his teeth. The bay horse, startled out of a three-legged doze, snorted and shook his head.

Seated, Aurelia could not see the door, but from the way Ballantyne half turned, she surmised someone had approached whose presence, without a single word, was enough to send everyone scurrying.

Everyone save Christopher Ballantyne.

"Good evening, MacKinnon," the American said in greeting, confirming her suspicions.

"Ballantyne, isn't it?" Joshua responded.

He opened the door and stepped in, so she could see at least his rain-spattered boots until he had moved around the horse. He gave the animal a wide berth as it craned its neck to follow him.

"What are you doing out here, Aurelia?" he asked. The slight start in his voice made her wonder if he was surprised to find her not only in the stable but also in Ballantyne's company—and if he disapproved of both.

"Miss Phillips was exercising her dog," Ballantyne answered for her, "and rather than wait in the cold for him to finish his run, she joined me while I ready my horse for my departure."

Had it been anyone else answering so brazenly for her—or anyone else asking so impertinently about actions for which she need make neither excuse nor explanation—Aurelia would never have allowed such an imposition on her independence. Ballantyne's cleverness, however, piqued her curiosity.

"I'm sorry you're leaving us so soon," Joshua commented. Did he intend to sound so blatantly sarcastic, Aurelia wondered, or was this another sign of his growing arrogance? Did he believe his position as the next duke of Winterburn allowed him to insult with impunity?

"I wouldn't want to overstay my welcome."

Aurelia had to restrain her lips from forming a triumphant smile. Her guest was capable of giving as well as he got.

"And since I've completed my business at Nethergate, I've no reason to tarry."

"You spoke with my grandfather?"

Joshua's exclamation echoed the astonishment Aurelia barely kept from her own tongue. Had Ballantyne, she worried, found his way to the duke's quarters and forced his way in? Was that why he said he did not want to be disturbed?

The American answered without defensiveness, without any emotion present in his voice.

"My business is concluded, yes."

A lie? Or a careful telling of a very different truth? Aurelia withdrew at least part of her earlier accusation but refused to absolve Ballantyne completely. If he led one to believe falsely even though he himself told the truth, was that not the same as a lie?

Whether it was or not, Joshua seemed comfortable with it. Or at least with the prospect of Ballantyne's departure.

"A shame you must go so soon, for the weather appears to be breaking and we'll no doubt have fine shooting tomorrow. But I suppose you'll want to take advantage of the weather for traveling."

"Precisely."

They could have been two prizefighters facing each other in a market fair ring, circling, assessing, though neither moved a step. In such a match, Ballantyne would have the clear edge. Taller, broader through the shoulder, he seemed unafraid to reduce any quarrel to a physical contest. In this game of wits, of half-lies and less than truths, their skills might be more evenly balanced.

Yet it was Joshua who backed off. Did he consider himself the victor? Aurelia could not tell. He made no further remarks and had turned to leave when a rapid scratching at the door and another startled snort from the bay horse heralded Galahad's arrival.

Aurelia reacted as quickly as she could, but even that was

not quickly enough. Joshua had left the door off the latch, and before she could shut it, the dog bounded gleefully into the stable. The horse tried to rear; only its tether to a stout post prevented serious injury to the man who leapt to grab its halter. While Galahad darted playfully to a reunion with Aurelia, Ballantyne calmed the horse with soothing words and rhythmic pats of a firm hand on its neck.

"Down, Galahad!" she commanded. "Sit!"

The deerhound complied, allowing her to snap the lead to his collar once more. Tongue lolling, he sat docilely at Aurelia's knee. He had left wet, muddy paw prints on her cloak and the skirt of her dress, but no further damage. And by the time she looked up, Ballantyne had the bay under control as well. With a final nose-to-tail shake, the horse was once more settled.

It had taken only an instant. And in that instant, Joshua had disappeared.

Aurelia breakfasted alone. The dowager marchioness of Whiston and Lady Moresby were leaving the breakfast room as Aurelia came in; both Charlotte and Serena, late risers, customarily had trays taken to them in their rooms. The men, including Lord Moresby, had headed out for the day's shooting at dawn.

She would have preferred company, for being alone left her no diversions from her thoughts, and they, no matter how she tried, strayed inevitably to Christopher Ballantyne.

Servants had informed her that he and Emil Drew had ridden away from Nethergate not long after the hunting party set out. She found herself more than a little disappointed that he left behind no word of farewell, not so much as a note thanking her for her hospitality. On the pretext of taking Galahad for an early morning walk, she made her way to the shabby room where the Americans had spent the night.

She stood for several minutes in the empty chamber.

Only light from the corridor penetrated, so that even on a sunny morning, the place was gloomy. Cold ashes filled the fireplace; neither lamp nor candle chased the shadows.

Though she had never thought him a thief, Aurelia's quick inventory of the furnishings proved Ballantyne had taken nothing but what belonged to him. Nor had he left anything behind.

Except this feeling of unshakable apprehension that lingered, through her usual morning tasks, her solitary breakfast. Normally she would have spent the morning with Joshua in the increasingly futile effort of trying to familiarize him with the workings of Nethergate and the other Winterburn properties, but because he had gone with Adam Braisthwaite and Freddie Denholm for a day's shooting, she was left to her own devices.

Even her grandfather chased her grumpily from his company, once she had assured him Ballantyne was indeed gone.

"You're certain?" he asked, looking up at her from his chair by the fire. He did not ask her to join him.

"His room is empty, and Guthrie said they rode out almost on the heels of the hunting party."

"Then there's no harm done by the lying thief," he said, so quietly he might have been speaking to himself. And he sounded unconvinced as he stared blankly at the flames.

She wanted to ask him what harm Christopher Ballantyne could have done, and how he knew the American was a liar and a thief, but she hesitated to pursue a subject she sensed he was reluctant to discuss. And he did not look well, with deeper shadows under his eyes that spoke of a sleepless night, not a restful one. Aurelia noted too that there was another bottle on the table added to the collection of potions and tonics Dr. Robbins, the village doctor, had prescribed. Dr. Ward, the physician Serena brought with her from London, must have concocted this latest elixir, but it did not appear Charles had taken any, for the bottle was full despite the spoon lying beside it.

Aurelia was searching for words to continue the conversation, to break the silence, to keep her mind from dwelling on Christopher Ballantyne and at the same time seek answers to the questions plaguing her, when the duke suddenly growled, "Have you nothing better to do than sit and watch an old man die?"

"But, Grandfather, you know I—"

"You're as bad as the rest of 'em," he interrupted with a rude wave of his hand. "Go on, go on with you. Leave me alone. Let me live—or die—in peace. And see to it that Ballantyne never sets foot in Nethergate again."

His attitude was an unnerving combination of childish petulance and imperious command, followed by a morose silence. Aurelia welcomed the dismissal even as she worried at the changes in both his physical condition and emotional state.

Perhaps it had been a mistake to let Christopher Ballantyne escape without getting answers from him.

But it was too late to do so now. Rather than wander the halls of Nethergate like some restless shade or sit in her own room as glum as the duke in his, Aurelia bundled herself in cloak and boots and, with Galahad straining at his lead, decided to expend some of the excess nervous energy she had felt building within her all morning.

She did not give the dog the freedom to run off the lead for fear Adam or Freddie or even Joshua, who claimed to know little of hunting, might mistake the deerhound for a deer. When Galahad, who could not understand the reason for his restraint despite Aurelia's explaining it to him often enough, insisted on running, she added, "Besides, even if he did recognize you, Joshua is as likely to shoot you anyway. I've never seen an Englishman, even a colonial, as afraid of a harmless dog as he is."

Not knowing in which direction the hunters had set out, she listened for sounds of gunfire but heard nothing. In contrast to the day before, the late morning was brilliant and clear, with an electric blue sky overhead and not a single cloud. Frost clung to the ground in the shadows, but where the sunlight had melted it, everything glistened with tiny droplets. Birds that had not flown to warmer climes chirped and twittered, and even a rabbit hopped across the path, to set Galahad pulling so hard Aurelia needed both hands to hold him back.

But for all the beauty of the day, the air was cold, especially when the path twisted its way into the woods. When the cottage, built for a MacKinnon spinster a century or so ago and abandoned until Aurelia claimed it as her own refuge, came in view, she let Galahad pull her toward it. Inside she could light a small fire, brew a cup of tea, and spend the rest of the day in the same peace and quiet her grandfather had requested.

She might even, she thought, be able finally to put Christopher Ballantyne out of her mind.

The stone building nestled like a hibernating mouse in a wooded fold between two hills. A low wall, of the same rounded fieldstone as the house and notched by an ornamental iron gate, enclosed a grassy yard. An icy, spring-fed stream gurgled a few yards away, crossed by an arched stone footbridge to take the path into the trees. Another road, wider but no more heavily traveled, followed the water's course and led, by an easier but more circuitous route, back to Nethergate's front door.

Isolation cocooned the place. The unkempt yard was littered with dead leaves that should have been cleared away weeks ago. The rose climbing a trellis beside the doorway was as brown as the stones and added to the sense of abandonment. Even the birds seemed quieter, letting the rush of the brook sound louder in contrast.

Galahad shattered the spell with a sudden spate of riotous barking. The ring of keys Aurelia had taken from her pocket went flying as she struggled to keep the dog from running headlong across the bridge and into the woods. She thought she heard a sound, the breaking of branches, slow hoofbeats, even voices, but the echoes of Galahad's yelps and howls reverberated off the hills until she could hear nothing else.

And then she saw the horses, moving unevenly as they came down the road through the trees. The brown mare's rider sat slumped and swaying in the saddle, as though the slightest nudge would send him toppling to the ground. The bay gelding limped slowly, cajoled into making each step by the man who walked between the two animals.

He wore neither coat nor hat, and his white shirt was stained with what could only be blood.

5

HAD THE DOG NOT SET UP SUCH A FURIOUS BARKING, KIT WOULD never have seen the cottage or the path that led over the bridge to the gate. The weathered slate and rounded stone blended well into the shadows of autumn-browned woods on the hillside. The way the road curved, too, helped hide the building. He had passed this way only a few hours ago, but had seen nothing.

Now, perhaps, he had found a haven, if he could get the terrified gelding under control.

"Easy, easy," he crooned to the animal, and cursed the dog under his breath. He wished he could pat the horse's lathered neck, but he dared not let go of the mare's bridle. A single misstep would pitch Emil to the ground, and if she bolted, there would be no way to move the injured man any further.

"Hold on, Emil," he called over his shoulder. "It's going to be rough for a bit, but I think we're almost there."

The huddled figure, shrouded in Kit's much too large

coat, emitted a low moan but did not ask where "there" might be.

The barking faded, and Kit watched, still struggling with the wild-eyed bay, as Aurelia tied the dog's lead to the gate and then headed with military determination in her stride toward the bridge.

The quaintly attractive span was too narrow for the two horses to cross abreast. With a quick, deep breath to steel himself against more misery, Kit dragged them down the rocky bank and into the rushing water. His feet were already wet and the stream was no more than two or three paces wide; it was a matter of the numbness now reaching halfway to his knees instead of merely to his ankles.

He had nearly brought the mare and gelding up the slippery slope on the other side when the bay stumbled again. His fingers clenched so tightly around the bridles for so long, Kit couldn't immediately let go to keep himself from falling. Even as he felt the ground sliding away beneath his feet and lost his hold on the mare, the hem of Aurelia's cloak entered his field of vision.

"I have the mare!" she cried. "Can you manage the other?"

He could not speak, only nod and hope she understood. He was on his knees in the icy water, his left arm about to be separated from his shoulder by the panicked gelding—or worse if the animal bolted and dragged him to kingdom come.

Aurelia screamed again. "Let him go before he kills you!"

The horse snorted and thrashed his head, but Kit hung on, managing to get to his feet on the slippery rocks at last. He was soaked to the skin now, too cold even to speak beyond a bitter laugh and a croaked, "Someone else has tried and failed. I'll not give a dumb beast the pleasure."

He said nothing more until they had tied the horses at the gate and taken Emil into the cottage. They had a devil of a time getting him up the narrow stairs, with Aurelia insisting there was more risk of aggravating his injury if Kit carried him, but finally Kit overruled her and picked up his friend for the last half-dozen steps. With a brief moan, Emil protested, then lapsed into unconsciousness.

Aurelia turned back the coverlet on a bed in one of the bedrooms and Kit laid Emil down as gently as his own shivering muscles could. She was a model of efficiency and calm, for which he had to admire her.

"I'll bring in your valise while you strip out of those wet clothes. As soon as I've started a fire and made you some tea, I'll fetch the doctor."

Without looking at him, she headed for the door.

"That won't be necessary," he said, pulling the blankets up to cover Emil's still form. "My coat's dry, if a bit bloody, and as soon as I've changed my clothes I can ride the mare to the village—"

She turned sharply.

"There's no doctor in the village now, and if there were, you are in no condition to go after him."

She was looking at his face, at the blood he felt drying there. He touched the knot on his forehead and the small cut beginning to scab over. He had done worse bumping into low doorways.

"I'm fine. Where *is* the nearest physician?"

"At Nethergate."

The tone of her voice told him she knew he had been ordered never to set foot in the place again and that the servants would refuse him entrance—and that she also knew he had been returning there despite the ban.

"You're quite safe here, Mr. Ballantyne. The cottage is mine."

He tried to laugh through chattering teeth as he slowly descended the stairs. She was a picture of Quaker simplicity and innocence, adjusting her cloak around her shoulders after having pushed it back to settle Emil in the bed. He almost hated to alter that innocence, but had no choice.

"It's good to know you won't kick me out the way your

grandfather did, Miss Phillips, but I'm afraid that hardly makes me feel 'safe.' Didn't you hear me a few minutes ago? Someone tried to kill me."

The man was an accomplished liar. There was no reason for Aurelia to believe his accusation. Had he not told her last night that this Emil Drew was a poor horseman? A purely accidental fall, attributable to his own incompetence, might have caused his injuries, which Christopher Ballantyne then seized upon as a convenient justification for retracing his steps to Nethergate. Despite that rationalization she let him lead her outside without protest.

"It was very cleverly done," he explained as they walked toward the gelding and mare dozing in the noontime sun. "A little more clever and I would undoubtedly not be here to talk about it."

He cautioned her to remain inside the gate, where Galahad immediately tried to jump on her in greeting. She smacked his nose and made him sit at her heel while she watched Ballantyne unsaddle the gelding, who tried to prance out of the way and laid his ears back in warning.

She noticed blood on the gelding's flanks and at first thought it caused by spurs. A quick glance told her that Ballantyne wore none. And, she saw when he had untied the valise from the saddle and let it drop to the ground, the source of the bleeding appeared too high, almost on the horse's back.

"Last night, I told Guthrie I didn't know exactly when Emil and I would be leaving, so he needn't saddle the horses. Yet we found them waiting for us in the stable yard this morning." He began pulling the straps free, and the horse whinnied with a sound akin to panic. His eyes rolled and Ballantyne had to stop to pet the beast calm. "With your other guests demanding attention, Emil and I chose to be on our way."

She very nearly told him Joshua and his friends were not her guests at all, but kept silent while Ballantyne continued.

"I didn't ask who had readied our mounts or why. The saddles were secure and a final inspection revealed nothing amiss. But I had not checked everything."

He eased the saddle away from the gelding's back, and what Aurelia saw brought an angry gasp from her.

A raw wound oozed fresh blood, and the underside of the saddle was soaked with it. Ballantyne dumped the jumble of leather and wool padding upside down on the stone wall before he probed at the torn flesh. Again the horse tossed his head menacingly.

Aurelia's first close look at the bloody saddle revealed an ugly bit of metal formed of several twisted nails embedded in the wool. Only after a few miles' riding it would have worked through to begin the painful digging and cutting into the horse's skin.

Ballantyne pulled a wrinkled handkerchief from a pocket and tried to wipe away some of the blood. "A less competent rider would have been thrown when the gelding tried to rid himself of what he thought was the cause of his pain—namely, me. While I dismounted to find out what had happened, he spooked the mare."

She remembered what he had said last night about the servant's dislike of horses and how the stable boys had laughed at the stories. Did Ballantyne feel as guilty now as she did? She suspected so, from the tone of his voice.

"Poor Emil lost control of the mare, and he was the one hurt, not I."

"But who would do such a thing?"

"That is precisely what I would like to know, Miss Phillips."

His question came easily and without a trace of emotion. In his eyes, however, she detected something that felt very like an accusation. He stared at her without blinking.

"Perhaps if we knew *why* someone would do it," she said, meeting his stare with no guilt, "we would have a better idea of the *who.*"

Did that answer, with its ambiguous "we," imply she

believed him? She thought he took it that way, for he seemed to relax slightly, like a man who does not realize his fear until it has passed.

Not knowing herself whether she believed him, she opened the gate and untied the mare. "Let me go to Nethergate," she implored. "Whether the servants would let you in or even carry a message from you to the doctor, you are soaking wet and in no condition to ride." When he did not protest, she drew a deep breath and went on. "The cottage is not stocked with food this time of year, but there is tea and you might find some brandy."

He said nothing as he offered her a leg up so she could mount astride, but looking down at him, she sensed an air of conspiracy, secrecy, reluctant trust. She tucked skirts and petticoats around her legs as best she could, then dug her heels into the mare's flanks.

Galahad barked twice before he let out a mournful howl that not even the steady thud of hoofbeats could cover.

She arrived windblown and disheveled in the stable yard, where the lack of activity assured her Joshua and his party had not returned. An astonished Guthrie emerged from the building to help her dismount with as much dignity and decorum as she could muster. The instant her feet touched the ground, she began snapping orders.

"See that this horse is properly cared for and saddle another for me at once. I shall also need a mount readied for one of the doctors. Then send someone immediately to my cottage to fetch Mr. Ballantyne's gelding."

"Mr. Ballantyne?" the old man repeated slowly. "Begging your pardon, Miss Phillips, but I thought—"

"And I want to know who was responsible for saddling his horse this morning," she went on, ignoring Guthrie's question. She imagined he must be staring at her in disbelief at her brusqueness, but she had no time to waste. If she so much as stopped to address him face-to-face, she would confess everything, including her knowledge that the American had been banished from Nethergate. "You'll also need to send word to Mr. Atkins, the innkeeper, that his horses have not been stolen and will be returned to him shortly. The gelding is injured, but whether you tell Mr. Atkins that or not is up to you."

Did Guthrie gasp at that last? Aurelia nearly did herself; she had never condoned, much less encouraged, deceit in her life.

With a muttered dismissal, she sent him on his way. There were more important things to worry about than whether a groom told the whole truth about an injured horse.

The problem must have bothered her more than she expected, for she did not, a few moments later, even remember entering Nethergate. She stood, enveloped in silence, inside one of the doors leading from the garden. Her pounding pulse and rapid breathing told her she had run, but she did not recall that, either.

She could not recall the last time she had run, for any reason, except last night when she fled Christopher Ballantyne and his kiss.

She wanted to wait, in the familiar quiet, until every trace of haste had left her. She wanted the calm, ordered existence that had been hers all her life to return, to wrap her in the warmth of routine and security. She wanted to erase Christopher Ballantyne from her mind, for in less than twenty-four hours he had destroyed that security.

Not one of her wishes could come true. She had no time to catch her breath, for a man lay injured and awaiting the medical attention she had promised to bring him. The pattern of her life had not been disrupted solely by the storm-swept arrival of a handsome colonial last night, nor even by his frightening accusation of attempted murder and the evidence she had seen with her own eyes. If anything, the installation of Joshua MacKinnon as the heir to Winterburn more than a month ago posed a more serious threat to her peace and serenity. He, too, disturbed her, with his lies and his laziness, his disregard for others, especially for the estate his grandfather had recalled him to.

And she suspected that even if she never saw him again, Christopher Ballantyne was already indelibly etched in her memory. How could she ever forget the rush of warm desire that filled her at that first touch of his lips on hers? That he knew at least part of her secret and found it more amusing than threatening was enough to make her overlook some of his own dishonesty, but was it enough to allow her to trust him further?

Her footsteps echoed in the vast silence of Nethergate. When had silence become so uncomfortable? Had a single race from the cottage, with the rush of the wind and the heart-echoing rhythm of hoofbeats in her ear, destroyed forever everything familiar? Aurelia tried to slow her pace and quiet the rapid cadence of her boots on marble floors, but she also had to fight an urge to scream, to shatter this suffocating stillness, to call out for Dr. Robbins and send him to the cottage and lock herself in her room alone with only Galahad's devoted company and . . .

Elegant in a simple gown of pastel blue, Serena appeared at the open door to the drawing room and broke into Aurelia's thoughts.

"Whatever is the matter, my dear? My gracious, we heard running feet and assumed the house was afire or Bonaparte had invaded."

Aurelia glanced into the drawing room and saw Lady Whiston, Lady Moresby, and Charlotte gathered near the fire. The dowager marchioness stared with unabashed curiosity and cupped a hand to her ear to catch any conversation. Charlotte, her shoulders hunched as if to hide the expanse of chalky white bosom exposed by her magenta gown, studied the hands folded on her lap. Lady Moresby slurped tea noisily.

A lie, a simple, innocuous lie, should be so much easier than the truth, with its concomitant explanations. In Aurelia's mind, the words were there. She had only to say,

"Nothing is the matter; please excuse me for disturbing you," and she could be on her way.

Instead she stammered, "I must find either Dr. Ward or Dr. Robbins at once."

Serena's tiny gasp could not screen the glitter of anticipation that entered her eyes. Her hand reached for the long strand of pearls and stroked them with a slight tremor.

"Nothing has happened to His Grace, I hope?"

"Not that I know of. There's been an accident. Mr. Ballantyne's servant was thrown from his horse and has been injured."

The glitter faded, then flared more brightly. Did it mean Serena had anything to do with the metal burr placed under the gelding's saddle? Or was she delighted at any reason that brought Christopher Ballantyne to Nethergate?

"I believe Dr. Robbins may have been called out, but Dr. Ward should be in the library this time of the day." She twisted the pearls around her fingers, then laid her other hand on Aurelia's arm with a conspiratorial squeeze. "You've done what you must, my dear. Why don't you prepare rooms for Mr. Ballantyne and his poor servant while Dr. Ward and I take the trap to bring them back to Nethergate?"

Aurelia shook her head emphatically. "Grandfather has forbidden him to return."

"Oh, la, child, I know that. Both he and his secretary have made it clear to everyone in the house. Do you think I care a fig what a dying man forbids? If I wish to invite Mr. Ballantyne to join our party, I shall do so. Charles gave me leave to invite whomever I thought would best prepare his grandson to step into his inheritance. Perhaps Mr. Ballantyne can teach Joshua . . . something." Her laughter lacked all pretense at humor, and her grasp on Aurelia's arm tightened. "Now, tell me where I may find our injured *guests.*"

Even as she pulled free of Serena's grip, Aurelia stood fast. Though Christopher Ballantyne had lied on more than one occasion, he had at least made the attempt to justify his actions as being for someone else's benefit. There was no question in her mind that Serena lied far more frequently and with only her own interests at heart. If she must choose between acceding to Serena's wishes and protecting the American, Aurelia readily sided with Ballantyne.

Keeping her voice low, she said, "I do not recall asking for your assistance, Serena, but only if you knew where I could find one of the doctors. Since we may be gone most of the day, I'm sure you will be more comfortable remaining here."

Her heart was pounding and her palms felt sticky with nervous sweat. Had she ever defied Serena so brazenly before? If so, she could not remember it, but Aurelia discovered she had enough courage after her surprising show of defiance to give Serena a final cutting stare. The older woman's blue eyes widened in shock. If they later narrowed with anger because Serena had not received the answer to her question, Aurelia did not see. She spun away, her cloak dramatically aswirl, and strode down the corridor to find Dr. Ward.

The terror of the battle did not leave her, and she knew there lurked the threat of reprisal, but mixed with the fear was a strange, new exhilaration, the sweet thrill of victory. She fairly ran to the library, where Dr. Ward informed her he would meet her in the stable yard in thirty minutes. Now the energy building within her was fueled by impatience as well. Unable to contain it, she hastened to her grandfather's room. He must, she reasoned, be informed of the truth of the morning's incidents before Serena had the opportunity to spread her lies. His Grace must be told that Christopher Ballantyne was once again under Nethergate's roof because he had no choice, and not because Serena wished him to be.

To avoid attracting unwanted attention, Aurelia slowed her pace so the tap of her heels on the marble floor did not announce her. As she turned into the intersecting corridor that led to the duke's apartment, she glanced at the wrinkles in her skirt. His fading eyesight would not likely notice her disheveled appearance, but nonetheless she tried to smooth the fabric into a semblance of decency.

Had she not been so uncharacteristically concerned with decorum, she might not have heard the duke's anguished query.

"Good God, man, are you certain? *Absolutely* certain?"

She stopped dead. Twenty feet away, the door to his apartment stood ajar, angled toward her. She would have seen it if she had not been worried about a few wrinkles. And now as another voice, filled with the same anxiety as her grandfather's, reached her, she could not go on, not even to make her presence known.

"A-absolutely certain, Your G-grace," Morton Sullivan repeated, the secretary's stammer a clear sign of agitation. "I w-would not have t-told you were I n-not."

Aurelia had never in her life eavesdropped on a private conversation. Was this, she wondered, wiping her damp palms on the wrinkled wool skirt, the same as lying? Yes, it must be, for she immediately turned to go back the way she had come before she heard any more. The two voices dropped to quieter tones that still sounded like arguing, both men speaking at once, so she walked carefully, silently, to avoid disturbing them. But she had taken only two stealthy steps when she remembered why she had come to see the duke—to keep Serena's lies from spreading.

She pivoted again and prepared to stride noisily down the corridor, announcing her arrival in no uncertain terms, when an angry outburst halted her before she could take the first step.

"You must tell no one, Sullivan, do you understand?" The duke wheezed a desperate bellow over the other's feeble protests. Had he not been an old man and weakened by his illness, his voice would have carried throughout Nethergate. "Nothing must come between my grandson and his inheritance."

"B-but surely Mr. MacKinnon himself m-must be told. Or M-miss Phillips?"

"No one, Sullivan! And least of all my granddaughter!"

Aurelia clapped a fist to her mouth to silence a gasp of horror. Biting down on her own knuckles, she tried to make her feet move, either to depart or to make her grandfather and his secretary aware that she was in the corridor. But she could not move except to flatten herself against the wall, though she knew she could not hope to escape detection if either Sullivan or the duke emerged from that room or even peered out into the corridor.

After a long pause, the secretary began to voice another protest, until a sharp thud echoed that Aurelia recognized as the duke's gold-headed cane being pounded against the floor. Sullivan's last word ended with a squeak, followed by a heavy silence.

"Now that Ballantyne's gone, she'll believe whatever I tell her," the duke growled, his voice breaking into a fit of coughing. Aurelia knew she should use that to cover her escape, but something beyond mere curiosity kept her quiet where she stood and waiting to hear more. The coughing eased, and after a brief silence, he continued. "No one will doubt *her* honesty. The girl does have her uses."

6

STARING OUT THE PARLOR WINDOW AT THE FADING AFTERNOON, Kit rolled the bit of twisted metal on his palm. He did not dare close his fingers over it or the sharpened spines would cut into his flesh the way they had into the gelding's skin. One thumb had already taken a painful puncture when he extracted the vicious device from the saddle.

Behind him, Aurelia Phillips coughed softly, as though to remind him of her presence. He had not, however, forgotten her.

"You have no choice, Mr. Ballantyne," she said. Her old imperiousness had given way to uncertainty. Her voice was softer, each sentence more a question than a statement. She looked the same as when she had left the cottage three or four hours ago, but she did not sound the same. "Mr. Drew has been seriously injured. Dr. Ward said there is some risk even in moving him to Nethergate, but if you insist on—"

"I know what the doctor said, Miss Phillips. A broken collarbone and several broken ribs, a concussion, a bruised hip, and multiple minor injuries. I also know what your grandfather told me last night. I'm not welcome at Nethergate, as this 'gift' proves."

Kit had presented his case and his evidence in a brief interview with Charles MacKinnon last night and been summarily dismissed. The duke of Winterburn assured him that David MacKinnon, the elder brother who should have come into the title, died in what was then the colony of Pennsylvania in 1763. Though his body had not been recovered, witnesses testified to his bravery and the severity of his injuries that prevented his leaving the battlefield. With his troops under fire, no one had been able to retrieve the body, and the territory had fallen to the French for several weeks. Given David's reputation, if he had indeed survived, he would not have abandoned his title and its responsibilities.

The old man then ordered his unwelcome American guest to depart from Nethergate and never return. After offering apologies for disturbing His Grace and assurances that he would do as requested, Kit left the gloomy chamber, and this morning he had left Nethergate as well.

Then why the attempt to injure or even kill him? Had he not done as ordered? Or was his mere departure not enough?

He turned, tossing the entwined nails casually into the air. Aurelia followed the object with her eyes, up and down, up and down. She swallowed delicately, discreetly, but not without Kit's notice.

"His Grace is not an unreasonable man. Under the circumstances, I'm certain he can be persuaded to—"

"And how will you persuade him, Miss Phillips? By telling him he'll have more opportunities to do away with me?"

She flinched, like a child expecting a blow, and said not a word in her own defense—or her grandfather's.

Because she could not lie, and because the truth held no defense?

No, Kit was certain, it was something else that held her

tongue, something that had happened during the hour or so she had been gone from the cottage. When she returned with the doctor, there had been no time for questions, only for tending to Emil, who now slept, swathed in bandages and splits, in an upstairs room. But the impression of change permeated even her efficiency in assisting the pompous, impatient physician. She obviously had experience caring for the sick, yet she seemed hesitant, unsure—almost, Kit thought, preoccupied. Not at all the confident chatelaine who had greeted him yesterday afternoon when he entered her domain nor the self-possessed beauty who did not lie.

Watching her now, as she stood with the fireplace behind her and the dog at her feet, Kit tried to determine exactly what about her was different.

And could see nothing.

She stood as straight as yesterday afternoon when she opened the door to Nethergate and admitted, albeit reluctantly, two storm-tossed travelers. Her hair was braided and coiled as sleekly around her head, framing a composed face that betrayed no hint of emotion. Her green eyes met his unwaveringly. She held her hands demurely clasped in front of her, until Kit took a step toward her. The dog rose to his feet, tail wagging slowly, and pushed his head against her knee. When she reached to pat Galahad's head, Kit noticed how that hand trembled. Not the way it had yesterday when she dropped the candle. That, he recognized, was nerves. This was far more intense.

When she spoke, breaking what had become a tense silence, each word came distinctly, as though only great effort kept her voice steady. He did not think she had ever had such difficulty before in her life.

"Whoever was responsible for what happened today, I do not believe His Grace would do such a thing."

"Someone did."

"Not my grandfather!"

The parlor was the largest room in the cottage, but in

another three strides Kit would have crossed it to stand directly in front of Aurelia. He was angry enough to do it, angry enough to grab her by her shoulders and shake the whole truth from her, but the sudden light in those green eyes halted him—and cooled his temper. She was, he now understood, as confused and unsure of the truth as he.

He drew a deep breath and asked, "Then who?"

"I don't know!"

The dog growled, either alarmed by Aurelia's cry or by Kit's approach. Then he barked once, a friendly yip while he continued to wag his tail, but Kit knew Galahad was capable of tearing a man to pieces, even one who had released him from his short lead and given him water and scratched his belly, even one who let him lie in front of the fire instead of in the cold, wet grass. Cautious, Kit left a space of half a yard between himself and Aurelia.

"I believe you, Miss Phillips." He let himself look into her eyes as he spoke, capturing her attention. Now it was she who moved forward to narrow the distance between them. "But I also believe it would be risking my life to spend another night within the walls of Nethergate."

He caught the movement of her hand as she sank her fingers into the scruff of the dog's neck. Galahad whined, not in pain but with a childlike excitement and eagerness. In contrast, the dark light in Aurelia's eyes spoke of fear. Kit extended his own hand and let the dog sniff his palm before he scratched a tufted ear, and then curled his fingers over hers.

"What did you say to my grandfather last night?" she whispered.

"Didn't he tell you?"

Aurelia fought the urge to clasp the hand that covered hers. This man had come a stranger into her life only yesterday, had lied to her and kissed her, and aroused a desire in her she had thought no one could. Was it that unexpected attraction that frightened her, while at the same time it thrilled her? In some way she could not comprehend,

Christopher Ballantyne threatened everything she held dear. He had come between her and the only anchor in her life, to leave her feeling lost and adrift. What flawed instinct drove her toward him when she ought to flee? What made her lean into his touch when he brushed her cheek with his thumb?

She shook her head, and Ballantyne moved his hand away, but not far. "He told me nothing."

But it was a lie, was it not? The duke *had* told her something when she overheard his conversation with his secretary, even if he himself did not know it nor she know what it meant. Did that absolve her? Or was she splitting hairs over nothing?

And what of Ballantyne? He had not answered her question, save with another of his own, and now his knuckles grazed her jaw to force her to tilt her head back. Her heart was pounding so that she could hardly breathe and something in those dark eyes of his told her he was going to kiss her again. As her eyelids drifted down, shutting out sight and heightening her other senses, she felt the warmth of his breath on her lips.

"Thank God," he whispered.

Her eyes flew open, and she staggered back, knocked off balance as Galahad leaped free of her desperate hold. There was no opportunity to ask Christopher Ballantyne why his whisper echoed the cryptic words he had spoken yesterday evening under eerily similar circumstances. The dog launched himself across the room and now jumped at the door, his barks and snarls filling the cottage and drowning any question Aurelia might have voiced.

But there was more holding her silent than Galahad's uproar. Only Ballantyne's grip on her hand had kept her from falling into the fire. He pulled her roughly toward him in a gesture of instinctive protectiveness, then positioned himself between her and the danger he undoubtedly believed Galahad presented. With her cheek pressed to the rough fabric of his coat, her eyes open with shock as well as confusion, she saw through the parlor window what caused the dog's frenzy.

Half a dozen horses, steaming in the afternoon chill, milled and stamped outside the gate as riders dismounted and grooms hurried to take charge of the animals. With a long-barreled firearm aimed at the cottage door, Joshua MacKinnon led Freddie Denholm and Adam Braisthwaite through the gate. They, too, carried weapons, and Aurelia knew they were far more experienced in the use of those weapons than Joshua.

A wordless cry streaked from her throat as she broke free of Ballantyne's embrace. He clutched at her arm, and though that did not stop her, it kept her from holding her skirt high enough to run. She stumbled on the hem and managed to keep her balance only long enough to fling herself at the last possible moment against the dog. He grunted at the impact, and with her last breath she shrieked a command for him to lie down, but both sounds were lost in the explosion from the other side of the door.

Deafened by the shot, Aurelia heard the ensuing tumult as if from a distance, distorted and muffled by the ringing in her ears: men's shouts, the shrill neighs of startled horses, the low rumble that might have been the thunder of an approaching storm but was in reality fists pounding on the door a few feet away. She did not even hear Galahad's whines; she knew he made them only because he always whined when he licked her face, and he was swiping her cheeks eagerly with a warm, wet tongue.

She had known, even at the instant she watched Joshua raise the gun, that the thick oak of the door was more than enough protection. The shot intended to bring down pheasants and leave enough left to eat would do little damage to the stout wood.

But her fear had been instinctive, as well as her willingness to sacrifice herself. Now, assured that the dog had not been harmed, she wanted to bury her face in his rough fur and weep with relief. Relief, however, gave way to rage as the door opened and cold air rushed over Aurelia's exposed ankles and calves.

She scrambled to her feet, aware as she did so of a steady hand that gripped her arm and helped her up, of another that thrust a leather strap into her free hand. But she gave all her attention to the man who stood before her.

Joshua MacKinnon held another gun leveled at her, then slowly lowered the barrel to point it directly at Galahad.

"You imbecile," she hissed. "Get out of my house."

Beside her, Galahad rumbled a steady, menacing growl. She tightened her grip on the dog's collar, both to hold him and to gain control over her own murderous fury.

With a belligerent thrust of his chin toward the man whose presence Aurelia now felt close behind her, Joshua asked, "What's *he* doing here?" He did not alter the aim of his gun, however. "I thought Grandfather ordered him off Winterburn land."

Before Aurelia could reply, Ballantyne moved from behind her and with a single swift motion grasped the barrel of the fowling piece to shove it harmlessly upward. It spun out of Joshua's grip and would have landed on the slate floor had the American not snatched it from the air at the last second. He examined the weapon briefly before cradling it in the crook of his arm. Without a word, he stepped back to stand beside Aurelia.

"This isn't Winterburn land." Aurelia snapped her attention to Joshua and to Freddie Denholm and Adam Braisthwaite, who crowded in behind him. It must have been Adam's gun Joshua lost to Ballantyne, for the viscount's son reached forward as if to reclaim his possession. Something, perhaps a glare from the American's dark eyes, halted him.

"It's part of the estate until the duke dies," Joshua countered with an arrogant tilt of his head.

If he thought that statement would rally his companions to his support, he was to be disappointed. Adam had already lost his weapon, and Freddie, holding his by the barrel, lowered the stock to the floor. Aurelia did not dismiss either of them as a threat, though she felt more secure since Ballantyne's action had evened the odds.

The silence tingled. The door, disfigured by dozens of splintery pockmarks, still stood open; the parlor, so cozy a minute or two ago, had grown cold. Ignoring the shivers that tried to set her teeth chattering, Aurelia tugged on Galahad's collar until the dog sat, then she addressed Joshua as if the others, including Christopher Ballantyne, did not exist.

"The cottage is mine as of my twenty-fifth birthday, Joshua, which I achieved without celebration four months ago. I suggest, therefore, that you quit the premises immediately. And take whatever game you've bagged today to Nethergate at once. Mr. Ballantyne will be joining us for dinner, and I'm certain you'll wish to impress him with your sporting expertise."

Freddie leaned over Joshua's shoulder and whispered something to him that Aurelia could not hear over the pounding of her heart and the still annoying ring in her ears. Joshua's face contorted in a malevolent scowl. Aurelia realized that what Christopher Ballantyne had given her was Galahad's leather lead. She kept her gaze unwavering ly locked with Joshua's while she clipped the strap to the dog's collar and then let him take a single step toward Joshua.

Exhausted in mind as well as body, and feeling the ache of the bruises her tumble with Galahad had brought to her knees, Aurelia laid her hand lightly on her grandfather's arm and braced herself for the ordeal of dinner.

She had told the duke only enough of the afternoon's events that he consented, with evident reluctance, to grant Ballantyne and the injured Emil Drew shelter until Drew could be safely moved. She would have gone on to detail the discovery of the metal burr under the gelding's saddle, but she sensed her grandfather's withdrawal from the present.

More than once she caught him mumbling to himself, as if lost in his thoughts instead of listening to her.

He was, she admitted, eighty-two years old. It was not surprising, in light of the tale she had heard from Ballantyne, that Charles MacKinnon would occasionally slip into memories resurrected no doubt by the confrontation with the American.

Nor was it surprising that the duke insisted on being escorted to dinner at the same time he rudely dismissed Aurelia from his company. Such childish petulance, Dr. Robbins had told her upon her exit, often manifested itself as a symptom of age and illness. If Aurelia had not noticed this change from his usually affable disposition, she had only to remind herself, as she led him into the dining room several hours after that uncomfortable interview, that both his recent illness and her increased duties since Joshua's arrival had combined to diminish the amount of time she spent with him. And during their infrequent meetings she was often, as last night, preoccupied with other matters and could have missed the foretelling signs.

Upon her first glimpse of the guests already assembled in the dining room, she abandoned her last hope of avoiding disaster.

The duke walked slowly, covering his reliance on the cane with an air of heightened dignity. "Moresby's drunk," he observed under his breath. "And that wife of his best not take a deep breath or she'll burst her gown and have her bosom on her plate."

Chatter had covered the first part of his whisper, but his entrance brought almost instant quiet. Aurelia was certain everyone heard that last remark. Lady Moresby did gasp and flushed an unattractive red, but the strained fabric held.

Serena, resplendent in gold satin and the ever-present pearls, broke away from her conversation with Joshua and Lincoln Gould, the attorney Joshua had engaged in London, to glide with elegant grace toward the table.

"It's so wonderful to see you, Charles," she purred. "Are

you feeling much better now? Yes, of course, you must be. And how fortunate that you can join our newest guest, Mr. Ballantyne."

She made even the act of sitting appear seductive, Aurelia thought as she relinquished her grandfather's arm. And the quick glance Serena gave Ballantyne while she spoke left no doubt as to the object of her seduction. When the American failed to react, and also failed to read Serena's signal that he was expected to sit beside her, she curled her fingers around the rope of pearls until her knuckles turned the same creamy white. Aurelia waited for the strand to snap.

Instead, Adam Braisthwaite broke the tension.

"It appears I have the honor and pleasure of your company, Mrs. MacKinnon," he said, taking the place next to Serena.

The blatant lust in Adam's voice so horrified Aurelia that she was not for a moment aware that Christopher Ballantyne had come to stand beside her.

"Are you not going to sit, Miss Phillips?"

"What? Oh, yes, of course. Forgive me."

"There is nothing, I'm sure, to forgive," he murmured as he held the chair for her. The warmth of his breath on the back of her neck raised the fine hairs with tingling sensitivity.

Serena, directly across the table, shot Aurelia a deadly glare before turning to Adam and asking, "Did Freddie best you at the shooting today? Or are you still our champion?"

The viscount's son choked on his wine. "I'll beat him tomorrow," he vowed, turning a very ugly shade of red. "He had the better gun."

Ballantyne reached for his own goblet with what Aurelia was certain was a smile. "What a sad waste of birds," he remarked quietly.

A stunned silence fell over the table, broken as suddenly as it descended by Lady Whiston's cupping her hand to her ear and asking in a too-loud voice, "What did you say? Speak up, Mr. Ballantyne."

Like the duke's eyesight, the elderly marchioness's hearing had faded, but she turned bright, alert eyes on the American. Almost, Aurelia thought, too bright.

"I said, my lady, what a sad waste of birds to shoot them simply to see how many one can shoot. Unless," Ballantyne drawled, his attention and smile fixed firmly on the marchioness, "the stakes are high enough."

Recovered from his spate of coughing, Adam challenged, "And what do you mean by that remark?"

"He means," the duke cut in before Ballantyne could answer for himself, "that it is stupid to kill every grouse and partridge and sparrow on Winterburn land for no other reason than to prove you can do it."

For all its anger, his voice was hardly more than a whisper, and the outburst left him wheezing. One of the servants stepped forward and Aurelia began to push her chair back to aid him, but the duke waved away assistance.

"What the hell else are we supposed to do in this godforsaken corner of England? Or are we even in England anymore?" Adam asked. "Seems to me—"

A squeak and a sniffle from Charlotte Braisthwaite drew her brother's attention—and caustic comment.

"Oh, Lottie, what *are* you sniveling about now?"

Aurelia turned to her left, intending to offer the girl a smile of encouragement or at the very least sympathy. She found herself instead staring into Christopher Ballantyne's dark eyes. His glance was so swift, so cold, she almost gasped aloud. Yet it was also so brief that she might have dismissed it except for the touch of his booted toe on her ankle.

Did he mean her to keep her silence? And if so, why? She tried to meet his gaze again, but he seemed intent now on the interplay between Adam and his unfortunate sister.

"I'm not sniveling," Charlotte replied in a voice trembling on the edge of tears.

"Ought to be grinning from ear to ear, you ungrateful

chit," her father grumbled. "Another new gown, I see. Shows too much of a bosom you ain't got enough of, if you ask me. Don't you think so, Mr. Ballantyne?"

The pressure against Aurelia's ankle became a gentle stroking. A slow, delightful warmth began to smolder within her, as if Ballantyne's bare toes were tickling up her leg. She felt—and quelled—an urge to smile, giggle, laugh aloud, and waited for his response to Lord Moresby's question.

"I'm afraid I know nothing about ladies' fashions, my lord," he answered.

Aurelia knew once again with sickening certainty that he lied. When she tried to pull away from his continued toying with her foot, he pinned it between his and one of the chair legs.

"I assure you, James," Serena volunteered, "I have done everything in my power to dress your daughter in the latest styles. Surely you are aware that it is not uncommon for a young lady, especially one of marriageable age and station, to—"

"To strut herself like some Haymarket doxy?"

"That was uncalled for, James," Lady Moresby admonished her husband. "Serena offered to help. I've never paid much attention to fashions, and Lottie's not like most young ladies."

He belched. "The gown is hideous, makes her look like a tuppenny whore, and a dying one, too. Yellow ain't her color."

With that Aurelia had to agree, but she said nothing. Anything she said would only have made matters worse, especially for the hapless Charlotte, whose sallow skin appeared almost green in contrast to the bright buttercup yellow satin. Perhaps the seamstress had nothing else, or perhaps Serena chose the unbecoming shade intentionally, to diminish a potential rival.

Perhaps Ballantyne's behavior, too, was intentional. Aurelia began to see a purpose in his apparent goading of the others, even in his lie. He was deliberately drawing out the worst in them. Someone had set out to kill him today, quite possibly someone who now sat with him at this table. What better way to find out who wished him dead than to provoke that person's anger again?

Charlotte sniffled, louder this time. "Papa, please. Mrs. MacKinnon is only trying to help."

"Help at what?" Adam asked, unable to hide a drunken leer. "Help you seduce Freddie here? Or Joshua?"

"Adam!" Lady Moresby snapped.

The viscount's son would not be rebuked.

"Well, if it's true she's dressed like a whore, isn't it also true that she's here to snag a husband? There she sits, pimply little bosom and all, right between Freddie Denholm, whom she drooled over last Season and who wouldn't look twice at her, and Mr. Ballantyne, the mysterious stranger."

"Papa, make him stop!"

But there was no stopping the hideous tableau. Charlotte's voice rose to a shriek as she attempted to drown out her brother's lurid accusations, while her parents shouted and screamed at each other. The dowager marchioness, seated between Adam and his father, swiveled her head back and forth until Aurelia thought the old woman would grow dizzy and swoon. Joshua, at the end of the table opposite the duke, leaned in his chair and watched with a glint of savage amusement in his eyes.

Serena, too, seemed to find the entire debacle entertaining. She kept her gaze trained on her plate, ostensibly ignoring all that went on around her, but Aurelia caught the flicker of a smile on those perfect lips, the sparkle of wicked delight in the crystal blue eyes.

Both the sparkle and the smile faded when Charlotte shrieked and threw down her spoon with such force that it bounced across the table and landed on her mother's plate. Everyone except the duke froze in stunned horror as the girl burst into hysterical tears and fled the room. Aurelia watched her grandfather's reaction. He displayed no awareness of what had happened, except to raise his eyes from a blank stare at his food and, for a brief moment, to look quizzically at Christopher Ballantyne.

Charlotte's sobs slowly faded as the doors swung shut, and the duke continued to stare, much as he had in his room a few hours ago, blankly, so lost in his thoughts he was oblivious to much that went on around him. Aurelia, disturbed by his unwavering attention to the guest he had previously dismissed, tried to conceal her own curiosity, but it was impossible. Serena, too, she noticed, was watching the old man's obsessive stare.

As if the portion of the conversation preceding Charlotte's departure had never taken place, the duke quietly asked, "Do you shoot, Mr. Ballantyne?"

"Not for sport."

Not so much as a blink of an eye separated question from answer. And though Ballantyne spoke casually, Aurelia felt the warning shivers down her spine. When he moved his foot from hers, she felt a different kind of chill.

By the time the absurd spectacle of dinner came to a conclusion with Serena's announcement that it was time for the ladies to retire to the drawing room, Kit acknowledged two clear facts. Everyone at Nethergate, with the possible exception of Aurelia Phillips, would much rather have been almost anywhere else. And everyone at Nethergate, with a few suspicious exceptions, hated everyone else.

Socializing in such malevolent surroundings was not his idea of an entertaining evening.

With a respectful bow to his host, he excused himself.

"Gentlemen, Your Grace, it is with great reluctance that I forgo the pleasure of your company. I wish to look in on Mr. Drew and then, it having been a very long day, I believe I will retire." Much as he disliked the superficial politeness of the formal phrasing, it came easily to him. He supposed, with a wry mental smile, that the others considered his speech as sincere as any they themselves might have made.

Joshua, who had settled himself once more in his chair, puffed deeply on a slim cheroot.

"Good night to you, then, Mr. Ballantyne. Will you come shooting with us in the morning?"

"You forget, Josh. Mr. Ballantyne doesn't shoot for sport," Freddie Denholm said.

"Perhaps he could be persuaded."

If the Winterburn heir expected the challenge in his suggestion to be irresistible, Kit took enormous satisfaction in disappointing him.

"No, I cannot be persuaded. Good night."

Making his way to the comfortable room where he and Emil were lodged, as proper guests this night instead of wayfaring strangers, Kit listened for footsteps behind him. More than once he turned to see for sure that no one had followed.

He had more of a sense of the place now, having seen at least the front of Nethergate in daylight, but much of it remained a labyrinth of short corridors and oddly placed stairs, the result of centuries of construction and reconstruction. In that respect he understood Adam Braisthwaite's sarcasm as to whether Nethergate were indeed within the borders of England; the atmosphere permeating the ancient house was decidedly unmodern, much more reminiscent of a medieval castle on the fog-shrouded moors of nearby Scotland than the glittering mansions of London under the influence of the Prince Regent.

Of the two, Kit much preferred Nethergate, but as he opened the door to the room where Emil, to judge by his snores, slept soundly, he wished he could have spent the night at the cottage at the edge of the woods.

Circumstances dictating otherwise, he would make do as best he could.

The door, he noticed, had a lock, but he had been given no key.

"An intentional oversight, I'm certain," he muttered, mimicking the prim and proper Miss Phillips. He made his way to the small desk and searched the drawers, but he found nothing save a broken quill and a pearl button.

He considered lighting the lamp but worried that it might disturb Emil's rest. The room was small, the furnishings few, and if the key had been placed anywhere, he ought to be able to find it by the light coming in from the corridor. Only a pair of candlesticks were on the mantel, another likely place to leave a key. He headed to the wardrobe, where efficient servants had already hung his clothes. His boots had been polished, too, he noticed.

As grateful as he was for these favors, there was something to be said for a life without servants. His privacy had been invaded in the name of hospitality. Even Emil would never have gone into his carpetbag without asking.

But this was not Kit's first experience with English hospitality. He reached into his pocket and withdrew the ebony box he had dropped there before going down to dinner. It, at least, had not been handled, opened, and even gossiped about by Winterburn's people.

A shadow fell across the room, but too briefly for him to look up and see who had passed by in the corridor.

"One of these ubiquitous servants, no doubt," he muttered, since all the guests save Charlotte Braisthwaite were at the evening's entertainment.

Even so, he walked to the door and peered out, but saw nothing and heard only the closing of another door, though he could not determine which of several along this corridor it might have been.

Despite the preoccupation with Emil's welfare that had demanded his attention earlier this afternoon, Kit had taken some notice of his surroundings, enough to orient himself with the parts of Nethergate he had ventured into last night. Now, after listening for any other sounds of intrusion, he decided only a fool would pass up the opportunity to explore further.

The room Aurelia had settled them in was at the end of a short hallway, one of several that led from a gallery overlooking the entrance hall. He pulled the door closed, leaving Emil to his snores, and set off to discover what more he could of Nethergate, and of its occupants as well.

Like many truly ancient homes that had been occupied by a single family through the centuries, Nethergate had been frequently altered but never completely rebuilt. Though newer than the room where he had spent last night, the wings that joined at the entrance hall were at least a hundred years old, perhaps more, and he had seen nothing in his midnight wanderings that appeared more recently constructed.

Fingering the small box in his pocket, Kit leaned over the oaken railing to peer down into the darkness of the foyer where he had first stepped inside the walls of Nethergate. He let his questions drift at their own pace through his mind as he sought those whose answers lay in the house itself.

Why had the present duke maintained the house so carefully that a spiderweb spun one day was gone the next but never left his own mark upon the building in the fifty years and more that he had held the title? Poverty left subtle signs, as Kit knew, and he had seen none of them at Nethergate. Servants were well dressed, horses well fed and cared for, lamps filled, and corridors brightened with candles. Yet Charles MacKinnon had used none of his wealth to change a single stone of the sprawling jumble.

Another door opened and closed, a distant echo in the silence. Kit listened, trying to trace its source, and could only determine that someone in the main wing had entered or left a room. It was the first indication that he was not the only person abroad in the house. He pushed away from the gallery rail and set off in the direction of that door.

The corridor he followed eventually widened into a broad

chamber imbued with the oppressive atmosphere created by the dark oak paneling and furniture so distinctive of the Tudors. A dozen or more portraits of the various dukes and, in some cases, their duchesses hung in heavy frames on the walls. Last night he had passed through quickly, intent upon finding the duke himself. Now, with more time on his hands, Kit studied each of the portraits until he found the most recent.

He recognized none of the four figures in the family group, seated in a summer garden with a willow-bordered pond in the background, but he knew who they must be. In scarlet coat, satin breeches, and powdered wig, Robert, duke of Winterburn, stood behind the garden bench where his wife Margaret spread wide the pale blue skirts of her lace-trimmed gown. At His Grace's side stood his elder son David, a tall youth of thirteen or fourteen, who even in the stiff formality of a painting seemed impatient to be doing something.

The younger boy could not be more than five or six years old. Fair as his brother was dark, and fragile in comparison to David's vitality, Charles MacKinnon stood at his mother's knee, his hand in hers, as though she wanted never to let him go.

Kit had no idea how long he stared at the portrait, fascinated by the possibilities his mind conjured of what had happened to the dark-haired youth, but the swish and rustle of a lady's skirts and the tapping of a cane on the floor heralded the arrival of others and brought him out of his musing. He smiled, regretting the time he had wasted, but somehow pleased to discover Lady Whiston and Aurelia Phillips entering the gallery from the opposite corridor.

"Ah, Mr. Ballantyne!" the dowager greeted him, her booming voice intended to carry to any others who might share her affliction. "Admiring the family, so to speak?"

She was taller than Aurelia by several inches, and heavier, though what had once been the robustness of youth had given way to the soft, puffy flesh of age. Her bright eyes, glinting in the light that illuminated the portrait gallery, studied him without ever seeming to hold still.

"Yes, I was," he answered quickly, not knowing why he felt there was more to her question than mere curiosity. "It's one of Gainsborough's, isn't it?"

The old woman grinned.

"No one else was good enough for the duchess of Winterburn," she laughed. "Margaret brought him up from London. Charles was so sickly, you know, she refused to travel with him. Rushed into his room every morning to see if he'd survived the night, then hurried him out to the garden to have his portrait done lest he die the next night. Look at the way he clings to her hand, and she to his, as if they are about to be parted at any instant by angels taking him to heaven."

"I'm sure Mr. Ballantyne isn't interested in Grandfather's childhood illnesses," Aurelia interrupted. She met his eyes with an apology, perhaps for the marchioness's deafness that necessitated raising their voices to a shout, perhaps for the intrusion.

"Quite the contrary. As a matter of fact, I'm very interested. Not, of course, that your ladyship could have known His Grace at that age."

He took the old woman's hand in his and raised it gallantly to his lips. She rewarded him with a grin and then slapped his wrist in mock chastisement.

"For a colonial, my boy, you've got pretty manners. David flirted like that, too, with every woman he met, rest his soul. A flatterer as well as an adventurer. Charles, on the other hand . . ."

Her voice faded with each slowly enunciated word. Her attention seemed to have been utterly captured by the portrait, but when she took another step toward it, away from Aurelia's steadying hand, the marchioness swayed. Only Kit's hand under her elbow kept her from falling.

He waited until Aurelia had once more taken the old woman's arm before asking, "Are you all right?"

"Yes, yes, my boy, I'm fine." Her smile this time was less enthusiastic, and he thought he detected a trace of confusion in her voice as well as her eyes. "A bit too much port, I'm afraid. And my knees, you know. They aren't what they used to be."

Again Aurelia entered the conversation. "Which is why you decided to retire," she reminded Lady Whiston as she began to guide her away from the portrait and toward her room. "Molly will have hot towels waiting for you. If you'll excuse us, Mr. Ballantyne?"

"And not escort you? My country's honor is at stake," he said with a wink that earned another grin from the ancient marchioness.

It was not smiles he bargained for, however. Gwendolyn, dowager marchioness of Whiston, had known David MacKinnon in his youth, known him well enough to remember his gallantry. Had she, sixty years later, recognized something of David MacKinnon, once the heir to Winterburn, in Christopher Ballantyne? Was that recognition what sparked her interest in the guest the others would just as soon have ignored?

He was grasping at straws, and the notion irritated him, but not nearly so much as Lady Whiston's silence on the matter all the way down the long hall to her room. She chattered about Charlotte Braisthwaite and her infatuation with Freddie, about Lady Moresby's own lack of taste in clothes, which had obviously visited itself upon poor Charlotte, and about Adam Braisthwaite's overindulgence of alcohol.

She was, in other words, making it perfectly clear to Aurelia, and to Kit himself, that she did not want her nephew marrying into the family.

She said not another word about David MacKinnon.

Disappointed, as well as angry with himself for letting an impossibility generate something akin to hope, Kit paced outside the door after Aurelia and the marchioness bade him good night. He had no reason to stay, and more than enough reasons to continue his exploration. After forcing himself to begin walking on down the corridor in the general direction of the duke's quarters, he paused; and when Aurelia emerged a few minutes later, whispering a last good night to the marchioness as she backed out the door and into the corridor, Kit knew he had been waiting for her.

7

For the space of three or four seconds, she remained unaware of his presence. She pulled the door to until it latched with a soft click; then, with her eyes closed, she arched her neck, stretching out the exhaustion that drew her brows together and created a tiny furrow between them.

"Ahem, Miss Phillips."

She turned abruptly, the crinkle above her nose now a scowl of irritation rather than weariness. As he strode to her, he wanted to reach out and stroke it away.

"Did you want something, Mr. Ballantyne?" she snapped.

"The name's Kit. No one calls me Mr. Ballantyne, not even Emil, and only my mother calls me Christopher."

Her expression did not change, except that she glanced at the door she had closed as if contemplating it as a means to escape.

"I hope you'll allow me to apologize for my earlier rudeness," he continued.

"And which occasion would that be, Mr. Ballantyne?"

The exaggerated politeness with which she spat his name told him more clearly than anything that she did not intend any familiarity between them. “When you sneaked into my grandfather’s room last night? When you accused him of plotting your murder? When you insulted everyone at dinner tonight?”

He was tempted to mock her manners but did not. There was no sense aggravating an already awkward situation.

“No, Miss Phillips, I meant none of those. If I had, I would have apologized to your grandfather or your guests.”

She had marched off a few steps, though Kit was not sure if she were trying to escape from him or merely draw him and their argument away from the marchioness’s door. To Aurelia’s back he added, “I wanted to make amends to you, personally.”

She kept on, but her pace slowed, as though she were beset by a temptation to face him once again. He had no choice but to pursue her, and perhaps that was exactly what she wanted. Another corridor joined this one, short like the others but without the soft shimmer of candlelight to dispel the shadows. Kit realized, when Aurelia finally halted, that she had not been leading him away from Lady Whiston’s door; the marchioness would never have heard them anyway. Aurelia Phillips had been heading instinctively for the sanctuary of her own room.

“You don’t understand even now, do you?” he asked when she paused, poised to turn down that corridor.

“I understand that you’ve come to my home and disrupted it. I understand that someone in my family may have a reason to try to kill you.” Did she struggle with that confession? He thought he detected a slight stammer but could not be certain. She still refused to face him; he wanted to reach out to her, turn her around and look into those misty eyes where he suspected tears hovered.

“Self-righteous indignation is such a perfect defense, isn’t it, Miss Phillips?”

“I—I don’t know what you mean.”

No hiding the stammer that time. And the suspicion of tears was confirmed with a sniffle, followed by a telltale straightening of her shoulders.

The urge to touch her grew stronger, but beneath it lay a strange combination of emotions. Her obstinacy angered him almost as much as it attracted him. He wanted to scoff at her naïveté at the same time he wanted to protect her innocence.

"You claim you never lie, but apparently your honesty is only directed outward. You seem to find ready excuses for concealing the truth from yourself."

"I beg your pardon!"

He thought she would turn on that exclamation, but even when she steadfastly refused to face him, he pressed his advantage.

"Now we're getting somewhere. At least we know it is possible to insult some part of your dubious honor."

"Mr. Ballantyne!"

She did not turn; she whirled. And her eyes did not spark; they smoldered.

"If this is the way you spoke to my grandfather last night, it is no wonder he threw you out of Nethergate."

"On the contrary, Miss Phillips. I was very polite to His Grace. It's really only to you that I've exhibited a remarkable lapse in manners." The crease reappeared between her brows; this time he could not resist skimming it once, very lightly, with the tip of his finger. "No matter how much he desires a lady's silence, a true gentleman would never imprison that lady's foot against her chair."

She blushed, and turned from his touch. The rosiness in her cheeks should have faded as quickly as it blossomed, but perhaps it, too, of itself was embarrassed for her, for after the first rush of color, another, more subtle and more lingering, suffused her features.

Unwilling to see her habitual pallor return, Kit continued his harassment, albeit in a more gentle, more tender tone.

"And certainly no gentleman, even if he is but a poor

colonial, should ever be so forward as to take a lady's chin in his hand and steal a kiss."

She felt the roughness of his finger stroke across her cheek to her temple, then down the curve of her jaw. That same queer eagerness curled and coiled in the pit of her stomach as she tilted her chin upward in anticipation of another of those stolen kisses.

Then he pulled away abruptly, leaving her with an even more furious blush when she realized she must look an absolute wanton. Christopher Ballantyne was indeed an uncouth colonial, and she was about to tell him so in no uncertain terms when a rhythmic noise reached her through the pounding of her own pulse in her ears.

The sound was footsteps, climbing the stairs at the far end of the gallery.

"Ah, Miss Phillips, there you are," Morton Sullivan called, wheezing only slightly after the exertion. "And Mr. Ballantyne, too. How fortuitous."

Aurelia composed herself as best she could in the few seconds it would take her grandfather's secretary to stroll the length of the gallery and reach her. Ballantyne must have heard Sullivan's approach before her, but the glance she stole told her that though he might be far more skilled and experienced in such matters, he, too, struggled to erase the evidence of that almost-kiss.

"Fortuitous, Mr. Sullivan?" he echoed.

"Yes, quite," the secretary said, still walking toward them. He slowed his pace as he approached, but never truly stopped. "I have messages for both of you and now need not search any further. His Grace wishes to speak with Mr. Ballantyne immediately, in his study. And you, Miss Phillips, are requested to attend His Grace first thing in the morning."

When Sullivan had delivered the summonses, he nodded briskly before quickening his steps again and disappearing down the corridor.

Aurelia suffered a moment of speechless humiliation,

until Ballantyne shattered the silence with a low, decidedly wicked chuckle.

"Sir, I fail to see what you could possibly find—"

"I haven't been caught in the act, so to speak, for at least fifteen years."

Feeling her face flame, Aurelia sputtered, "You think I have? That I'm accustomed to being . . . *fondled* in front of my grandfather's secretary?"

She thought she saw a look of apology cross his face, but all that mattered was the smile he could not seem to erase. She felt naked, as if he knew more about her at that moment than she did about herself.

She put enough distance between them that he could not touch her, but the impression remained of a man more than willing to sacrifice his reputation to his desires. As furious as that impression made Aurelia, she had to confront her own lack of self-control. She had been eager for his kiss and had conveyed that eagerness earlier, when she granted him those silly intimacies under the dining table. Silly, perhaps, but she could not hide another blush at the very thought.

"We'll talk later, Aurelia," he said, daring with colonial audacity to use her given name. It rolled off his American accent like a caress, slow and silky, and it was all she could do not to fall victim to the seduction of hearing her name from a man's lips. "I suspect a summons from the duke of Winterburn is not to be taken lightly."

She had opened her mouth to speak, but he silenced her with a kiss, quick and soft, and stole every thought from her head. Only after he had gone, through the long gallery and down the stairs, did she find her voice again, and then it was far too late to call him back and warn him that she had told her grandfather only part of what happened that afternoon.

Galahad, perhaps because of his exercise during the afternoon, was more energetic than usual when Aurelia slipped into her room after parting from Christopher Ballantyne. This was not the first trying day she had had in the past months, and though she frequently lost patience with the dog, such impatience did not last long. His unconditional affection always won her over quickly.

But this night she welcomed his assault, his joyous whine and yips, the swipes of his warm tongue on her hands, even the sting of his ropelike tail slapping against her legs as he cavorted in front of her. When she knelt on the hearth to tend the fire, he lay beside her, not quiet and comforting as she might have wished, but playfully shoving his wet nose under her elbow to demand attention.

He did not belong locked in this room day after day. Before Joshua's arrival at Nethergate, Aurelia's time was her own, to do with as she wished, and so she and Galahad spent many hours out of doors every day. In the past months, however, too much had changed. She could adapt to the changes, unpleasant as they might be; this devoted companion who did not understand the changes could not.

The fire flared, but she sought instead the warmth of the furry form beside her. Eventually she would strip off the velvet gown she had worn to dinner, don her cloak, and snap Galahad's lead to his collar. For now, however, she buried her face against his rough coat and wept.

Aurelia was cold and utterly exhausted by the time she returned to the old kitchen door to let Galahad and herself within the close confines of Nethergate. For her own selfish reasons she had not loosed him as she normally would; she took great comfort from his nearness, even from his tugging on the lead. It seemed that they walked for hours around the ruins of what had been, too many years ago to count, the great castle of Winterburn; and perhaps they had, for only a few of Nethergate's windows still gleamed with light. Aurelia guessed the hour to be near midnight, or even later.

It was not unusual for Serena to be up nearly until dawn. She claimed she was too accustomed to London hours and saw no reason to change. Joshua, too, often blamed his nocturnal habits on a lifetime spent in the tropics, where the heat of the day sapped strength and energy and forced one to be active only after the sun had gone down.

What surprised Aurelia tonight was that she detected the faint but unmistakable glimmer of lamplight around the drawn curtains of her grandfather's study windows. She glanced up to the room where Christopher Ballantyne and his injured servant had been housed. The blank stare of darkened glass told her nothing. Emil Drew could be sleeping soundly while his master argued in the study with the duke.

Had she, Aurelia wondered with the beginning of a lump of fear in her throat, left her grandfather at the mercy of this colonial interloper? She tugged the old door open and pulled it tightly to behind her, then raced through corridors cloaked in shadows.

Galahad thought it a game and began barking ecstatically. She tried to quiet him but eventually had to stop and slow her pace to a brisk walk or he would have wakened everyone in Nethergate.

The stillness assailed her. Her every footstep echoed loudly in the utter absence of other sounds as she passed room after darkened room, all silent. Occasionally a banked fire popped on the grate, and once or twice she thought she heard the skitter of a mouse, but no wind moaned in the chimneys or rattled the windowpanes. Nethergate slept.

Then, as she drew nearer the study, she began to hear what sounded like furtive whispers. A word or two, no more, so brief she could not even be sure they were in fact words. She listened, straining her ears, and moved steadily closer, until at last other sounds distinguished themselves. The rattle of a drawer pull, the rustle of papers, the slap of a book being dropped atop another.

Aurelia stood close enough to the door that the light escaping underneath it glistened on the droplets of dew on her boots. Holding her breath, she waited for the persons on the other side to speak again.

"Damn! Nothing here at all!"

Her heart sank at the recognition of Joshua's voice. She was not surprised that he dared to rummage through the duke's private study, but she knew the knowledge would crush her grandfather. She should, she knew in that first instant of revelation, have never kept secret from him that his grandson and heir was as lazy and ne'er-do-well as the son who had been disinherited years ago.

A moment of silence followed, and she could easily imagine Joshua and his unknown companion surveying the study in search of other hiding places for whatever it was they had not found. Drawers rattled again, and then heavy footsteps crossed from the desk on the far wall toward the door.

Galahad's growl was too deep for human ears; she felt the rumble when she curled her fingers around his collar. Had it not been for Joshua's caution in locking the door, she would have been discovered at her eavesdropping. But the key clattered from the lock and she had time to back far enough away that when Adam Braisthwaite threw the door open, Aurelia and Galahad were at the edge of the light spilling from within.

Adam gave her a dismissive sneer.

"Up a bit late, ain't you, Miss Phillips?"

She could not miss the stink of alcohol that surrounded him.

"I took Galahad out for a walk, as I do every evening."

The dog sat obediently at her heel, ears erect, tail curled neatly over his front paws like a cat. She tightened her hold on him when, over Adam's shoulder, she saw Joshua.

He staggered around the room, snuffing candles but not bothering to straighten the piles of disordered papers on the duke's desk or the tumbled stacks of books on the floor. For all the whispering and apparent secrecy, he did not seem to care who knew what he had been doing.

Beneath Aurelia's hand, Galahad continued to growl softly as a purring cat.

Holding a candle high, Joshua came up behind Adam.

He, too, reeked of brandy. Even by the flickering light she could see the long stain discoloring the front of his shirt.

"I saw lights and thought Grandfather was awake," she volunteered as bravely as she could.

"Went to bed hours ago," Joshua replied with a sniff and a rude yawn. His speech was badly slurred, so much so that the slight colonial accent he tried to cover up slipped in, not like Ballantyne's soft, easy drawl but more the nasal twang of a Cockney. He hiccuped, then pushed Adam out of his way and pulled the door closed behind him. Not that Aurelia could have seen anything beyond the mess they had made, for both of them blocked her way and Joshua had put out all the lights save the one he carried.

They bade her a gruff good night before pushing past her and heading for the stairs that would take them to their rooms. Adam gave her one last leer that sent a shiver down her spine, but they were quickly gone, leaving her and Galahad alone in the dark.

She shrugged off their rudeness as the result of drunkenness. She could easily fetch a taper or lamp from the study and light her way, or wait until her eyes once more accustomed themselves to the dark of the house. Certainly she was familiar enough with Nethergate to find her own room even blindfolded. So she chose to wait, not only for her sight to return after the glare of Joshua's candle but also to put some distance between herself and him.

She even contemplated going into the study to straighten up the mess they had made. But Christopher Ballantyne's words echoed in the silence left when Adam and Joshua's footsteps finally faded. He had told her she did not understand, that she was willing to lie to herself when she could not lie to others.

Something cold raced through her and she began to shiver. Galahad whimpered and rose to his feet, nudging her knee with his nose. The shaking did not stop, and she felt such terror grip her heart as she had never known before in her life.

What sight she had regained now blurred, as tears filled her eyes and spilled over. Her mind's eye, perfectly clear, spread out before her memory that horrible scene when she arrived at Nethergate after the disaster of her interrupted Season in London years before.

She had simmered over a fire of righteous indignation and defense of the truth, no matter how brutal, on the whole long journey. Her mother and stepfather had gone ahead in another carriage, because the weather was cold and their vehicle, being smaller, was also warmer and faster. Aurelia was left to shiver, to contemplate the error of her honesty.

She had seen no error, no matter how she analyzed the ugly situation. And she felt no shame at being cast out of London society for her actions. She hated the artificality of it, the posing and preening, and especially the lies. Yet because she could not lie, because she dared to reveal the truth, they had left London in disgrace. And in the storm that overtook her parents' road to Nethergate, their carriage had overturned. They were killed instantly.

Would lies have saved them? Never, in the dark days that followed, had she believed she did wrong. Tonight, as she stared blindly into all-enveloping darkness, she felt the first pang of doubt, sharper for the years in which it had honed itself deep within her.

Had she lied to her grandfather when she failed to tell him the truth about Joshua? Or had she lied to herself by believing her actions justified? How proud she had been in her hypocrisy!

The American had been right; she did not understand. That confession wrenched a sob from her, as painful as the knife of guilt and doubt twisting in her heart. Somehow, stumbling more than Joshua and Adam in their drunkenness, she groped her way from the study. She nearly fell, and if Galahad had not led her on, she might have spent the night in a crumpled heap at the bottom of the stairs.

There was a light above her, but after the dark, it burned

her eyes. She shut them to shut it out, though nothing stopped the weeping. She gathered her skirt in her fist and, still clutching Galahad's collar, staggered up the steps.

At the top, a disheveled Charlotte Braisthwaite stood, holding high a quivering taper. Her mousy hair hung in two thin plaits on her shoulders; her wrapper had been buttoned crooked.

"Good mercy, Miss Phillips, what's happened?" she asked, backing away from Galahad.

"Nothing," Aurelia blubbered, trying desperately to compose herself. "It's awfully late, Charlotte. Shouldn't you be in bed asleep?"

Galahad, tail wagging slowly, approached her with his nose twitching. There was a childlike curiosity about Charlotte that made Aurelia think she wanted to make friends with the dog. And she recognized, too, a kinship between the viscount's daughter and herself. She at least had Galahad to provide unquestioned sympathy and affection; Charlotte Braisthwaite had no one.

"I—I was hungry," Charlotte stammered. "I didn't eat much at dinner and I thought maybe I could find something in the kitchen."

Aurelia was about to hasten her on her way when a door opened down the hallway and Lady Moresby poked her head out.

"What are you doing there?" she snapped.

Aurelia did not wait to hear the rest of the conversation between mother and daughter. She took the opportunity to drag Galahad toward the sanctuary of her own room.

She had taken a different route through Nethergate to investigate the lights in her grandfather's study, so to reach her room she had to pass through the long expanse of the portrait gallery. A single lamp, turned low, burned at the far end. Still choking back sobs, she maneuvered past the staring eyes of the dukes and duchesses of Winterburn.

At long last, she reached the corridor to her room. Fumbling in her pocket for the key, she did not see the shadowy figure waiting by her door until it was too late. She cried out once as Galahad broke free of her desperate grasp and then suddenly she was wrapped tightly in an embrace from which she never wanted to escape.

8

CURSING STEADILY UNDER HIS BREATH, KIT GATHERED AURELIA into his arms. The anger that had simmered in him for the past two hours or more vanished like so much steam when the lid is lifted, but the pot continued to boil.

Something clattered to the floor—her key from the sound of it—but he did not bother to retrieve it. With the faithful deerhound at their heels, he half led, half carried her to the gallery. He sat her down beside him on a settee pulled close to the fire that, banked for the night, gave little enough warmth.

He noticed the chill only because of the trembling creature who clung to him. She was cloaked in thick wool, with the hood pulled over her hair and hiding her face almost entirely, yet the sweet heat of her kindled an answering glow deep within him, making the fire unnecessary. And of course there was the anger. He could not, even with her weeping and vulnerable in his arm, forget why he had waited for her return.

A great shudder rippled through her, followed by a long sigh. Then, to Kit's surprise and, he realized too late, disappointment, Aurelia pulled gently away from him.

She did not, however, rise from the settee.

"Forgive me, Mr. Ballantyne. I am not usually so . . . so . . ."

"So honest?" He expected her to jump up and flee at the mockery in his accusation. She tensed but held still and he dared to stroke her hair as he pushed back the hood. He felt the silky smoothness of her braids and wondered if there were as much tightly controlled passion in her hair as in her soul. "I saw young MacKinnon and his friend a few minutes ago, just ahead of you. If they accosted you, you have every right—"

"Joshua and Adam? Accost me? No, they're much more interested in—"

She cut herself off as abruptly as she had him. There was too little light for him to read her features. Instead he read bitterness in her voice and impotent anger in the way she lifted a hand to wipe away the tears. Anger not unlike his own.

"They're interested in your aunt, aren't they? Like young hounds after a bitch in heat."

She stiffened. He had gone too far, but at least one suspicion was thereby confirmed. The deplorably honest Miss Phillips did not deny the obvious truth. He regretted, however, having brought her guard up once more.

"You are a guest in this house, Mr. Ballantyne," she reminded him.

"And an unwelcome one, as my conversation with His Grace this evening made only too clear."

"If you understand that, then why do you challenge our hospitality?"

"In what way have I challenged it? By not allowing myself to be killed on request?"

She sighed with obvious frustration and less obvious

weariness. "By sneaking around and forcing yourself on my grandfather last night. By mocking the others at dinner. By insulting your hostess. By accosting me in the dark."

Kit did not respond to that last accusation, but neither did he ignore it. "Serena MacKinnon is not my hostess. I'm not sure what she is, or why that withered old conniver tolerates her, but I am certain she has little to do with my being granted accommodations while Emil recuperates."

"That gives you no cause to insult her. She is my grandfather's daughter-in-law. If he offers her a home at Nethergate, as he has me, who am I to question him?"

"Then why did you not jump to her defense?"

She said nothing. In the quiet, even her breathing grew loud, punctuated by a discreet sniffle from leftover tears. Arguing with her, venting some of his anger, he was able to keep under control the treacherous rise of desire. Now desire gained the upper hand. Again Kit caressed her hair, finding a pin that had worked its way loose. He pulled it free and held it in his hand, then searched for another.

He had just started to wriggle the next pin when Aurelia got to her feet. She turned to face him, and almost instantly the dog rose from his spot in front of the fire to stand at her heel.

"You ask so many questions, yet you answer none," she said. "Why are you here, Mr. Ballantyne? Why did you come from Charleston, South Carolina, to Nethergate? Why have you gone seeking an old man who does not wish to see you? Why were you waiting outside my door at an hour when—"

"Because, dammit, someone tried to kill me!" he exploded as he, too, stood up. Aurelia retreated from him, but not before he clasped his hands around her arms and pulled her close. "Because I want to know which of the various denizens of Nethergate was responsible. Because I want to know why the duke of Winterburn feels it necessary to make me a pawn in some scheme you and he have devised to—"

A low growl from Galahad interrupted him. There was no threat in the dog's stance at Aurelia's knee, no baring of his teeth. Just a warning Kit did not ignore.

With a long sigh, he released what he discovered was a crushing grip on her arms, then ran his fingers through his hair in a gesture of exasperation. The dog had no way of knowing Kit meant no harm to his mistress. Kit himself had not realized until he let her go how close he was to turning a string of bitter accusations into a passionate embrace. Even now the urge to forget everything else and crush her against him was so strong his hands shook with it.

"I'm sorry, Miss Phillips. Very sorry. I have no excuse."

He expected a disdainful sniff and an imperious dismissal, but Aurelia Phillips stood frozen motionless in front of him. Was she as confused as he? Had she, too, felt the lightning surge that blasted all else to glittering dust?

No, apparently not, for an instant later she turned and walked away, Galahad at her heels. Kit watched her go, watched how she squared her shoulders and stiffened her spine, and when she entered the brighter light shed by the lamp in the hallway, he noticed for the first time that one of her braids had come completely loose.

He ought to leave, go to his own room and Emil's deafening snores, but he waited, letting his emotions cool for the few minutes it would take Aurelia to find the dropped key and open her door. Galahad's display of protectiveness assured him she was in no immediate danger.

But he heard no metallic clink of key in lock, no creak of hinges, only a soft epithet that might have been a curse. She must have lost the key completely in the dark.

He reached the light before she did and took it down from the hook to afford better illumination into the dark corridor. He spotted first a tiny gleam of some small object in the far corner, but then the light fell on the key where it had slid across the floor and come to rest leaning against the molding.

Aurelia bent to retrieve it, her loose braid swinging free. The soft curl at the end brushed the floor, but when she rose, it showed not the faintest trace of dust.

"Thank you," she whispered, though she did not look at him as she fit the key into the lock.

The dog trotted ahead of her into the waiting darkness of her room. Then, before Kit could say another word, even a polite good night, she closed the door.

After a sleepless night that ended much too soon, Aurelia dressed in her usual somber clothes, stoked up the fire, and took down Galahad's lead. He had been lying patiently on the rug at the foot of her bed, chewing on some small object. When she approached him with the lead in hand, he abandoned his toy, which skittered out of reach under the bed.

"I do not know where you keep finding these pebbles," she scolded aloud before making certain her key was in her pocket. "At least this one is out of the way and I shan't worry about stepping on it in my bare feet the way I did the last one."

As if he understood every word, the dog laid his neat ears back against his head and looked at her with what could only be described as contrition.

She took her cloak from the wardrobe where she had hung it last night. She had fought every urge, in that horrible hour after locking her door against Christopher Ballantyne, to fling herself on her bed and sob out her pain. Tending to routine matters of housekeeping—putting her clothes in the wardrobe, scooping ashes from the fire—had restored a semblance of calm that enabled her to climb into bed without tears, but now that calm was being eroded by memories.

She sought to regain it out of doors on an overcast morning that promised snow before noon. But running with Galahad beyond the wildest of the castle ruins did not settle her rampaging thoughts. Her bruised knees were stiff and sore, and twice she stumbled trying to clamber over fallen stones of the ancient curtain wall. Galahad barked as he jumped and cavorted ahead of her, his breath forming little puffs of cloud in the biting air. She heard the distant echoes of guns and did not set the dog loose, and that only reminded her of yesterday, of a shot fired at an oaken door.

Only a man unfamiliar with guns and hunting would have intentionally fired at so impenetrable a target, and Joshua had claimed from the beginning to have neither experience nor knowledge of firearms. They were, he insisted, not as much a necessity in the Islands as they were in England. Had he fired deliberately, hoping in his ignorance to pierce the stout wood and injure or kill whomever might stand on the other side? Or was his act an accident, the result of fear or anxiety?

She had had no clear answer yesterday when she left the cottage and so she had said nothing even of Joshua's appearance there to her grandfather. To speculate, she reasoned, would be a kind of lie, since she did not have the truth.

But to say nothing also meant she did not tell the duke of Joshua's later actions, when neither accident nor ignorance explained his pointing Adam's gun at Galahad.

Another lie of omission, and for what purpose? To shield her grandfather from the truth about Joshua? And why should she do otherwise? Telling Charles everything would change nothing, nor would it make his last days any easier. Above all else, she would not repay his kindness over the years to her with unnecessary cruelty.

Breathless, a skinned knuckle and smudges of dirt on her gown and cloak evidence of her hoydenish behavior, Aurelia returned to Nethergate and her appointment with the duke.

To her mild surprise, Morton Sullivan himself met her at the back entrance she used.

"His Grace is waiting for you," the secretary intoned.

She followed his gaze to Galahad, who sat, tongue lolling,

at her side. The dog's paws were muddy and the first few flakes of snow clung to his rough coat.

"I'll take Galahad with me," she replied. "My grandfather does not mind him."

The secretary sniffed but did not argue.

A second surprise awaited Aurelia when she walked into the study. Not only had her grandfather taken his customary place behind the imposing desk, but that desk was as neat and tidy as ever it had been. There was no sign anywhere in the room of the depredations Joshua and Adam had wreaked last night. The duke, dressed in black save for a stark white shirt and silver-gray waistcoat, appeared to be examining one of the account ledgers, which, apart from a lamp and a pot of ink, was the only item on the desk. The books that had been piled on the floor were now back on their shelves.

Aurelia glanced to the crystal decanter and glasses that graced a console table in front of the single window. The decanter was full, the glasses clean and sparkling in the muted light that came through the windowpanes.

"You may leave, Morton," the duke ordered. He looked up from his contemplation of the ledger and scowled at Aurelia. "Where have you been?"

She waited until the door closed to take the chair in front of the desk and answer, "I was outdoors with Galahad."

"Dogs belong in kennels."

She said nothing.

After her exertion in the fresh, cold air, she found the study stuffy and overheated. Or perhaps it was the duke's silent, penetrating stare that made her feel uncomfortably warm. She wished she had removed the heavy cloak, but she could not do so now without drawing more unwanted attention to herself.

"But I suppose after I'm dead and buried you'll take that mangy cur with you to the cottage, so it won't do me any good to exile him now, will it?"

He had made similar comments before in jest, but this

time Aurelia detected no amusement, no lightness in his tone. And his eyes, so pale and filmy she was certain he could see almost nothing, never wavered from her face.

Behind the dim curtain, however, gleamed a spark unwilling to die.

"I've a favor to ask of you, Aurelia. Consider it the wish of a dying man, if you will."

She wanted to leap to her feet and protest, to assure herself as well as him that he was not dying, but she knew the truth. She saw it in his hands, the transparent skin over bone fragile with age. She heard it in his voice, not soft but weak.

"I shall try, Grandfather."

"No, not 'try,' Aurelia. You will *do* this, for me."

The heat was making her dizzy and sleepy; she had to concentrate to pay attention, to combat the hypnotic drone of his words and her own exhaustion.

He began talking of Joshua, of his plans for the child of a prodigal son who never returned. She had heard it before, too often, and no matter how hard she tried to pay attention, her mind wandered. A word or two reached her consciousness, but more and more her thoughts strayed from Joshua MacKinnon to another colonial, to Kit Ballantyne, whose mother alone called him Christopher.

Thoughts of him as she lay in the dark had kept her awake; now she could hardly keep her eyes open. She blinked and forced herself to listen to her grandfather.

". . . a life of laziness and luxury and knows nothing else. It was unfair to think he would change in a few weeks, but I fear we have run out of time."

She wanted to apologize for her failure, to tell him she had done her best despite Joshua's lack of interest in his responsibilities. She stared out the window at the increasingly thick fall of snow and tried to find the right words, but the snow reminded her of the cold lust of greed in Joshua's eyes last night. She had not failed, and to confess to a guilt that was not her own was as much a lie as any deliberate falsehood.

Was that what Kit Ballantyne meant last night when he told her she did not understand? Had he seen what she refused to admit: that her grandfather, without being told, knew how unsuited Joshua MacKinnon was to accept the role of duke of Winterburn? Had she lied to herself far more than to His Grace? Was Kit showing her a truth she herself had denied?

Aurelia blinked, afraid she had indeed fallen asleep. Why else, even in the privacy of her own thoughts, would she have referred to the American so familiarly?

More important, why was the duke discussing the man himself? What had her grandfather said, while she was daydreaming, that she missed?

"Ballantyne will agree, because he trusts you. By the time he learns of your betrayal, it will be too late."

"Betrayal?" she echoed in confused disbelief. Dear heaven, what had he said while she drifted in oblivion? "What are you talking about?"

She bit back further outburst, though a protestation against any kind of betrayal quivered silently on her tongue. The light film of sweat on her body now felt icy, and the chill penetrated deep, beyond any ordinary sensation of cold she had ever experienced before.

"He claims his mother was my brother David's child."

The last trace of mental fog cleared away, as if chased by the same wind that now swirled the storm of snow outside the study window.

"You told me your brother died and left no heir."

"He did," the duke agreed with unexpectedly bitter vehemence. "He went off to the colonies in search of adventure, he said, and told me to keep watch over 'his' Nethergate until he returned. But he did not return."

His pale eyes fired for a moment and he lapsed into an oppressive silence, his skeletal hands caressing the ledger page his only sign of life. Aurelia took the moment not to clear her thoughts, for that was impossible, but to order the barrage of chaotic images assailing her. From the portrait of the young brothers and their parents to Lady Whiston's intense study of it. From Joshua's fowling piece aimed at Galahad to the bloody wound on a horse's back. From Serena MacKinnon's seductive smile to Charlotte Braisthwaite's cry of mortification. From her own denial of a connived scheme to Kit Ballantyne's whispered "Thank God" just before he kissed her. Now, she suspected, she was hearing that very scheme for herself.

"I was here, in this very room, when they brought the news to my father. David died bravely, the messenger said, defending English women and children against the murderous French and their savages. My father looked at me, at his sickly second son, and *then* he wept."

He began coughing weakly, as though prolonged speech had robbed him of strength again, but when Aurelia started to rise to assist him, he gestured her to sit down. She sank back onto the chair, her hands now gripping the arms to help her hold on to reality. This whole scene had become something out of a nightmare.

"I was sickly, but I survived," he rasped, his fevered glare now focused on her. "I took care of Nethergate, of all Winterburn, exactly as I promised David I would. *I* kept my promise; he didn't keep his." Again she heard that childish whine; it set her nerves on edge, but she said nothing as he continued, "And when my father died, *I* became the duke of Winterburn. I had earned it, and I will see that Joshua does as well. My grandson, not some boorish colonial with ridiculous stories."

"But even if the tale were true, his uncle is still alive, and Kit could not inherit through his mother."

Such a simple statement of simple fact should have reassured him. Instead, he snapped at her, "Do you think I don't know that? But you will tell them otherwise."

"I? Tell whom? And you cannot expect me to lie, Grandfather."

At any other time, she might have laughed at the absurdity of it, but not this morning.

"That is exactly what I expect, Aurelia. You will tell Joshua there *is* a way, that he must earn his inheritance as he has never earned anything in his life. Or I will name Christopher Ballantyne my heir."

"That is outrageous! I—I cannot do it!"

Galahad, sleeping at her feet, lifted his head at her outcry. When she reached down to reassure him with a scratch behind his ears, she felt the subtle vibration of a low, almost soundless growl.

Her grandfather said nothing. The subtle shift of his gaze from her face to the dog, however, told her without words that he had made his threat. A dying man's last wish, she recalled. And while he lived he could take away the one hope she had for her future.

A disturbance outside the closed study doors reached her ears. Someone shouted, a good distance away, and perhaps that, rather than her own agitation, had startled Galahad.

He growled again.

"Why, Grandfather?" Aurelia stroked the dog's slender head and sleeked back his ears. "You know I would do anything in my power for you, and the cottage is all I—"

More shouts drowned the rest of her statement. Galahad stood, hackles raised, as the study door opened without a warning knock.

Aurelia turned in her chair, her fingers sunk deep into the deerhound's coarse pelt. Morton Sullivan, his ordinarily pale features bleached a sickly gray, separated himself from a knot of whispering servants clustered outside the door.

"What is it, Sullivan? By what right do you—"

"Ruth has just been in to take Mrs. MacKinnon her morning chocolate, Your Grace." The secretary's monotone quivered with nervousness, as though he kept some frightful emotion barely controlled. He walked up behind the chair to Aurelia's left and gripped the back of it until his knuckles went whiter than his ashen face. Even that, however, failed to still a trembling that grew ever more violent.

"Mrs. MacKinnon is dead, Your Grace. Strangled. Murdered."

9

NOT WAITING TO HEAR WHAT ELSE THE SECRETARY HAD TO report, Aurelia left both her grandfather and Morton Sullivan in the study and raced with Galahad at her heels to Serena's room. Breathless, her heart pounding with dread, she shouldered her way through the crowd of morbidly curious servants, giving each of them instructions to be about their normal duties. She dispatched one to find Joshua's hunting party, and another to fetch both Dr. Ward and Dr. Robbins.

Dr. Robbins, however, was only a few steps behind her, and when they entered Serena's bedchamber, the portly and as always disheveled country doctor strode on ahead.

"No question but she was murdered," he said before he reached the bed.

Aurelia thanked providence she had not had time for her own breakfast.

Serena's abigail, a gaunt, usually quiet woman named Ruth, sat sobbing on a chair in the far corner of the room. A large wet chocolate stain on her apron and the shattered porcelain on the floor testified to the shock she had endured. Aurelia signaled to two maids hovering by the door. If they could not get Ruth to leave the room, they could at least shield her view of what lay on the bed.

Aurelia forced herself to look, not from idle or morbid fascination, but to satisfy herself of the truth.

The mortal remains of Serena MacKinnon sprawled amidst tumbled bedclothes, evidence of a struggle against her assailant. Her arms were flung wide, with one hand extended, palm upward, over the edge of the bed. From the white fingers hung a piece of heavy string; a dozen pearls on her palm were all that had not scattered when the necklace broke. The others lay everywhere, on the bed, on the floor, even on the tangled blond hair fanned behind her on the pillow.

Her thin linen nightrail, provocative but utterly impractical this time of year, was twisted about her thighs in a macabre semblance of decency.

There was no blood.

"Thank God," a familiar voice murmured behind Aurelia.

"Are you thanking Him because a woman has been brutally slain in her own bed, Mr. Ballantyne?"

"No, I'm thanking Him that *you* are all right. You are, aren't you?"

Was she? At least facing him meant she could turn from the hideous sight of Serena, her sightless eyes bulging from the bloated, purplish distortion of what had been such perfect features. But she could not turn away, not even when Ballantyne's steady hand on her shoulder applied unsubtle pressure.

"I am as well as can be expected under the circumstances."

She watched the village doctor, shorter and far less elegant than his London counterpart, take two pennies from his waistcoat pocket and place them over the staring eyes.

"She's been dead for hours," Ballantyne whispered.

Now Aurelia did turn, just her head, to look up at him. "How do you know?"

But before she had her answer, the pressure of his fingers increased and he was guiding her from the room.

"Where can we talk?" he asked as soon as they were in the corridor and far enough from Serena's chamber that no one would hear. "Privately. Without fear of interruption."

Surprised that her thought processes still functioned, Aurelia dismissed several locations.

"The room where you stayed two nights ago," she said and stepped ahead of him enough to free herself from that hand on her shoulder.

To reach the old servants' wing on the other side of Nethergate, she had to lead him through the portrait gallery, where now all those long-dead eyes seemed to stare at her, with questions, accusations, palpable malice.

"How did you know she's been dead so long?" she asked again, to add voice to the rhythm of their footsteps.

"He couldn't close her eyes. Rigor mortis does not take hold until several hours after death, and then it is gradual. Especially in a room as cold as hers."

Other voices, agitated but low, drifted up the main staircase. There was, Aurelia knew, no way to reach the distant wing without descending those stairs and confronting whomever was gathered there.

She was surprised, however, when Ballantyne took hold of her elbow and pulled her to a halt. With a finger to his lips he held her silent. In an instant, she had recognized the voices and strode to the top of the stairs. Ballantyne hung back, out of sight, but she knew he heard every word.

"What's going on?" Joshua called up to her. "Where in blazes is everyone?"

"Place is like a bloody tomb," Freddie Denholm added, brushing snow from his shoulders. "Did His Grace finally die or something?"

As she descended the stairs, Aurelia told them, "I thought you were hunting; I sent someone to find you."

Adam Braisthwaite gave up a futile attempt to unfasten his coat buttons and looked up at her.

"Too damn much snow. Couldn't see a bloody thing." Then, after a disparaging glance at Joshua, "Oughtn't to have listened to a man who's never seen snow before in his bloody life."

Joshua shrugged off the insult. "How was I to know? Gould said it was too early in the season for heavy snow, and he's from London. I can't imagine him setting out if he thought he'd be caught in the storm."

"He's a bloody solicitor who never sees the light of day. How would he know anything about weather?"

How would Kit Ballantyne know anything about dead bodies and rigor mortis? Aurelia asked herself. One step at a time, she drew closer to the trio who had returned on their own from the abortive shoot. Not one of them would meet her eyes. Freddie seemed the most nervous, casting her furtive glances and then looking away. Adam returned to fumbling with his buttons and swearing with a deplorable lack of imagination. Joshua, after another shrug, turned from the stairs as if searching for the servants.

She waited until she had reached the last step but one before telling them, "Serena is dead."

It was impossible to watch all three of them for their individual reactions, but Aurelia caught glimpses of each. Freddie paled so suddenly she thought he might faint. He stumbled forward to the bannister and clung to the newel post for support.

"When? How?" he whispered.

"Last night. Someone strangled her in her bed."

Adam's face, too, had lost its color. Now a sickly greenish tinge crept into his pudgy cheeks. With a strangled cry, he bolted past her. She made no effort to stop him and hoped Ballantyne, too, had let him go. Apparently he had, for

Adam's thudding footsteps continued long after he had reached the top of the stairs.

That left Joshua, frozen like one of the marble sculptures that graced this room. Aurelia held her breath, waiting for his reaction, and tightened her grip on Galahad's lead. The dog did not sit as he usually did, but stood quietly, ears alert, tail motionless.

Only Freddie's desperate gasps broke the silence until Aurelia heard steady footsteps on the stair behind her, the measured cadence that should not be familiar and yet was.

Then Joshua turned. Though red from the cold out of doors, his cheeks had gone pale with shock. Twin streaks of tears glistened in mute testimony to grief.

"She was my only friend," he murmured like a frightened child.

Aurelia moved toward him, to offer what comfort she could, but with the speed and intensity of summer lightning, he lunged toward her. If she had not had a good grip on Galahad's lead, the dog would have been at Joshua's throat long before his hands reached hers.

"Damn you, you sanctimonious parson's daughter!" he raged, retreating from the dog's bared teeth. "And that hound from hell of yours, too! You did this to her! You killed her!"

"Joshua, please, I did nothing of the kind. Someone else, we do not know who—"

"Yes, yes, you did!" He danced around the hall, his arms outflung almost exactly as Serena's were. "You raised the others up against her! You made them hate her, just as you hate me!"

He came at her again, his eyes wild, his hands curled now into claws. Aurelia did all she could to control Galahad, who snarled and snapped each time Joshua came close.

Ballantyne, standing behind her, ordered, "Take the dog and I'll meet you in the other room," then he went to take control of the hysterical Joshua MacKinnon.

But by that time, Joshua's wails and screams had brought servants, too, including the man Aurelia had sent to find the hunting party. In a few seconds, Kit had Joshua on the floor and was calling for someone to administer a heavy dose of laudanum to calm him. That was what they had tried to force on her when her parents died. She had refused it, and her grandfather had not let them hold her on the bed and pour it down her throat.

Too many images, too many memories. She blinked them away, only to see Ballantyne look up at her, an angry scowl darkening his face. He yelled at her to go, that he would find her later, but she hesitated. There was still poor Freddie, oblivious to the tumult around him, who clung to the newel post.

"Dammit, Aurelia, get out of here! There's nothing you can do now!"

Galahad no longer strained toward the combatants, and his growls settled to a deep steady rumble, but she had no difficulty dragging him from the scene. She stared at Joshua, spittle flecking his lips as he shrieked obscenities at her, and only from the corner of her eye did she catch a glimpse of Freddie, glassy-eyed, reaching into his coat and withdrawing a short, sharp-bladed knife.

As Freddie lunged at her, slashing wildly, she screamed and ran, and did not look behind her.

His nocturnal explorations proved valuable, and Kit made his way to the tiny chamber unerringly. The corridor was dim but not dark, for the high, narrow windows let in little of the winter light, but at the end the glow from an open door beckoned.

He stopped in the doorway, certain Aurelia had not heard his approach, but he had not counted on Galahad. The dog immediately rose from his resting place in front of the fire and trotted toward the door, tail slicing the air merrily. Kit extended his hand to a cold nose and a warm tongue.

"He trusts you." She had taken a steaming kettle from the

hob and was pouring tea into a single cup. She did not look at him.

"And you do not?"

"No, Mr. Ballantyne, I do not. Now, if you will excuse me, I have a great deal of very unpleasant work to do."

He waited, watching the stiffness of her movements as she returned the kettle to the fire and snapped her fingers at the dog. Whether she knew it or not, she teetered on the edge of the same hysteria that had driven a distraught Freddie Denholm to lash out at the nearest target, before he turned his weapon on himself. Kit saw it in her exaggerated calm, her attention riveted to the commonplace act of pouring tea into a cup. Denholm had been restrained before he did any damage; would physical force be needed to protect Aurelia, too?

Kit waited until she had attached the lead to the dog's collar and was about to leave. She still had not looked at him, but when he blocked her escape with his hands firmly on her shoulders, she finally tilted her head back and met his eyes with hers.

"I must go," she murmured.

"There are servants," he insisted.

"There is no one to tell them what to do."

"His Grace is ruler of this domain. Let him do it. Or his secretary. Or Lady Whiston. With her voice, she'll have them jumping in no time."

His feeble attempt at humor failed miserably, except to distract Aurelia enough that Kit was able to push her backward a step at a time. When at last he had her sitting in the chair again, he went down on one knee, his hands on her shoulders. Beneath them, she had begun to shiver in the aftermath of too many shocks.

He had seen the same reaction before. Another ugly death, a different woman left to cope with unanswered questions and an uncertain future. And he himself was so much younger then, so frightened. Experience had taught him well.

"Can you hear me, Aurelia?"

For a moment he thought she had slipped into a kind of waking trance, but slowly she nodded her head once. Gently, soothingly, he stroked his hands down her arms to her wrists, then turned her palms upward. They were icy yet damp with nervous sweat.

"Then I want you to listen to me very carefully. We have only a few minutes before someone comes for us."

Her vacant stare gradually focused and then without warning she asked, "How did you know about rigor mortis? Are you accustomed to examining corpses, Mr. Ballantyne?"

In the interest of time, he decided to forgo gentle explanations. Nor did he fight when she pulled her hands free. He placed his on the arms of the chair, keeping her just as effectively held.

"My father hanged himself when I was fifteen years old, Miss Phillips. I found his body the next morning. My mother wanted it to be a murder, so she wouldn't have to accept responsibility for driving him to his death, but there was no evidence, no likely suspect."

That brief recitation caused little pain, and even less anger, except when he saw the pity it stirred in Aurelia's green eyes.

"I'm terribly sorry. How selfish you must think me."

"Malcolm Ballantyne was a foolish man who married an even more foolish woman. I sometimes wonder how I ever gained an ounce of sense coming from such a union."

"That's a terrible thing to say about your mother!"

He could have laughed or at least smiled, but he chose instead the cruelest reply of all.

"But, Miss Phillips, it is the truth. And it has nothing whatsoever to do with the situation we find ourselves in. Serena MacKinnon was murdered last night while you and I were in the gallery. I believe the same person who tried to kill me killed her and now intends to pin the crime on me."

"And I, Mr. Ballantyne, believe you are suffering from a very active imagination." She snatched her hands free and tried to hide them in her skirt.

"Am I, Aurelia?"

He grabbed her right wrist and turned her palm up again. She closed it into a tight fist, but when he reached into his pocket with his other hand and held it over hers, she slowly opened her fingers. He dropped a small white object onto her palm.

Then he let her go.

She stared at the pearl for the space of two or three deep breaths before she looked at him again.

"Where did you get this?"

"In the hallway outside your room. When I brought the lamp to help you find your key last night, the light fell on it."

"You could be lying. You've lied to me before. You could have picked it up from Serena's room. The pearls were everywhere." As if realizing what she held, she suddenly handed the bead back to him. "Or perhaps you are only saying you found it by my room. Perhaps it came into your pocket when *you* killed Serena."

"Or perhaps it was caught in *your* clothes when *you* killed her. Did anyone see you while you were walking your dog last night, Miss Phillips?" Horror at the notion of such a thing being believed blanched her features, and he could not stand to let her suffer. "No one in his right mind would suspect you, Aurelia."

She took a deep, cleansing breath.

"But suspicions and accusations are very different things, are they not, Mr. Ballantyne?"

This time a ghost of a wan smile turned up her mouth, and when he offered her his hand, she took it between both of hers and closed her fingers tightly around his.

Yet she said nothing, and some of that eerie vacancy returned to her green eyes. Kit imagined she was weighing the alternatives, searching for the one she could label "true" and thereby tidily discard the rest. None of them, however, would fit so perfectly to the exclusion of all others.

"What you are saying, I think, is that we must trust each other, while at the same time wonder if we are not walking into a trap from which only the guilty will emerge."

"*Skeptical* is the word, my dear."

Touching her was like playing with one of those electrical toys all the rage in London. Someone cranked the thing up while you put your hand near the brass ball and then suddenly a sizzle and a snap and a bluish flash of light jumped across to your finger and jolted you to your toes. When he held her wrist the sleeve of her dress insulated his fingers, but when he dropped the pearl onto her palm, nothing protected him from the surge of current. Now there was no resisting the magnetism of her touch. With a quick twist of his wrist he held both her hands gently prisoner and brought them to his mouth for a kiss.

"Does this seal our relationship in some barbaric colonial fashion, Mr. Ballantyne?" she commented when he raised his eyes to hers again. "Am I now committed to you for my own self-preservation? A woman lies cold and dead, murdered in her own bed. Another narrowly escaped a similar fate at the hands of a knife-wielding madman, and you expect her to let you, who could very well be the murderer, take her hands in yours and cover them with passionate, seductive kisses?"

Her breathing altered even as she spoke, becoming more shallow and rapid.

"Are they passionate, Aurelia?"

He closed his mouth over one of her knuckles and grazed it with the edge of his teeth. Aurelia moaned softly but did not pull her hand away.

"Are they seductive?"

Desire mounted in him like the static electricity in one of those parlor toys. He kissed the back of her hand, closed now into a tight but trembling fist. The spark was ready to explode within him, until a canine whine and a raking paw on Kit's knee broke the fragile contact.

Still holding Aurelia's hand, he looked down into a pair of dark, pleading eyes.

"It appears Galahad does not approve of my kisses, seductive and passionate or otherwise."

She blushed so furiously Kit felt the heat rush into her hand before she pulled it free. She could not know how that blush transformed her, how it melted her austerity into innocence, how it proved the depth of the hidden passion she tried so hard to control.

"He must think we're . . . playing," she murmured.

"Then I fear I must revise my opinion of his judgment, for I assure you, Miss Phillips, I was most serious."

Even had she not had the cloak fastened around her, her modest gown would have concealed the extent of the furious crimson that overflowed her cheeks. How would such a rosy glow look, Kit wondered, if Aurelia chose a gown as daring as what Serena had worn?

"Far too serious, Mr. Ballantyne," she breathed, "and under the circumstances, most inappropriate."

He stood and pulled her to her feet. She offered little resistance—perhaps because she dared not admit her own response was every bit as inappropriate as his advance? Because her knees had gone too weak to hold her and she needed his strength?

"Serena is dead," he said, curling her against him in anticipation of her protest, "and we are alive. Very much alive. Under those circumstances, I do not consider a moment of appreciation for the fact inappropriate at all."

She leaned back in his arms and looked up at him with eyes darkened by a passion beyond her innocent power to deny. Yet she did not give in to it. Her heart pounded against his; he watched the echoing pulse at the base of her throat. He waited for the feathery lashes to descend as she finally surrendered to the storm of emotion that swept away all thought, all reason.

"Why have you come here, Christopher Ballantyne? What was in the letter you sent to my grandfather? What did you tell him that turned him against me?" she whispered. "And tell me no more lies."

Too late, he recognized his error. The passion that beat within her was anger, not desire.

"I have not lied to you, Aurelia. I want you to trust me, to help me—"

"Help you?" Calm so cold it shivered frosted her echo. "Help you steal what is rightfully Joshua's? Is that why you came here? Is that why you tried to seduce me? Is that why you lied to me?"

Good God, what had the old man told her?

"Dammit, I haven't lied to you, Aurelia."

"You asked me where we could be alone to talk, and you have said nothing. You only wanted a place to seduce me. And to kill me, too, the way you did Serena."

"I didn't kill her! And I didn't lie to you! Why won't you believe me? You have no monopoly on truth, Aurelia Phillips."

More frustrated than angry, he thrust her from him, hard enough that she lost her balance and had to grab for the chair to keep from falling. Galahad was already at her side, hackles raised, ears laid flat against his skull.

"I came out of idle curiosity and because I had nothing better to do."

She laughed. "No one comes to Nethergate by choice, Mr. Ballantyne."

"Well, I did!" She was driving him beyond endurance, and if he did not get hold of himself he was likely to do something worth regretting.

The energy roaring through his veins demanded physical release. Pacing the small room was not the outlet Kit would have chosen, nor did it fully satisfy certain needs, but it helped. And it put some distance between him and the woman he was not sure what to do with.

"I told you my father killed himself, leaving me to

support my mother. A Charleston shipbuilder, William Cooke, gave me work and promises. Six months ago, after I had put fifteen years of my life into his company, Cooke sold out to pay debts I never knew he had. My expectation of a partnership vanished. So did the interest of a young woman I had intended to marry."

Something flickered in Aurelia's eyes at that comment. Why was he telling her what he had never revealed even to Emil? Sarah Wadsworth's betrayal was a private pain, yet it was also one Kit had healed from more quickly than the other. Perhaps he wanted to spark a bit of jealousy—and perhaps he had.

"Your grandfather could have told you this. Or has he already? Are you testing me to see if I can tell the same tale twice?"

"My grandfather told me you claimed to be his brother's son, which is of course absurd."

"Of course. His brother was my grandfather, not my father. His *elder* brother."

"That's a lie!"

"Is it?"

In losing her temper for that brief outburst, she had given him the control of his. Kit reached into his pocket for the ebony box.

With surprising calm he admitted, "I didn't believe it either, and I'd heard it all my life from my mother. That her father should have been a duke and walked away from half a kingdom, a castle, a fortune. I sometimes think she drove my father to his death because he could not meet her dreams."

A tiny gasp escaped her, and she turned exceedingly pale. Whatever he said that had affected her, she recovered in an instant, becoming once again cool and still.

"After the loss of my prospects with Cooke, I considered going to sea with Captain Cornelius Trethevy, whose ship we had built. I made the mistake of inviting the captain home, and my mother pounced on him like a terrier on a rat. Told the poor man the whole story of her life as the duke's daughter, raised in poverty on the frontier because her uncle had stolen the title from her father."

The retelling sounded absurd, not as it had last night when he recounted his history to Charles MacKinnon, the very man his mother had reviled. Once started, however, Kit knew he must finish the tale or it would mean nothing at all.

"Trethevy believed her story, not so much because she charmed him but because he knew a bit more of it even than she. His trade in the Caribbean had introduced him to most of the planters, including one Michael MacKinnon, who had been disinherited and then reinstated as the heir to the same duke of Winterburn."

"Joshua's father. But he died nearly two years ago," Aurelia said.

Her anger seemed to have faded, replaced by what Kit took to be acceptance. He did not waste the opportunity.

"Yes, Michael had died and according to Trethevy left a spectacularly worthless son. Gossip being as valuable an item of trade as coffee, molasses, or tobacco, Trethevy also informed my mother that there was no other heir, that Charles MacKinnon's other sons had died without issue."

"So you *did* come here to steal Joshua's inheritance!"

"I most certainly did not." He noticed with some wry satisfaction that she had not jumped to Joshua's defense. "I'm an American citizen, Miss Phillips. We did away with hereditary titles when we did away with British rule over forty years ago. I came to England because Trethevy suggested I join him as partner and seek investors in London, now that the two countries are at peace again. Before I left, my mother made me promise I would seek out the duke of Winterburn and get the truth from him at last."

He snapped open the silver clasp on the box and lifted the lid.

"You asked me what I wrote to your grandfather," he

went on, taking from its velvet nest a broken bit of black stone. "I wrote only that my name was Christopher Ballantyne, that I came on behalf of my mother, Mathilda MacKinnon Ballantyne, and my uncle, Jeremiah MacKinnon. Jeremiah had given me this signet and said he remembered the day it was broken. I then sealed that brief note with this."

Kit set the ring on its velvet cushion and handed the box to Aurelia, hoping that the display of trust would engender some reciprocation.

She took it from him gingerly. Was she, like he, afraid to risk the slightest contact? He realized then, watching as she removed the signet to examine it in the lamplight, that through the turmoil she had not tried to leave the room. The door stood open, exactly as he had left it. She could have escaped at any time while he paced and was preoccupied with telling of the events that brought him to this snowbound charnel house. He would not have stopped her.

Yet she had stayed.

Perhaps she trusted him in spite of herself.

In the lamplight, the details of the tiny carving stood out clearly, a snarling wolf's head cut from a single piece of black onyx. Though most of the ring's shank was missing, the bit that remained and the almost intact signet were enough to indicate that the whole was made to fit a small hand. Christopher Ballantyne could never have worn it. Even Charles MacKinnon in his youth might not have been able to slide the circle over his knuckle.

Yet the signet itself was as large as any man would wear. Aurelia held it on her palm to admire the intricacy of the work. The missing corner had taken an ear, but the bared teeth, the curled lips, the savage eyes comprised a miniature masterpiece.

Then, as she turned it slightly the ring rolled over, and on the inside, on the small portion of narrowed shank, she saw a single letter, a capital *A,* incised into the stone. Part of a name? Surely not an endearment on such a blatantly official signet. Perhaps a motto.

Ballantyne watched her for a moment, then, as though consumed with an unconquerable need for action, began moving around the small room again.

"Before I left Charleston, I visited my uncle," he told her, taking up the poker to stir the fire. "He lives in a simple cabin, as did his father, in a rather wild part of Pennsylvania."

Setting the signet back in its box, Aurelia asked, "And did he tell you how the ring came to be broken?"

"No. He told me to ask Charles, and I did that first night. Charles said he had never seen it before, knew nothing about it.

Sparks raced up the chimney, and the blazing logs popped. Aurelia tried to estimate how much time had passed since Christopher Ballantyne had joined her here, but she had lost all sense of time. By the burning of the logs, she suspected at least an hour had passed since she laid the fire. Surely someone would be looking for them by now.

Aurelia glanced at the open door. Ballantyne turned his back to her to add another log to the fire, leaving her free to walk from the room if she so desired. He could, she supposed, catch her if she ran, but she also supposed he would not try. Not even if she confronted him with the worst of her suspicions.

"You hunted him down and accused him of stealing his title and estate from a brother he thought was dead. You knew he was incapable of defending himself, so you did not wonder *why* someone tried to kill you the next day, only *who* had done it."

He walked to her but to her mild surprise he said nothing. Nor did he ask for the box and ring, which she held open in her hand. She snapped it closed and fastened the tiny silver clasp before offering it to him.

"The answer to the one would tell me the answer to the other," he said. "I believe, however, that the opposite is true with the unfortunate Serena. If we knew *why* she was killed, we should have a very good idea who did the deed. And in learning who killed Serena, we will discover why that same person wants me dead as well."

10

"I'M NOT CERTAIN I UNDERSTAND EXACTLY WHAT YOU MEAN, Mr. Ballantyne. Are you implying it is up to us—you and me—to unmask Serena's murderer?"

He closed his long fingers around her hand to repossess the ring box. In contrast to the way he had given it to her, he seemed to want to extend the contact. Aurelia felt herself drawn toward him, not so much into a physical embrace as into an alliance. A preposterous, possibly unholy alliance.

"I am implying precisely that, my dear Aurelia, and a great deal more as well."

He slipped the ebony box into his pocket. The removal of his hand around hers left her feeling vulnerable and exposed. She wanted to regain the sense of protection he offered, but at the same time she remained wary, not only of him but also of her own wishes.

"Why?" she asked. "Why is it suddenly our responsibility?"

"Because we alone know we are innocent."

"Do we?" She sensed far more arrogance in his statement than innocence.

"I most assuredly did not try to kill myself by putting a metal burr under a horse's saddle, nor had I any reason to hurt poor Emil in the process."

"Unless you needed a reason to return to Nethergate."

To her surprise, he smiled and nodded with what she took to be approbation. "An excuse at best, but not a reason. I had no reason to return, and every reason to leave a place I knew I was unwelcome. I came back only because of Emil."

Another lie, or part of one. Surely Ballantyne had not forgotten how insistent Serena had been that he stay, not only upon his arrival but the next day, after the accident. Now Serena was dead.

Or, Aurelia wondered as a headache of desperate confusion began to throb in her temples, did Ballantyne dismiss Serena's eagerness? But how could such a dismissal constitute a reason to kill her? Surely a man did not kill a woman simply because she desired him and he did not return her affections.

She shuddered, recalling the scene of the dead woman, the broken strand of pearls, the rumpled sheets that hinted at an intimate liaison. It made no sense to imagine Ballantyne returning to Nethergate at Serena's command, unless he was a far more skilled liar than Aurelia thought. But could she believe him, when he carried the evidence of the pearl in his hand? That tiny bead conjured in her mind the image of Christopher Ballantyne and Serena MacKinnon, locked in the most sensual of embraces, and yet something else immediately erased the picture like chalk from a slate. Was it because she could not bear the image? Or because there *was* no possibility?

She pressed her fingertips to her temples and closed her eyes in an attempt to order her thoughts. She must not allow herself to offer defenses when the evidence was to the contrary. She must not let her own emotions, her own desires, take control of the truth. Even as the questions tumbled into her mind like pebbles down a hillside, undermining her already precarious balance, Aurelia resisted the temptation to trust.

Ballantyne said nothing, as if he meant her to take the lead rather than direct her. She listened to the quiet sounds he made, his footsteps going toward the fire, the hiss of cold tea tossed into the flames, his lifting the steaming kettle and the soothing ripple of the cup being refilled.

She opened her eyes when she knew he stood in front of her, offering her the scalding drink.

"It wants a good shot of brandy or whiskey," he told her, "but I've neither. Still, this is strong and hot and . . ."

She took the cup from him, allowing their fingers to brush and acknowledging the sensation such a touch sent through her. To deny it would be the worst kind of lie.

"It's much too hot," she whispered.

"The other was much too cold."

The seduction in his voice could not have been more blatant. Aurelia, her hands occupied with cup and saucer, found herself defenseless when he walked behind her and began methodically removing the pins from her hair.

"Mr. Ballantyne, I must request that you not—"

"You have a headache," he interrupted. "I am merely attempting to alleviate the symptoms."

His calm, matter-of-fact tone contrasted so sharply to what Aurelia had heard as seduction just seconds earlier that she believed she must have imagined it. She felt profoundly—and inexplicably—dismayed.

"You cannot expect to think clearly with a headache, and as we both know, you must have all your wits about you."

The cup was so full she could not take so much as a step without the risk of spilling tea over her hands, much less turn around to escape his ministrations. He had loosened one thick plait from the tight coronet and now worked on the second. The effect was so soothing, so relieving of the pain in her head that words of protest became impossible.

Instead, she agreed with everything he said.

"I want you to drink your tea, and then we shall find someone to help with the necessary arrangements. Lady Moresby? The dowager countess? One of the servants?"

She shook her head, amazed at how light she felt without the constriction of the braids pinned to her scalp.

"No, not Lady Moresby. If she is not prostrate with shock, she will be hysterical, and of no use in either case." The words came automatically, without thought. The throb of the headache had eased, too, to little more than a sensation of pressure at the base of her skull. Coherent thought returned, along with a consciousness of the responsibilities that devolved upon her. "Lady Whiston is a marchioness, not a countess, but I would sooner expect capability from her, despite her age, than from the others."

Yes, yes, she was able to think again. There were so many things to do, things she had forgotten about in her shock. And though she did not believe an uncomfortable coiffure had kept her from being rational, she admitted Christopher Ballantyne's remarks had merit. She felt much better with her hair loosened from its pins. The first sip of barely cooled tea also helped. It burned, but it also warmed, deep inside where there had been such coldness before.

Ballantyne came around to stand in front of her, his dark eyes narrowed as he looked down at her. She was reminded again of his height, of his raw, masculine, somehow peculiarly American strength. He rested his left hand on her shoulder, then lifted his thumb to stroke the corner of her jaw.

"I did not lie to you, Aurelia. I did not bring you here to seduce you, for the word implies deceit and coercion. I cannot, however, deny wanting you."

He raised his other hand and she saw that twined around his fingers was a wavy lock of her hair.

She could not think. There she stood, an ordinary, commonplace cup of tea in her hands, and this man, this stranger, lifted a lock of her hair to his lips and kissed it. She did not know he had even loosed the braids.

"I could accuse you of the worst kind of deceit," he murmured, "in hiding this extraordinary beauty."

"Kit, not here, not now. Please."

A faint smile turned up his lips. She thought at first he was going to kiss her, and discovered with some shock that she wanted him to. She remembered what he had said about celebrating life even in the face of death, and now she knew exactly what he meant.

But he didn't kiss her. He nodded silently in the general direction of that very mundane cup of tea. She drank again.

"When you've finished that, we will go together to His Grace and tell him—"

Aurelia dropped the cup to its saucer with a clatter; had she not been holding both of them, she was sure they would have shattered on the floor.

She had forgotten. In the horror of Serena's death, in the shock of Joshua's reaction, in the violence of poor Freddie's attack, she had forgotten the single most frightening event of that hideous morning. Now she remembered, and not even the tea could melt the ice of dread that formed within her.

Her grandfather had demanded she lie, that she declare this man standing before her an equal heir to Winterburn, though she knew it could not be true. Charles MacKinnon would never have done that save under the most extraordinary of circumstances. Aurelia had done what she could to keep him from knowing the truth about Joshua, about his laziness, his lack of interest in the estate save for how quickly he could spend its fortune, but Charles MacKinnon had not reached the age of eighty-two without acquiring some insight into human nature. He knew the truth about his grandson. He knew that she had failed, but far worse, he also knew that she had, in her own way, lied to him.

Serena had polished Joshua into a proper Englishman. She had brought her friends to Nethergate to teach Joshua the social skills he would need as duke of Winterburn. They had succeeded. Aurelia had failed.

She realized now that her grandfather, the one person she had been able to trust all her life, saw that failure as a betrayal. This, then, was to be her punishment. A fitting punishment. Forced to lie, then forced to betray not only the victim of her lie but herself as well.

She wanted to scream at the unfairness of it. Instead, she gathered the cold that curled inside her and wrapped it around her like a cloak.

"I do not know what you told my grandfather that turned him against me, Mr. Ballantyne, nor do I know how I will tell the lies he has asked me to tell, but I will do it. I will leave the search for Serena's killer to the constable or whoever is responsible for such things."

"Who will you send to the village for the constable in this weather?" he asked. "And isn't your grandfather, as lord of the manor, the magistrate and therefore responsible for the investigation of all crimes committed within his jurisdiction?"

He spoke the truth, but nevertheless Aurelia felt manipulated. She could not, on her own, call in the local constable without the duke's authority, and she was quite certain His Grace would never consent to bringing in an outsider anyway.

"Whoever is in fact responsible for such investigations, Mr. Ballantyne, surely it is not I, and even more surely it is not you. In any case, I would not ally myself with you in such a search for fear I would be looking in vain."

"Are you accusing me of murdering that woman?"

His eyes were hard, staring down into hers, but Aurelia thought she saw within them a kind of pain. She told herself, however, she was only seeing another of his lies.

But he had asked a question she could not answer, not without lying.

She could not trust him, and yet she had no one else to trust.

He took the cup and saucer from her and set them on the table.

"If I had wanted Serena dead, or your grandfather, or anyone else in this bloody cold heap of stone, don't you think I'd have done it two nights ago and been long gone when the sun rose on my deeds?"

He made perfect sense. But so had his lies to Serena that very first night.

He shook his head and finally turned away from her. He ran his hands through his hair, tousling it further. Aurelia grasped at her own unbound tresses and tried to twist them into some semblance of a civilized coiffure, but she could find no pins to hold it.

"I told him his plan to lie to Joshua was a waste of time," Ballantyne finally said, "that I wouldn't go along with it and neither would you. Apparently I was wrong."

Her heart skipped a beat and her breath caught in her throat.

"You don't understand," she began, aware of the note of pleading in her voice and unable to silence it.

"No, Aurelia, you are the one who does not understand, because you are the most innocent of us all. You trusted a man who was willing to use your trust for his own ends. And in your innocence, you who cannot lie, you will betray us all."

He came back to her with astonishing swiftness and took her face ungently in his hands. She had no time to cry out, only to open her mouth before his descended upon it, strangling her protest.

His kiss was hot and brutal, but too ferociously honest in its passion to be a lie. Could a man feign such hunger that his hands trembled as they caressed her cheeks and jaw? Could counterfeit desire draw from her a response so powerful it caused physical pain?

As suddenly as he kissed her, he drew away, though his hands still circled her face. She felt the hot shimmer of tears in her eyes, the burning of strangled breath in her chest, the incandescent fire in her blood.

What had he done to her? Dear sweet God, in that

moment she would have done anything for him, so long as he did not let her go. The words were on her tongue, to agree to the lie, to betray everything she held sacred. She would have risked her very soul.

"You have never been kissed like that, have you?"

She could only shake her head, and did not even blush at his discovery of the depth of her innocence.

"You know that what your grandfather wants is impossible, don't you? Lies, even yours, will never turn Joshua into what Charles wants him to be. He is clinging to an unrealistic dream."

"Perhaps, if I—"

"No, Aurelia, don't even try to lie. Not for him. Not for me."

He let go of her so abruptly she felt as if he had shoved her away from him.

"Don't let him use you."

The echo of an overheard conversation chilled the already fading heat inside her. "The girl has her uses," she had heard her grandfather say.

She steadied her breathing in the next moments of silence. Ballantyne, too, appeared to be regathering his control. A marshaling of strength before battle. And Aurelia suspected she would be wise to do the same.

Ballantyne walked away from her with never a look back. But his steps were slow, measured, granting her time. Aurelia consciously held her breath, willing him not to leave, and he stood, framed by the doorway. Then, slowly, perhaps against his will and controlled by hers, he turned. He stretched out his hand toward her and she obeyed the summons, not with the automatic obedience of a mindless slave but with the purposefulness of a woman making her own choice.

"You are a touchstone," he whispered, "proving the ultimate truth. Don't let him take that from you. Don't give the aura of truth to his lies. Not even for me. Most of all, not for me."

The very honesty that had made her an outcast elsewhere was here, in Christopher Ballantyne's arms, accepted, even cherished. But she could forget his falsehoods no more easily than she could forget Serena, and therefore she could not ignore the chance that he harbored even more lies. For the moment, however, she would take what comfort and strength his embrace offered. Only, she reminded herself sternly, for the moment.

They parted with the awkwardness of reluctant lovers, Ballantyne excusing himself to check on Emil Drew while Aurelia sought Lady Whiston's assistance in preparing for Serena's funeral. By shortly after noon the arrangements had been secured. There remained only the tasks of informing the family and guests—and confronting the chilling reality that one of them could very well be the killer.

Seated by the roaring fire, her hair confined in a less severe chignon at her nape, Aurelia watched as the members of the Nethergate household assembled in the drawing room. Lady Whiston and Dr. Robbins arrived first, as expected. The dowager marchioness sat down and spread her skirts like a debutante on the small sofa; the village physician stood behind her, his pipe clenched in his teeth.

Charlotte Braisthwaite, Aurelia suspected, came more out of curiosity and a desire to be with Freddie Denholm than anything else, but she obeyed the summons dutifully nonetheless and sat beside the glassy-eyed Freddie on the other sofa. Notable by her absence was Lady Moresby, who according to her husband was prostrate with grief and shock and brandy. She was not missed.

Adam, pale and unable to sit still for three seconds, paced in front of the windows. He mumbled curses at the weather, which had become a veritable blizzard. Wind howled incessantly in the chimney and lashed the windowpanes with brittle blasts of snow. There would be no escaping Nethergate, not for the murderer, not for the victim.

Aurelia wondered which role Adam Braisthwaite would play.

What a frightening tableau they presented, she thought as Joshua, the last to arrive, entered the room. One among them could be a cold-blooded killer, and any of the others his—or her—next victim. When a servant closed the doors, no doubt to hunker down in the corridor and listen to every word spoken within and pass it on to his fellows below stairs, Aurelia did not try to suppress a shudder.

Joshua took his place on one of the elegant brocaded chairs beside a small table laden with decanters and glasses. There was a sense of isolation about the way he held himself physically aloof. Like Adam, he was pale, but his calm seemed more a drugged lethargy than Freddie's stunned catatonia. He alone availed himself of the liquor. He might have chosen the chair for that reason.

"I believe we are all here," Aurelia began, her voice low and steady. She could not resist, no matter how much she wanted to, a single reassuring glance toward Christopher Ballantyne, who stood in the far corner, almost invisible in the shadows. Emil Drew, his arm in a white sling that glowed eerily in the softly lit room, sat on a chair in front of Ballantyne. Lines of pain etched the wiry sailor's mouth, but he appeared alert and clear-minded. "His Grace begs your indulgence. This has come as an enormous shock to him, as of course it has to everyone, but given the state of his health, Dr. Ward advised him to rest."

A few whispers drifted through the air, punctuated by a snort Aurelia believed came from Dr. Robbins. The village physician, puffing vigorously on his briar, certainly looked as if he had just snorted.

Aurelia knew from her experience with him during the early days of her grandfather's illness that Robbins was a gruff, practical man, rarely elegant and frequently so blunt in his speech and manners as to be cruel and even crude. His animosity toward Dr. Ward, the London physician who had accompanied Serena when she returned to Nethergate with Joshua, had no doubt been aggravated this morning by the latter's insistence on seeing to the duke while avoiding the gruesome unpleasantness of dealing with Serena.

"There will be a brief service for Mrs. MacKinnon tomorrow morning. Should His Grace, as head of the family, not be able to preside, that duty will fall to Joshua." She waited until she received an almost imperceptible nod from him before continuing. "It does not appear we will be able to reach the village and the churchyard in this weather, so a temporary interment in the old chapel will be prepared."

"What you're saying is that none of us is to leave Nethergate," Adam interrupted. He did not stop pacing.

Freddie sighed and said, "I believe the weather has made that decision for us."

"God, but I hate this bloody cold place!"

Uttered with violent disgust, Joshua's oath drew everyone's attention.

"And we're trapped here with a murderer!" Charlotte's voice rose steadily to a panicky shriek. "Any one of us could be his next victim!"

She grabbed Freddie's hand and would have clutched it to her bosom had he not jerked himself free.

"Who says a man killed her?" he replied, giving Charlotte an icy stare that was his first display of emotion since drawing the knife. "You hated her; maybe you're the killer."

Aurelia watched the exchange with a sense of detached curiosity. She had only a moment or two left of the private knowledge Dr. Robbins had given her earlier; once he had shared it with everyone, she would lose the minuscule advantage of knowing what no one else did.

Charlotte gasped and sputtered, but said nothing. Freddie's accusation had hit its mark with such deadly accuracy it killed any other defense Charlotte might have mounted.

"The killer was most assuredly a man," Dr. Robbins

interposed, moving from his inconspicuous post behind the marchioness to stand at the opposite side of the fireplace from Aurelia. "Mrs. MacKinnon's throat was crushed, and the bruises left on her neck indicated the killer's hands were large as well as strong. A man's hands, not a woman's."

"Are you accusing one of *us?*" Adam asked.

Now he did stop his pacing, to advance toward the doctor. Lord Moresby rose from his chair to take hold of his son's arm.

"*Someone* did it," the viscount reminded him with a touch of horrified weariness to his voice.

Adam shook off his father's hand, but retraced his steps toward the windows and began pacing again. "It could have been one of the servants. God knows there are enough of them around, and she treated them as rotten as she treated everyone else."

"Each of us had reason," Aurelia said. "Even I."

Freddie's anguished, wordless cry shattered what remained of the afternoon quiet.

"I loved her!" he protested, evading Charlotte's restraining grasp to get to his feet. "I would never have harmed her!"

"You silly fool, you've no idea what love is!" Lady Whiston scolded. "And have you never heard of jealousy as a motive for murder? You'd not be the first besotted imbecile to do away with a woman whose devotion fell short of his."

Watching them, Aurelia discovered, was like watching a very badly acted play. Each had rehearsed a certain number of lines but in no particular order, and had no idea what the other actors were going to say or do.

"Don't be an ass, Denholm," Joshua added. He stared steadily into the glass of brandy he held, never raising his eyes to Freddie, who had come to stand directly in front of him. In contrast to his flagrant display that morning, Joshua showed no emotion at all. "At least not over a woman."

"You're one to talk!" Adam exploded from the other side

of the room. This time his father could not stop him, and he headed toward Joshua. "You were panting after the whore just like Freddie!"

"Serena was no whore!" Freddie wailed, grabbing the front of Joshua's coat and pulling him out of his chair. The brandy splashed both of them equally before the glass fell and shattered on the floor.

"Braisthwaite said she was, not I!"

Aurelia jumped from her seat and in two strides had reached the nearest available weapon, the decanter from which Joshua had poured his brandy.

"Stop it!" she screamed, and threw the contents of the heavy crystal bottle onto the three combatants the way she would have tossed water on snarling dogs.

Some of the potent liquor splashed into the fire and flared with a brief blue roar that drowned the echoes of her cry and bathed the room and all within it in a ghostly glow. As quickly as the flames blazed they died, but by then the shock had registered.

Freddie and Adam blinked in surprise and offered no resistance as Lord Moresby escorted them from Joshua. Charlotte rushed to Freddie's side, her handkerchief ready to dab at the drops on her beloved's face and coat, but he pushed her rudely away and stomped from the room. Undaunted, the girl ran after him. Pity for Charlotte's unrequited infatuation touched Aurelia's heart.

"Maybe she did it," Joshua said.

She had forgotten him in her attention to the others.

"Don't be absurd," Lord Moresby said.

"Why not? If Denholm could be consumed with jealousy, why not your daughter?"

Though half the room separated the viscount and the duke's heir, Aurelia positioned herself between them.

"Now is not the time," she said. "We are upset and not thinking clearly. I believe it would be best if I cancel the usual dinner and have trays sent to everyone."

"*You* believe it would be best?" Joshua echoed. "How

quickly you've taken over the running of the household, Miss Phillips."

She knew what he was going to say next, even knew that he would not wait until Lord Moresby and Adam had departed. Perhaps he wanted them, along with Lady Whiston, as witnesses.

"Think about what you're doing," Aurelia warned him, but his answering grin, with brandy spattered on his face and hair, told her he had no intention of heeding her.

"I've already thought, more than I care to. But that's exactly what you'd like me to do, isn't it, Aurelia? You'd like me not to think, not to wonder, not to question. Because the question you don't want me to ask is who had more reason to be jealous of poor Serena than you, our quiet little Aurelia, the parson's orphan. And we all saw you in the corridor last night with your backwoods paramour."

She glanced imploringly at Ballantyne in his distant corner. He had leaned over Emil's shoulder, apparently to whisper something to the servant, and she could not be sure if he saw her silent plea. Joshua must have seen her seeking help from the stranger, for he grabbed her shoulders and spun her to face him.

"If any of us had the strength to crush a woman's throat, it's he." He spat the words in her face, but she did not turn away from his accusation. Not even when she knew there was worse to come. "And if Freddie or the Braisthwaite chit were jealous, there was none of us under this roof who hated Serena more than you."

11

JOSHUA MACKINNON STOOD ONLY A HEAD TALLER THAN Aurelia, enough to look down on her with a sufficiently disdainful glare before making his grand exit from the drawing room. Dumbfounded at the viciousness of his accusation, Aurelia watched silently as he left, then as Lord Moresby, with equal scorn and condescension, shepherded his furious son in Joshua's wake. Dr. Robbins, after a questioning glance at Lady Whiston, followed them.

"Fools," Lady Whiston barked when the doors shut behind them. "Dangerous, of course, as fools frequently are, but fools nonetheless. Oh, don't gape at me, child, and do tell that fine young American to come out of his corner to where he won't have to yell for me to hear him."

Kit, who had left Emil when the others departed and had been standing behind the sofa through most of Lady Whiston's monologue, now walked around to face her.

"Your wish is my command, milady." He raised her hand with exaggerated gallantry.

She did not laugh but waved him away with the same

hand and exclaimed, "Balderdash! What if I wish to be sixteen again? Can you make it so?"

Aurelia felt excluded from this exchange, and at the same time knew Lady Whiston would not have allowed her to depart. Was the old woman playing some kind of game, baiting her with this flirtatious intimacy the way Joshua had with cruel innuendoes and blatant accusations?

Kit shook his head. "You'd not be happy being sixteen again," he told her. "I suspect you were wiser than all your beaux then. Think how much worse it would be now."

Lady Whiston sighed and folded her hands on her lap.

"I was married at sixteen," she grumbled, staring at her hands, twisting them nervously, "and did not like it one bit. If word hadn't come that David was killed, I might have left my husband and gone after him."

"Then you did know him," Kit asked.

He pulled Aurelia's chair closer to the sofa and gestured her to sit, then dragged Joshua's next to hers and took it himself. Closeness to him and to Lady Whiston did not lessen the feeling of being a detached observer rather than participant, but Aurelia realized that was precisely what Kit wanted.

She realized, too, how much better he understood what had happened than did she. Joshua's accusation had linked them in everyone's eyes, not only because both she and Kit were outsiders, but also because another bond had been forged. She had used the boyish diminutive of his Christian name before, that morning when he pulled the pins from her hair and loosed both it and one more of her tightly controlled inhibitions.

She straightened her shoulders and mentally shook off the implication. She would not, could not allow herself to fall in love with Christopher Ballantyne. She knew nothing about him, at least nothing that recommended him. He had proved himself a liar, and she did not doubt that his goal, no matter what else he said, was to gain possession, by fair means or foul, of Nethergate.

"Yes, of course I knew David. Cut a fine figure in his uniform, he did. I was fourteen when I last saw him." She leaned forward, her hands on her knees, her elbows bent out at graceless but determined angles. "Unless the reports of his death were false and he lived to a very hale old age, I'd guess you're his grandson, not his son. And by your name either a bastard or a daughter's child. Either way, no threat to Joshua's inheritance."

Aurelia watched as a slow smile lit Kit's face.

"You are very perceptive, milady. As my mother tells the tale, David MacKinnon, heir to Winterburn, was wounded in fierce fighting, not killed, but abandoned when his troops fled the field. He was retrieved later by a colonial family and nursed slowly back to health."

"And fell in love with the daughter, no doubt."

"No, with the wife. A few years later the husband died, and my grandfather followed his natural inclination."

"He had no sons?"

"One, my Uncle Jeremiah."

He went on with the story, filling in details Aurelia knew as well as others she did not, until finally he drew the ebony box from his pocket and opened it.

The elderly marchioness stared for a long, silent moment at the broken ring on its cushion of velvet. She made no move to touch it until she reached out to close the lid.

"I don't recognize it," she said, "nor do I know its significance. Perhaps Miss Phillips, who knows more about Nethergate than any of the rest of us, knows the story of the ring?"

Aurelia shook her head. "I know nothing. Grandfather has never said a word, not even after Kit confronted him with it."

"And what do you think of young Mr. Ballantyne's story? Do you believe him?"

An instinctive "yes" tried to force its way to Aurelia's tongue, but she bit it back. When she looked at Kit, his dark eyes met hers, not with pleading or warning but with a sharp demand.

"Tell the truth, Aurelia," he said.

She took a deep breath and stammered, "I—I don't know. He's lied before, on several occasions. For good reason, I'm sure, at least in his own mind, but he does not deny lying. Yet when he says he comes here only to satisfy his curiosity, and admits he has no claim on Nethergate or the Winterburn title, how can I not believe him?"

Aurelia scratched Galahad's ear with one hand and locked her door with the other. She ought to have found the quiet and solitude of her own room welcoming after the events of the morning and early afternoon. She always had before. Here there was no one to castigate her for her stubbornness or cast fearful glances her way.

Now she felt a strange loneliness, unassuaged by Galahad's affection.

Because Lady Whiston had come to the drawing room with Dr. Robbins, the old woman had forgotten her walking stick and was forced to rely on Aurelia's assistance to return to her room. Kit was likewise burdened with Emil Drew, and so they had parted, with no personal exchange, no whispered plans for an assignation.

She smiled with bitter humor.

Dear God, she *was* falling in love with him.

"No, I shan't give in to such foolishness," she told Galahad as she poured water from her pitcher into a crockery dish for him to drink from. While he lapped the water, she knelt beside him, stroking his shaggy hide. "As Lady Whiston said, fools are dangerous, and I'd be a very dangerous fool if I fell in love with the first man who kissed me."

The dog raised his head, water dripping from his slender jowls. With his ears laid back tightly and his tail wagging, he appeared to be smiling indulgently at her.

She got to her feet to escape the censure in that canine grin.

There were other chores to tend to. The room was cold, the fire banked carefully while Aurelia was gone. Before Joshua's arrival and the influx of guests, there had been no problem allowing Galahad the run of the house. He rarely wandered far from Aurelia's side. Keeping him confined to her room, however, left her to do her own housekeeping.

It was a small price to pay for his continued companionship. She knew the dog would have adapted to the kennel, but she could not have stood the utter aloneness of life without him.

She stoked up the fire, warming her hands by the leaping flames. She stared half mesmerized into the light to clear her thoughts completely before she began a mental list of the things she needed to do. There were meals to order for dinner and the final details of Serena's funeral. She had spoken to Morton Sullivan earlier but not to her grandfather, and she must compose herself for that confrontation. Nor could she put it off, lest Joshua strike the first blow.

"Oh, Galahad, I wish it could be the way it was before," she said, sighing.

When she looked around for the dog, expecting him to be within reach as he usually was, she discovered him standing by the water dish. He faced the door and, with his sleek head cocked to one side, appeared to be listening.

First instinct sent her toward the door to learn who might be outside, but another, deeper sense froze her in her footsteps.

The deerhound was no watchdog, neither by breeding nor by training. Devoted and loyal, he was a friendly animal eager to please and to return affection. At the moment, however, he was neither eager nor friendly.

The crackle and hiss of the fire, the whistle of the wind in the chimney, and the rattle of ancient panes in the window all made it impossible for Aurelia to hear what Galahad's more sensitive ears heard. She watched the narrow strip of light under the door to see if anyone crossed in front of it, but the light in the room was brighter than in the hall, and so she could see nothing.

Still, she trusted the dog's finer senses and inched toward the fire to retrieve the poker as a potential weapon. No sooner had she reached it and curled her hand around the cold metal than the dog suddenly relaxed and trotted up to her with tail wagging.

She dropped the poker and ran to the door, then fumbled with the key she had left in the lock. Surely no more than a few seconds had passed, but when she pulled the door open and dashed into the corridor, she saw and heard nothing until, a heartbeat later, the soft thud of a distant closing door rippled through the stillness of Nethergate.

Kit stepped away from the window and let the curtain fall.

"A frontiersman like Uncle Jeremiah would undoubtedly laugh at the absurdity of being snowed in by this, but I'm afraid that's exactly what we are, my friend," he said to Emil, who was once again propped up against a heap of pillows on the bed. "How's the shoulder?"

"A good bit better, sir. Maybe by tomorrow, if you can put me up on a horse, we can—"

"We'll be here longer than that, whether we want to be or not, unless someone suddenly steps forward and announces he—or she—is the killer."

"Oh, come now, sir, ye can't mean anyone would truly believe *you* had anything to do with that poor woman's death!"

"Joshua MacKinnon certainly does, and you know as well as I he was only voicing an opinion everyone in that room held."

"But ye had no reason! A man doesn't go about murdering women in their beds without a reason."

"You heard them. They gave me a reason."

Emil snorted, then grimaced. Kit wondered how much

pain his friend was in, and how much he tried to conceal. Emil was a tough old sea dog who had spent nearly his entire life on one ship or another, incurring along the way his share of injuries. But broken bones on a man well past his fiftieth year were not to be taken lightly, nor his recovery rushed.

"Then why didn't ye let me speak out?"

Kit experienced a quick pang of guilt. He had known Emil was about to leap to his defense this afternoon and had squeezed the poor man's shoulder in warning. If he had not been so intent on apologizing to Emil, he might have been able to help Aurelia. Except that she had not needed his help. He even had to smile at her resourcefulness. Only a woman accustomed to dealing with problems on her own would have had the presence of mind to douse a trio of belligerent young bucks with brandy.

"I took you with me this afternoon because I didn't dare leave you alone, not because I needed someone to defend me. The last thing we need is to arouse any more suspicions, and denying the obvious would do exactly that."

Emil grinned, deepening the creases in his face.

"Ah, so that's how the wind blows. Meself, I prefer my women a bit warmer, but . . ."

He shrugged, which brought on another grimace.

Kit considered correcting Emil's opinion of Aurelia, but the feverish passion she had displayed was not a thing he wanted to share. Unlike the brilliance with which Serena had snared Freddie Denholm and Adam Braisthwaite and even the preening Dr. Ward, Aurelia's desire was dark, subtle, infinitely more intimate. And more fragile.

He piled the fire high with fresh logs that would keep the room warm for a good long while, then returned to the window for one more glance at the swirling snow.

He could escape, he could even take Emil with him. It might be a hard trek, but he was certain they could elude any pursuit. There was even the possibility that the real killer would not mount a search, would instead be content to let an absent Christopher Ballantyne take the blame. Kit shuddered at the thought of being branded a murderer, of Aurelia thinking him guilty and his not being able to prove—to *her*—otherwise.

He had too many reasons not to leave. And behind them lay the woman with the midnight hair and misty eyes.

He let the drape fall once more and reached into his pocket. Instead of drawing out the ebony box that held the wolf's-head signet, he fumbled for a much smaller object that had fallen into the corner. Without looking at the pearl, he closed his fingers around it and headed for the door.

The chapel at Nethergate was rarely used. Restored at about the time of the Stuart kings, it was one of the few authentically medieval structures to survive the depredations of time and modernization. It sat squat and sturdy in a small private garden, sheltered by three massive oaks that made it virtually invisible to those who did not know of its existence.

Shivering, Aurelia pushed open the ironbound door and stepped out of the cruel wind. Galahad shook snow off his coat, then sat down to lick his paws dry.

"If Christ Himself was born in a stable, there should be no harm in bringing a dog into a church," Aurelia whispered.

She walked down the center aisle, past the five short rows of pews on either side, to the bier awaiting Serena's casket in front of the altar. None of the candles had been lit; the only illumination came from the narrow windows and the wan daylight. A gently funereal gloom pervaded the place, softening the shadows.

Two men in rough work clothes walked out of the vestry. The whole building was too small for them not to have heard the sounds of Aurelia's entry, so she was not surprised when both of them came out together. Everyone on the estate was bound to be nervous. But when neither of these two servants, whom she had known nearly since the day she arrived at Nethergate, said so much as a word of greeting, she knew the tale of Joshua's accusation had spread quickly.

"Will everything be ready by morning?" she asked, refusing to use their names. If Will Carmer and Horace Gilliam could so easily believe her guilty of murder, she would not dignify this meeting with a reminder of old friendship.

"Aye, Miss Phillips," Will replied. "Seems a lot o' trouble to go to fer the likes o' her, but mebbe someone else has need o' the proper blessing?"

That accusatory question mark in his tone stiffened her back, but Aurelia said nothing, for Will's words echoed the conversation she had had with her grandfather only a few hours before. He, too, believed funerals were not for the dead but for the living.

She mumbled something to the men about getting on with their work, then jerked on Galahad's lead to make as rapid an exit from the icy chapel as she could. The dog had loosened a tiny pebble from the snow stuck to the fur on his paws and was playing with it, but dropped it to trot eagerly after her.

Anger and hurt and not a small dose of fear lengthened Aurelia's strides. A dozen would have brought her to the door, but before she had taken half that number, the door creaked inward. Snow swirled across the ancient flagstones, and a shrouded figure entered.

"Miss Phillips? I think you'd best come here."

Though she could not remember ever seeing the groom so bundled in coat and knit cap, she recognized Guthrie's voice at once. She also noted the alarm in it, and the urgency.

He held the door for her, then pulled it closed with a secure thud. The wind had risen during those few minutes she spent inside the chapel's sheltering walls. A particularly cruel gust chose just that moment to curl around her and slash through the feeble protection of her cloak. It pulled her hood off and loosened strands of hair from the knot at her nape. She could do nothing but fight the storm.

Then, as if tired of its torment, the wind relented. Aurelia kept her hands beneath her cloak and let the last stirrings of snow and frigid air clear her hair from her eyes.

Before her, shoulders hunched against the storm, stood the red-haired stable boy who had laughed at Emil Drew's inept horsemanship. He held the bridle of an obviously exhausted gray mare. Her knees were torn and bleeding, and red dripped from her mouth to the shifting snow at her feet. A single short length of one rein dangled from the bridle to snap in the wind.

"Take her on back, Robbie," Guthrie ordered. "You know what to do."

The boy bobbed his head. "Aye, sir. Like she was me own mother."

A second later, he and the limping mare disappeared into the snow.

"What happened?" Aurelia asked, afraid she knew the answer. Everyone in the household was accounted for, save one.

"That's the horse Mr. Gould set out for London on early this morning. Fer a man who sat behind a desk or in a courtroom all day, the lawyer were a good rider, and the mare steady as any at Nethergate. Storm's bad, but not to keep a man from reaching the village by noon."

Aurelia could not stand still. The cold and wind propelled her toward the house as surely as the horror growing in her mind as Guthrie continued to tell her what she had already concluded for herself.

"If he reached the inn there, he'd have had the mare stabled. Surely he wouldn't have gone on, not in this weather, and if he had, she wouldn't have found her way home this soon."

The broken rein hanging from the bridle reminded Aurelia of nothing so much as the last bit of pearl necklace dangling from Serena's dead fingers.

Aurelia glanced at the sky, letting the snowflakes fall on her numbed cheeks. She made her decision quickly.

"I'll tell Joshua what has happened. You may ask some of the men if they wish to go out in search of Mr. Gould, but I will not order them out in this weather so late in the day. It's far too dangerous."

He touched the edge of his cap with a gloved forefinger.

"Aye, Miss Phillips. Don't be frettin' what those London folk say, even Mr. MacKinnon. They don't know you."

The man's loyalty touched her and eased some of the distress she felt at abandoning Gould to whatever fate had befallen him.

"Thank you, Guthrie. I knew the gossip would travel, but I—"

"And that's what it be, gossip. Now, I know it's not my place, but a man who's spent his whole life around dumb animals gets a special sense about which ones to trust and which ones never to walk behind. If I were lookin' for a horse to carry me into battle, so to speak, that colonial stallion is the only one I'd give money for. The others are just for show."

Aurelia would have blushed had the cold not frozen her blood in her veins. Guthrie's forthrightness was welcome; she, too, trusted an instinct she could not explain.

He escorted her across the main courtyard to the kitchen door she preferred, though it was a longer walk than necessary in the bitter weather. Aurelia voiced no complaint, however, for she was able to make her entrance with less risk of attracting attention.

The contrast between the blustery weather outdoors and the dim quiet within Nethergate's ancient walls should have offered some instant comfort, but instead Aurelia found herself shaking violently. The cold went too deep, beyond even her bones into her soul. Hoping to reach the safety of her own room before having to speak to anyone, she raced through the labyrinthine halls. Galahad barked wildly and slipped on bare floors and snapped at the edges of her cloak, as if this were some new game.

His voice echoed in the stillness. She should have slowed, quieted him, then proceeded with proper decorum as befit the occasion, but she could not control the panic. She grasped a handful of skirt, heavy and wet from the weather, and ran up the stairs. From the corner of her eye she saw someone in the gallery, seated by the fire. She did not stop to find out who.

Breathless, fingers trembling, she found the icy metal of her key and fitted it into the lock. Cold tears of frustration burned her cheeks as the key refused to turn.

"Damn, damn, damn," she swore, withdrawing her hand to blow desperate warmth onto her fingers.

At last the lock gave and the door swung open. Galahad leapt into the room, dragging Aurelia with him. She let go his lead and turned to close the door, only to find Charlotte Braisthwaite standing there.

"May I come in?" she whispered. "The dog won't bite, will he?"

"No, he won't bite."

Aurelia swore again, a single muttered syllable, this time for the invasion of her sanctuary. But something told her Charlotte's visit was not entirely voluntary, that something had happened to force the girl against her will to venture into what must seem the lion's den.

Her eyes were wide with fright, her cheeks pale. She twisted her hands together incessantly. Even her breathing was unnatural and nervous; each time she inhaled with a slight gasp, as if she were about to reveal a monumental secret and then suddenly changed her mind, so that she exhaled with a loud and irritating sigh.

Aurelia suppressed her other emotions to concentrate on Charlotte's distress.

"Come, sit by the fire and be comfortable." She ushered

the tall, awkward girl further into the room, not to the chair closest to the hearth, for Galahad lay on the warm stones and might frighten Charlotte. "I regret I cannot offer you tea, for I've just come in myself, but if you like I can ring for some to be brought to us."

Charlotte shook her head vigorously.

"Mama will come for me if I'm gone too long," she said.

Aurelia removed her cloak and draped it over the chair for the fire to dry the melting snow. She would have walked back to close the door, but a slight widening of Charlotte's already terrified eyes changed her mind. Galahad was content to stay, to lick his paws dry and then nap before the fire; Aurelia was more concerned about who else might enter her haven than about the dog running out.

She sat down, aware that her heart had not stilled its pounding. From the exertion of her flight through the house she had been given no respite before Charlotte's visit.

"Now, tell me why you've come."

The girl looked down at her hands, still twisting and wringing as if she had no control over them. Aurelia noticed that those hands, like the rest of the viscount's daughter, were large—and long-fingered. Neither Lord Moresby nor his wife was of delicate build, and certainly Adam had inherited the sturdy frame and inclination toward portliness. If Charlotte had not yet developed her mother's impressive bosom, she could not be described as dainty.

As the silence after Aurelia's question lengthened, those overwrought hands calmed, until at last they lay motionless on Charlotte's lap. She rested the back of the right one on her knee and with trembling slowness opened the tightly clenched fingers.

"I found this on the floor outside your door," she said.

On her palm lay one of Serena's pearls.

12

AURELIA STIFLED A GASP THAT COULD EASILY HAVE BECOME A scream. She must not, she warned herself, give in. Not now.

"I do not think you are telling the truth, Charlotte."

"Oh, but I am! I swear to you, I am! I found it on the floor, just a little while ago, while you were out with—with your dog."

It was not possible. Yet the evidence was plain, gleaming in the indistinct light on Charlotte Braisthwaite's sweaty palm.

"M-maybe it fell out of your dress or something after—after you were in *her* room."

Aurelia shook her head.

She had been nowhere near Serena's body, where most of the pearls lay. The loose ones were scattered on the bed and the floor, and if it was conceivable that one or more might have been disturbed and found their way into someone's clothing while the body was being prepared for burial, Aurelia had left that grisly chore to Serena's abigail, Ruth, and Dr. Robbins.

There must be another explanation for a second pearl's being discovered so close to her own quarters. She closed her eyes, blocking out the sight of the incriminating bead, but even then no logical thoughts came to her.

When she opened her eyes again, the room had grown darker and Charlotte had grown more silent.

A quiet voice drawled in a now-familiar accent, "Miss Braisthwaite is lying. I can prove it very quickly."

"I beg your pardon, Mr. Ballantyne, but I most certainly am *not* lying. I found this—"

Kit walked into the room and did not, to Aurelia's surprise, close the door. Instead, he approached Charlotte and took the pearl from her. She gave it up without a fight, which Aurelia ascribed to guilt over the lie.

But Kit's assertion that he could prove the pearl had not been found outside the door aroused Aurelia's curiosity. When he headed for the door, she instinctively followed him.

What he did was simple. She watched in astonishment.

He turned, facing her and Charlotte, who now sat with her head hanging in guilty embarrassment even before the proof had been presented. Then he opened his hand and dropped the pearl to the floor.

It bounced once, then rolled merrily to the end of the corridor and came to rest against the wall. He retrieved it, knelt to drop it from a few inches above the floor rather than waist height, and again it rolled to the wall.

Charlotte began to weep.

"How did *you* know she was lying?" Kit asked. He leaned against the door frame rather than entering her room after they had returned a distraught but contrite Charlotte to her own quarters. He could watch the corridor this way, as well as watch Aurelia without being too close to her. Even from this distance, the effect she had on him was disturbing.

"I didn't know for certain, but it did not make sense."

Charlotte had mentioned that Aurelia had taken the dog

outdoors. Galahad had greeted Kit like an old friend and then went sniffing about the room in search of whatever amusement was available. Kit found further confirmation of her excursion in the cloak hung by the fire, and the dark patches of damp on her skirt indicated she must have been confronted by Charlotte before having had time to change into dry clothing.

He was not therefore particularly surprised when Aurelia interrupted her explanation to go to the wardrobe and take out a pair of soft leather slippers and dry stockings. But when she unselfconsciously placed one foot on the rung of her chair, raised her skirt and petticoats to her knee, and proceeded to remove a wet boot and stocking, he had to force himself to concentrate on her words.

"If she really had found the pearl outside my room, why offer it to me? That would eliminate the damning evidence as well as put her at risk. It seemed more likely she had found the thing somewhere else and simply wanted to get rid of it."

"Before it pointed a finger at her."

"Precisely. There was also the matter of Charlotte's dislike for Serena beyond Freddie's infatuation. Lady Moresby constantly compared the poor creature with Serena and found her lacking, as you were forced to witness at dinner."

Aurelia Phillips, on the other hand, lacked nothing by comparison. She balanced on one foot with the toes of the other curled on the chair rung while she unrolled a dry stocking. They were long toes for such a small foot, he noticed, but perfectly proportioned to her slender ankle and sleek, firm calf.

"And Charlotte is not unaware of her physical attributes. I daresay her hand is as large and strong as Joshua's."

Dear God, did the woman have no sense of what she was saying? Kit turned his back on her and released a silent groan.

"Then how do you suppose the pearl found its way to her

room? Could Charlotte in fact be the killer? We know she was awake last night at an hour close to the time Serena was murdered."

Remembering last night was no less disturbing than watching Aurelia remove her other boot and stocking. Did a similar memory cause her momentary silence? He hazarded a glance over his shoulder.

And met her staring back at him.

He stepped into the room and closed the door.

She ran into his arms, and for a moment he had the exquisite satisfaction of holding her, of knowing she had come to him honestly and willingly. He wanted more, oh, yes, much more, but what he wanted was only hers to give, not his to take.

He sensed her trust, more precious now than anything else. She took a deep, gasping breath, then let it out with a long sigh and rested her cheek against his chest.

"Kit, something else has happened," she said, not moving away from his embrace. Indeed, he discovered to his delight that she had slipped her arms under his coat. "Joshua's solicitor, Mr. Gould, set out for London early this morning. His horse returned an hour ago without him."

"Have you told anyone? Joshua? Your grandfather?"

"No one. There wasn't time. Charlotte came and—"

She shivered, and for her own good he set her away from him. She was too vulnerable now, and no matter how much she trusted him, he trusted himself not at all.

"Put your other shoe on," he told her, "and I'll take you to see your grandfather. That's where you're headed, isn't it? To tell him about Gould's horse?"

"You don't need to."

"I *want* to, Aurelia. What I do *not* want is for you to be alone, do you understand?"

And he wanted to kiss her, to crush her tender mouth beneath his and drink all the sweet honesty of her passion until he was giddy with it.

"But I shall be alone at night, Kit."

He watched her lips and wanted each word they formed to be his name.

"Not if you don't wish to be."

He brushed his thumb slowly across her lower lip. Her eyes darkened until only a narrow band of misty green remained.

Then a tiny sound wedged its way into the silence between them.

"Galahad has found another stone," Aurelia whispered. Beneath Kit's thumb, her lips turned up in a tremulous smile. "I believe he has saved us from making fools of ourselves."

She slipped out of Kit's arms and went to the dog, who was indeed playing with a pebble. He ducked his head away and laid his ears back in a wordless canine plea to keep his toy.

"He had one this morning and I thought it was out of his reach under the bed," she said as she knelt beside him and pried his jaws apart. "I should have known he'd find it."

Kit pulled four or five deep breaths into his lungs and let each out slowly. He ought to be grateful the dog had interrupted. Thirty more seconds of Aurelia's erotic innocence would have taken him beyond any hope of control.

There was nothing erotic about watching her reach into the deerhound's mouth to extract the pebble. When the dog finally gave up the fight and Aurelia had the stone in her hand, Kit expected her to toss it into the fire. There was no reason for her to remain on her knees, staring at the thing.

He was beside her in an instant, ignoring the dog, who scrambled to get out of the way, and grabbed the tight fist she held out in front of her as though she wanted to fling her hand into the flames along with the stone.

At the first touch of his hand on hers, she opened her fingers to disclose another of Serena's pearls.

"He had it this morning, Kit. It was here, in my room,

before we ever knew she was dead. Someone must have put it here during the night."

Joshua poured more brandy into his glass. The decanter had been full when he began, a little more than an hour ago. Now he offered it, half-empty, to Kit, who declined with a curt nod. When the duke, sitting across the desk from them, made no response to a similar offer, Joshua stretched forward to set the bottle down on the polished mahogany with a rude thump. After throwing half the contents of his glass down his throat, he slumped in his chair and belched.

"I think it's a diversion," he announced with a noticeable slur. His eyelids drooped, as if the light from the single lamp irritated his eyes, red and swollen. "Gould killed her, left early according to the plans he told me about last night, then met with a confederate who had another horse waiting. It's no wonder none of Guthrie's men found any trace of him. He's long gone."

He downed the rest of the brandy, then took a handkerchief from his sleeve and blew his nose.

Kit glanced from the pathetic display of Joshua MacKinnon's grief to a frighteningly stoic Aurelia.

The strain of the unrelenting ordeal had taken its toll, no matter how she tried to deny it. He had not let her out of his sight since the discovery of the third pearl, and not for one minute since then had she found the least opportunity to relax, or to give in to the mounting horror he saw so clearly in her eyes.

He had accompanied her to Charles MacKinnon's apartments, the same room where he confronted the old man that first night at Nethergate. Charles had defied him then, much as Kit supposed he had defied all who opposed him over the years, including death itself. Two days later, he looked like a man who wanted to die and could not.

He had taken the news about Gould with little reaction, save to order both Kit and Aurelia to meet him in the study at six o'clock. He also charged her with informing Joshua of the lawyer's disappearance.

She did so with an efficient detachment unlike anything Kit had ever seen. She ordered meals for the guests and gave instructions to the workmen building Serena's coffin. She settled a childish dispute between Freddie and Serena's abigail over which gown to bury the woman in. As each small crisis arose, she dispatched it—and went on to the next.

The first sign of strain was a simple pressing of her fingers to her temples during that silly argument. If she had still had her hair in those spinsterish braids, Kit would have snatched every pin from her head and thrown them in the nearest fire. But she had abandoned the more severe style for a softer chignon, from which long strands straggled free.

More hung loose now, inviting Kit's touch, but she was beyond his reach. Joshua sat between them, squarely across the desk from his grandfather, with Kit on one side and Aurelia at the other. She had moved her chair closer to the duke, giving Kit a clear view of her, but thereby increasing the torment of his not being able to touch her, comfort her, stroke away the lines of worry between her brows.

They had been there since the stroke of six; the mantel clock had struck quarter past seven. Charles, his skeletal hands steepled in front of him, stared into the darkness beyond the lamplight. Kit wondered if the old despot was aware how exhausted his granddaughter looked—or if he cared.

"What reason had Mr. Gould to harm Serena?" she asked in a distracted tone as though she were speaking more to herself than to anyone else, thinking aloud more than seeking an answer.

"Perhaps she spurned his advances," Joshua suggested. "She was a beautiful woman."

His sneer made the implied comparison blatant.

Aurelia said nothing. She nodded in mute agreement,

with a dazed look in her eyes as though her thoughts were already far away from this close, silent room.

She was, Kit realized, utterly exhausted, beyond rational thought. He knew she had had neither dinner nor luncheon, and probably no breakfast before that.

"If I may beg Your Grace's indulgence," he said as he rose from his chair and went to her. "Miss Phillips is what we Americans would call dead on her feet."

He offered her his hands, and when she had placed hers within them, he pulled her gently to her feet.

"Where do you think you're going?" Joshua demanded.

She swayed, as though she had risen too quickly and experienced a rush of lightheadedness. Kit gave her a moment to steady herself.

"I am taking Miss Phillips to her room. This has been a difficult day for her, and I for one believe she's done enough."

He expected Joshua to reply with a whining reiteration of his own grievances, but instead it was the duke who rasped in his parchment-rough voice, "We have all been through a great deal today, Mr. Ballantyne. And do remember that Miss Phillips is a member of the family only by marriage."

She sagged as if he had struck her a blow, not a mere insult.

Kit did not wait for her to recover. He scooped her up like a tired child and, after fumbling for a moment to unlock and open the door, carried her out of the study.

The shock took only a moment to wear off, and then confusion set in, followed by bitterness.

"Why would he say something so hurtful?" Aurelia wondered. "It is as if he is a different person."

"I cannot begin to answer that one," Kit replied, heading up the stairs. He had never met Charles MacKinnon before coming to Nethergate and had no idea what the duke was like, but if he had indeed changed, Kit suspected the transformation was of recent origin, perhaps as recent as his own arrival.

Compared with the morose darkness of the study, the rest of Nethergate blazed with light. And if the servants were quiet, even silent, they were abundant. At the top of the stairs, Kit waylaid a bashful young girl.

"I want a tray sent to Miss Phillips's room at once," he ordered her. "A hot meal, not some cold tidbits. And a bottle of wine. No, make that brandy."

The child looked at him, then at Aurelia, ensconced in his arms.

"For both of ye, Miss Phillips?"

Kit interrupted, "No, just for Aurelia. I can—"

"For two, Rose. Mr. Ballantyne has been helping me all day and has not had any dinner either."

The girl bobbed a half-curtsey and dashed off.

Aurelia wanted to tell Kit to set her on her feet, but it felt good to give in to his strength, if only for a while. She liked, too, the vindication that bubbled like champagne deep inside her.

"You could have had brandy earlier," she said. "Joshua offered you some."

"This is for you, my dear, not me. You need a good night's sleep."

Before they reached her door, he had to put her down so she could get her key, but he took it from her the instant she had it out of her pocket. She was about to warn him to be careful of Galahad when an angry voice called her name.

"Miss Phillips! I've been looking everywhere for you."

Ruth, holding something in her apron, bustled down the main corridor. She spared Kit a brief censuring glare before she rounded on Aurelia.

"I have a very serious problem, Miss Phillips."

Aurelia could not contain a weary sigh.

But Kit positioned himself between her and the determined abigail and asked, "Is someone injured or ill, Ruth?

Is the drawing room afire? Have Viking raiders come ashore at Bamburgh? If not, your problems can wait until morning."

In spite of herself, or perhaps simply because she had gone beyond her own limits, Aurelia began to laugh at the idea of Vikings invading Nethergate.

Ruth, however, was not amused.

"Have you no respect?"

"For the dead? If you call arguing over what to dress a corpse in 'respect,' then I'm afraid I do not have any." He inserted the key in the lock and opened the door enough for Aurelia to squeeze through. She could not suppress a giggle, even though she knew it was highly inappropriate. "On the other hand, I have great deal of respect for this young woman, who is not only alive but very tired and very hungry. Now, if you will excuse us."

Then he, too, passed into the room. Aurelia, struggling to hold an exuberant Galahad, looked up to catch a last vision of the abigail's silent gasp of outraged astonishment as Kit slammed the door in her face.

Galahad broke loose and descended upon Kit with as wild a welcome as any he had ever given Aurelia. She sank exhausted and slightly dazed to the floor where she sat, legs ungracefully crossed beneath her tumbled skirts, and watched as man and dog tussled affectionately.

She smiled, even while an irrational twinge of jealousy flashed like a brief falling star through her.

"You were very rude to Ruth."

"She deserved it," he answered with a last scratch to the dog's ears.

Galahad trotted to Aurelia and stretched out beside her, his chin on her knee.

"Ruth has been with Serena a long time," she said, stroking the rough-coated head. The devotion in the dog's eyes chased her earlier merriment and brought a lump to her throat. "You're not familiar with the ways of servants, Mr. Ballantyne, but they have certain expectations, too. An older woman—such as Ruth—with a young mistress expects to be taken care of for the rest of her life."

"So we're back to 'Mr. Ballantyne' now, are we?"

She blushed. He stood over her, his hand stretched down to assist her up, and she could not wipe away the red stain that burned her cheeks.

When she did not take his proffered hand, Kit lowered himself to the floor, to sit where Galahad formed a barrier between them. The dog looked up once, wagged his tail, then put his chin back down on her knee.

"There's a great deal I don't know, Aurelia. Why you didn't set everyone straight about Joshua's remark this afternoon, for instance."

He knew the answer to his own question. She could tell by the way he stated it. She had committed another lie by omission and been caught in it. Unable to deny it, she let him continue.

"You didn't usurp Serena's place as mistress of this household, did you? The responsibility has been yours for a long time, while she basked in the glory and glitter, greeted the guests, and seduced their sons."

"Adam? Are you saying you believe Adam—no, I won't credit it."

She shook her head, and another of the pins holding her hair came loose to slide around her neck, over her shoulder, and down the neckline of her dress. She felt the pin too late to stop it, or to stop the thick knot at her nape from unwinding.

Nor could she stop Kit from leaning toward her to remove the other pins caught in the long hank of her hair.

"Think of it, Aurelia. A beautiful woman, no longer as young as she was, isolated for whatever reasons here in this gloomy house."

She shivered, not only because the hairpin down her dress was poking painfully into her flesh but because Kit

Ballantyne, in that deep seductive drawl, could have been describing her as well as Serena.

"She's a widow, dependent on a dying old man for her support, and along comes a young man, heir to a title, who wears his appetites like a fashionably tied cravat."

"A widow—or an orphan? Why don't you accuse *me* of seducing Adam, or Freddie Denholm for that matter?"

She would have gotten to her feet and shown him the door, except that both he and Galahad were sitting upon her skirts. Kit had no way of knowing how often her grandfather had suggested she set her cap for the viscount's son or Lady Whiston's nephew, or even for Joshua himself.

"Because I don't think you did it, that's why."

"And you think Adam did?"

He shrugged, and twisted the end of her hair around his fingers.

"I think he's as likely a suspect as any. You saw how he ran the instant he heard she was dead. Lost his breakfast on the way, too, before he saw the—what was in her room. I'm quite certain you would have no idea, but to me, her bed indicated she'd not spent the hours before her death alone."

Aurelia felt a subtle tug at the back of her head and realized Kit was winding her hair like a winch, drawing her nearer even while he discussed the possibility of Adam Braisthwaite being Serena's lover *and* murderer. The scenario was macabre and revolting—and decidedly absurd.

"Kit, really, if you think to divert my attention with an examination of so morbid a subject while you seduce me . . ."

He had brought her close enough that even with the dog between them, he could kiss her. His dark eyes told her he wanted to, the same as his sudden freeing of her hair told her he knew she would not move away.

"I can think of many more effective—and more pleasurable—ways to divert your attention, Aurelia. In fact, I would much rather—"

A furious pounding on the door and unintelligible but distinctly female shouts cut him off an instant before the unlocked door burst inward. As though she had not expected the door to open so easily, a florid-faced Lady Moresby tumbled into the room, with a horrified but slightly sanctimonious Ruth right behind her.

13

TIME FROZE FOR TWO OR THREE HIDEOUS SECONDS, LONG enough for Aurelia to impress every detail into her memory.

She half sat, half lay on the floor, with her neck on Kit's thigh and her hair wrapped like an ebony rope around his wrist, the very picture of either a wanton in her pleasure or a victim of a madman about to be strangled with her own unbound tresses. Kit leaned over her, his lips inches from hers, his eyes dark and stormy with desire—or madness. The grisly irony, rather than any fear that Kit might actually harm her, brought more incongruous laughter to the surface.

She struggled mightily against it.

Beside her, Galahad growled a preliminary warning and Kit simply growled, "Get out."

Lady Moresby screamed. And screamed again.

Galahad bared his teeth.

Aurelia lost the battle with laughter.

"Hold your dog," Kit ordered her as he unwound his hand from her hair and stood.

"Murderer!" Lady Moresby shrieked. *"Murderer!"*

Wiping away tears of uncontrolled laughter that held no merriment, Aurelia wrapped her arms about Galahad's neck and fumbled to hook one hand under his collar. Too tangled in her skirt, on which the dog still stood, to rise, she watched as Kit clapped his hands on Lady Moresby's shoulders and shook the viscountess sharply once.

To no effect.

"Oh, dear God, he's going to kill me next!"

He raised one hand as if to slap her, then settled for shaking her again and bellowing above her hysteria, "Shut up, you silly cow! I'm not going to kill anyone!"

Lady Moresby continued screaming. Such a tumult, Aurelia realized, could not fail to draw the attention of others in the household. Already she heard doors opening and feet running down hallways.

She managed somehow to shove Galahad off her skirt without letting go of his collar, so she could stand and restore some measure of decorum. The pricking of the hairpin inside her bodice served as a reminder of how ludicrous and yet dangerous this situation was.

There were too many weapons in Nethergate, and too many fears. She had no idea what had happened to the knife Freddie Denholm had tried to turn on her, and she had already witnessed both Adam's and Joshua's willingness to use a gun.

With Galahad to clear a path for her, Aurelia insinuated herself between Kit and Lady Moresby, who finally stopped shrieking.

Lord Moresby, in nightshirt and cap despite the early hour, ran up, bare feet slapping on the floor.

"What in blazes is going on? Good God, there's not been another . . . ?"

"It's a simple misunderstanding," Aurelia explained, edging the viscountess and the maid into the corridor.

Adam, brandishing a poker, and his valet joined the assembly next, followed by Freddie and a white-faced

Charlotte, plus several of the Nethergate staff. Aurelia noted among them a kitchen maid who had no business in this part of the house—and whose dress was buttoned crookedly, an indication she had donned it in as much haste as Lord Moresby pulled on his nightshirt.

Ruth, resisting her expulsion from Aurelia's room, stretched out an arm to point a long, bony finger at Kit.

"I saw you! You threw her to the floor and had your hands on her throat!"

There were so many of them now, including Dr. Ward, who carried a stout walking stick. Everyone, it seemed, except Joshua and her grandfather. Aurelia dismissed a flicker of apprehension.

"I did no such thing," Kit denied Ruth's accusation as he tried to pull Aurelia back into the room.

She placed her free hand on his arm and whispered, "Please, let me handle them," then turned to the others and said, "I assure you, there is nothing to worry about. I was tired and Mr. Ballantyne brought me to my room. I stumbled and fell, I believe. Something was very funny. I was laughing."

A strange sensation came over her, like walking into a sudden bank of fog on a sunny day. She saw Lady Moresby and Ruth clearly, right in front of her, but the others blurred to a vague, multihued mass surrounded by a rapidly encroaching darkness. Everyone was talking at once, yet she heard nothing until a single voice escaped that gathering gloom.

"For God's sake, get out of the way! Give her some air, you fools!"

In the wake of that authoritative voice came the sharp odor of smelling salts, strong at first, then weaker as the vial was passed under her nose and removed. Why would someone put smelling salts under her nose?

She blinked several times, expecting to see Lady Moresby and Ruth still glaring at her. Instead, Kit's face, drawn into a worried scowl, filled her entire field of vision. She realized then that she lay in his arms, her own looped intimately around his neck.

"Dear heavens! Whatever have I done?" she exclaimed sheepishly.

"Your virtue remains unsullied, Miss Phillips," Kit said, the worry easing to a relieved smile. "I did not take advantage of your very brief indisposition."

"I have never fainted in my life. Never!"

"If it is any comfort to you, you did not swoon dead away. Close enough to give some of us a good scare, however."

She became aware then, albeit slowly, of activity around her. Ruth busily turned down the bed, and another servant was laying out a dinner tray. Dr. Ward chased the last of the onlookers, including a still-furious Lady Moresby, back to their rooms or, in the case of curious servants, back to their work.

It was he, Aurelia presumed, who had produced the smelling salts. She rubbed her nose to relieve some of the sting.

Kit set her down so she sat on the edge of the bed. Galahad immediately jumped up and lay down beside her.

"At least now I needn't worry about tripping over him," Kit said, though Aurelia thought she detected a hint of jealousy. "The dog never strayed an inch from me the whole time I held you."

Aurelia nearly laughed aloud again. She was trembling with fatigue and shock, but nothing was so important as the fact that Kit Ballantyne was jealous of Galahad because the dog slept in her bed. She wanted to tell him Galahad rarely stayed more than a few minutes, but then she remembered Ruth had not yet left.

The woman was, in fact, standing at the foot of the bed.

"Will that be all, Mr. Ballantyne?" she asked in the awkward tone of a woman who had not dealt enough with men to be comfortable speaking directly to them. "Shall I help Miss Phillips ready herself for bed or—"

"Yes, Ruth, please do," Aurelia interposed. "At least help

me with the buttons on my dress, and my nightgowns are in the wardrobe."

Her face flamed with abject mortification, but she met the older woman's icy stare without flinching. She would not cringe under Ruth's censure. She had no reason to.

Five minutes later, before her dinner had time to grow cold, Aurelia sat in bed, an enormous pile of pillows behind her, her dinner tray across her lap. Galahad, anticipating a tasty tidbit or two, lay neatly beside her. His eyes—and nose—followed every morsel she put into her mouth.

"Eat slowly," Kit admonished from the chair he had moved beside the bed. "If you eat too quickly you'll be sick, or feel full before you've had hardly anything."

She ate dutifully but had little appetite. She wanted only to close her eyes and drift off to sleep and forget the nightmares of waking.

Yet there were strange pleasures, too. How odd it was, she thought, to have someone taking care of her. No, not so much taking care, for Kit did not argue when she refused Dr. Ward's recommended dose of laudanum. Nor had he insisted she eat more than she really wanted. When she sent Ruth on her way and undressed herself without the abigail's annoying assistance, Kit gallantly turned his back and tended the fire. She wriggled out of her drawers and chemise and ducked into a warm flannel nightgown as quickly as she could.

Then Aurelia settled herself on the bed and pulled the covers over as much of her as possible, given that mound of pillows.

Because all she could think about was her plain flannel nightgown. It was warm and comfortable. Hardly romantic. No frill of lace at throat or cuff. No ruffles down the front. Spinsterish.

And beneath the soft fabric, her skin longed for something very different.

She did not want Kit taking care of her. She wanted him

to care *for* her. She had thought—hoped—he did. But when he looked at her, in her plain nightgown . . .

A sharp rap at the door brought her out of a light doze. She could not have but closed her eyes for a few moments, yet the room was dark and the tray gone from her lap. She must, she realized, have slept for some time. Had she, in fact, even heard that single knock, or was it the product of a dream?

As she listened closely for any other sound, she grew aware of other changes in her surroundings. Galahad no longer slept beside her, but another, heavier form lay stretched out on top of the counterpane. Indeed, the dog had wakened and was padding quietly to the door.

Whatever had wakened her and Galahad also disturbed Kit's rest, for he rolled closer to her and whispered, "Don't make a sound. The door is locked; whoever it is will go away when they can't get in."

She was cocooned in blankets yet still felt the vital warmth of his hand on her shoulder. Protective. Reassuring. Seductive.

Galahad sniffed noisily along the bottom of the door, then jumped back at a second knock.

"Mr. Ballantyne, I know you are in there with Miss Phillips. If you do not wish me to wake everyone in Nethergate, I suggest you open this door at once and do not keep an old woman waiting."

Kit was off the bed in an instant. Aurelia barely had time to throw back the covers and snatch her wrapper from its usual place at the foot of the bed before Kit had the door open and ushered Lady Whiston in.

She hobbled to the chair Aurelia set before the fire and waited while candles were lit. Kit offered her a glass of brandy, which she accepted and drank in a single swift gulp, then he placed the decanter on the small table beside her chair before he crossed to stand by the fire. Galahad greeted her with little apparent interest, accepted a desultory pat to his head, then lay back down.

"Always preferred spaniels myself," the dowager stated, "though they tend to be yappy. I brought you something."

Her directness, combined with the lingering effects of a few hours' desperately needed but not completely adequate sleep, left Aurelia confused. That confusion changed to shock when the elderly woman held out the empty glass and dropped a pearl into it.

"I caught Freddie with it," she said, handing the glass to Kit. "Said he found it in Serena's room after they'd taken the body out. He wanted it for remembrance."

Aurelia watched Kit remove the pearl from the glass and wipe off the sticky brandy on his handkerchief. She knew Freddie had lied. She suspected Lady Whiston knew it, too.

Kit dropped the pearl into his pocket and said, "I hope you don't mind if I keep this."

"Not at all. I certainly don't want Freddie caught with it."

"Then you are aware no one was allowed in Serena's room while—she was being taken care of, and that the door was locked after—she was taken out." Aurelia could not bring herself to speak of Serena as a "body." Not this soon.

"Oh, perfectly aware, my dear. After Freddie made such a fool of himself with that knife of his, I wasn't about to let him see her, so I made sure he never went near her room. Really, Mr. Ballantyne, you need not sleep in your boots. They are a fine gesture but hardly proof that you've not engaged in improprieties with Miss Phillips. And they do dreadful damage to the bedclothes."

He had the temerity to chuckle, but at least he did not lie.

"It was exhaustion, not gallantry, milady. But to return to the question of Mrs. MacKinnon's pearl, how do you think your nephew came into possession of it?"

He spoke not loudly, as did most who knew of Lady Whiston's hearing loss, but rather more slowly and distinctly than usual, and made sure he faced her. Aurelia admired the cleverness of his tactic; the marchioness compensated for her disadvantage by using her keen eyes to read his lips as they formed each word.

Lady Whiston offered a shrug. "There is always the possibility that he took it when he murdered her, or that it found its way into his pocket or a fold of his clothing while he committed the act. I prefer, however, to think the real killer dropped it and poor Freddie found it. The boy was enslaved by the unfortunate woman and probably capable of doing anything she asked him, but I find it very difficult to believe he would continue mooning over the slut if he'd killed her. And I do not want the future Lord Whiston found guilty of murdering a former Haymarket whore."

After a long silence, she said, "Oh, dear, child, you mean he doesn't know? And you've not told him?"

"No. There hasn't been time—or necessity."

Lady Whiston hoisted herself out of the chair and took back the brandy glass from Kit.

"I suggest you do so now. Make yourself comfortable, Mr. Ballantyne. I believe we may be up for hours."

Aurelia shook her head.

"No, Kit, there isn't that much to tell. Not that's important, at any rate."

Lady Whiston snorted and said, "I shall fill in the details this child leaves out."

With a deep breath, Aurelia began the story she had sworn not to tell, and hoped that breaking an old promise was not the same as a lie.

"My Uncle Henry was the duke's eldest son, charming and educated and witty. Next to my father, I adored him above every man I'd ever met. He played games with me, read me stories, taught me to ride even before my mother said he could. He let me watch when one of Grandfather's bitches whelped her first litter.

"His only failing, which I did not see as a child but came to understand as I grew older, was that he did not care for the business of the Winterburn estate. Joshua is like him in that regard, and apparently it is a not uncommon trait among the MacKinnons. Henry also seemed reluctant to choose a bride and continue the family. His Grace was furious and often went down to London or sent angry letters threatening to disinherit Henry."

Her hands began to tremble and a tightness in her chest made breathing difficult. She tried to swallow the lump in her throat but it stuck, until Kit pressed another glass into her hand and ordered her to drink.

The brandy burned her throat, much like the smelling salts had seared her nostrils, and like the ammonia, the liquor cleared her head.

She began again, more slowly, though she knew she need not for Lady Whiston's sake.

"Henry arrived at Nethergate one spring morning, with a bride. She was beautiful and elegant, everything the next duchess of Winterburn should be. The duke was ecstatic and ordered a grand celebration, only to have Henry halt all plans. They had a terrible fight, but in the end Henry won. There would be no celebration, he said, because there was nothing to celebrate. Grandfather did not speak to anyone for days, would not leave his rooms. We knew nothing, except that Henry had once again taken up residence here. He gave up his life in London, his friends, his clubs, everything, and became a virtual hermit, with Serena, at Nethergate."

Lady Whiston nodded, a signal Aurelia took to mean the marchioness had nothing to add and that she might continue.

"They fought constantly. She hated Nethergate, hated my parents and me because we liked it. She wanted to live in London, but Henry said she had what she wanted. She had wed the heir to Winterburn; she would someday be his duchess. The issue seemed to be the duke's grandchild. When Serena conceived and bore a son, Henry would take her back to London."

"And she never did."

Aurelia shook her head, aware as she did so that tears were streaming from her eyes.

"She had blackmailed him. For years, Henry kept a lover in London, a young man he was devoted to who happened to be a younger son of a powerful family. Serena was a common prostitute who plied her trade in a place where Henry and his lover frequently met. The price of her silence was marriage to Henry.

"They had been married a little more than a year when Henry received word that his lover had died. The young man had, in fact, sent him a letter, saying he could no longer go on after Henry's abandonment. He hanged himself. The next day, with the letter in his hand, Henry put a pistol to his head."

How long, Kit wondered, had Aurelia lived with the secret, the loss, the hurt? A truth she could never tell, now told.

He walked silently to her and placed his hands on her shoulders. She was not one, he understood, to give in to the hard, cathartic sobs that cleansed pain, only the silent streaks of tears.

"You knew all of this, didn't you?" he asked the dowager marchioness, who calmly poured herself another splash of brandy. "She's been through enough today. Couldn't you have told me yourself and spared her?"

Aurelia shook her head and rested a tear-wet cheek on the back of his hand, but it was Lady Whiston who answered, "I knew only that Henry MacKinnon was homosexual and that Serena blackmailed him in hopes of becoming a duchess. Charles, of course, tried to keep the whole story quiet and agreed to support Serena in an appropriate style as his son's widow provided she allowed no further scandal and denied the truth."

Beneath his hands, Aurelia winced. He leaned down to kiss the top of her head and whisper, "No more, dearest. This is enough."

"No, you must know it all. I've come this far."

She accepted his handkerchief and blew her nose and wiped her eyes. Then, after a deep breath and a long sigh, she went on.

"Grandfather swore me to secrecy. I must never tell anyone, he said, why Henry killed himself. I never did, until tonight. But with Henry dead and Michael disowned, my stepfather became the heir to Winterburn. He said I must have a Season in London, and though I did not want to leave Nethergate, Mother and Robert and I made the pilgrimage."

"She was the success of the Season," Lady Whiston added.

Aurelia disagreed sharply. "I most certainly was not. I hated all of them, the men, the women, the husband-seeking mamas and their grasping daughters. No one ever told the truth, and when I did, they laughed at me. One night, at a particularly disgusting assembly, a very drunken young man asked me if it were true that Robert, my stepfather, engaged in the same perverted vices as Henry. I was furious. I told them—"

She faltered, swallowing the tears that choked her but with a stern wave of her hand refusing any more brandy.

"I told them the truth, not all of it because I had sworn not to, but I defended Henry as he deserved to be defended. He was kind and intelligent and funny and loving. They made him into a monster."

The last words were a hoarse, nearly unintelligible whisper.

"Society cut them, even though Robert was to be the next Winterburn," Lady Whiston finished for her. "They were welcome nowhere. There was no sense attempting to deny that what the girl said was true, and no one wanted to be around her for fear what indiscretion she'd reveal next. They left London within a few days, Robert and his wife in one carriage, Aurelia following with the servants and baggage. Her parents were killed in a carriage accident before they reached Nethergate."

The silence that descended after the marchioness's pronouncement was a healing silence. Kit let it hang, like a warm rain that washes away the grit of a dusty summer afternoon. A tension he had not noticed before had left Aurelia's shoulders, as if a physical burden had been lifted.

He knew the guilt she had experienced, the sense of helpless frustration. He had blamed himself for his father's death, too, as well as struggled against the anger and hatred that became part of the guilt. If he had not been so determined to overcome his father's legacy of failure, he might have seen the problems that eventually led to Cooke's financial collapse and the loss of his own future—another grievance he might have laid at his father's feet.

Unlike Aurelia, however, he had shaken off the guilt and gone on. Why, then, had she not?

The question begged an answer, and there was one dangling just beyond his mind's reach. Before he could stretch for and grab it, Lady Whiston brought an end to the contemplative quiet.

"Now that you know one of Charles's uglier secrets, I shall ask you to explore a small mystery for me. Whether it has any bearing on the present mystery of who strangled Serena MacKinnon, I do not know." She got to her feet with effort, leaning heavily on her cane, and she accepted Kit's offer of assistance with resigned gratitude.

"Nethergate is one of my favorite places," she said, her hand clutching his arm for support as she led the way to the door. Aurelia jumped ahead to unlock it and hold it open to the dark and quiet corridor. "Oh, I know it's a dreary old place, but so many of the grand homes I knew as a girl are gone now, or so changed by 'modernization' that I wish they had been razed by Cromwell. It would have been a kinder and more dignified death. Nethergate, however, never changes."

Kit remembered his own thoughts on the remarkable preservation of the past he had witnessed. There was a sense of enshrinement about the place.

The marchioness continued down the hall while Aurelia relocked the door. Kit listened to the click of the lock, then the soft slap of Aurelia's bare feet on the floor. She had not put on slippers.

She had, however, brought Galahad. Kit smiled without the slightest twinge of jealousy for the undivided devotion she lavished on the one creature she dared to trust.

"Charles never changes anything, does he?"

"No, nothing," Aurelia answered.

She seemed on the point of saying more, but the echoes of those two words, like laughter in a cathedral, provided an eerie reprimand. Every sound, the tap of Lady Whiston's cane, the scrape of Galahad's claws on the floor, was magnified to preternatural clarity in the dark silence.

Only the elderly Lady Whiston dared defile it.

"Charles never needed to change anything. He rarely invited guests, and there were few who were inclined to venture this far from the comforts of London. He cared nothing about following fashion, and with neither guests nor family to wear anything out, everything remained the same."

She hobbled to the gallery, where the light from the candle Aurelia held shone on the immobile forms and faces of the MacKinnon portraits. For Kit, they were more alive now, fighting against the bonds of time and death and forgetfulness to tell what they knew, what they had seen.

Lady Whiston halted before one of the smaller paintings, of a dark-haired young man in uniform, and gazed at it for a moment before snapping at Aurelia, "Bring the light, child."

Aurelia moved closer, while Kit brought one of the chairs for the marchioness. She never took her eyes from the portrait but lowered herself with a groan to the chair.

"Do you recognize this young man?" she asked.

"No, but I do not know most of the people in the portraits."

"He is, or rather he was, Major Sir Littleton Wood-

Spendley, of His Majesty's dragoon guards. Lost an arm in that colonial revolt that gave birth to your United States of America, Mr. Ballantyne. Littie, we called him. He died fifteen years ago. In Canada."

Kit watched her ancient face become a grotesque yet fascinating mask of distorted shadows and sharp highlights as Aurelia lifted the candle higher to examine the painting.

"Why is his portrait here in Nethergate?" she asked. "Is he a relative?"

"Not at all. And considering that he left England for the colonies before David MacKinnon, I doubt Charles ever met him. What I consider most curious is that this portrait, a second-rate work by an untalented disciple of Gainsborough, now hangs where David MacKinnon's did."

14

A COLD, WET NOSE PRESSED TO HERS WAKENED AURELIA FROM A deep, dreamless sleep. She rolled away from the dog's uncomfortable greeting and opened her eyes to a room gray with morning light seeping through the curtains—and cold enough she fancied she could see her breath.

"Good morning, Galahad," she whispered, snaking an arm out of the warmth to scratch the dog's chin. Then, shivering, she burrowed once again into the comfort of her bed. She dared to stretch her left foot tentatively toward the far side until she encountered, with more relief than surprise, Kit.

She smiled. Though her eyes still ached from last night's tears, she recognized their cleansing power. He had taught her that much.

He lay on his side, his back to her, but she did not think he slept. She ran her toes exploringly along the bottom of his stockinged foot and got the expected response. He jerked his foot away, and grunted.

He had shed only his boots, coat, and waistcoat last night

before crawling, at her insistence, into the bed beside her. She still wore her nightgown and would not have removed her wrapper except that it became so horribly tangled as she tried to make herself comfortable with the unfamiliar presence of another body in her bed. She squirmed out of the robe shyly, conscious despite her exhaustion that Kit steadfastly paid her no attention.

Caught in the act, she remembered him saying the other night. They had been "caught" twice since then, yet here they lay, fully clothed, in her bed, with nothing between them but a few kisses. In the cold light of day, reality returned with bitter humor. Christopher Ballantyne had spent the night in her bed and never once touched her.

Galahad whined, intruding on her thoughts. There was nothing to be done but get up and brave the chill of her room as she did every morning, dress quickly, and take him outside. She would stop in the kitchen and order breakfast sent to her room, for herself and Kit.

If he chose to stay.

She threw back the covers and gasped at the cold.

His voice rough and warm with sleep, Kit asked, "Where are you going?"

"To take Galahad outside. To get breakfast. To make the last arrangements for—for Serena."

She felt the movement of the bed as he turned toward her and then a soft glow suffused her as he pulled the bedclothes up again.

"Don't go—yet," he whispered.

A week ago, even three days ago, she had given up all thought, much less hope, of sharing the rest of her life with a man, a husband, a companion, a lover. She could not have conceived the notion of what it would be like to waken in the morning with someone beside her, to go through the day with that someone's attention and care, his voice and touch. She had been content with her lot, accepting of her situation.

If not the rest of her life, at least she had this morning.

He wrapped her in his arms, drawing her against the warmth of his body that chased away more chills than all the fires and comforters in Nethergate.

"Did you sleep well?" he asked, nuzzling the top of her head while she snuggled closer into his embrace.

"Yes. And you?"

"Not a wink."

Aurelia drew back in alarm and looked at him.

He lay his head on the same pillow as she, his face with its lazy, drowsy smile only inches from hers. A dark stubble shadowed his cheeks and chin.

"I couldn't sleep for wanting you, Aurelia," he said.

She slipped one hand up between their bodies to touch his jaw, then stroked a finger across his lips. He snapped at it, catching it playfully between his teeth, then curled his tongue around the sensitive tip.

Glittery tingles flashed all through her, like the sparkles of fireworks. But instead of winking out into darkness, these grew and coalesced in a single bright heat.

She would not ask him for love, for promises, for anything. She would give him neither reason nor opportunity to lie.

And she had already given him her answer to his silent queries. She wanted him as much as he wanted her.

He inched his hand from the small of her back to the curve of her hip. Through the fabric of her nightgown she felt the heat of his touch, the rough texture of the calluses on his palm, the trembling and tender strength of his fingers.

"A cold morning and a warm bed are temptation enough, but you, ah, Aurelia, I cannot resist you," he murmured. "I tried all night, told myself a hundred times I was a fool to stay here, that I should get up and sleep in the chair like a proper English gentlemen. Except that I'm not a proper English gentleman at all. But you know that, don't you?"

With a slow circling caress, he pulled the only garment between his hand and her flesh higher until there was nothing separating them. The first intimate contact of male to female startled a gasp from her, but that gasp changed almost at once to a subtle moan.

"I know nothing," she answered, "only that I have never felt like this before, never wanted this way before."

He slid his hand higher beneath the bunched-up fabric, slowly, inexorably moving toward the aching fullness of her breasts. Following an instinct awakened for the first time, Aurelia reached for the fastenings on his clothing, seeking the same connection with him that he had made with her.

When the buttons on his shirt opened and she slipped hesitant fingers under the soft linen to touch the hair on his chest and finally to press her hand against him as he did to her, Kit, too, groaned.

"Did I hurt you?"

He groaned again, and laughed, a soft, intimate lover's laugh.

"'Tis the sweetest pain in the world, and my own fault, not yours."

With the pressure of a kiss, he eased her onto her back. Her hands were free now to touch and explore him, to pull the shirt off his arms and over his head, and then to stroke down the naked skin of his shoulders.

How marvelous was this sense of touch! Eyes closed, Aurelia tried to take in every nuance of each new sensation that threatened to overwhelm her. It was more than the cool, smooth power of a man's muscles rippling beneath her palm while he divested himself of the rest of his clothing. More even than the weight of his body pressing her into the softness of mattress and pillow. It was the coarse stubble of his beard scraping her cheek, the sinewy length of his thigh molding to her own curves, the slippery satin of his tongue probing for entrance to her mouth, the pleasure so sweet it was almost pain of his thumb—she knew it was his thumb and yet did not know how she knew—brushing across her nipple.

A shiver of ecstatic anticipation lightninged through her as he trailed a line of searing kisses down her throat. She thought she would cry out when through the fabric of her nightgown he swept his tongue over that same sensitive bit of flesh his thumb caressed. Chill followed warmth, then warmth descended again. He suckled gently, yet even gentleness made her writhe with desire.

Frantic to eliminate all barriers between them, she wriggled free of the nightgown and her very nakedness heightened every new sensation.

With his face buried between her breasts, he stroked one hand down her belly to the warm, secret place where all her longing centered. Now she did cry out, first with shock and then with deepening pleasure, as he opened her like a precious flower.

She felt the swollen length of his manhood against her thigh, hot and sleek and thick, all eagerness and hunger she did not understand but could not deny. With his knee he nudged her legs apart, then settled his weight between them.

She moaned softly at his first tentative entry. There was only a slight pain, a tightening, as part of her wanted to deepen the intimacy of this connection and another resisted.

"Ah, yes," he whispered, kissing first one corner of her mouth then the other. "Let it be easy, my sweet. Don't rush, don't hurry, not this first time."

But his words made no sense, not when her body screamed for completion and she knew his did as well. His heart pounded against hers, and even those tiny kisses trembled with suppressed urgency.

"Kit, please, I can't—I don't know—"

"Hush, and let me show you."

He withdrew, dragging from her a whimper of abandonment that abated only when he slid within her. He would have ignored his own rampant, irrational need in order to spare her, but Aurelia herself drove him on. She arched to him with all her virgin passion and took him completely, deeply, sweetly within her.

* * *

In the gray silence, she lay curled against him, his arm around her shoulders so her head rested on his chest. Beneath her ear, his heart beat steadily, and his fingers idly twisted a strand of her hair.

Rational thought returned, to replace the spinning ecstasy to which Aurelia had gladly surrendered a few minutes ago. At first it had frightened her with its demanding and total control of her mind and body, but she had been as powerless to defy it as she had been to resist her craving for Christopher Ballantyne.

She did not know if she loved him; she did know she had wanted him, not only with her body but with her heart, too. Was that love? Or was this golden glow that both filled and surrounded her nothing more than the aftermath of sexual rapture?

And what of Kit? Despite her inexperience, Aurelia had seen simple lust, both the kind that drove Adam Braisthwaite to compete for Serena's favors as well as the more casual variety his father indulged in with the kitchen maid. Was it lust that had brought Kit to her bed last night and aroused him to touch and caress and kiss and finally make love to her this morning?

Perhaps it was, for he suddenly slid his arm out from under her and threw back the covers to sit on the edge of the bed.

She wrapped her arms around herself against the cold of her room and against the cold of a future without Christopher Ballantyne.

"You must allow me some privacy," she begged while he shrugged into his shirt and pulled on his breeches. She glanced at the clock on the mantel to discover it was almost half past seven. The entire household would be up and about by now, with no hope of concealing the fact that she had not spent the night alone. Someone would undoubtedly see Kit, unshaven, in rumpled clothes, leaving her room. She should have been embarrassed, ashamed. Instead, she blushed with pleasure.

Fastening the buttons on his waistcoat, Kit replied, "Half an hour, no more. If you don't meet me in the gallery by eight o'clock, I shall come looking for you. Now, where are my boots?"

"By the chair," she answered, and watched as he stretched the muscles she had felt flex beneath her hands. He had slumped onto the chair and reached for the first boot when Galahad trotted to the door and began sniffing along the bottom, exactly as he had yesterday. Aurelia felt her blood run cold.

A heavy fist pounded on the door, followed by Ruth's imperious voice demanding, "Miss Phillips, I need to see you immediately. I know you are in there. I know you have that man with you."

Scrambling out of the bed, Aurelia snatched her nightgown over her head and tied the ribbons at her throat while she raced for the door. Her fingers slipped on the cold metal of the key and she scraped a knuckle on the wood. Wrenching the door open with one hand, she grabbed the insistent abigail by her arm and dragged her into the room.

Ruth's smug expression remained intact as she looked from Aurelia to Kit and back again. Kit, dressed except for his coat, stirred the fire to life and then lit the candles with the nonchalance and self-possession of a man who had every right to be where he was, with no apologies.

From his attitude, Aurelia took her own composure. "You may think and say what you like, Ruth. Mr. Ballantyne and I have no secrets."

The supercilious smile slipped, but only for a second.

Ruth reached into the deep pocket of her skirt and, with dramatic slowness, withdrew the long strand of Serena's pearls. A needle and stout thread dangled where the maid had not finished the task of restringing the scattered beads.

"Ought to be two hundred of 'em," Ruth said. "Twelve be missing."

Aurelia's heart stopped beating and only began again

when she felt Kit come up behind her. He leaned over her shoulder to kiss her cheek and to whisper a voiceless "Shhh" in her ear.

Then he reached around her for the necklace, not to take it from Ruth but to drape the pearls over the back of his hand. They gleamed in the faint light that suffused the room, spectral gems to grace the throat of a dead woman. Aurelia shuddered, but Kit's hand on her arm squeezed gently and she did not draw away.

He let the pearls roll back to his wrist and said, "It seems a shame to bury them with her, but then I don't suppose anyone else would ever want to wear them. And I don't suppose Mrs. MacKinnon is going to miss the other twelve when she has all these."

He gave them back so that Ruth had to hold them in both hands or risk their coming unstrung again.

"They were hers, given to her by her husband. She ought to have all of 'em with her."

Aurelia expected Ruth to complete her statement with a remark about Serena meeting Henry beyond the grave, but apparently the abigail thought better of such inanity.

Kit, however, seemed more than eager to send the woman on her way.

"Ruth, my dear, I assure you Miss Phillips has no idea where the twelve missing pearls are, and neither do I. We have not found any, but if we do, we will surely let you know."

He maneuvered her toward the door, which still stood open, and then out into the hall. She had not been able to put the pearls in her pocket; they threatened to spill out of her hands, and Kit guided her as if they might at any second go rolling and skittering in a hundred directions.

"Eight o'clock, Miss Phillips," he called over his shoulder, then pulled the door closed.

Aurelia looked down at the key she still held in her hand.

He had lied again.

"To protect me?" she asked of Galahad, who sat neatly in front of her to whine and wag his tail. "Or to protect himself?"

She locked the door, and at the same time locked away the emotions that had accompanied her wakening on this dreadful day. She could not, however, ignore her responsibilities, so she turned with renewed purpose toward the wardrobe.

And spied Kit's coat still draped with intimate casualness over her chair.

Anger as well as wild hope surged through her. She snatched up the heavy garment and reached into first one pocket then another. All were empty. She found neither the pearls nor the ebony box in which Kit had put them.

Kit nicked himself twice while shaving. He swore, dabbed at the red spots on his jaw with a clean handkerchief, and swore again.

"It's too damn cold," he muttered, grasping for any excuse. "I'd make a miserable Englishman, Emil. I find this weather deplorable. Even Charleston's mosquitoes are to be preferred over this incessant cold."

The sailor turned valet was up and about better today, though his splints and slings left him incapable of providing genuine assistance.

"Young MacKinnon doesn't seem bothered by it," he observed, holding Kit's other coat with one hand.

"Joshua's been here longer and had time to adjust. And he's the heir. Besides, he *wants* Nethergate, which gives him good reason to adjust to the place. I, on the other hand, have none."

Emil sniffed and helped him into the coat.

"Spendin' the night with Miss Phillips ain't a reason, I take it."

The remark deserved no reply, primarily because Kit was unsure he had one sufficient to squelch any debate on the subject. Of all the things he either hoped or expected to find at Nethergate, the very last was a woman like Aurelia. A woman utterly free of pretense. A woman whose only measure of a man was his character. A woman so sweetly innocent she did not even know enough to be frightened by the explosive passion she unleashed in him.

A woman as honest in her own passion as in everything else she did.

A woman he would have to walk away from, as David MacKinnon had walked away from Nethergate.

That was not, he admitted, an accurate comparison. David had, Kit was sure, intended to return. According to Jeremiah, he had done so. But Kit might have no opportunity to return for Aurelia, and he did not think he could leave her, knowing that he might never see her again.

Could one night and one morning in her bed have had such a profound effect upon him that he was thinking in terms of "never"—and "forever"?

No, it was more than making love to her that had him thinking this way, just as it was more than the prospect of making love to her that had put him in her bed last night.

He settled for scowling at Emil, who backed away with an awkward shrug and exaggerated grimace.

After checking his chin in the mirror one more time, Kit patted his pocket where the ebony box lay. It was far more comfortable there than in his boot. Though not long, the walk from Aurelia's room to his had been enough for the damn box to rub a raw spot on his ankle.

He wondered if Aurelia had discovered its disappearance. Was she so honest she would attempt to catch him in a lie about finding the pearls by showing them to Ruth or even to her grandfather? He half suspected she was, which was why he had taken the box out of his pocket and dropped it into his boot. But she would have had to search his coat, and the thought of her slipping her hands in and out of his pockets was enough to make him smile. He was jealous of his coat.

He arrived at the gallery precisely at eight, but saw no sign of her. Annoyed, but not really surprised, he paced back and forth in front of Major Sir Littleton Wood-Spendley's portrait for five long minutes, then went in search of her.

He found her an hour later in the stables, examining the gray mare Gould had ridden out of Nethergate the previous morning. As usual, Galahad was with her, snuffling about the mare's stall while Aurelia stood patiently off to one side. Guthrie, on his knees in the straw, was rewinding the bandage around one of the mare's forelegs.

"'Twas nothing too serious," he said. At Kit's entrance, he looked up but did not leave off his work. "Ah, good mornin', Mr. Ballantyne. The gelding's comin' along right well, if you'd care to see. I've not had the chance to tell ye how sorry I am. I blame myself for not—"

Kit cut him off sharply.

"It wasn't your fault. I should have checked everything myself."

The words came without thought, the apology, the dismissal, the polite shifting and acceptance of blame, when all Kit wanted to do was either bellow his fury at Aurelia because she had worried the devil out of him for nearly an hour—or crush her in an embrace from which she would never escape and kiss her within an inch of her life and then make love to her until they both felt they had died.

Once this morning had most definitely not been enough.

Instead, he kept up the inane chatter with the groom, even squatted down to examine the lacerations on the horse's knee himself. Yet he was aware of Aurelia's pointed effort not to acknowledge his presence.

When she tugged on Galahad's lead to leave, Kit blocked her exit.

"May I be allowed to accompany you, Miss Phillips?" He managed to avoid gagging on the overly polite phrases, but only with effort, and only because what he wanted to tell her could not be voiced where others might hear. "I had hoped to speak with you earlier but we seem to have missed each other."

A brief flare brightened her cheeks.

"I have no time for idle conversation, Mr. Ballantyne."

She drew the comment out long enough to make her exit from the stall, and Kit held off his reply until they were well beyond Guthrie's hearing.

"I am not interested in idle conversation, Aurelia, as I suspect you well know."

Galahad jumped at Kit, eager to play and have his ears scratched, but Aurelia jerked on the lead to bring the dog to her other side.

"Whatever the cause for your anger, my dear, don't take it out on an innocent animal. If *I've* done something, at least give me a chance to defend myself. Why didn't you wait for me?"

She marched with her usual self-righteous determination out of the stable and into the snow-carpeted courtyard of Nethergate.

He had timed his speech well. Several boys were at work with brooms and shovels clearing a wide path from the main entrance across the courtyard to the old chapel. Aurelia would not, Kit was certain, put on a display in front of servants. The wind, too, biting and laden with fine particles of snow that stung exposed skin, made any kind of communication difficult. Galahad, who took great delight chasing the swirls of snow across the cleared flagstones, added to the difficulty, especially when he chose to pounce on one of the piles of white fluff the boys had heaped to the side of the walkway.

Perhaps in defiance of Kit's chiding, Aurelia repeatedly pulled the dog back, until Galahad went sprawling.

She was on her knees at once, arms around the beast's neck while he licked her face with unquestioned forgiveness.

"You lied to me," she blurted to Kit, never looking at

him, never breaking stride as, head down against the wind, she resumed her royal progress toward Nethergate.

He let the wind cover his sigh of relief. If she was hurt and angry enough by what she took to be a lie that she even unthinkingly hurt Galahad, then Kit had every reason to believe she felt at least some of this strange, exhilarating, frightening emotion that he dared not yet give a name to.

Instead of the main entrance, she entered one of the side doors, one Kit guessed would take her to her room by the least public route. With servants and guests alike preparing for the memorial service, no doubt she wished to save both herself and Galahad further delays.

The longer walk should have afforded Kit a chance to explain his actions, but it was clear Aurelia was in no mood to talk now, and the bitter weather was hardly conducive to rational discourse. Nor, he realized as a particularly nasty gust swept snow and frigid air inside his coat, was the open territory of the courtyard the proper place.

He was, however, able to study the whole of Nethergate for the first time, and from a most intriguing angle. Accustomed as he was to building ships and envisioning the completed vessel from a drawing, or to mentally peeling away a hull to expose the underlying structure, he instinctively matched his earlier exploration to this, his first real look at Nethergate.

Its birth as a fortress barbican was clear from the courtyard side, though the interior had obviously been gutted and rebuilt to match the Jacobean entrance front, by which he and Emil had entered the maze a mere three days ago. Here, however, the medieval stones and arches still stood, as in the two remnants of curtain wall that hinted at the outlines of the vanished castle. In one of those wings, which even more from the outside than within gave evidence of having been converted to servants' quarters, he had spent his first night.

The other, in far worse repair, held true to its Norman beginnings. Some of the windows showed light behind them, evidence of a collapsed roof. The others were dark and lifeless.

He could recall from his previous forays no sign of entrance to this silent vestige from within Nethergate Hall. Perhaps, while Aurelia was safely surrounded by the rest of the household at Serena's funeral, he might venture to do additional exploring.

But a shout from across the courtyard interrupted his thoughts. He discovered, too, that Aurelia and Galahad had managed to reach the door several strides ahead of him. He quickly closed the distance between them as Joshua hallooed again from the arched stone shelter of Nethergate's medieval entrance.

The Winterburn heir hung back, as though hoping they would come to him, but when Aurelia stood fast, Joshua walked out into the wind and cold and headed for them.

Galahad whined, then emitted a single low growl. Kit reached down a gloved hand to pat the dog's head and encountered Aurelia's already there. She withdrew slowly, leaving Kit with an impression of reluctance to break the contact despite her anger but also reluctance for the liaison to be witnessed.

She could not—and if he knew her at all, she would not —deny what they had shared, but he sensed that she wanted to hold it privately within her, rather than flaunt it. It made no difference that probably every chambermaid and stable boy in Nethergate knew the American stranger had spent the night in Miss Phillips's bedroom; Aurelia would keep the secret truth to herself.

Which Kit recognized was further evidence of the depth of her feelings.

Joshua, who may or may not have seen the gesture, came no closer than necessary to deliver his message without shouting. With neither a preliminary greeting nor in any way acknowledging Kit's presence, he said, "Grandfather wishes to speak with you immediately, Aurelia."

Kit felt the scorn in Joshua's flagrant snub, but shrugged

it off as little different from what he had experienced at the hands of London Society a few days ago. Aurelia's reaction, however, was very different.

She took a single step back, whether to increase the distance between herself and Joshua or to take advantage of Kit's nearness, Kit himself did not know. When he put a hand on her shoulder, he felt the tension tighten her muscles like string being pulled at both ends.

A string that could too easily break.

"I shall attend His Grace as soon as I return Galahad to my quarters," she said, her voice as tight as the cords of her shoulder.

Joshua sneered. "That animal belongs in the kennels," he snapped. "When I am—"

Beneath Kit's hand, Aurelia vibrated with anger like a plucked harpstring. He could not see the expression on her face, but something cut Joshua's threat short.

"I shall attend His Grace as soon as I return Galahad to my quarters," she repeated, each word low and distinct.

Joshua did not back away from her, either physically or emotionally. If anything flickered behind the blank mask he drew over his features, it was vague confusion. But Kit had no time to evaluate so fleeting and fragile an impression, for after a brief glance, Joshua turned to retrace his steps.

Aurelia pulled the other door open and strode inside, leaving Kit to close it and shut out the cold and wind. He half expected her to continue without waiting for him, and indeed she did take two or three more steps, but they were hesitant and halting, and finally she stood, her back to him, her shoulders squared.

They had entered an old scullery, a small, dim room that, like the chamber where Kit had spent his first night, had not seen the meticulous care lavished on the rest of Nethergate. It smelled of damp and dust, and the glass in the single high window was cracked behind a curtain of cobwebs.

It was exactly what Kit had expected of Nethergate. But

nothing, he reflected as he cautiously approached Aurelia, since he entered its walls was what he had expected.

He touched her shoulder gently, afraid to frighten her. When she displayed no reaction, he walked around her, pulling back the hood of her cloak as he did so.

She partly turned her head at that, giving the faint light from that grimy window full play on her features. Her expression was stony, as pale and cold as a marble cameo, but no confusion lingered in her eyes.

For several long moments he did nothing but hold her, stiff but unresisting. He found it difficult to imagine the rigid creature in his arms was the same he had held little more than an hour ago. But she did not try to escape his clumsy embrace. She simply stood, mute, unmoving, her cheek resting against his shoulder, within the circle of his arms.

Though the scullery was unheated, at least the wind did not whip about them to steal what warmth their bodies generated. Some of the ice began to thaw.

"Come, I'll take you to your grandfather," Kit offered.

If she had not found another reservoir of determination, he would have been content to hold her for hours, until the repressive stiffness melted. However, she sighed with a great shiver, then extricated herself from his embrace. At first her steps were hesitant, as when she had come through the door and entered this tiny room. But she drew into herself a ferocious strength, manifested in a lengthening of her strides and a steady quickening of her pace as she made her way from this room to another.

She had spurned him but not rejected him. She did not trust him, but she did not hate him either.

Kit could only follow and wait for the proper moment to explain.

The chapel shimmered with the light from dozens of tall candles on the altar and around the bier. The draft from opening and closing the door sent the tiny flames into wild gyrations. Aurelia paused for a moment while her eyes adjusted to the dancing shadows after the glare of weak sunlight on snow.

The few household servants who had chosen to attend gathered in knots to whisper softly, but even those conversations died as Aurelia made her way past familiar faces toward the front of the chapel. She clutched the duke's Book of Common Prayer in cold hands; she had forgotten her gloves in her haste.

Futile haste, for she was still the last to arrive. Joshua, his head bowed in an attitude of prayer, occupied the chair nearest the head of the black-draped casket; Freddie Denholm sat at Serena's feet.

Even Kit Ballantyne, whom she had distinctly told at the last minute after she left her grandfather's room to stay away from the chapel, stood off to one side, unobtrusive yet making no secret of his presence.

"Damn you," she muttered under her breath, and at the same time she sent up a silent prayer of thanks that he had not followed her orders.

She approached Joshua, who raised his eyes at the sound of her footsteps. He stood, but only after glancing around, as though to make sure she had come to him alone. On his feet, he could look down on her; he could not do the same to Kit Ballantyne.

"Grandfather is unable to read the service," she told him simply, holding out the book to him. "He requests that you do it, and if you are not willing, the honor is to go to Mr. Ballantyne."

He glared at her, opened his mouth to speak, then snapped it shut again, but there was no hiding his fury. When he would have snatched the book from her, she held on tightly.

"Does Ballantyne know?"

She nodded and released her hold on the prayer book.

The duke's directive made no sense. By rights Lord Moresby should have read the service in the duke's absence, drunk or not, and Aurelia noted that the viscount, seated with his family, seemed quite frighteningly sober this morning, perhaps in anticipation of being called upon. Even Lady Whiston, who had braved the cold and the unheated chapel, raised an eyebrow when Joshua began flipping through the pages. The old woman sat with a heavy robe over her legs and what appeared to be a flask of brandy tucked under the edge.

Aurelia swallowed a great lump of unease and turned her footsteps in the direction of the shadowed corner where Kit stood. She caught a snippet of disapproving whisper from Lady Moresby but did not bother to acknowledge it.

Lies and secrets and threats, and now the finality of a death. She tried to make sense of it but could not.

She was no more than two or three steps away from Kit when Joshua cleared his throat, preparing to begin. The chapel fell into silence, so that the soft rustle of her skirts, the patter of her last footsteps, echoed clear. But if any attention turned toward her, it soon veered in a different direction, as with a creak of rusty hinges and the groan of ancient timber, the door to the chapel swung inward.

Again the candle flames leapt into wild motion, more like the greedy fires of hell hungry for a new soul than the pure luminescence of heaven they were meant to symbolize.

Aurelia instantly recognized the silhouette framed by the wide entrance. Only a matter of gravest concern would prompt Guthrie to interrupt the solemn business of Serena's funeral.

"Well, man, speak up!" Joshua called. "What do you want?"

"It's Mr. Gould, sir."

Whispers rippled, and several of the candles snuffed out in the draft.

"He's returned?"

"In a manner of speaking, sir."

Aurelia slipped further into the shadows to make her way along the wall, around the gathered mourners, and inch toward the door.

"What do you mean? Either he's back or he isn't."

"What he is, sir, is dead."

15

THERE WAS NOTHING ANYONE COULD DO FOR EITHER LINCOLN Gould or Serena MacKinnon, yet Aurelia felt everyone in the chapel staring at her, waiting for her to make a decision. Anger charged her. Why did they not ask Joshua? He was to be the duke, the master of Winterburn and lord of Nethergate, and no one, neither Guthrie and the other servants nor Lord Moresby himself, considered Joshua the one to take charge of the situation.

No one—except Christopher Ballantyne.

The chapel was small, and though the others who clustered around her were taller than she, still Aurelia could see Kit standing where she had left him. She became aware then of his calm, even in the face of this latest disaster. She could easily have turned to him for assistance, for guidance, and he would have stepped in with his innate competence.

"Dr. Robbins, would you mind accompanying Guthrie and taking care of whatever needs to be taken care of?" she asked the physician. Dr. Ward, too, pushed his way through the tiny crowd. "I shall join you when we are finished here."

Guthrie nodded, first to her and then, perhaps as an afterthought, to Joshua, who had joined them rather belatedly. He still held the prayer book open.

There had been a perfunctoriness to the service prior to Guthrie's intrusion and the news of the lawyer's death. Now a kind of desperation settled over the assembly. Aurelia felt it, heard it in the fervent responses. Freddie Denholm relit the candles that had blown out, as though the light would chase the demons that troubled them all.

Joshua's performance surprised her. He read the service in a clear, steady voice worthy of any pulpit. The duke would, Aurelia thought, have been pleased. Yet she could not forget the indecision that had plagued the heir to Winterburn a few minutes earlier. Perhaps Joshua's true calling lay in the Church, and perhaps someone else should rule Nethergate.

She glanced in Kit's direction. She had thought he would go with Dr. Robbins to examine Mr. Gould's body, since he seemed to know a great deal about such things, but he remained. She took enormous comfort from his presence. He had displayed utmost confidence in her, yet he had not demanded anything in return. He trusted her, but would not have thought any less of her if she had asked for his assistance.

He confused her—or perhaps she confused herself.

Her mind wandered too often, brought back to the present now and then by Joshua's oddly compelling voice or the unison replies of the mourners. At last, the final amen rang through the chapel. Lady Whiston had to direct Lord Moresby to pull Freddie away from the casket, and it appeared there might be a scene, but Aurelia did not stay to watch or resolve it. She was on her way to the stable.

The body lay on a carriage robe in the straw of an empty stall. Dr. Robbins hunched over the still form.

Aurelia walked past Guthrie and gazed down at the dead

man. In contrast to the gruesome bloating of Serena's face, Gould looked peaceful, his eyes closed, his features composed. Except for the large stain of blood on his collar, there was no obvious indication of injury.

"Shandy found him," Guthrie explained. "I let him go visit his mother two days ago and he was walking back this morning. Found him just above the old shepherd's hut."

She knew the place well. Only three walls remained standing of the tiny stone structure; it offered little shelter save from the wind. A man who had lost his horse might have survived the storm with a fire, but there was no source of firewood near the hut.

Even that was not what set the hairs at the nape of her neck prickling.

Joshua, with Freddie and Adam shuffling behind him, entered the stable, but none of them came into the stall. Adam, indeed, hung back where he did not even have a view of what lay on the carriage robe.

She directed her question to Guthrie, but she was glad Joshua had come in time to hear it.

"I thought Mr. Gould was on his way to London. That old hut is several miles due north of Nethergate, in the opposite direction."

Joshua was quick to answer.

"I rode with him a short way, nearly to your cottage, then joined the others for the shooting," he said. "I told him I was worried about the weather, that it appeared to be worsening and he should not ride on. He laughed and suggested I accustom myself to the English climate, that snow was hardly uncommon in this part of the country and easily navigated. I left him in perfect health, I assure you, or do you accuse me now of murdering my lawyer, too?"

"Someone killed him." Dr. Robbins grunted and rolled the half-frozen corpse onto its side to expose the back of the head. The flesh above the coat collar was battered to a hideous pulp, with what could only be bits of bone stuck in the clotted blood. Whatever weapon had been used had torn the fabric of the coat. No mere fall could have done that. "If he had fallen, even if he hit his head on a rock, the wound would be higher, closer to the top of his head. As you can see, there is no wound to the head. It's his neck that's broken."

Aurelia forced down the sour nausea. Once again, Kit's hand on her shoulder and the now familiar colonial lilt to his voice steadied her.

"If Lord Moresby has not already done so, I believe His Grace must be informed. Will you, Mr. MacKinnon?" Though softly spoken, the question taunted Joshua to the edge of his endurance.

Had Kit challenged him deliberately? Was this his way of goading Joshua into fulfilling the role he must play when he came into the title? Aurelia looked over her shoulder at him, but she could read no answer in his expression.

She could, however, take the initiative Joshua failed to.

"I will apprise His Grace at once," she announced, eager to be away.

She could hardly breathe until she had left the stable behind and once again stood in the cold biting air. The sky had lightened further, and behind only a thin veil of clouds, the noon sun on snow blinded her. She shielded her eyes with one hand and struggled to pull up her hood with the other, but her hair had come loose, and in the wind, she finally had to give up. The moments she lost in the effort, however, afforded both Kit and Joshua time to join her.

She would have preferred to accomplish this task alone.

"What reason had I to kill him?" Joshua wailed defensively, striding at her left.

"No one has accused you," she reminded him.

"Yes, you have. You all have. Just as you accused me of killing Serena. With your whispers and your glances."

He sounded like a spoiled child expecting to be excused for some petty misdeed.

Aurelia was numb with cold by the time they reached the

duke's study—and found Morton Sullivan waiting for them. The secretary silently ushered them into the room where Charles MacKinnon sat behind the desk as if he had been carried down from his room and placed in that position like a posed doll.

"So there's been another death," he said.

Aurelia nodded and walked closer, explaining, "One of the stable boys found Mr. Gould on his way to Nethergate after a visit to his mother. Dr. Robbins says he was murdered."

His Grace had grown more frail in the two short hours since she last spoke with him in the dim comfort of his room. Here, with the study brightened by sunlight and snow glare streaming in the windows, the ravages of age and illness and the telling events of the past few days stood out clearly.

How much longer, she wondered, could he last? A day? A week? How long could the rage and hatred she saw in his eyes sustain him?

And at whom was that rage directed?

Not at Morton Sullivan, who went to stand beside the duke as though guarding him against attack. It must have been the secretary who told him of Gould's death. Aurelia remembered Sullivan's being in the chapel earlier but whether he stayed after Guthrie's interruption, she did not recall.

Nor was the duke angry at Joshua, who railed against fate and unseen, unknown enemies.

"What have I done to deserve this?" he cried, pacing to the windows. "First Serena, the only person in this household who treated me with kindness. And now my solicitor, an honest and honorable man who committed no crime save to be engaged in looking out for my interests. How can you possibly accuse me of having anything to do with their deaths? What had I to gain?"

He had nothing to gain, because he already had everything, Aurelia admitted with a glance to Kit. On the other hand, Christopher Ballantyne was the interloper, coming to Nethergate with nothing.

She tried to placate Joshua with the same words she had used before.

"No one has accused you of anything. You yourself admitted that you rode out with Mr. Gould, that you were probably the last to see him alive."

"But I did not kill him!" He threw his hands up in the air and crossed to one of the bookcases, where some of the household ledgers lay. He stroked a shaking hand along the leather binding, the most interest he had shown in them of his own accord since Aurelia had tried to teach him the accounts. "And why do you take the village charlatan's word for gospel? Why is it not possible that Gould's horse threw him and dragged him along the ground? Would that not account for the same kind of wound?"

When the duke asked no questions, Aurelia understood the terrible mistake she had made by not coming immediately to her grandfather with the news of Gould's death. Sullivan had not stayed in the chapel for Serena's service; he had gone with Guthrie and then taken the tale to his employer. Instead of seeing to the living by tending to Joshua's needs—and perhaps his protection—Aurelia had gone on with a funeral that could make no difference to anyone, least of all the heir to Winterburn. She had given the duke evidence of her changed allegiance, her betrayal.

The full weight of the discovery settled on her with such crushing force that a short, anguished moan escaped her.

It was she whom Charles MacKinnon, duke of Winterburn, hated with such passion that he fended off even death.

Holding on to a last shred of dignity, she granted him a bitter curtsey.

"If you will excuse me, Your Grace," she murmured.

"And where do you think you're going?"

The mockery in his voice, a voice as frail as the body that produced it and every bit as hate-filled, sent ice through her veins. She understood the threat only too well—that there was nowhere for her to go.

Yet she could not stay.

"Come back here, Aurelia Phillips!"

She ignored the duke's feeble shout and made her way to the door Sullivan had not locked. As soon as she was safely in the corridor, she ran.

She ran as she had never run before in her life, with but one thought in her mind. Ignoring the shouts and running footsteps behind her, she pushed an unlucky servant out of her way and sent flying both the girl and the tray she carried.

At the foot of the main staircase, Kit caught her, grabbing her arm and spinning her around to face him so swiftly she nearly fell.

"Running will accomplish nothing," he told her, "except to give the killer a scapegoat."

"Do you expect me to ignore what we both saw in that room? My grandfather hates me. He has threatened to take from me the one hope I have for anything but a life of poverty or dependence on charity."

He began leading, almost dragging, her up the stairs. She had no doubt that if she resisted, he would indeed haul her like a dead sheep wherever he wished to take her.

"I expect you to ignore everything, to act as if nothing untoward has happened."

She tried to shake off his grip but he only tightened it even as Lady Whiston's maid Molly passed them on the staircase.

"Then I suggest, Mr. Ballantyne, that you do the same," she snapped. "This kind of behavior in front of the servants . . ."

"I don't care about servants. I only care about catching a killer. Give me your key."

"I beg your pardon!"

"Dammit, Aurelia, don't argue with me! Give me the key!"

He did not let go of her wrist as he unlocked the door and pulled her inside. Galahad danced around their ankles, but he did not leap on Aurelia as was his wont. When Kit snapped an order, the dog trotted over to his rug in front of the fire and lay down.

"Thank you for unlocking the door. Now, if you will please excuse me, Mr. Ballantyne, I have packing to do."

When she looked back at Kit, she saw the most unexpected smile on his face.

"So, you are human after all," he said. "You can react emotionally, without thought, like the rest of us. You are capable of misjudgment and even—forgive me, love—stupidity."

"*Stupidity!* I beg your pardon, Mr. Ballantyne, but—"

"Yes, Aurelia, stupidity. Think for a moment. Where would you go? What would you do? You've lived your life in the shelter of your grandfather's malignant generosity. He took care of you only so he could use you."

She winced as if he had read her mind and shoved a page in front of her she had tried to ignore.

She shook her head, not wanting to believe it yet knowing it was true.

"I can go to London. I am educated enough to find a position as a governess."

"Not without references. I may not know much about servants, but I do know about references."

He was making her think rather than feel, even when her feeling was anger at him for being right.

"I will ask Lady Whiston." That would mean a further delay, when a few minutes ago she could not have spared ten seconds, so desperate was she to flee.

"She may refuse. Even if she does not refuse, who will hire you? Who will trust you in their family, with all the petty secrets any family harbors? Isn't that why you immured yourself here in the first place?"

He was asking the questions she should have asked and answered for herself long ago. He forced her to face the ugly reality of her one weakness—blind loyalty to the man whom she had believed loved her—and challenged her to find new strengths.

She sought them only because she knew he would not have done so had he not known they were there, somewhere.

"I must speak with your grandfather—alone," he said, pressing the key into her hand once more. "I shall be gone no longer than an hour. Wait for me."

He curled her hand around the key with that intimacy of touch she remembered far too well.

Unable to control the need rushing through her, Aurelia threw her arms around his neck, her fingers clawing their way into his hair to pull his mouth down to hers. He groaned with an echoing hunger and crushed her to him. She felt the heat of him, from the hands he stroked down her spine and curved around her buttocks to mold her to the hard evidence of his arousal pressed so demandingly to her belly.

He bruised her lips in the act of forcing them apart, but she felt no pain, just took his savage tongue deep into her mouth. The taste of him, of his desperation, sent wild arcs of desire through her.

This was not like earlier in the morning. He had taken her carefully, cautiously through the discovery and the passion, and if she went beyond the bounds of her own control, she blamed her innocence—and his experience.

Now she sensed a complete absence of control, his as well as her own. Now there was only the passion, the need.

He untied her cloak and let it fall to the floor, then began on the long row of buttons.

She broke far enough away from his mouth to gasp with her last breath of sanity, "No, Kit, don't let them find us like this. Please, stop."

"I don't care about the damn servants," he growled against her throat as he pulled her dress lower, almost baring one breast.

"But I *do* care, Kit! Dear God, for better or worse, I must live here with them!"

The ferocity of her outburst must have chilled his passion, for he released her abruptly.

"Oh, Kit, you were right, so right. I have nothing, not even any hope, for the future. I wanted so little, and I thought Grandfather had given it to me. Joshua would inherit the title and Nethergate and the Winterburn estates, but I would have the cottage, and Galahad, and a small income to live on in peace and quiet."

"You think he lied?"

"I *know* he lied! Did you not hear him? He all but told me I was a prisoner here, at his mercy now and at Joshua's when he is gone."

She looked around her at a room that had been her sanctuary for so many years, each object familiar and commonplace and dependable. When had it become a prison? When had everything she believed in, everyone she trusted, turned on her like a rabid dog in the most vicious of betrayals? And why?

Everyone had lied, and now she wondered if perhaps she had been manipulated into lying for them.

"I *was* his touchstone, wasn't I?" she asked aloud.

Kit came to her and lifted her chin with a finger curled under it. When she tried to avert her countenance, he kissed her cheek and she looked into his eyes once more.

"Aurelia, my innocent Aurelia, people aren't like bits of gold or silver, to be proven genuine by scratching the surface. The worth of the human heart lies deeper than that, and the truth of a person's soul deeper still."

He kissed her lips this time, with such consummate restraint that she felt the passion vibrate within him. Deep within him, she knew, and the lesson was driven home.

"You came here in search of a simple truth, Mr. Ballantyne, and I believe you have uncovered nothing but a wealth of lies."

Again he brushed his mouth across hers, lingering long

enough to set her heart pounding and leave her first breath a gasp.

"Then I must simply dig deeper," he said. "But I fear I have little time, and unless someone is willing to help me . . ."

"I will do whatever I can."

"Whatever?"

"Yes, whatever! Oh, Kit, don't tease me! Tell me what I can do to help you. Even if it is too late for me, even if he takes away the cottage and leaves me at Joshua's mercy, let me at least redeem myself for all the trouble I've—"

The brush of Galahad against her skirt interrupted her. As he had in the past, the dog trotted to the door and put his nose to the narrow space beneath it.

She looked down at the key lying on her open palm, then met Kit's hard, silent gaze. He knew as well as she how unprotected they were, and how much they owed to the dog's more sensitive hearing and innate curiosity.

They had wasted precious time indulging in frustrated passion. Aurelia would do what she could to regain those moments, and a few more if possible.

The knock on the door came as no surprise, nor did the voice on the other side, demanding entrance. Before Joshua put his hand to the latch to find it unlocked and open, Aurelia let every muscle in her body go utterly limp and fell into Kit's arms in a dead faint.

16

"For God's sake, MacKinnon, don't just stand there! Find her maid, or that corsetted fop who calls himself a physician!"

"Aurelia doesn't have a maid," Joshua muttered.

He had opened the door, perhaps a bit surprised to find it unlocked, but he came no further into the room than to stand in the doorway. Galahad, hackles raised but displaying no other sign of hostility, barred his progress.

Kit carried Aurelia to the bed and laid her down upon the counterpane before he bellowed, "Then get the damn doctor! And close the door behind you so the dog doesn't get out!"

That last was, Kit thought, a stroke of genuis; it purchased a few extra seconds.

Aurelia opened her eyes the instant the door latched.

Kit kissed her full on the mouth, gladly wasting those extra seconds all over again.

"You're a fine actress, my dear. I almost believed you myself."

"What's important is whether Joshua did. And you should have found out what he wanted before you sent him away."

"I've plenty of time to do that later. At least he's gone on an errand that ought to keep him occupied for a few minutes. First things first."

He looked down at her, lying exactly as he had placed her, as if she had indeed lost consciousness. Only the trace of color on her cheeks, the moist gleam on her swollen lips where she had licked them before speaking, and the rapid pulse at the base of her throat betrayed her.

"And what does come first?"

"The portrait of David MacKinnon."

She tried to sit up, a natural reaction, but Kit gently forced her down. She apologized at once.

"I'm sorry. Of course it's important to you."

"No, not just to me. That portrait is the only thing Charles MacKinnon has removed from Nethergate in sixty years. There must have been a compelling reason. A *very* compelling reason, for he not only removed his brother's portrait, he also hung another in its place to disguise the disappearance."

"The brother he adored and for whom he promised to preserve his estate. The brother who should have inherited but never kept his promise to return." The words came from her slowly but with painful conviction. "The brother whose grandson has now come to Nethergate to remind Charles of his own betrayal."

Kit saw the pain in her eyes as she allowed herself to begin accepting an unwelcome truth.

"If it were only a reminder of David, I do not think Charles would have removed it," he added, and the brief lowering of her eyes told him she agreed. "I think there is something very special about that portrait, something that will help us answer a great many questions."

* * *

Lady Whiston leaned on Kit's arm and hobbled from her bed to the chair by the fire. Charlotte Braisthwaite held a lap robe as close to the flames as was safe, then draped it clumsily over the marchioness's legs.

"That will be all, child. Your assistance has been greatly appreciated. Now go, change out of that hideous black that does not become you, and join your mother. And remember, no more of those silly ringlets. They are less becoming to you than mourning."

Charlotte hid a furious blush behind a curtsey before she departed, leaving Kit to close the door.

"You are a most remarkable woman, milady," he said with a nod.

"I ought to be, after all these years, even if I am foolish enough to go out in the cold and then have to suffer for it. Damn these old knees!" She tucked the rug more tightly about her before gesturing to Kit to pour her another brandy. "Aurelia needed someone trustworthy to look after her until she recovers from this brief 'indisposition,' so who better than my Molly? And if Charlotte is to continue making calf eyes at Freddie, she might as well dress and act the part. Now, tell me why you want the portrait."

He had been confined and inactive too long for a man accustomed to spending his days in a shipyard. He wanted to pace, but knew it was far more important to face the elderly woman not only so she could interpret his words without his raising his voice, but also so he could maintain her trust.

"In part to prove I am who I say, but more important to prove I'm innocent of killing Serena MacKinnon."

"And you think a portrait of David MacKinnon can do that?" She snorted her disbelief. "Assuming it still exists, of course."

Kit cocked his head in acknowledgment of Lady Whiston's astute perception, but he deliberately avoided responding to it. The portrait's very existence was a major part of his theory. He simply allowed the dowager marchioness to know that he had considered the possibility that the portrait had been destroyed—and discarded it.

"I never met my grandfather, but I can understand why he left the restrictions and responsibilities of Nethergate and why he would stay away. I have no designs on Winterburn."

"Humph. Easy for you to say when the title's not yours."

He shrugged.

"It's as good a reason as any. What *you* said, however, may have been more important than either of us suspected at the time. To prove my theory, I need that portrait. And I need you to tell me what to look for."

"When do you plan to explain this theory of yours to me? After you've found David's painting, I suppose."

He grinned and refilled the glass she held out to him. "My theory is worthless without proof."

"In other words, you have no theory. And you won't until you find poor David's portrait." She fell silent, lost in thought, then said, "I recall it only as a typical likeness of a young man in uniform, similar in arrangement to the one Charles hung in its place. Nothing out of the ordinary except, of course, for the subject." She smiled, and when he acknowledged the compliment, she added, "Do you really believe a painting can tell you anything?"

"I will know that when I find it." He hesitated, then decided there was no reason to withhold anything, even a question, from the one person who might have answers—and the one person besides Charles himself who had known David MacKinnon. "You called him 'poor' David. Why?"

Lady Whiston sighed.

"Because I'd believed him dead all these years. Instead he was probably the only one of us who found happiness. He'd have done his part as Winterburn, and done it well, but he would never have been content. Knowing he survived, I'd like to think he enjoyed a life of adventure and freedom, exactly as he wanted."

Lady Whiston twirled the glass by its stem.

"Brandy does not ease the pain the way laudanum or other drugs do," she observed. "In fact, it does not ease the pain at all. It merely makes you feel as if the pain isn't important."

She poured the amber liquid down her throat and swallowed once. When Kit offered her more, she shook her head and made him take the glass from her.

"You resemble him a great deal, but the likeness is not exact. I would never mistake you for him. Never." She gave him another tiny smile, then resumed all seriousness. "You already know, from the family portrait, David looked nothing like his brother Charles. Why do you not simply ask Charles where the bloody thing is? Oh, no, don't bother to answer. Forgive my stupidity. If Charles wanted you to have it, he'd have given it to you."

Kit nodded.

"Or not taken it down in the first place."

Without a word of explanation from him, the dowager marchioness had followed his line of thought precisely. His logic, he felt confident, held true.

Aurelia rested her hands on the polished surface of her grandfather's desk. She could not stop trembling. The door was open, she made no secret of her presence, yet she felt as guilty and terrified as if she had committed the most grievous sin.

But she had not lied—not yet.

If no one interrupted her, she would not have to.

And how ironic, she thought as she leaned down to open the last of the drawers, that after carefully crafting a believable lie to cover her actions, she had not needed to use it.

Irony, however, did not still the shaking of her hands. Nor did irony provide the information she sought. Everything her grandfather removed from Nethergate was carefully accounted for. There must be a record of the missing portrait.

"What are you doing here?"

Joshua, dressed for riding, walked into the study. How long he had been watching her from the doorway, she had no way of knowing.

"I asked you a question, Miss Phillips."

He strode around the desk and rested one booted foot on the open drawer.

"I was looking for information on whom to notify of Mr. Gould's death," she said. "His family, his partner."

"Leave it to Sullivan. Isn't that his job?"

"Yes, of course, but I thought I could—"

"Don't trouble yourself, Miss Phillips. Really, are you certain you should be up and about after this morning?"

His oily solicitousness as he took her arm and helped her from the chair would not of itself have frightened her. Joshua could be extremely pleasant when he chose to be, and she blamed her momentary revulsion on her own guilt.

He led her past Adam Braisthwaite, whose leering grin and "Not feeling vaporish this afternoon, are we, Miss Phillips?" prompted her to snap, "At least I did not spew my breakfast all over the carpet." She wanted the words back, not because they were a lie or because she had intentionally and maliciously embarrassed Adam with the truth, but because of the vicious hatred—she dared in her own mind to call it murderous—that twisted his grin into a glower. Adam frightened her, but she passed by him without hesitation.

It was Freddie Denholm whom Aurelia feared to approach. While Joshua came to escort her from the study and Adam came in to watch, Freddie waited in the corridor.

Since that horrible moment on the stairs when he learned of Serena's death, Freddie had not spoken a word to her, but she was constantly aware of his eyes on her. She knew too little about the passions of men to know if his rage came because he held her in some way responsible for that tragedy or if he feared she would expose his own guilt.

She would never have thought Freddie capable of such an

obsession. Adam, yes, for there was so much about him that spoke of indulgence in excesses. Kit's words regarding the importance of the portrait haunted her, even as she allowed Joshua to escort her to the drawing room where Lady Moresby and Charlotte busied themselves with that superficial pastime of elegant ladies—embroidery.

Lady Moresby made room for Aurelia to sit beside her on the settee; Charlotte, head bowed over her work, sat across from them.

The difference in Charlotte's appearance amazed Aurelia. She would never be beautiful, nor even what might be called handsome. Lady Whiston and Molly, however, had effected a simple and remarkable transformation. Gone were the childish curls and ringlets that suited most girls her age but looked ridiculous on Charlotte. The subdued mauve of her gown was only partly due to mourning; the color toned down the sallow tints of her skin and at the same time lent a bit of richness to her hair. She might never attract Freddie, but at least she had hopes of attracting someone.

Joshua quite literally handed Aurelia into Lady Moresby's care.

"The weather has proven so advantageous that we are going to ride out to the place where Gould was found and see if there is any evidence to be discovered," he explained. "Do keep an eye on Miss Phillips, won't you? Until we return."

The viscountess looked from Aurelia to her son and said, "Must you go? I should think you would be worried about finding the murderer and ending up his next victims."

Adam puffed out his chest. "We shall be armed, Mother. And Freddie is a dead shot."

Charlotte winced but did not look up.

It was still early, for Aurelia had heard a clock chime twice while she walked with Joshua from the study, and even this time of year, on a sunny day, there were several hours of daylight left. She understood the need for action, too. Her own frustration at not being able to do anything gnawed at her nerves.

Joshua forestalled further conversation with a sharp "The snow is melting. If we expect to find anything, we'd best go now."

She wondered what he expected to find.

For several interminable minutes after Joshua's departure with Adam and Freddie at his heels, she sat without moving. Lady Moresby made desultory chat about the weather; Charlotte said nothing. Aurelia noticed a spot of red on the linen handkerchief Charlotte was embroidering; she had pricked her finger enough to make it bleed. Over nervousness because Freddie had been present? Anger that he had not paid her the slightest bit of attention? Guilt?

Aurelia could not look at anyone without speculating on his or her possible guilt. She knew she was seeing only the surface, scratched now and then, but the heart lay hidden. She had seen the obvious motives and dismissed most of them. But were there others?

The clock tolled three times. She realized she had been sitting in a trancelike state for nearly an hour.

The drawing room had darkened ominously. Lady Moresby and Charlotte, intent on their needlework in lamplight, probably had not noticed the changing atmosphere, but as Aurelia came back to full awareness of her surroundings, she realized the sky had gone from blue to gray.

She turned to Lady Moresby and said, "If you will excuse me, milady, I must take Galahad outside. I fear we are about to have another storm."

The viscountess turned her attention to the far window. "Oh, dear, I do hope Adam has enough sense to come in."

Aurelia left her ruminating on her son's intelligence and made her escape.

Galahad was all joyous barks and excitement when she returned to her room, as though Kit's absence permitted him to indulge in his old playful habits. She scratched his ears and let him lick her chin affectionately while she fastened her cloak around her.

"We're going exploring," she told him as she snapped the lead to his collar. "Just the two of us. I *know* I can trust you."

She encountered no one on her way through a silent Nethergate and out to the courtyard. Galahad walked obediently beside her, trotting ahead every so often to sniff as dogs are wont to do, and then leaving his mark. She was tempted to release him to run, but Adam's parting words about Freddie's skill with a gun echoed in her thoughts. Though Joshua and his friends were likely miles from Nethergate by now, Aurelia took no chances and kept Galahad close.

The sky was indeed lowering, and the absence of the sun made the afternoon cold as well as dreary. It made the stark expanse of the ruins even more forbidding than usual. Aurelia had left her room with excited anticipation of entering the tumbledown remnant of ancient Winterburn Castle and finding the missing portrait, but that anticipation was turning to apprehension as thick clouds drifted overhead.

She led Galahad away from the ruins and headed for the stables. Long before reaching them, she heard the sound of a hammer and knew that someone inside was building Mr. Gould's coffin.

Ignoring her own unease, she entered the brisk, sweet-smelling damp of the stable. The quiet sounds of the horses welcomed her, if no one else.

After securing Galahad, she entered the stall where the brown gelding dozed. He turned his head and blew softly as she ran her hand down his back to feel where the ugly wound had scabbed over.

"'Tis healing nicely, Miss Phillips," Guthrie greeted. "The lawyer's mare, too, if you'd care to look."

Aurelia rubbed the gelding's nose and regretted she had

not brought an apple or carrot for him, then followed Guthrie down the wide aisle.

"Curious thing," he said, opening the door and preceding her. "Careful now, she's a mite skittish."

The mare stood in the corner, ears back, eyes showing white. Guthrie approached her quietly with low words meant to calm, and within a few seconds she returned to her normal placidity.

She allowed him to run his hands down her bandaged forelegs.

"What's so unusual?" Aurelia asked, her own curiosity aroused.

Guthrie plucked off his cap and scratched his head before answering with slow consideration, "That meadow where Shandy found the body ben't more'n three mile from here. Why did it take so long for the mare to make it home?"

Her mind raced from that simple question to a dozen possible explanations so quickly she could not evaluate any of them. Some made clear sense and others only raised further questions, to none of which she had answers.

"I'm sure there is a logical explanation," she said, giving voice to the first thought that came to her mind, "as there is for all that has happened. Perhaps Joshua and his friends will discover it."

Whether Guthrie accepted that logic or understood the response as a hint that Aurelia was not about to discuss the matter further, she did not know. He might, she thought, have been every bit as perplexed as she and hesitant to appear more inquisitive than one in his station ought.

There remained, too, the possibility that he trusted her to take his simple question and build from it the rest of the truth.

She felt foolish that the question had not risen in her own mind, and yet her lack of astonishment at the concept made her wonder if she had not in fact come up with it but, because of circumstances, forced it behind other, more pressing issues. She was, she told herself sternly, perfectly capable of running the Winterburn estate with no more help than a bit of advice from the duke or Morton Sullivan, so much so that His Grace had entrusted her, rather than the secretary, with training Joshua in his duties.

Had the trauma, unexpected delight, and unimagined pain of falling in love with Christopher Ballantyne, of surrendering to the physical joy of being a woman, addled an otherwise competent mind?

No, she could not believe that, and as she went about the seemingly innocent routine of exercising Galahad, she put these notions of weak-mindedness behind her. She also put Nethergate and its environs under subtle surveillance.

The afternoon had grown dreary and cold after the brief respite of sun and warmth. The frigid puddles had started to freeze, making the flagstones slick. A fine, sleety snow drifted on a light wind. As Aurelia began one more circuit of the courtyard, more and more of the windows around her gleamed yellow in the faltering daylight, and the air grew pungent with the smoke of many fires.

Charlotte and Lady Moresby had no doubt been joined by Lord Moresby prior to the serving of afternoon tea. Aurelia expected Lady Whiston to join them, and Dr. Ward as well. Though Kit had said he intended to avoid the others by spending the afternoon with his injured companion, Aurelia trusted he, too, would emerge from that seclusion if for no other reason than to keep an eye on the others.

After all, he did not know Joshua, Adam, and Freddie had ridden out in search of "evidence."

She was quite certain they would find nothing.

She only hoped her search for David MacKinnon's portrait was more fruitful.

By the time she reached her destination, she was numb with cold. She skirted around the chapel, using the old oaks as shelter and concealment, but the distance added to her discomfort. Under the trees, the ice was slicker, and the snow had not been cleared from the corner of the courtyard where the ruined wing of the old castle had once joined the chapel. While Galahad enjoyed digging in the white stuff and pounced gleefully on whatever poor creatures scuttled beneath an increasingly crusty surface, Aurelia found each step an effort.

Nearer the wall of the ruins there was no snow, only a slippery shelf of ice that left no trace of her passage. Shortening Galahad's lead so the dog walked beside her on the dangerous path, she made her way cautiously in the shadows between the chapel and the ruin. Despite the cold, the lack of light, and the treacherous footing, she had no difficulty locating the low, arched doorway, half filled with rubble and leafless vines, that gave forgotten entrance to the remains of Winterburn Castle.

The archway appeared to be nothing more than ornamental stonework, but in fact it concealed a cleverly offset inner portal and a passage that angled through the wall. After crawling as much as walking over fallen, broken blocks of stone, she entered a low-ceilinged space that had once served as a storage area and crude barracks for the armed men who protected the fortress of Winterburn. Squat, massive pillars supported the ceiling and the two floors above. Around one of those pillars curved a flight of worn stairs littered with dust and dead leaves that had blown in through that hidden entrance. Aurelia, holding Galahad close to her, made her way toward the stairs.

Though the ancient walls protected her from the wind, no warmth penetrated the stones of Winterburn. The only light came from two small windows, one at either end of the hall. Except for the detritus of leaves and dust, little seemed changed from the days when, as Henry MacKinnon had told her years ago, Winterburn was a Plantagenet stronghold against the Scots.

The same Plantagenets had wrought most of the damage when York fought Lancaster, and neither side won. The chapel and the lower barbican—the Nethergate—survived, and the last remnants of Winterburn's glory fell into ruin.

Aurelia heard echoes of long-forgotten battles as she felt

her way up the silent stairs. At the top, the massive oaken portal stood partly open on its ancient hinges. She pulled the door further open, hoping to shed light for her return. She was disappointed to find the second floor nearly as dark as the stairwell. Though the doors to the rooms were open, the leaded windows set deep into the thick stone walls allowed only dim light into the chambers, and what spilled out into the corridors was hardly more than gloom.

She entered the first room, farthest from the stairs, but found it virtually empty. Still, she searched, with Galahad at her heels, and wished she had thought to bring a candle at least. A lantern or lamp would have attracted too much attention and so she had taken neither, but she also had not expected such darkness in midafternoon.

She had expected to find more than the single wooden chest that sat, its lid thrown open on one unbroken hinge, in the middle of the second room. Beside it lay a heap of dust-coated fabric, barely recognizable as the predecessors of the draperies that hung in the dining room.

"I thought Grandfather put everything in these rooms," she muttered to Galahad, who scratched at the drapes then poked his nose into the chest and stirred up the dust that lay within. "I thought the upper floor was utterly ruined and unfit even for storage of the things Grandfather could not bear to throw away."

She paused, emerging from the second room, to run her hand over the enormous stones that framed the doorway. That a structure as substantial as Winterburn Castle had fallen into decay disturbed her, and reminded her of how transitory everything was, especially life.

She admitted she could have been wrong, that her memories of exploring this ruin as a child had not served, but she could not give voice to those thoughts.

She had not, she realized, been in Winterburn since before Henry's death and that very thought raised goose-flesh on her arms. Her sense of hearing heightened, Aurelia listened closely while she reoriented herself. This dim light that cast no shadows was eerie enough, but like the solidity of the walls that echoed with decay, so the silence was shadowed with sounds: the ghostly wind that whispered in empty chimneys, and mice that skittered invisibly in the dark.

She shook off these childish fears and quickened her pace toward the third room. Halfway there, however, Galahad set up a soft whining and pulled on the lead. She stopped, thinking something had frightened him, but found him straining more with eagerness and curiosity toward the stairs.

"There's nothing there," she told him, "unless one of the cats has followed us in here." The half-wild creatures were plentiful around Nethergate, feeding on rats and mice and other vermin. Galahad found them amusing, more willing to play with them than they with him.

"We'll look for it later," she promised when he continued to tug on the lead.

An instant later, she heard what could have been a purr or a hiss or some other feline sound. Expecting to see a wiry tabby or fight-scarred tom emerge from the stairwell, she watched in horrified fascination as the door, pushed from the other side, slowly closed.

She ran to stop it, but though the distance was short, she could not reach it in time. With a groan of ancient wood, the door closed tight.

17

KIT TUCKED THE BRACE OF PISTOLS INTO HIS BELT AND REACHED for the greatcoat slung over the chair. Standing watch at the window, Emil said, "They ain't much against three men with muskets, but 'tis better'n naught at all."

"That they are. No sign of the hunters' return?"

"None. Nor of Miss Phillips neither. Weather's worsening, though, so you'd best be about it if you want to do yer snoopin' before they come back."

Kit peered over Emil's shoulder to the vista of snow-covered garden and courtyard below. If not for the invalid's attempt to relieve his boredom by watching out the window, they would never have known of Joshua's departure with the others, or of Aurelia's disappearance. The central wing of Nethergate blocked Kit's view of the old castle, so he could not see how she had entered the ruin, but he had no doubt that was where she had gone not a quarter of an hour ago. He had watched her saunter across the courtyard with Galahad, her image blurred by the snowy mist in the air, and disappear behind the chapel. She had not reappeared.

Forewarned, as the saying went, was forearmed, and when Emil suggested the pistols, Kit readily agreed.

"Damn her!" he swore softly, turning from the window.

"For not waitin' for ye?"

"For a hundred reasons, Emil. For not waiting. For lying. For telling the truth."

Aurelia threw her weight against the door one more time, with the same result. As old and hard as the oak was, it had swollen with damp and age and would not be budged.

And someone had done this to her deliberately.

She rubbed her sore shoulder and looked down at a patient Galahad.

"Who was it?" she whispered, as though that person might be on the other side of the door, listening. "Not Joshua, for you don't like him and would have let me know. Nor Kit, for you *do* like him."

The dog had always displayed far more eagerness when Kit approached, but was it possible that eagerness was tempered by the stealth with which Kit had crept up the stone steps and then closed the door?

She shook her head.

"He has no reason, not if he wants to explore these ruins himself."

For unless he followed her, and she was certain he had not, he had no idea there was any other way into the castle than what she had promised him she would reveal tonight.

Still she shivered. She had made no extraordinary attempt to hide her activities from anyone and merely relied on the absence of Joshua and his cronies and Kit's word that he was going to spend the afternoon with Emil. Only her grandfather's rooms and the suite that had been Serena's offered unobstructed views of the Winterburn relic.

But if whoever had followed her intended to trap her, he did not know the structure as well as she.

Galahad pawed at her skirt.

"Come on, then," she sighed. "We'll have to climb down the wall, which I don't much fancy in this weather, but we've no other choice."

There was another choice, but she determinedly ignored it. To open a window in one of those empty, haunted rooms and call for help would be to give away a secret she intended to keep.

At the end of the hallway, another flight of stairs climbed upward. Once enclosed within the very wall of Winterburn, these steps hinted at the greater devastation that awaited above, for here the wintry light was brighter with no roof to block it. Where the roof had fallen in, old beams and broken blocks of dark granite littered the landing.

A nimble child could clamber over the debris and reach the remnant of exterior stairs that, though likewise damaged, afforded a negotiable descent. Aurelia remembered the days, long past, when she had done just that. It would be more difficult now, but not impossible.

Even so, she proceeded with caution. She slipped the lead off Galahad before she picked her way over the rubble of the fallen wall and climbed to its uneven top. She thanked providence that there was no wind to speak of to whip her skirts and cloak about her. The icy coating and crevice-concealing snow made the scree below her even more treacherous.

Darker clouds had rolled in while she searched the ruins, diminishing the daylight. She felt less exposed than she would have in bright sun, but the ominous gloom reached into her soul.

The worst part of the descent was the first drop, from the top of the wall to the uppermost of the remaining stairs. Though the distance was no more than ten feet, the landing was littered with loose, slippery chunks of stone of unknown stability.

Aurelia lowered herself to lie on the cold rock, then swung over the wall and hung by her hands. Her fingers, already numb, fought for purchase. Galahad jumped to the top of the wall and tried to lick her face as she scrabbled for toeholds in the crumbling masonry.

She wondered, for a split second, if she had done the right thing. Would it not have been easier to open a window and call for help? Why had she so foolishly insisted on getting herself out of her predicament?

She knew the answer. She reminded herself that she dared trust no one in Nethergate, before she let go to fall to the landing.

She was running the thought through her mind like some litany to banish her fear or protect her from injury when a shot shattered the afternoon silence. Only when snow and bits of rock from the wall above her head exploded from the impact did she realize someone had shot at her.

By the time Aurelia's feet hit the slippery surface and she could cover her head against the rain of granite splinters, three or four more shots echoed in her ears.

Throwing the spent pistol to the ground, Kit jumped to scale the uneven ruin of the wall. He managed to reach the lowest of the broken stairs and hauled himself to his feet, then scrambled up them toward the sound of Aurelia's cry. He heard shouts and the clatter of hooves but ignored everything. Not even the possibility of another gunshot slowed him.

His hand still vibrated from the single pistol shot when he reached her. Crouching over the crumpled heap on the narrow ledge, he asked frantically, "Are you all right? My God, what happened?"

She stirred, but slowly. He brushed snow and slivers of stone from her cloak and her hair, exposed when the hood had fallen back.

She looked up at him, her eyes dark and enormous in the waning light, and asked, "Where is Galahad?" She was every bit as frantic as Kit had been when he had asked after her own safety.

A sharp bark overhead alerted Kit, and as if hearing his

name was a signal, the dog gathered himself and leapt down.

The broken stair became very crowded.

Kit helped Aurelia to stand, no easy task with the deerhound cavorting in canine ecstasy around their feet, and said, "I suppose I should not be surprised you expressed no concern over *my* well-being. Are you certain you're not injured? That's quite a drop, you know."

"Yes, I'm fine, thank you," she replied, but he noticed that despite her calm response, she trembled and clung to his arm more desperately than he had known her to do before.

Shouts from below, however, grabbed his attention.

"Don't try to come up," he warned, a bit more threateningly than he intended. "Miss Phillips is unhurt, and the footing is precarious."

Kit himself had not realized how steep and difficult the climb was; he did not remember scrambling up the almost sheer wall nor crawling over the fallen stones that all but buried the stairs. His one thought had been to reach Aurelia. And when her first words bespoke her worry for the wet-nosed whirlwind that threatened to knock them off their tenuous perch, he could do nothing but laugh and hold her.

Until he glanced down and saw Joshua MacKinnon standing on the ice-coated bottom stair pointing a gun at his head.

"Put that bloody blunderbuss away, MacKinnon, and let us off this damned parapet," Kit demanded, "before we fall to our deaths."

"You shot at me first," Joshua insisted.

Had he not started to slip on the ice, Joshua might have made good whatever threats he intended, but the uncertainty of his footing gave Kit the advantage. As he had done two—or was it three?—days ago, he disarmed the Winterburn heir, this time by grabbing hold of the barrel. Rather than risk being flung backward down the ruin, Joshua wisely if unwillingly relinquished the weapon.

"We'll debate who shot whom after we get Miss Phillips and Galahad safely down," Kit added, "or we could well be here until darkness falls."

Kit found only bitter satisfaction in being proven right. The debate, held over tea in the drawing room, dissolved into argument from which no conclusion could be drawn. Darkness had indeed fallen, tempers had grown short, and nothing was resolved. Only the appearance of the duke himself restored calm when, in a fading voice, he demanded an explanation from Joshua.

"I believe it was a matter of misunderstanding," the heir said. He was the only one of the group who had abstained from tea and now, after assisting his grandfather to a chair and adjusting a rug over the old man's knees, he helped himself to a brandy. "I'm not sure we will ever know who fired the first shot, and we should be glad that no one was hurt in the exchange."

A moment ago Joshua had been most belligerent in trying to lay blame; now he seemed intent on giving quite an opposite impression to his grandfather. Because he was lying?

Someone was. Kit tried to determine who the liar was, but there was no more evidence to convict Joshua over Freddie or Freddie over Adam than there was to tell who killed the lawyer.

He knew only that at the same instant he spotted Aurelia lowering herself from crumbling Winterburn Castle, a shot rang out, and from the splatter of rock above her, it had been aimed at the very wall to which she clung. He turned in the general direction from which the gun had been fired and saw the three riders, widely separated, entering the grounds of Nethergate. He had no time to try to determine which if any of them had discharged a firearm, or even the order in which they rode; after firing once to warn them off, for he had no hope of hitting anyone at that distance with

Emil's pistol, Kit climbed the ancient stairs and, to his great relief, found Aurelia and Galahad safe.

"What were the three of you doing out there with a murderer running loose?" the duke asked. "And with guns, no less! If one of you were guilty, he could have—"

Whether Charles MacKinnon lacked the strength to continue his reprimand or simply chose to leave the balance hanging in the air like a sword, the effect was marked.

"We went to look for evidence," Adam admitted, mollified after an hour of insisting he had only fired his fowling piece in the general direction of the castle ruins because he had heard at least one other shot.

"Like some amateur Bow Street runner?" His Grace sneered.

Freddie, who had kept control of his temper a bit more than the others earlier, launched into an outburst of frustration. "What were we expected to do, sit here until someone else is killed?" But his spite was short-lived. "Of course we found nothing. The wind had swept the meadow nearly clear of snow, and most of that was melted by the time we arrived. If there were any tracks, we covered them with our own."

How fortuitous for the murderer, Kit thought.

The calm that had settled over the assembled Nethergate residents was one of exhaustion and fear as much as confusion. Lady Moresby and her daughter had wept when the argument reached its peak, but they had not left the room. Nor had the viscount himself, though as he tried to comfort and calm his wife and daughter, he went as green around the gills as his son had a day ago.

Everyone claimed innocence, even those who had not been accused.

Except Aurelia. She claimed nothing, said nothing.

In the aftermath of the shooting, she had accepted Kit's assistance in getting her inside Nethergate, but she had said nothing to him, not even to answer his hastily whispered question about why she had gone into the ruin. And once inside the warmth and safety of the manor house proper, she disappeared, Galahad trotting at her side, before Kit could escape the questioning and quarreling of the others.

She reappeared half an hour later, dressed not in mourning black but in a rich brown velvet that accentuated the warm paleness of her complexion and the smoky green passion of her eyes. Adam was trying to explain the muddled sequence of events as he recalled them, with Freddie and Joshua angrily interrupting at every phrase, when she slipped almost unnoticed into the room.

But Kit did notice, and through the rest of the battle and the calm that followed, he could hardly take his eyes off her.

She, in turn, would not look at him. Nor at anyone else.

Adam Braisthwaite drew Kit's attention from Aurelia when he picked up where Freddie had left off. "We realized there was nothing to be found, and as the weather turned colder than we expected, we turned back. Denholm challenged us to a race, which he knew he'd win because he had the better horse."

He did not need to point out that Freddie's horse also carried several stone less than Adam's. But why, Kit wondered, would Joshua be so easily dismissed? The horses in the Nethergate stable were, even to Kit's inexpert eye, more than passable mounts, and a Caribbean planter's son should be a fair horseman. Why assume Freddie would automatically win?

Aurelia, too, must have been puzzled by the same question, for her brow furrowed and she tilted her head at a quizzical angle.

"I should think it very dangerous to race on muddy, slippery ground," she said quietly.

Freddie opened his mouth several times, saying nothing, then finally shut it. He glanced at Lady Whiston, perhaps hoping his great-aunt would come to his defense, but she seemed not to have heard.

Joshua held his brandy glass up to the light of the lamp at his side and agreed. "Precisely why I didn't participate."

And that, Kit recognized with a cold start, was the most patent lie he had heard all afternoon.

The proof lay in the covert glance Joshua gave his grandfather.

"And why, Mr. Ballantyne, did you not join my grandson and his companions on this search for evidence?" Winterburn asked, as though he had not seen Joshua's subtle plea for approval. You have as much reason to fear being found guilty as the others."

Resisting the temptation to see what, if any, reaction Aurelia had to this direct address, Kit calmly answered, "I was not informed, Your Grace, of their expedition, or I would indeed have gone. And of course there is also the fact that the mount I hired in the village is injured."

Was that tiny whisper a sigh of relief from her? He did not look to verify the assumption, but when Charles MacKinnon himself turned in Aurelia's direction, Kit had the verification he needed.

"And you, Miss Phillips, what were you doing in the old Winterburn ruins?"

"I was curious," she replied. Not a lie, but not all of the truth either. She said nothing about the portrait, which could have been her only reason for venturing into the old castle alone, and if there was guilt in her voice, there was also defiance. Trusting no one, she was clearly determined to solve the riddle on her own.

"Curiosity damn near got you killed," the old man grumbled. "You'll stay out of them in the future, do you understand?"

She nodded compliantly with downcast eyes, as though hiding a secret acknowledgment that understanding was not the same as obeying.

Dinner went no better than tea, but not even the quarrels, threats, accusations, and denials that accompanied a meal no one ate—save Adam—prepared Aurelia for what she discovered upon returning to her room.

She stared at the small white object on the palm of her hand and considered for a moment the wisdom of throwing the pearl into the fire.

"When did you find it?" Kit asked.

"Half an hour ago." What had seemed unreal, dreamlike at the time, became more coldly real in the telling of it. "I went to the door that leads into Winterburn and found it padlocked. I don't know when it was done, whether today or if it's been there for weeks, even years. Did Grandfather bar me because he no longer trusts me? Or did someone else? I thought to go to you directly, but I was afraid of being followed, I think. Or perhaps afraid you had something to do with it."

She looked at him, trying to find a sign that he felt the pain of her doubt, but he retained an understanding calm when he asked, "And the pearl was here when you returned?"

She took two or three deep breaths to order her thoughts once again.

"Yes. Carefully set under the door, so it would neither roll down the hall nor be picked up and played with or lost by Galahad. Oh, Kit, I don't understand it at all anymore! Nothing is as it was, or as I thought it would be."

She dropped the pearl into the open ebony box Kit had put on the table. There were five of the missing twelve. Kit told Ruth they had not found any, and he had not, in fact, lied. He himself had found one, in the hall, but he alone did not constitute the "we" he had used in dismissing Serena's maid. Charlotte had given another to Aurelia, and Lady Whiston had turned over the one she took from Freddie. The fourth was Galahad's discovery. Aurelia could no longer say she had found none, and if asked she would have to tell the truth.

Beside the box lay the large black key that should have opened the door from Nethergate to the Winterburn ruins. She ran her finger down the cold metal, then drew back as if burned.

"I went looking for the portrait this afternoon," she said. There was no easier way to begin the explanation than to answer the questions she knew Kit wanted to ask.

"I thought we were going to do that together—tonight. Why didn't you wait?"

For that she had no ready response.

"I'm not sure. Perhaps because, as I told Grandfather, I was curious. Perhaps I wanted to find it myself. Perhaps because I no longer trusted anyone."

"Not even me?"

Involuntarily, she glanced at the bed and knew he was thinking the same thoughts as she.

"No, Kit, not you, not my grandfather, not even myself."

She began to wander about the room, stopping to straighten small items on her dressing table, opening the wardrobe and then closing it, poking at the steady fire. Everything was in order except her thoughts.

"Two people are dead, and whatever Joshua may say about Mr. Gould's being killed falling from his horse, I do not believe there was any such accident. Is Joshua lying? I don't know. But I cannot trust him."

"Why should he kill his own lawyer?"

"I don't know! And I'm not accusing him of it. But he had no reason to kill Serena, either. Freddie did, because he was insanely jealous. And Freddie was the one who wanted to race back to Nethergate this afternoon. Why? To put himself ahead of the others to dispose of evidence from Serena's murder? More of the pearls? It seems a great deal of trouble to go to. Or was there evidence at the scene of Mr. Gould's murder? Though what reason Freddie would have to kill Joshua's solicitor, I cannot imagine." She was rambling, indulging in wild speculations based on the flimsiest of facts. "When he saw me on the wall, did he take advantage of the opportunity and try to kill me? He is an excellent shot and no doubt he would not have missed, so perhaps it was Adam."

"At least you're not accusing me."

"I could." She faced him squarely, expecting a flippant reply, but he made none, as though he knew the truth as well as she. "No, I couldn't," she admitted with a sigh. "I couldn't even tell you how many shots were fired. Freddie, Adam, and Joshua each admit to firing once, and you, but there might have been more; I can't be sure. And without proof . . ."

"Proof is very different from trust, Aurelia."

"Do you think I don't know that? But everyone I've trusted has betrayed me."

"Have I?"

Again she paused, unable to lie but not wanting to tell the truth. And the pause, she knew, was truth enough itself, but it was much too late to defend herself.

"I don't know," she said bleakly.

"For God's sake, Aurelia, if I had wanted you dead, I could have let you fall this afternoon and no one would be the wiser."

She had known that, too.

"I could have strangled you in your sleep last night."

She shivered and looked once again at the pearls. It was time for another confession.

"*Someone* wants me dead. While I was in the castle, someone closed a door on me, a door I could not open." The shivering did not stop. The fear, like a banked fire given air, roared to life. "It could not have been Joshua or Freddie or Adam, for they were not yet back at Nethergate. Charlotte and her parents were in the drawing room. Lady Whiston is confined to her bed."

"I was with Emil, which is the same as having no alibi at all."

"You begin to understand, Mr. Ballantyne."

A quiet knock interrupted her. Kit, who stood nearer, scooped up the box with the pearls and the broken ring before he opened the door at her nod of assent.

Charlotte, her hand poised from knocking, blushed furiously.

"Excuse me, Miss Phillips, Mr. Ballantyne," she mumbled. "I didn't interrupt you, did I?"

"It's quite all right, Miss Braisthwaite," Kit greeted her, taking her elbow with practiced grace and guiding her into the room. When she glanced at the door, he pointedly left it open. "Is there something we can do for you?"

Aurelia noticed then that Charlotte held a folded piece of paper in her other hand. She held it up and looked at it as if she had forgotten its existence, much less any message that came with it. Then she crossed the room and placed the note in Aurelia's hand.

"I wanted to thank you, Miss Phillips, for suggesting I speak with her ladyship about my wardrobe." She intoned the words like lines from a play, memorized but repeated without emotion. "I should not speak ill of the dead, but I do believe Mrs. MacKinnon did not understand that what suited her would not necessarily suit me."

Aurelia gave her a puzzled frown, then realized this was Charlotte's poor but sincere attempt at discretion. She had kept the note hidden, which no doubt came from Lady Whiston, and now, should anyone be listening, they would hear only an innocent message of appreciation.

"You are welcome, Charlotte," Aurelia told her, hoping to convey to her that she meant every word. For different reasons, they shared a common bond, a sense of ostracism. Aurelia would, if possible, spare her some of that.

She left with one more exaggerated glance at the note.

When she was gone and Kit had secured the door once more, Aurelia lifted the piece of heavy paper and touched the neat circle of red wax that held it closed.

"Are you going to read it?" he asked.

The trembling of her fingers was less noticeable when she put them to work, even at so small a task as breaking the waxen seal and unfolding the paper. But after scanning the cramped handwriting, Aurelia felt such a tremor ripple through her she stumbled to the chair and fell, boneless with shock, onto it.

Before Kit had time to react, to snatch the note from her hand and read it himself, she recited the words, aware that she did so in the same flat monotone Charlotte Braisthwaite had used.

"'I am sending this via C. They have given me laudanum, so I must be brief. I received communication today from London that there is no solicitor named Gould. He is a fraud, an impostor.'"

18

THE LAST DAMNING WORD HAD SCARCELY ESCAPED HER LIPS when Kit snatched open the door he had closed only a moment ago.

"Stay here!" he ordered as he ran into the hallway.

Aurelia made no move to rise from the chair, much less leave the room.

All the calm order had gone out of her existence, replaced by turmoil and uncertainty. Nothing was what it had been or seemed. But with the upheaval had come a challenge and an unlooked-for affirmation. It was as if, to borrow Kit's own analogy of the touchstone, she had scratched the surface and found dross and now had to dig deep within her own soul.

There was no need to follow him; she knew where he had gone and that he would return soon. She would have only a minute or two in which to collect her thoughts and preserve them from the chaos.

Charlotte, more frightened than before and more like the unsure child than the mature young woman her appearance suggested, entered ahead of Kit. She glanced nervously to Aurelia, then to the man who closed the door behind her.

"Here, Charlotte, please sit down." Aurelia offered her her own chair. Again Charlotte glanced from one to the other and back again. "You've done nothing wrong, as I hope Mr. Ballantyne told you. We only wish to talk to you about the note Lady Whiston sent."

"Every tiny detail could be important, Miss Braisthwaite," Kit added, in the soft, seductive tone Aurelia knew would calm Charlotte and elicit from her any information she held.

The girl sat on the edge of the chair.

"After dinner, Freddie—that is, Mr. Denholm—and I helped her ladyship to her room. She was in such pain, could hardly walk at all. He cursed a great deal, blaming her for going out in the cold when she knows it hurts her so. I've never seen him so angry." She paused, and this time there was a plea for assurance in her questioning glances.

"He told her she should have stayed in London, that *he* had been invited here, not she."

Now the questioning look came from Kit, but Aurelia could reply only with a shrug that neither confirmed nor denied the truth of Freddie Denholm's statement.

"He was dreadfully angry, Miss Phillips. When we brought her ladyship to her room, he chased poor Molly to fetch Dr. Ward at once and then demanded the doctor give her ladyship something to ease her pain."

Kit prompted, "And did Dr. Ward give her something?"

Charlotte nodded. "He gave her a bottle of laudanum and told her how much to take and then he left. She told Freddie—I mean, Mr. Denholm—that he needn't wait around, that she would take the drug as soon as she had dealt with the letters she had received in the post."

"When did she receive these letters?" Aurelia asked. "No one has delivered mail here in days, nor has anyone gone to the village since before—Serena died."

"I don't know!" Charlotte cried, bursting into tears. "Oh,

please, Miss Phillips, I know nothing about any of this! Her ladyship had three letters on her dressing table. Freddie snatched them from her and told her he would burn them if she did not take the medicine at once." The words raced from her as if they had a life of their own and she could not control them. "She told him she knew who the letters were from and it didn't make any difference if he threw them in the fire, but she took the medicine anyway."

"And you saw all this for yourself, Miss Braisthwaite? You weren't listening at the door?"

Charlotte shook her head and wiped away the tears streaming down her face before looking at Kit and answering his question.

"I was there," she insisted with impassioned intensity. "She took the medicine and he gave her the letters, then she told him to leave. I wanted to leave, too, but she told me to stay."

Aurelia walked to her dressing table and found in one of the drawers a clean handkerchief that she handed to Charlotte.

"It's all right, Charlotte. Please, try to calm yourself, then continue."

"There's nothing else! Molly helped Lady Whiston into her nightclothes, and when her ladyship was in bed she excused Molly. Then she told me to bring her the letters and a dispatch box that she kept under the bed. She read the letters very quickly and put them in the box."

She had to pause then to blow her nose, and Aurelia took advantage of the break in Charlotte's tale to ask more questions.

"Where did Lady Whiston keep the key to the dispatch box? Did you see what else she kept in it?"

"I don't know where she had the key, nor did I see what she did with it after she put the letters away, because she told me to bring her the writing box from the desk. When I did, she handed me the dispatch box and I put it back under the bed. She was getting very sleepy and I asked if she would like me to write the letter for her, but she said no, she could do it herself. I had to melt the wax for her, though, and I had to hold her hand when she pressed her ring into it. She bade me take the letter to you at once and to be sure I told no one about it until I had, especially not Freddie."

She blew her nose again, then added, "I know I've made it sound as if Freddie might have killed Mrs. MacKinnon, but I swear to you, he couldn't have. He just couldn't!"

By the tension in Kit's jaw and the narrowing gleam in his eyes, Aurelia knew he was of the same mind. Charlotte had told everything she could; they would have to confront Lady Whiston if they wished to learn the rest.

Galahad paid little attention through most of the discussion, though at Charlotte's more vocal outbursts he lifted his head and, ears forward, cocked it to one side. But when both Aurelia and Kit strolled to the door to escort Charlotte to her room, the dog was immediately at Aurelia's knee, whining in a voice she could almost call human.

She did not want to leave him, not because she feared for his safety, but because he alone had given her no cause to doubt his loyalty. A flush of shame washed over her as she recalled the warning she had ignored. Had she heeded Galahad's instincts, she might now know who had tried to trap her in the castle ruin.

Or she might be dead.

She leaned down to brush her cheek affectionately against his rough-coated head before bidding him good-bye and promising to return shortly.

Charlotte, unable to hide her nervousness, hurried ahead while Aurelia locked her door. There was no need for words, not even after delivering the girl safely to her own quarters. In silence Kit and Aurelia headed for Lady Whiston's.

Aurelia reached into her pocket and gripped the hard metal of the key to her own door. She had keys to nearly every room in Nethergate, save her grandfather's study and Joshua's apartments, on a heavy ring that lay in a drawer in her wardrobe. She rarely carried them for she seldom needed them. But as she raised her hand to beg entrance to the dowager marchioness's room, she wished she had brought at least that one.

Before she could knock a second time, Molly, the faithful abigail, opened the door.

"Come in, come in," she whispered, ushering both Aurelia and Kit into the chamber. A pair of candles gleamed in a silver candelabrum by the side of the elderly woman's bed, another pair on a table between two chairs by the curtained window. "I'm afraid my mistress isn't quite herself, but I b'lieve she was expecting you."

A soft uneven snore came from the figure sunk deep into the pillows. The great four-poster dwarfed her, making her appear at once very, very old, with only her wrinkled face visible above the sheets and below the white linen cap that covered her hair, and very young, as small as a child.

Something, perhaps a shadow crossing her eyes, wakened her. The bright eyes opened at once.

"David?" she asked with the false alertness of one coming out of deep sleep.

Had she been dreaming? Had the drug that eased the pain of stiff, swollen joints also taken her deep into her memories, or was the resemblance that strong?

"No, not David," she mumbled, her eyes widening as she tried to focus them. "You're Ballantyne, aren't you? Not David at all."

The disappointment in her voice brought a lump to Aurelia's throat, but Kit seemed unmoved. He pulled one of the chairs close to the bed and sat down. How well Lady Whiston could hear or see under the opiate's influence, he could not tell, but he obviously did not want to raise his voice louder than necessary.

"Yes, I'm Kit Ballantyne, not David MacKinnon," he began, as though helping her to orient herself. "I need to know what you can tell me about the letters you received. About Mr. Gould."

She thrust out her chin and shook her head back and forth vehemently on the pillows.

"Fraud. Never heard of him."

"Who never heard of him?"

She laughed, her eyes closed as if she slept and spoke in her dreams.

"Ah, David, you should never have left. Nethergate is unchanged, exactly as you left it, but it's a damn cold and lifeless place. A fit tomb."

Aurelia shook her head. She was certain this interview was hopeless, but Kit persisted with unexpected patience.

"Think, milady. Concentrate. There was more you wanted to tell us."

And at that, she looked at him, her brow puckered as she struggled to follow his orders.

"I'm a widow, you know. Have to watch out for myself. My solicitor, Mr. Poole, advised me not to come to Nethergate."

"But you came anyway."

He spoke softly, and Aurelia watched with admiration as he kept the dowager marchioness talking, though surely the drug must have put her to sleep long ago.

"George Poole thinks I came here to die. He's afraid I'll die and he'll not be here to take care of matters. Fussy old bird, George Poole is."

"Lawyers are like that."

"I told him not to worry, that Joshua MacKinnon's solicitor was here. I told George about him, but now George says there is no lawyer in London named Lincoln Gould. Funny, isn't it, that I thought to tell you before I told Joshua or even Charles? But then, I always was half in love with you, my dear David. Or perhaps more than half."

Again she laughed, a dry, daft old woman's cackle that floated into a gentle snore.

Aurelia stood behind Kit, though she did not remember going to him. She might have been drawn by Lady

Whiston's soft voice, or by his own hypnotic command. She placed her hands on his shoulders and felt a ripple of relief flow through him.

"She'll sleep the rest of the night and into the morning now," he said.

To Aurelia's surprise, he rested his elbows on his knees and then buried his face in his hands.

On the other side of the bed, Molly snuffed the candles.

"She won't die tomorrow, Mr. Ballantyne, if that's what ye fear. Nor likely day after. But she's lived her life full, and she'll take no regrets to her grave."

Aurelia asked, her voice low, "How much do you know of her ladyship's affairs?"

"Little enough." Molly shrugged. "'Tis not my place to pry. Her husband left her an income and she had some from her mother, too. Mr. Poole handles it, though she has her fingers in everything, much to his dismay."

Kit slowly got to his feet, deftly taking one of Aurelia's hands in his, as though he, like she, did not want to break a fragile contact from which each drew strength.

"You've been a great help, Molly," he said.

The maid bobbed a curtsey and smiled.

Aurelia felt a gentle tightening of the fingers enclosing her own. Although her curiosity was aroused and she desperately wanted to see the letters in Lady Whiston's dispatch box, she supposed Kit was right. There was little more they would learn here.

There was, however, another source of information.

"I want to talk to my grandfather," Aurelia said after they had left Molly to finish dousing the light. Lady Whiston herself was snoring audibly, and Aurelia took comfort that, though her own curiosity might be unsatisfied, the elderly marchioness was sleeping peacefully.

Kit stepped in front of her, blocking her progress down the hall and back to her room, though he still held her hand.

"Do you trust him to tell you the truth? If not, then you must tell *him* nothing."

"I ought at least tell him about Mr. Gould."

He must have sensed the fierce and loyal resistance in her, for instead of arguing with her, he sighed and pulled her close in a tender embrace.

"Dear God, Aurelia, what have I done to you? I've destroyed, for no other reason than idle curiosity, your whole world. And now I would turn you against your grandfather."

She rested her head on his shoulder and for the first time in days felt safe, though she knew the feeling was insubstantial, momentary. She would dash it herself.

"It was a world in which I was not very happy," she confessed. "And you could not turn me against my grandfather. Only he could do that."

"Then come with me, Aurelia," he whispered, his breath touching her hair. "Not just for tonight, though God knows I don't think I can be parted from you for so much as a heartbeat. Come with me to Charleston."

A bitter weight settled in her chest. This was no heartfelt profession of love and devotion, no proposal of marriage. And in truth she had not even thought in such terms—until Kit spoke quite the opposite.

Had she sacrificed those undreamed dreams last night?

She brought her hand up to caress his face, to trace the lines of his lips that had spoken of desire but not of love.

"I cannot leave, Kit. Everything I have . . ."

"You need nothing, Aurelia. Nothing but this."

He did not give her time or breath to deny him. Hot and hard, he kissed her, the seductive thrust of his tongue opening her mouth as he pulled her tightly against him. She offered no resistance, but accepted his passion as greedily, as gratefully, as parched desert accepts rain.

How *could* she refuse him? He had shattered the lies and falsehoods that imprisoned her in a safe but loveless existence. Freed of those shackles, she had dared to taste another life and found dangers and betrayals at every turn.

She did not surrender to Kit; she took what he offered

because she wanted it, needed it, craved it as essential to life itself. As he slid his hands up to her shoulders and then slowly down her back, she let the heat from within her sweetest core melt her body against his.

She could never resume the life he had destroyed.

He broke the kiss, leaving her with unquenched desire, and buried his face against her neck. Each breath was labored, uneven, as he struggled to control what he believed she could not. His effort, however, brought her to reality.

"Dear heavens, Kit, please stop!" she cried. "Any—anyone could see us!"

He chuckled, his breath warm against her skin, stirring fine hairs behind her ear.

"Mustn't be caught in the act, must we?"

With obvious effort, he set himself away from her, but Aurelia knew this was only a temporary interruption. What they had started must be finished.

Still, she was embarrassed at how easily he aroused her, as well as at her inability to conceal the effects. She tried to brush away his hand when he smoothed loosened tendrils of her hair. When he caught her hand in his and placed a gentle kiss on her palm, she found no strength or will to pull away.

"Forgive me, innocent," he murmured.

"No, not so innocent anymore."

He turned her hand over and grazed her knuckles with his lips.

"Far too innocent, no matter what you say," he insisted. "Now, come, we'll go to your grandfather—"

"No, Kit, I must do this alone."

"Why? I don't like it, Aurelia. I don't trust him."

The words nearly stuck in her throat. "But he trusts me, or at least he did." Instead of a quick retort, Kit's only reply was a stony silence. She endured it for a long moment, then said, "Yes, he perverted that trust when he demanded I lie, but at least *I* never betrayed it."

Until now. By falling in love with Kit Ballantyne.

She began walking again, amazed that her knees did not

buckle. Still her heart fluttered within her breast and the taste of Kit's kisses lingered on her swollen lips. Were the signs as visible to others as they felt to her? Surely, she thought if she entered her grandfather's room with Kit, even those faded eyes would see the evidence.

And if His Grace the duke of Winterburn did not see, Aurelia was certain Joshua would.

The door was closed, not partly open as it had been the other time she inadvertently eavesdropped. Even so, she heard the voices, not loud but angry. Afraid for her grandfather, she poised her hand to knock, but Kit stayed it. With a finger to her lips, he lowered her fist and bade her listen.

The words were mere jumbles of sound, only one or two distinct enough to identify and those too few to piece together a thread of conversation. Aurelia was on the point of suggesting to Kit that one of the speakers might be Morton Sullivan or one of the doctors, for the duke was well known to argue with his physicians, when Joshua's laughter clearly identified him.

"You can't threaten me, Your Grace," he announced, the words sounding clearer as he approached the door. "I know what you want, and without me, you can't have it, can you?"

19

THEY HAD LITTLE HOPE OF HEARING WHAT REPLY, IF ANY, THE duke made to his grandson's challenge, nor was there any sense in waiting to be discovered in the very act of eavesdropping. Kit, holding Aurelia's wrist, dragged her from the door, down the hallway.

"Do you think you can climb the castle wall in the dark?" he whispered, finally coming to a halt well out of hearing of anyone in the duke's apartment. "I don't know how you managed it in the daylight, but—"

She rested a hand on his chest and shook her head.

"No, Kit, not at night. It's too dangerous."

"We may not have another chance!"

He took her face between his hands, his fingers dark against her pale cheeks, and lowered his mouth to take hers in a kiss meant to sear away her resistance. She moaned and fought him, but he tasted the beginning of capitulation.

Then all of Nethergate disintegrated around them as a soul-burning scream from one of the nearby rooms sliced through the night's silence. A woman's cry, terrified then muffled, then stronger than before, followed by a man's bellow.

Other sounds of struggle, of furniture being overturned, grunts of pain, a woman's fervent pleas for help while a key grated in a lock, located the source as being in the next room down the hall, but Kit had no idea which of the guests occupied it until one by one, other doors opened and white, frightened faces peered out: Charlotte Braisthwaite, in her somber gown; her brother Adam with a poker in one hand and a riding crop in the other; Lady Moresby, unsteady and bleary-eyed from more than sleepiness.

Then the woman who had screamed burst out of her temporary prison. Clad only in a plain chemise such as a parlormaid might wear, she ran into the hall and, pointing at the room from which she had come, shrieked, "He's the one! Him! Lor' Moresby himself! He done it!"

Joshua, running from his grandfather's room, grabbed the girl by the shoulders and shook her.

"For God's sake, get hold of yourself!" he ordered.

This was not, Kit realized, a servant frightened by the unwelcome advances of a titled gentleman. Her chemise was not torn, and her hair, though loose and tousled, had more the look of careless abandon. She bore no marks of violence upon her exposed arms and shoulders, as though she had been willing enough earlier but something had caused her to change her mind.

A crowd was beginning to gather as servants and guests alike now spilled out of rooms and into the hall. Across the way, Kit spotted Freddie Denholm and Dr. Robbins, but Joshua had taken center stage.

"What's the meaning of this?" he demanded again of the sobbing, hysterical girl. She broke from him, stumbling against the wall, and he let her go as though her touch had defiled him. "How dare you accuse Lord Moresby of—"

A collective gasp interrupted him as James Braisthwaite, Viscount Moresby, staggered to the open door and slumped against the frame.

"Good God, Moresby!" Joshua exploded.

"Father, for the love of Heaven!"

"Papa!"

Stark naked, with the white mass of his belly hanging almost to cover his shriveled manhood, Moresby seemed oblivious to both his nudity and the gawking, horrified crowd around him. A thin trickle of blood streaked his forehead, where the lump from a blow already swelled beneath his few wisps of hair.

"Where did the wench go?" he grumbled as if to himself. He looked first to one side, then the other.

"Murderer!" the maid shrieked again.

The viscount grinned lopsidedly at the sound of her voice.

"Ah, there ye are, m'dear. Come, stop yer caterwaulin' 'n' come on back t' bed."

But the girl did not move, only stared at the grotesque figure that reached out a hand and beckoned to her.

On the palm of that hand lay a round, gleaming pearl.

With the disorientation typical of a man who has drunk too much and then been hit on the head, Moresby stared at the pearl with stupefied confusion. An instant later, the grin was on his face again.

"I found it, ye silly chit. This morning, when I come back from the slut's memorial service, it were on the floor. Did ye think I killed her? Bah! The bitch weren't worth it."

Kit tensed, waiting for a defense of Serena's reputation by the man who professed to love her. But none came.

As if she had noted Freddie's appearance and then disappearance as well, Aurelia tugged on Kit's sleeve and pulled him away from the crowd. Adam had torn off his own coat and handed it to his father. In a minute or two, the diversion would be over.

Aurelia whispered with frantic urgency, "Meet me at the cottage as soon as you can."

"Are you insane?"

"No, I'm perfectly sane, but we've not much time. Go,

now, and if I'm not there before you, wait. Dear God, Kit, I'll explain later. Just *go.*"

He was tempted to demand an explanation now, before he headed off in the cold and dark to a locked cottage, but something in her smoldering green eyes, in the way she slipped her hand free of his, told him as strongly as her words that there was indeed no time.

"What about Denholm?"

"I can handle Freddie," she insisted, already moving away from him. After a pause, she whispered, "Trust me," then lifted her skirts and ran.

Freddie Denholm waited, as she expected, in the corridor outside Aurelia's room, hands sunk in his pockets, a glum expression on his face. Inside, Galahad whined and scratched at the door but did not bark.

"May I help you with something, Mr. Denholm?" Aurelia asked, hoping her anxiety was not obvious to a man preoccupied with his own.

"I want the pearl."

"I'm afraid I don't—"

"Dammit, Miss Phillips, I've already searched Aunt Gwen's room, including her precious dispatch box. She wouldn't give it to anyone but you. Please, give it to me?" Near tears, he grabbed her shoulders, but she felt only his grief and desperation, not a threat. And he must have realized he had gone too far, for he released her almost immediately and turned away with a quiet, "It's the only memento I have left of her. Besides, you can't believe I killed her, not now that Moresby's received one of her pearls, too."

"'Received' one?"

"How else do you think I came by it? The real killer must have rolled it under the door, no doubt to get rid of incriminating evidence as well as put suspicion on someone else. Adam has one, and I think his sister, too. I wondered about Moresby himself, but I needn't wonder any longer."

Eager to be on her way to the cottage and anxious for Kit's safety, Aurelia nevertheless knew what Freddie had to tell her might reveal some valuable bit of information. She found enough patience to listen.

"His room is next to mine, as you know. I heard him and the girl enter nearly an hour ago. He's an insatiable old lecher, can't keep his hands off anything in skirts." He waited, perhaps for a shocked reaction from her, but Aurelia offered him none. "You know that's why Moresby and his family are here, don't you? No one in London will have him in their home; none of the servants are safe. When he runs out of parlor maids, he's not above soliciting the young boys, either. And of course there's that sot of a wife of his, forever pushing her daughter off on *someone.*"

Aurelia had never before thought to question the reasons anyone came to Nethergate. Serena had devised the guest list for a small group to make an extended stay to help with the grooming of the heir to Winterburn. Had others turned down the invitation? And if so, why had these, including Freddie Denholm, agreed?

"Tonight, however, Moresby must not have been in top form. The girl wanted more than the honor of sharing a viscount's bed. That's when the fool offered to give her the pearl. You heard the rest."

Brief though it was, Aurelia's sojourn in London so many years ago had given her a clear enough picture of the ways of Society. If not all peers of the realm yielded to their appetites as Lord Moresby did, enough indulged themselves that Aurelia found Freddie's tale disgusting but hardly surprising.

She dared to follow it with another, more dangerous question. "How do you know Adam has one of the pearls?"

He paced the short hallway several times, each time peering nervously down the main corridor in both directions, before answering.

"He told me he did. As if he knew I had had one and no longer did," he said, his voice low, almost breaking as he spoke again of the loss. "I challenged them to the race this afternoon because Adam is too frightened to try to keep up and Joshua is a dreadful horseman. With the slippery ground and the ghastly weather, I hoped one of them would fall and give me the time to search Braisthwaite's quarters."

"Adam's? Why?"

"To find the rest of the pearls! He has them! I know he does!"

With a sobbing groan, Freddie threw himself against the wall, arms folded in front of his face.

"He killed her! I know he did!"

Calming the distraught Freddie was, Aurelia supposed, much like calming a child, and she had little experience with children. She had no choice, however, but to do her best, for Lady Whiston lay snoring under the effect of a drug and Charlotte, who would have leapt at the chance to succor the object of her affection, was likely more concerned with minimizing the effect of her father's public disgrace.

Time was a precious commodity. Though Aurelia had hoped to escape from Nethergate and be on her way to the cottage before anyone discovered her absence, she had excuses she could use if seen. Kit, on the other hand, was a mysterious stranger in the eyes of the other guests as well as the servants, and he needed more cover than she. If anyone had noticed their leaving the scene of Lord Moresby's humiliation, it would no doubt be assumed they were together. By delaying any search Freddie himself might make, Aurelia could give Kit a few extra minutes.

She placed a comforting hand on Freddie's shoulder.

"What makes you think Adam killed Serena?"

A shudder went through him, a ripple of palpable malevolence so startling she withdrew her hand even before he turned around again.

"She baited him, seduced him, used him, tormented him, just as she tormented me," he hissed. Once again, that blank gleam of dementia glittered in his eyes. "Oh, God in Heaven, she made madmen of us all!"

Dissolving into incoherent moans filled with self-pitying despair, he slowly slid to the floor. He was no longer aware of Aurelia's presence, yet she inched warily away and did not take her eyes from him for a single second while she slipped her key from her pocket and fitted it into the lock. As quickly as possible, she squeezed into the room and closed the door, then locked it once more.

With no idea how long her confrontation with Freddie Denholm had lasted, she wasted no time. The banked fire, though only a dull glow of red coals, offered sufficient illumination for her purpose; she did not even light a candle. After gathering a few articles of clothing from her wardrobe, she wrapped them into a hasty bundle easily concealed under her cloak. She tugged on sturdy boots and tucked her shoes into the bundle of clothing, then took down Galahad's lead.

If Freddie asked, she was prepared to tell him an almost-truth.

"I'm going to take you for a walk, Galahad," she said, rehearsing the lines while she tossed her cloak about her shoulders and quickly fastened the frogs at her throat and down the front. "On the way, I shall look for Dr. Ward or Dr. Robbins and have them take care of Freddie."

She put her hand on the latch and turned the key for the last time. Charles MacKinnon was right; she had lived here because of his generosity, and that generosity could be withdrawn at any time. Without so much as a farewell glance to the room she had called her own for twenty years, and which she might never see again, she opened the door and let Galahad out into the hall.

There was no sign of Freddie Denholm.

Quelling the urge to run, Aurelia turned Galahad in the direction of the kitchen door they most often used. She had gone four or five steps when she thought better of her decision. Though it took her several valuable seconds, locking the door might gain more time should someone come looking for her. She turned the key, dropped it in her pocket, and this time ran.

Were it not for the unmelted snow that blanketed the ground in white, Kit would have had to grope his way from Nethergate to the cottage, but the narrow sliver of moon floating low in a clear, cold sky was enough to show him the double set of footprints. In another hour, even that pale crescent would be gone, and only someone with a lantern would be able to follow Aurelia and Galahad's tracks.

Not that anyone, finding her gone, would have any doubt as to her destination.

She must have known that, too, for when Kit came in view of the cottage, he saw soft light gleaming behind the curtains at the windows, and a silver plume of smoke rose from the chimney against the starry sky.

He would have increased his pace, but the last stretch was down a hill grown slippery with ice. A few seconds' delay in the name of caution was well worth the expense.

And to have the night alone with her was worth the cold, the tiresome trudging through ice-crusted snow, even the risk of leaving Emil.

If Aurelia and the cottage were a trap, Kit considered he was already caught at Nethergate. At least he owed himself and Emil an effort to escape. It might mean a charge of murder hanging over his head, but staying offered few chances of clearing his name, too.

She had shut the gate, perhaps because the screech of the iron as Kit opened it served as warning. Indeed, Galahad's familiar barks meant no one was likely to sneak up on the cottage. When, after relatching the gate, Kit turned toward the cottage, the door opened.

She was upon him before he reached the door, before he could see her in the light, before he could set the satchel safely down and have both arms free to embrace her.

"I've worried every second," she breathed between frenetic kisses, "and each one seemed a year."

The deerhound, each bark puffing a frosty cloud into the air, danced a greeting around their feet.

"Must we stand in the cold?" Kit teased. "I'm not accustomed to English weather, you know."

She laughed, though her laughter had a nervous edge to it, and taking his free hand in both of hers, she led him past the scarred door and into the parlor.

Only when they were securely inside did she wax serious and ask him, "Where is Mr. Drew? I expected you to bring him."

"So would anyone else," Kit answered, hefting the carpet-bag to the trestle table that separated kitchen from parlor. "But he's in no condition to make this trek, not at night. I knew it even before I'd made it myself; I'd have ended up carrying him most of the way and possibly killing him and myself in the process. He said he can do us both more good by delaying any search for us as long as possible."

While he talked, Kit removed from the satchel the items he had purloined from Nethergate's kitchen: a small ham, two roasted capons, a crock of cream, two loaves of bread, and a wheel of pungent cheese. And wrapped in one of his shirts, two bottles of wine.

"Do you mean that all the while I was here worrying myself sick, you were raiding the larder?"

"No, not *all* the while. A few minutes only," he answered. He found two glasses on a cupboard shelf and quickly filled them with wine. "I watched you at dinner; you ate nothing. If we're to climb ancient castle walls in the dark, I don't want your grumbling stomach to give us away."

He handed her a glass, careful to let only the tips of their fingers touch for the most fleeting of seconds. Any more and he would not have been able to control the need surging through his blood. Had danger and risk heightened his desire, or the joy at finding her eager and waiting?

"We shan't be climbing castle walls in the dark," she said, then closed her lips over the edge of the glass to drink.

When he gave her a puzzled frown, she added. "I hope that doesn't disappoint you."

"Not at all. One such adventure was quite enough for me." He realized then that he had made an erroneous assumption. "There's another entrance, isn't there? You said the door was padlocked and you came out over the wall, but that isn't how you went in, was it?"

Shaking her head, she slipped her arm through his and led him back to the parlor.

Between two facing chairs in front of the fire she had placed a low table on which was laid out a large sheet of paper, such as an artist might use for sketching or painting. As Kit allowed Aurelia to remove his coat, he began to study the series of drawings neatly spaced on the page.

"I've had to do most of them from memory," she explained. "Please, Kit, sit down. You're chilled and every bit as hungry as I."

He sat obediently and moved the two-branched candlestick closer as he leaned over the paper.

Aurelia moved comfortably about the shadowy kitchen to lay out plates and utensils, to cut the capons and slice the ham. The last residue of fear was leaving her, now that she could glance into the parlor and see Kit seated in front of the fire. He seemed to have forgotten whatever fear he had felt, if any. Eyes narrowed in concentration, he held his wine in his left hand and with his right forefinger traced the lines she had drawn. Occasionally he nodded, as though the sketch imparted some sage wisdom. How many years would she be able to hold that scene in her memory and her heart after he had gone? How long would be enough, before the loss of her first and only love became too much to bear?

She closed her eyes and smiled. Tonight she would make as many memories as possible.

With two plates and the open bottle of wine in her hands, she returned to the parlor and explained, "Uncle Henry claimed he found the other way into Winterburn when he was a boy and he never told anyone until he showed it to me. Most of it is filled with rubble and unless you go partway in, you can't tell there's any more to it than that."

"It makes sense. See, here, there must have been a cloister connecting the chapel with the castle itself." He pointed to the place on the drawing, but Aurelia's attention focused on his finger and his hand, strong and rough from hard work yet sure and steady with confidence. "This section of the wall inside the chapel appeared different from the rest, as if it replaced an older one."

Aurelia thought about bringing the other chair closer but decided instead to sit at Kit's feet. Galahad, with his customary eagerness for handouts, sat beside her, tail swishing on the slate.

"Whoever followed me into the ruins came by way of the cellar door," she said.

"You told me it was padlocked."

"It was—this evening. Grandfather could have had the lock put on within an hour of my return—or if the lock has been there for a long time, he could have given someone the key."

"Why didn't you go that way in the first place?"

The answer she had given him earlier was hardly sufficient, and she knew it. The answer she intended to give him now required considerable thought—but it would be all of the truth.

"There is a bar across the door that I can lower but not raise from the other side without difficulty. I did not want to leave it up and thereby alert anyone to my presence in the ruins. I thought that if I found the portrait and discovered what is so important about it that it had to be hidden, I could use the information to get answers from my grandfather."

"Isn't that blackmail?"

Despite the accusatory tone of his voice, he smiled at her when she looked up at him.

"Perhaps. But is that any worse than what he's done to

me? Forcing me to lie? Threatening to break his promise that the cottage was mine? No, that's unfair of me. He gave me a roof over my head, which is more than he needed to do. I was responsible for the death of a son he loved very much."

"Were you?"

"Yes, I told you what happened."

"You told me your parents were killed in an accident. How could that be your fault? Unless you contrived the bad weather, the slippery road."

"But had it not been for me, they would not have left London under those conditions."

"Were conditions bad in London when they left? Did they have any way of knowing what the road would be like three or four hundred miles away?"

"What are you saying?"

"I'm saying that I think your grandfather knew you had little real blame in his son's death. I think he also felt his own guilt for Henry's death, and saw the loss of Robert as divine justice."

"There's more, isn't there."

She had no reason to ask it as a question; his pause before answering confirmed her statement.

"I had a long cold walk this evening with little to keep me warm but my thoughts. Most of those thoughts were of you, and I must admit, they did indeed keep me warm."

She felt her own face flush as he cupped his hand around her head and brought her close, so her chin rested on his knee.

"But it struck me as curious, too, why Charles MacKinnon did not banish from his sight the person he ought most to hate. You cost him the reputation of his eldest son—and the life of his youngest. What, I wondered, made him do that?"

"He is not a cruel man. He knew I had nothing, nowhere else to go."

"Cruelty has little to do with it. Unless he is a saint, a

man does not willingly keep about him the reminder of his own shame and guilt, his own loss and failure."

"You're saying there was another reason? But what reason would he have?"

"Perhaps he had none. Perhaps someone else did."

"But there was no one else. Only Serena."

Time, like breath on a windowpane, had frozen into a glittering but opaque frost. Then a ray of sunlight touched it, and the cold, blinding beauty melted.

Aurelia rose slowly, with the deceptive calm that precedes shock, first lifting her head from Kit's knee, then gathering her feet beneath her. When he reached for her hand, she did not draw away, but neither did she let him close the distance between them.

"You believe she killed my parents."

20

"I THINK IT'S POSSIBLE, NOTHING MORE."

The thought horrified her, but she held it in the palm of her mind's hand and examined it with dispassion albeit with some fear.

"Serena was wicked and greedy," Aurelia admitted. "Grandfather blamed her for Henry's death, but he also blamed himself. He never accused her of killing my mother and his son, although I suppose one could postulate that by some strange sequence of events, their deaths were related to my defense of Henry, which I would not have given had he not taken his life because of Serena."

How complex, she thought, was the long chain of events that led to this moment. Was there a similar chain that had led Christopher Ballantyne to England and to Nethergate and, yes, to this cozy cottage parlor? And was Aurelia Phillips, who had wanted nothing more than to be left alone, now tightly bound in those chains?

Suppositions, even motives, were hardly enough to convict anyone of a crime. Aurelia pointed out to Kit, "Serena's seduction of Henry MacKinnon, even her blackmailing of the duke, hardly makes her a murderess."

"No more than it does you."

Kit's implacable gaze, his quick replies, seemed targeted at a particular response, but Aurelia was at a loss to understand his objective. "Besides, Serena had nothing to gain by killing my parents. There were times when I thought, with a child's jealousy, that she flirted with Robert, but he was her husband's brother and she could never have married him."

She picked up her plate and carried it to the other side of the table. Though she now sat no further from the fire than before, she felt a chill, and knew it was nearness to Kit that had kept her warm. Had that proximity also affected her logic? Kit's logic, if it could be called that, had too many flaws, but it made her uneasy.

"I believe our cold English weather has stimulated your colonial imagination," she said. "I have no idea what Serena's role, if any, in my parents' death can possibly have to do with our finding a portrait of your grandfather. Is that not what you came to do tonight?"

"No, it's not."

If Aurelia had not intended the slightly accusatory tone that ended her questions, neither did she expect the soft hint of seduction that filled Kit's reply.

"I came to Nethergate to lay a lie to rest," he said, serious once more. "I believed, despite my mother's fanciful stories and even my uncle's testimony, that my grandfather was a frightened soldier who, after his commanding officer David MacKinnon was killed, assumed MacKinnon's identity rather than be labeled a deserter. I thought it no more than an odd coincidence that half a century later, a friend should remark that I bore some resemblance to another MacKinnon, a Caribbean planter who was reputed to be the disinherited heir of an English nobleman."

"Did you not question this when you went to London?"

He shook his head and said, "During the two months I was in London, no one recognized me as the long-lost heir to Winterburn. No one remarked on a family resemblance. Again I dismissed it, but Emil insisted that we had come that far and we might as well go the rest of the way. So we came here, to this frigid shrine to an absent brother, to prove there was nothing to the story." He picked up a capon leg and sank his teeth into it with deliberate enjoyment.

Aurelia shivered. The silence while he ate was too much to bear. It was better to talk.

"But there would be very few in London who remembered David MacKinnon. And although I do not remember exactly what the circumstances were, I believe Michael left Nethergate as a young man. He would not be a well-remembered figure, certainly not in London Society." The conclusion was too obvious for her to ignore. "You found that instead of a neat, easily dismissed lie, the whole tale could very well be true."

He took another bite of the fowl, nodded, and said, "Precisely, Miss Phillips."

He clearly left her to make the connection with Serena and with the possibility that the long-held belief in Serena's innocence was another lie. But even after a long rumination, Aurelia could make no sense of it. To dwell on the other implications was to court disastrous folly.

"Supposing, for the sake of discussion, Serena did have designs on Robert and planned to kill my mother. To marry Robert, she would have needed an annulment of her marriage to Henry. How could she do that after his death? Grandfather would have banished her for making the truth public, if she had any way of proving it, and it would not have profited her a thing. Besides, Robert truly loved my mother, and he despised Serena. He would never have married her."

Something nagged at her, like a vague fragment of a memory, but when Kit spoke, the fragment vanished.

He shrugged and said, "Then there's an end to it. I had

thought there might be a connection and it might shed some light on this, but it's useless to try to find logic in the actions of murderers." He finished off the capon leg and reached for another. "We may not be scaling castle walls, but if we're to go back to Nethergate in the dark of midnight, you'd best eat something."

She blinked and shook her head to clear out the cobwebs of the past. The present offered challenges enough without dredging up ancient pains. Even if Kit were right and Serena had played some part in the deaths of Robert and Jeannette MacKinnon, Serena, too, was dead now. She would have to answer to the victims herself, and to an even higher power.

"We're not going to Nethergate tonight," Aurelia replied. "Anyone, including the murderer, could see our lights. We'll go at dawn, before the household wakens."

There were hours until dawn. Hours for what? Aurelia read the question in Kit's eyes—and the answer.

"We can reach the ruins just before daybreak," she explained, knowing the implication in her words, "and enter without being seen. Once inside, we need only wait for sunrise. The upper rooms face east, overlooking the courtyard."

"You're certain we'll find what we're looking for?"

She shook her head, then realized there was another meaning to his comment.

"No, not certain." Was that the response he wanted to his verbal seduction? She could not tell, but plunged on with her explanation. "Everything Grandfather removed from Nethergate he put in the old rooms."

She told him of finding old draperies in one of the rooms she had explored that afternoon. Worn and faded, they had been duplicated and replaced, perhaps more than once, but the originals were never discarded. Kit listened attentively, as if he were trying not only to discern some unrecognized clue in her words but also to prompt an even fuller disclosure from her.

But of what?

She was aware of his eyes never leaving her. By the time Aurelia reached the conclusion, she could barely sigh, "A man who carefully preserves bits of faded damask and velvet surely would not dispose of a valuable portrait of his own brother. Not when he is acting on that brother's orders to preserve the estate in his absence."

That much, at least, seemed to satisfy Kit. He nodded and gave her a few minutes in which to eat, then asked, "What of other entrances to the ruins? You said the one from Nethergate is padlocked, yet someone else was inside the castle this afternoon. How did he—or she—get there?"

Aurelia breathed a sigh of relief. The same question had plagued her, too, until only one answer seemed possible.

"I believe Grandfather ordered the padlock installed only after today's incident. As for the other lock, it is old and there could be a number of keys around Nethergate that open it. Someone else, someone less concerned with his or her presence being known, went in earlier. Then, when they became aware that I, too, was in the ruins, they decided to trap me, leaving them at liberty to raise the bar, if indeed they had not left it up in the first place."

"You're certain that person entered the ruins from Nethergate?"

Aurelia nodded.

"You already know how difficult it is to gain entrance via the wall. No one who was within Nethergate this afternoon is capable of it, not even Charlotte, who has never been here before and could know nothing of where the outside stairs lead. Besides, the only way to the lower stairs from the upper floor would have taken the person past the room where I was, and Galahad would have warned me."

"But if what you say is true, Charlotte might have known of the cellar entrance. Lady Whiston apparently knows the place well enough, and she could have told Denholm, who could have passed the information on."

"It's possible. But then, nearly anything is possible.

Serena might have told Adam, who might have told his sister. Joshua knew, of course, and he might have told Adam. Henry might even have told Serena about the entrance behind the chapel."

"But none of them knew what to look for once they were inside the ruins, did they?"

Aurelia wanted to weep with frustration. All the logic, the analysis, the questions led nowhere. Yet if she did not press on, there was nowhere else to go. Nowhere but into the icy, night-shrouded ruins of Winterburn itself.

She gathered what composure she had left. She was frightened, which she did not mind admitting at least to herself. There would be no more lies. "We don't know either, Kit. We could be searching for something that no longer exists, something Grandfather destroyed years ago. Or perhaps his father took the painting down when David was reported killed rather than be reminded of his loss."

She remembered Joshua's frustration only a few nights ago when he and Adam ransacked the study, unable to find whatever they were looking for. Not the portrait, surely, but something.

Kit listened without comment while Aurelia told him of the incident, then she added, "Perhaps *we* are looking in the wrong direction. Perhaps David MacKinnon's portrait has nothing whatever to do with anything else. Perhaps we will *never* know who killed Serena or Mr. Gould."

"Then you cannot go back."

He spoke softly, but with the calm conviction with which she had become so familiar.

"Whatever do you mean?"

"I mean the same thing I told you before. Leave Nethergate, Aurelia. Leave England. Come with me to Charleston."

He offered neither promise nor plea of marriage, which notion was at once absurd and impossible and heartbreaking. Aurelia had long ago accepted her own unmarriageability, but that was when she had never been in love. She had never wanted to marry anyone, and it was easy then not to mourn what one never had.

But now, sitting with him in the cozy parlor of the cottage where she had planned to spend the rest of her life alone, she knew the pain and futility of love.

A man does not want a woman who tells him the truth; he wants one who will flatter him or protect him when others would force unwanted truths upon him. She held no illusions about herself, nor about Christopher Ballantyne, who watched her with dark eyes over the edge of a wineglass.

Men, even brash colonials, marry virgins.

"And what would I *do* in Charleston, Mr. Ballantyne?" she asked with an arched brow and a whisper of sarcasm meant to shield her from the blow to come. "I cannot build ships or invest in your enterprise. No, my place is here, as I have always known it would be."

He coughed as though choking on a piece of chicken or a bite of dry bread.

"You seem quite able to manage your grandfather's business. I might need a good manager. Or secretary. I presume you can write a fair hand? And spell? And do simple sums? I'd pay better wages than you'd make as a governess."

How had the conversation drifted in this direction? Was he actually offering her honest employment? And why did such an offer hurt far worse than if he had asked her to be his mistress?

She drank more wine, aware as she did so that it might loosen her tongue. Silence might be a lie, but she had already faced the truth herself.

He waited patiently for her answer, which made her all the more uncomfortable.

"Of course, if you'd prefer, since you'd have no references in Charleston, I might be able to help you find another position. I've not the reputation or status of Lady Whiston, but I've no black marks on my record."

"But what of *my* reputation? And where would I live?"

She rose to take her half-empty plate to the scullery. "I fail to understand where this notion came from and I certainly do not know where it can possibly lead."

She heard his footsteps, slow, measured, patient. Galahad, hoping as always for handouts, pattered beside him. She set the dishes on the table, her hands trembling so much she was afraid she would drop everything with a clatter, that the plate would shatter into as many pieces as her heart.

"I am sorry, Miss Phillips. I'm afraid I don't have your facility for—"

She did not let him finish. Hands now free, she turned and threw her arms around his neck to bring his mouth down for the kiss that would tell him what she could not put into words.

She had barely felt the first pressure of his lips, answering as eagerly and hungrily as her own, when he scooped her into his arms like a child.

"Thank God," he murmured, his smile obvious even in his voice, "for an honest woman."

He deepened the kiss, but Aurelia broke it when she realized he was headed in the direction of the stairs.

"Kit, please put me down. What if someone followed you?"

He continued without breaking stride.

"Are you afraid of being caught in the act?" he teased with the now familiar phrase, then immediately dismissed her fear. "No one followed me, just as no one followed you. You really didn't expect anyone to, did you? Or you wouldn't have set out on your own."

"But I had no intention of . . ."

"You're lying."

He took advantage of her outraged gasp to steal another kiss and began to mount the stairs. She wanted to slap his face but her arms around his neck only tightened her hold on him, defying her own conscious wishes. And somewhere deep inside her that incendiary spark of secret desire blossomed again.

At the top of the stairs, he stopped and released her mouth, this time leaving her breathless with a different kind of outrage.

"I want you, Aurelia. And I know you want me." He kept his voice to a harsh whisper and carried her into one of the cold, dark bedrooms. "I can feel your wanting, I can smell it, I can taste it."

She licked her lips at the suggestive image.

"You cannot lie to me, Aurelia; do not lie to yourself."

He set her on her feet. Before she regained her equilibrium, he was busy with the buttons on her gown.

"Is it the anticipation of danger that arouses us so?" he asked. "Or is it the relief at having survived other threats?"

She recalled the moment of hearing the gunshots and then the instant of looking up and finding Kit with her on the castle wall. There had been an elemental need to touch him then, and it had not faded.

"I could have lost you," she whispered, helping him shrug out of his coat. Then, her fingers suddenly frantic to undo the buttons of his waistcoat, she added, "I could have lost you before I ever found you."

Beyond that there were no words, for she *had* found him, and he was here with her, lifting her cold and naked and carrying her to the bed.

They lay together for a long while after that shimmering blaze of ecstacy had faded to a safe and secure glow. Curled against Kit, her head on his shoulder as it had been that morning, Aurelia listened for every tiny sound in the dark stillness to imprint upon her memory for the future. She heard only the rhythmic beat of his heart beneath her cheek, the gentle rasp of his breathing, the faint rustle as he stroked the fine silken hair at her temple.

And then, "Of everything I imagined I'd find here, I never expected you."

"But there were women in London, weren't there? And in Charleston?"

He chuckled, a deep purr as powerful and mesmerizing as a tiger's.

"There are women everywhere, my dear Aurelia, but there is only one woman."

He pulled her closer, so she lay across his chest. In the faint light that reached the room, she could make out only the shape of him against the pillow, the rough splash of dark hair against the white linen. She had to touch him to discern the frown that creased his brow.

"Come with me to Charleston, Aurelia," he pleaded again. "I have nothing to offer you, no wealth, no fine manor, certainly no title. My house is not even as grand as this cottage, and I share it with my mother, who can be a trial to the most patient of souls at times, but if it will make you happy—"

"Hush," she whispered, resting her fingers across his lips. She must not let him utter the passion-spawned lies that would leave her with nothing. "We have now, tonight. And you have already made me happy." Then she bent her head down to kiss him. Her mouth soft and gentle, lips parted, she let her tongue seek his.

But this time he refused to deepen the intimacy. It was he who drew away.

"I want more than tonight. So do you; don't tell me otherwise."

He stroked his hands up her arms to her shoulders, then framed her face. She turned to kiss one calloused palm and tasted the salt of her own tears.

"Don't, Kit," she begged, "don't ask for more than either of us has to give."

"And why not? You said yourself that I came here with everything to gain. Then surely by asking you to marry me and come with me to Charleston as my wife I have nothing to lose, have I?"

Nothing to lose—and everything to gain. The two phrases echoed and re-echoed in her mind, louder than her rapidly beating heart, louder than her joy at Kit's proposal, louder even than his persistent entreaties when she failed to reply, until she cried out to silence them and him.

And when the silence had indeed returned, she breathed, her voice trembling with shock, "Dear heaven, what a mistake we made. We thought the murderer was the person who had the most to gain; what if he is the one with the most to lose?"

21

"JOSHUA?" KIT ASKED.

His answer came so quickly, so instinctively, that Aurelia trusted it at once. Within seconds, however, Kit himself dismissed the notion.

"I've met his type often enough before, and they're never easy to like. The plantation life made him lazy, and now he's inherited even more wealth, but that's not reason enough to charge him with murder."

He was right, and she knew that as instinctively as she had known he was right when he first said Joshua's name.

Her mind was a maelstrom. Fears over what they might find when they entered the Winterburn ruins vied with the ever-present uncertainty over her own future, Kit's proposal notwithstanding. She had almost forgotten he had asked her to be his wife, because there were so many other disjointed thoughts tumbling over one another.

That much, at least, hardly seemed real. She tried to remember his exact words as she curled beside him once more. She hesitated to give voice to her thoughts, even to ask him to repeat what he had said. Had she misinterpreted him? She knew, with a furious blush, that she had, and when he, too, lapsed into silence, she was certain he had only been caught up in the kind of passion that spawned what, when reason returned, proved to be lies.

Knowing that she had acted very foolishly for allowing that same passion to lead her to believe those seductive lies did not lessen the disappointment, but it did restore some measure of clearheaded reason. To follow Christopher Ballantyne to Charleston would only compound the recklessness, no matter what risks she faced by staying at Nethergate. She should, she concluded, push personal feelings aside and catch a few hours of sleep before they set out on their search for the missing portrait of David MacKinnon. Other problems and dilemmas could be addressed later, and if she recognized her own blindness in so delaying the inevitable, she knew also that to do otherwise would be a waste of time.

Two thoughts, however, kept her awake. No matter how she tried to rationalize them into silence, they screamed over and over. Joshua MacKinnon did indeed have a great deal to lose that he had probably never thought to possess—and Christopher Ballantyne could risk all, for he had nothing to lose.

Kit, too, must have been plagued by the possibility that they had overlooked something, for he suddenly asked, "What of Freddie? Did Serena pose a threat to his inheritance?"

"I—I don't know," she stammered, snapping out of a light doze, almost asleep. "The laws of inheritance are quite fixed, you know. Grandfather was never sure, in fact, if disinheriting his second son was valid. Not that it mattered, as things turned out after Robert died."

"And Adam Braisthwaite? I take it there is no doubt he is his father's son and heir?"

Aurelia assured him there was no doubt at all.

As they lay in the dark, Kit continued down the list of

guests at Nethergate, from Freddie and Adam to Molly, Lady Whiston's maid, and Dr. Ward, the London physician. After going over the details so many times, Aurelia began to yawn, until finally Kit pulled the blankets over her and told her to sleep while she could.

She drifted uneasily in and out of vaguely unpleasant dreams for a few hours, waking more than once to find Kit sitting on the edge of the bed. Each time, she coaxed him to rest again, but when at last she opened her eyes to find him dressed and quietly pacing the room, she knew there was no hope for further sleep. She, too, rose and dressed to wait out the last hour or so in the parlor, savoring if not truly enjoying the comfort of the dying fire.

"We've missed something," Kit insisted. He stood at the window, where the glimmer of starlight through the naked tree branches belied the waning of the night. "I've gone over and over it, from the instant Emil and I set foot in Nethergate, and there is no reason why anyone would have seen either of us as a threat. Yet we were the first assaulted, and that *after* we had left."

Aurelia poured the last of a strong, bitter tea into her cup and returned to her chair by the fire. She, too, had found herself reliving every moment of the past few days, searching for an anomaly. "Unless things are not what they seem," she mused.

"What do you mean? You just told me everyone is quite secure in his or her little niche in the world. Adam will be the next Viscount Moresby, Joshua will inherit the Winterburn title."

She laughed, with that odd humorless mirth that comes from mental as well as physical exhaustion.

"I meant you, Kit."

"Me? Why?"

Galahad, sitting beside her, rested his chin on her knee. Idly stroking the dog's head and narrow muzzle, she explained, "You came, a stranger from the storm, with a fantastic story. You had neither proof nor witnesses. You could have been anyone." Again she laughed. "You could, for that matter, have claimed to be Joshua MacKinnon, late of St. Gregory's Island in the Caribbean yourself, and no one would have—" The laughter died with the abrupt cut of her sentence. When she spoke again, a tentative fear slowed the words, separated them into distinct statements of their own. "No one would have been the wiser."

Kit took out his watch.

"We have time," he said. "Tell me everything about Joshua. Everything."

There were more details than at first she had thought, but she told him everything. The duke's decision to reinstate his second son had not come immediately after Robert's death, and then there had been a long, slow correspondence, from the first letters dispatched to St. Gregory's to the replies that told of Michael's death.

"I'd nearly forgotten. Joshua sent a miniature of himself a year or more ago," she added almost at the end. "I have seen it in Grandfather's room, and there has never been any doubt in my mind that he is the man in the portrait."

She did not have to say that those doubts were there now.

They put on cloak and coat and set out. There was no moon, and no light faded the stars on the eastern horizon, but dawn was not far.

Still, the lack of light made the going slow and treacherous. Hampered by her skirts, Aurelia gave Kit control of Galahad as she struggled through the ice-crusted snow. Her feet grew cold and then numb by the time they crested the hill between the cottage and Nethergate, but beneath her cloak she felt the icy sweat of exertion.

"Are you all right?" Kit whispered. "Perhaps we should have waited until daybreak."

She shook her head, not caring whether he could see.

"No. It must be now or never." She pointed to the dark

shape against the sky, the faint outline of Nethergate more an absence of stars than a solid image, like a void cut into the heavens. "The answers are there."

The void hung above them and slowly metamorphosed into the familiar dark granite bulk as they drew near. No lights brightened the windows, not even on the west wing where Joshua and the duke slept. If anyone knew she and Kit had left Nethergate, no one had mounted a vigil for their return.

By the time they slipped into the courtyard and began the short but dangerous walk to the hidden entrance, the sky above was blacker than the walls surrounding them. The stars, with a last moment of brightness, cast only the vaguest of shadows. In the shadow of the chapel and the oak trees, however, no illumination penetrated the darkness. Aurelia closed her eyes and noted she saw the same as when they were open.

She had to feel each step in front of her, and kept one hand to the uneven stone of the castle wall. The ice was as slippery as in the daylight, but blindness exaggerated every other danger. She rubbed her fingers together for what feeble warmth she could find, then pressed them to the stone again and walked on.

She felt the prick and stab of dried vines first, then the outline of the stones forming the archway.

"We're here!" she breathed, unable to contain her relief and excitement. When she turned to find Kit, she discovered she could see him, though faintly, even in the shadows. Daylight was growing.

Daylight did not reach inside the hidden passage through the wall of Winterburn.

She became aware of the pounding of her heart, deeper and more urgent than she had ever known before, as she made her way past the rubble that disguised the entrance. By daylight the passage was easy enough to navigate, but in the dark Aurelia felt the weight of the ancient walls close in on her, and the pressure of stone and centuries over her head seemed to crush her soul. Dead leaves and branches from vines and trees, disturbed by her passing, filled her nose and eyes with age-old dust. Behind her, Kit muffled a sneeze. Each sound was magnified by Aurelia's fear.

Then suddenly, instead of the press of sound and fear, only tomblike silence surrounded her. Beneath her feet she felt bare, uneven stones, not rubble, and if she had lost all sense of direction, at least she knew she had reached the guardroom.

Like a disembodied phantom, Kit's hand circled her arm and pulled her close. Galahad wedged himself between them and pawed at Aurelia's skirt.

"This is it?" Kit whispered. "Do you know where we are?"

She pivoted slowly, searching for anything that would give her her bearings in the blackness. If the emotional hours it had taken to gain the entrance were in fact only minutes, even those minutes had served to bring the light of the new day a bit brighter. Off to her left, Aurelia distinguished a faint rectangle of murky gray, the northern window. The southern, in the shadow of Nethergate, remained darker, but it too was visible. Oriented by them, she strained to make out the vague shapes of the columns that supported the rest of the ruins.

"Yes," she answered triumphantly. "The stairs leading to the next floor are on the other side of that pillar," she said, pointing straight ahead, "and the stairs to the cellars under Nethergate are this way."

She hung back, unexpectedly reluctant to venture further into the darkness. Climbing up to the second floor meant climbing toward the light; the door from Nethergate was at the bottom of another flight of stairs near that northern window.

"I wish we dared strike a light," she said. "If there are no signs of anyone having come through that door . . ."

Someone had opened the door at the bottom of those stairs yesterday and entered the ruins, and no doubt there was evidence of that entry. No amount of light, however, would tell them if that person—or someone else—had come in again.

"We have to make certain," Kit insisted. "If the door is open, or the bar not dropped on the other side, we'll at least know someone is already with us. If not, and we can find something to brace the door, we may prevent anyone from joining us later."

They made their way cautiously, feeling for each step in the darkness, toward the northern wall. Aurelia kept glancing at the windows, not only to keep her path straight, but because she felt unseen eyes peering at her, especially from the darker window that faced the invisible bulk of Nethergate.

Yet for all that sense of being watched, she could see almost nothing. She had to trust to memory and instinct to find the unprotected stairwell, and even then came within half a step of tumbling down the steep, narrow shaft.

"Stay here," Kit ordered, "while I go down."

He transferred Galahad's lead to her wrist. She could hardly pull her hands from his. He brought them to his lips for a kiss.

"Now, describe it to me again, since I won't be able to see anything."

Again, she relied on memory and even closed her eyes to bring back what additional details she could.

"I don't know how many stairs there are, but they're steep and run parallel to the wall; at the bottom is a short landing, with the door at the end and to your left. The hinges are on the right, so the door opens toward the end of the well. If it doesn't budge, don't try to force it; either the padlock is on or the bar, at least, is down."

The light had grown imperceptibly; she could make out the rough shape of him among the shadows, enough to reach up her free hand to his face.

"Be careful, Kit," she whispered, then added, "I love you."

He took her in his arms so ferociously she nearly cried out.

"Ah, God, how sweet it is to hear you say that," he murmured into her ear. "Now, wait for me, do you understand? Don't take off on your own the way you did yesterday."

Without waiting for an answer, he was gone.

She listened to his footsteps on the stairs, counting as perhaps he did. It seemed as if half of eternity passed, though it could hardly be more than half a minute, for there were thirty-two steps.

She kept counting even after that, thinking surely it would take him no more than another minute—another eternity—to check the door and return. But she reached sixty and then seventy and heard no returning steps on the stairs, only odd scraping noises coming from the bottom of the stairwell.

An icy sweat broke out on her palms. She knelt on the stone floor and drew Galahad close, for warmth as well as for comfort. The dog sat obediently and licked her cheek.

"He's all right, he's all right," she breathed, her face buried against Galahad's neck to muffle her fervent litany. "No one is there, he's all right."

When Galahad added his own plaintive whines, she hugged him harder to silence him, and when she felt a tap on her shoulder, she nearly jumped out of her skin.

"I'm fine," Kit said, bending down to help her to her feet once more.

"What took you so long? I thought you'd been down there forever!"

"I found some small stones on the stairs and wedged them under the door. They won't be as effective as a wooden brace, but they ought to make sufficient noise if anyone tries to come through."

"Unless that person is already here."

"We won't know that until we look, will we?"

He would have preferred to wait until the light grew

stronger so he could examine the door further, but they had little enough time. In the end it would make little difference.

The few minutes he had spent at the Nethergate cellar door had brightened the guardroom chamber by enough that they could now see the pillars plainly. Preserving as much stealth as possible, they raced to the center support and the stairs that wound inside it.

Here all was black again, but within the narrow confines, Aurelia felt more secure, more familiar with her surroundings. And at the top, where the heavy door had been closed upon her, she felt a surge of anger.

She guided Kit's hands to the icy iron handle.

"Wait," he said. "Let me see if your intruder did as I did."

He groped, not knowing what his hands might encounter, for a block of wood or a wedge of stone that someone might have used to secure the door. There were several loose bits of rock that could fit that purpose, for Kit encountered what felt like the score marks of stone against stone. This time, if the intruder were waiting for them, he would not have been able to bar the door from this side himself.

Aurelia and Galahad had to back down two steps to give Kit the leverage he needed to pull the door free of the frame. Even with nothing forced beneath it, it was stuck fast. Could a man have done that, pulling from the other side?

Kit supposed he could have. If Joshua MacKinnon had a perfect alibi for yesterday, he had none right now.

But Kit spent no more time speculating. With one foot braced against the door frame, he leaned his full weight into pulling the door free and finally, with a grunt from him and a groan from the hinges, the portal opened.

The second floor was gloomy but details could be discerned at last. Nothing seemed changed from yesterday. The doors all stood open on the empty rooms Aurelia had explored before. This time, with Kit beside her, she entered with no less caution and hardly less fear, for the knowledge even of a possible explanation added to the risk.

But they found nothing disturbed.

"If anyone was, or is, here, he's left no sign," Aurelia whispered after showing Kit the faded draperies. The dust lay thick in the folds exactly as it had the day before. The light had grown enough that they could see even that. As they ventured into the hall once again, she pointed to the brighter end and added, "The stairs to the top level are there."

Kit wrapped his arms around her one more time, but only for the briefest of moments. Or perhaps it only felt brief, for she wanted it to last much longer.

"We'll go up, then."

The roofless landing from which Aurelia had climbed down the wall yesterday gave a panoramic view of a sleeping Nethergate. No lights bloomed in the windows, though overhead the stars at last began to pale.

Kit studied the construction of this landing from which Aurelia had made her escape.

He had seen the destruction wrought in Washington by the British invasion some seven or eight years ago, and surmised that something similar had happened here at Winterburn. The solidity of the remaining walls suggested that force, not nature, had caused the collapse of the roof on what was, to judge by its size, not a landing at the top of the stairs but an anteroom of sorts.

The ruined outer wall showed the partial outline of a narrow window, so narrow as to be described as an arrow slit, set into the masonry. When shuttered on the outside and concealed by a curtain inside the room, it offered a sufficient hiding place for a man, so thick was the wall. In contrast, the courtyard-side wall was no more substantial than modern construction. The glass in it might have been broken by the branches of the oak tree that even now pierced the frame.

Through those branches, the eastern sky began to fulfill its promise of morning's golden glow.

As the sun came nearer to rising, so too did the breeze.

Aurelia, in the shelter of the interior wall and its remnant of roof, hugged herself against this added chill. Galahad, nose raised, sniffed the air incessantly.

"Tell me again what's inside," Kit asked, coming to stand beside her. "A corridor and two rooms, correct?"

"Two rooms," she agreed, "and no other exit but this, except for the windows overlooking the courtyard."

She needed say no more. From those windows the drop to the flagstones would prove fatal. No oak trees would break a fall.

Kit put his hand on the ancient iron handle bolted to the door, then leaned down to brush his lips across Aurelia's.

"Trust me," he whispered.

"I do, Kit." Then she was tugging on his sleeve, pulling his hand from the door. "Please, we don't need to do this."

"And if indeed that is not the real Joshua MacKinnon who calls himself the heir of Winterburn? Would you allow him to continue that lie?"

He watched in the growing light as she struggled to form the word, the answer she wanted to give but did not believe in.

"I want no lies, my love. Not between us. I would not have you wonder forever, nor have fear of the truth be the cause of any unhappiness." He studied her face, turned up to his, as the soft morning glow lent the first hints of color to what had been only differing shades of gray: now the blush of passion pinked her cheeks, and the warm green flashed in her eyes. "He would hunt us down, Aurelia, before we were a mile from Nethergate, and if he did not catch us then, he would never stop until he had."

Then it was she who grasped the iron handle and pulled the door open.

22

THE DARK OF THE CORRIDOR WAS BROKEN BY A SINGLE NARROW splash of diffuse light on the dusty floor where the door to the more distant of the two rooms hung partially open. Footprints traced in the dust gave evidence of the occasional invasion of Winterburn's solitude, but they were of varying age, and none appeared fresh.

"I've not been here since I was a child," Aurelia breathed. "It is so cold, so . . . hushed."

"And haunted, perhaps?"

She shook her head.

"There are no ghosts save the ones we carry with us," she said, looking up at him with a hint of a smile.

There being neither bar nor latch, they did not bother propping the door from the ruined anteroom open but let it swing shut behind them. The protest of its old hinges was muffled by the remaining walls so that anyone now awake in Nethergate would be unlikely to determine the exact location of the sound, and should someone else enter, that same creak would provide warning.

They elected to search the more distant room first.

On entering, Kit gasped, "My God! He never threw anything away, did he?"

Even Aurelia, who had known what to expect, gazed around in open-mouthed astonishment.

The room was huge and high-ceilinged. Gossamer strands of cobwebs hung from blackened beams to drift spectrally as the entry of two human beings and a single dog shifted the stagnant air. So thick and long were the webs that they cast pale shadows across the dawn light penetrating the mullioned windows.

Rolls of worn carpet leaned like symmetrical tree trunks against one wall. Their edges were gnawed by the rodents that inhabited the ruins, with the degree of destruction indicating the relative lengths of time the carpets had been stored. Aurelia recognized from some of the turned-back corners the familiar patterns that still graced the floors of Nethergate.

Four chairs, identical to those in the dining room where Aurelia had endured so many horrible dinners in the past several weeks, lined up in front of the carpets. One had a broken back, another a slashed brocade seat.

"He kept everything as his brother charged him," Aurelia whispered, running her hand along the dust-coated back of one of those chairs. "It became an obsession."

"Then the painting will be here, somewhere."

But it was not in that room. Aurelia found boxes of broken china, each plate or cup in its own partitioned cell against the day it might be repaired or presented to the returning prodigal as proof of his deputy's diligence.

Struggling to open the drawer of a chest, the duplicate of which now stood in Lady Whiston's room, she unclasped Galahad's lead to let the dog wander where he would. He scared up a mouse or two but could not catch them, sneezed at the dust his own explorations raised, and soon had cobwebs dangling from his ears and tail.

"It's a wonder we don't find every chicken bone and

rotten apple disposed of in the kitchen," Kit remarked, his voice reaching her from another corner of the room.

He had, in fact, almost disappeared among the stacks of crates. But Aurelia, feeling more and more uneasy in this graveyard of household items, quickly moved to keep the familiar silhouette in view.

A sudden movement to her right startled a tiny shriek of alarm from her, until she discovered an instant later that it was only her own reflection distorted in a shattered pier glass.

She turned from the eerie image and observed, "There are no personal possessions, only what would appear on an inventory of the estate."

She peered into a pasteboard box and found the irreparable shards of a painted vase, one she herself had broken as a child.

The collection was fascinating, but frightening as well. What could have driven a man to carry out a responsibility with such precision? And what else was a man of such precision also capable of?

She shivered and replaced the lid on the box with its pitiful bits of porcelain.

Galahad startled another mouse and chased this one out into the corridor. Aurelia could not help laughing when the dog skidded trying to round the corner in pursuit of his quarry.

"Galahad has the right idea," Kit commented. "There's nothing in this room, unless you intend to search every one of these crates."

Aurelia shook her head and waited while he walked around the various piles to rejoin her.

"I can't think Grandfather would pack it away. If the frame were broken or the painting torn, he might, but somehow that seems unlikely." She paused at the door to take one last look around the room. "I wish we had asked Lady Whiston other questions."

"Such as?"

"Such as when she last saw David's painting in the gallery. Did it disappear right after he left for America or not until he died, or perhaps not until after he returned with his son?"

And then, because there was no time now to have those questions answered, she followed where Galahad had already wandered.

He had not gone far. He stood with nose pressed to the thin crack of light beneath the door to the other room, his hindquarters raised and his tail wagging steadily. At Aurelia's approach he began scratching at the floor, but desisted as if he knew such digging was futile.

"His mouse must have squeezed under there," Kit said as he held the door open for Aurelia to enter.

Galahad bounded gaily ahead of her, but she noticed, as the first true sunlight burning through the grimy, web-curtained windows illuminated the entrance, that the dog had left distinct paw prints in the dust, along with her own and Kit's. Had there been other prints as well, now erased by their passing?

She glanced down at the floor inside the room before she entered.

"Is something wrong?" Kit asked.

"No, nothing. I thought there might be some clue in the footprints in the dust, but there are too many. Until a few days ago, I never paid attention to any activity here, but apparently the ruins have not been quite as abandoned as I thought."

"If your guests have been like most guests, they've broken things, and no doubt His Grace has had them brought here."

Aurelia shivered, remembering the broken cup and chocolate pot on the rug in Serena's room. She vowed that if she found a small box free of dust, she would not look inside.

And this room did contain boxes, hundreds of them. Boxes of threadbare linens and crates of faded draperies. A carton of books ruined by water, perhaps when a library window was left open during a storm. A lady's hatbox, but instead of hats this contained torn and stained linen napkins.

The detritus of normal life, worthless and at the same time precious to the man who had vowed to look after it, was gathered here.

His madness was the worst lie of all.

She wiped away an unexpected tear and took a deep breath before facing the search again.

And then she saw it. So startling was the sight of that corner of gilded frame that she hardly dared exhale for fear she would shout.

Because the painting had been turned to face the wall, she did not even tell Kit, afraid to raise his hopes as her own were. Until she saw the image on the canvas, she would hold her silence.

That corner of the room, not far from one of the three windows, proved difficult to reach. A small gilded chair that had once belonged in the drawing room sat in front of the portrait. Aurelia moved the chair, heedless of the noise.

"Have you found something?" Kit called. "Do you need some help?"

He was on the other side of the room, near the door. She looked at Kit, the cold winter sunlight full on him, before she turned the painting away from the wall. Would it be his face, his tall, broad-shouldered form on the canvas? Or was this just another painting, a landscape from one of the drawing rooms or the library, darkened by decades of smoke, its frame warped by changes in weather?

"No, I can manage." Her hands were trembling as she gripped the heavy frame and angled its face to the light.

And stared into the countenance of David MacKinnon.

She recognized him more from the family portrait still hanging in the gallery than from a resemblance to his grandson. In scarlet tunic and black boots, with his hand upon his sword, he posed with all the enthusiastic arrogance of youth. In time, she suspected, he lost some of that arrogance and acquired the patience and determination that marked Kit's features, but the artist had also captured that indelible stamp of English aristocracy, which in two generations had been replaced by native intelligence.

Behind him, against a pastoral sky that somehow mocked the blatant aggression of the military uniform, loomed the facade of Nethergate, painted from an odd angle that included, even in miniature, the very ruins in which the painting had been hidden away. In the light that came through one of those ancient windows, light too harsh and direct for an artist, Aurelia saw the livid scar slashed across the paint, disfiguring not the young man who stood bold and proud in the foreground but the building perched on its distant hill.

A knife would have made a clean cut, not a jagged smear such as this. Leaning closer, on the point of announcing her find at last to Kit, Aurelia recognized with a strange foreboding that only the thick layer of paint itself had been damaged, as if melted or burned by the application of a small, hot object.

An object that left, an inch from David MacKinnon's right hand, the clear imprint of a snarling wolf's head.

Assuming the scuffling noise behind her to be Kit approaching, Aurelia did not turn at the sound but continued to study the impression that could only have been made by the signet Kit carried in the ebony box. When at last she did look up and glanced over her shoulder, she found the barrel of a pistol leveled at her.

Kit, who had moved several boxes and inadvertently surrounded himself with them, was climbing over a particularly large wooden chest to make his way to Aurelia when he saw the odd shadow cross the wall.

"Don't come any closer, Ballantyne," Joshua warned, "or I'll splatter our dear Aurelia's brains all over your grandfather's lovely portrait."

Instinctively, Kit took a step back to brace himself against the cold stone wall and place himself in a position to take cover behind the very crate he had just climbed over.

Between the boxes and broken pieces of old furniture there was an uneven aisle that led from the door to the window, but it was too narrow for Kit to run through quickly. He saw that at once. Before he got halfway, Joshua would have made good his grisly promise.

Still, there was no reason not to plead.

"Let her go, MacKinnon. She's no threat to you, and neither am I."

Joshua held her in front of the portrait, blocking Kit's view, but he knew what it was. The brief flash of the crimson uniform was enough.

"Ah, but you're wrong, Ballantyne, and you know it. Now, if you'll just hand over the paper, we can be about our business."

Before Kit could ask what paper Joshua was talking about, the familiar clatter of Galahad's claws on the floor announced his approach from another corner of the room.

"Get the bloody dog!" Joshua shrieked, not in the voice of a cultured planter, but in the unmistakable inflection of a working-class Englishman. "Or I'll shoot him and throw the girl out the bloody window!"

Aurelia had frozen the instant Joshua appeared, but now she struggled, obviously willing to thrust herself in front of Galahad. The cold pressure of the pistol to her cheek halted her and gave Joshua the opportunity to pin her right arm behind her while he grasped the other in his left hand.

"At least let Galahad go," she pleaded, knowing she dared make no further effort to escape.

"He goes where you go, and everybody knows it," Joshua snapped. "If he got out, they'd be swarming all over this bloody stone pile."

With the rising sun behind them, they were little more than black silhouettes to Kit's eyes, and he knew Joshua could see that much better. There was no hope of drawing his own weapon, and though the open door was only a foot behind him, escape was equally out of the question.

He could, however, grasp Galahad's collar and hold the dog safely back. His years on the Charleston waterfront now stood him in good stead. He had heard a hundred tongues and twice as many accents.

"Where are you from, Joshua, though of course that's not your real name, is it? Were you born in London, or Liverpool? Or maybe Manchester?"

The man with the pistol laughed, and when he spoke again, the carefully aristocratic accent had returned.

"Why, Mr. Ballantyne, do you doubt I was born and raised on Saint Gregory's Island? Of course I'm Joshua MacKinnon, son of Michael, grandson of Charles. Now, where's the bloody king's writ?"

The gun never wavered from Aurelia's head, and until he persuaded or tricked Joshua into lowering the weapon, Kit had to proceed with utmost caution. He would not willingly sacrifice Galahad, not even to draw Joshua's fire.

"Give it to him, Kit," Aurelia ordered with more fortitude in her voice than Kit expected. "And tell him where the rest of Serena's pearls are. He'll need them to convict us of her murder."

"Clever, Miss Phillips, very clever. But I don't need the others. I still have five, and they'll do quite nicely."

Kit tightened his grip on Galahad's collar as a very risky plan took shape in his mind.

"Before you kill us, whatever your name is, and blame us for Mrs. MacKinnon's death, can you at least tell us whose scheme it was in the first place? Did she recruit you, or did you suggest the idea to her? And did the real Joshua MacKinnon die, or did you kill him, too?"

It worked, at least for a moment. The man lowered the pistol and shook it in Kit's direction, but before either of them could react, he had it tight to her temple once more, as if he understood Kit's subterfuge and flaunted his skill at evading it.

"He was a worthless bastard, just as she said he'd be. Fat, fatter than old Moresby. And whined. Hated the cold, he did." The Cockney was back, almost exaggerated. "'E weren't 'ard to off, neither. I didn't do it meself, you understand. Me old mate Gould did it, neat as you please."

"And Gould then blackmailed you into cutting him in on the deal, so you had to eliminate him."

"Did you tell him you had killed Serena?" Aurelia asked, quickly continuing the thread as if she knew Kit's strategy was to keep the false Joshua MacKinnon from thinking beyond his present situation. "Or did you let him think both of you were in danger of discovery by the unknown person who had done the deed?"

Kit wanted to smile and applaud her quick-wittedness. Even he had not thought so far into this madman's scheme.

"Gould was a simpleton. I told him you were undoubtedly the killer, and he believed me."

"So there is in fact no honor among thieves."

"None, Mr. Ballantyne, none at all." Joshua sidled Aurelia closer to the window. "Now, for the last time, where in bloody hell is the writ? I'd shoot you if I didn't think you have the thing in your bloody pocket."

Kit considered telling Joshua the truth, that he had no idea what the man was talking about, but he doubted Joshua would believe him.

Aurelia, however, had no such reservations. "We haven't found it yet," she said.

"I don't believe you! You know everything about this place, how many spoons there are, how many—what was that?"

Kit recognized the distant scrape of stone on stone as it echoed through the hollow shell of Winterburn. Someone had opened the door from Nethergate, a door Joshua had locked behind him.

Again it was Aurelia who answered.

"Tree branches in the wind. And you know I don't lie, Joshua. Serena told you that, and so did Grandfather."

After a tiny pause she repeated, "We haven't found the writ. Why else would we still be looking for it?"

That silenced him, but only for a short while. And he had not moved the gun from her head. Kit dared not make any sudden move.

Then Joshua shook his head and dragged Aurelia closer to the ancient glass of the window, making his horrible intentions clear.

"No, I don't believe you. The old man said you had it, said it proved Ballantyne had a better claim than I."

The man was mad, and only two more deaths would satisfy him. Kit calculated the distance between himself and Joshua for perhaps the hundredth time, and for the hundredth time abandoned hope. Joshua, no matter how poor a shot, could not miss at a distance of fifteen or twenty feet. It would then be a simple matter to push Aurelia, with the gun in her hand, through the window, eliminating the only witness as well as providing a plausible suspect.

Kit blinked, trying to ease the strain of staring directly into the rising sun, yet he hardly dared take his eyes from Aurelia.

"I have no claim and no proof," he insisted.

But Aurelia warned him, "Don't lie, Kit. Joshua knows the Winterburn title was conferred by writ of summons, granting it to the heirs whether male or female. You *are* the heir to Winterburn, Kit, whether the real Joshua MacKinnon is dead or alive. And you have the ring as proof."

She struggled to find more words, any words, to keep talking and keep Joshua from hearing any other sounds the intruder might make.

"What ring?" Joshua demanded.

She winced as he tightened his grip on her arm.

"The wolf of Winterburn ring. David MacKinnon took it with him to the colonies, expecting either to return with it or have it sent home in the event of his death. When he did neither, he simply passed it along to his heir." The cold metal of the pistol dug deeper into her flesh, but she continued to find words. "No one else would know its significance, except Grandfather and the rightful heir. When David returned to Nethergate and demanded his inheritance, he was refused, the proof itself dismissed by the one and only man who could do so, the man who had set himself up as the duke of Winterburn when his brother abandoned him."

"Bloody nonsense! There's no such ring, no wolf of Winterburn. If there were, Serena would have told me. There's only the writ, and I mean to have it."

She squeezed her eyes shut, expecting at any instant to have her life extinguished in a single flash and explosion. Instead, the man who had killed and then called himself Joshua MacKinnon continued to demand the precious document that had created the title he coveted.

"I went through every inch, every corner of that bloody study and I didn't find it," he swore. "When I caught you and our American cousin traipsing through the wreckage yesterday, I knew it had to be here. Now, once again, Miss Phillips, *where in bloody hell is it!*"

Had his shrieks covered the sound of another door scraping open, one closer than the first? Aurelia waited, slowly opening her eyes, while the ringing in her ears from his screaming demands subsided.

"Give it up," Kit urged Joshua again. "We don't have the writ, and you can't trust either of us to continue looking for it. If you shoot Aurelia, you're defenseless against me. If you kill me, you're at her mercy—and Galahad's."

Had Kit moved his hand a fraction of an inch closer to the pistol she knew he carried? And if he had, what good would it do him? He could never draw and fire it before Joshua pulled the trigger on his own weapon.

But Kit, like her, kept up a steady stream of words intended to plead a logical solution to the checkmate in which they had found themselves.

"I've no interest in either the title or the estate that goes with it, so I'm more than willing to give you a tidy sum and let you crawl back into whatever sewer you crawled out of."

The pressure at her temple eased enough for her to feel the trembling of Joshua's rage. Would Kit succeed in drawing the pistol in his own direction before fury alone fired Joshua's?

"I never crawled out of a sewer," he sneered. "I was an actor, and a bloody good one, too. How else d'ye think I managed to fool that pompous viscount and his pickled sot of a wife? Never questioned but I was Joshua MacKinnon. I daresay they'd probably seen me on stage."

He chuckled, a sick, maniacal laugh.

"Is that where you met Serena?" Aurelia asked.

She got no answer, for the unmistakable groan of rusty hinges suddenly rent the silence of Winterburn. Behind Kit, the dark hallway filled with light.

It was the distraction they had waited for and the only chance they had.

Sensing Joshua's momentary absorption with the arrival of an unknown intruder, Aurelia ducked her head away from the pistol and shoved herself free of her captor. Prepared as best she could be for the impact of the shot, she dove for the shelter of one of the wooden crates.

But the only sound that met her ears was the shattering of glass. She looked up to see Joshua, his balance upset, turn as he followed the descending arc of the pistol, surrounded by shards of ancient window, against the bright morning sky. She must have knocked it out of his hand when she escaped him, and now it fell, harmless as well as useless, to the snow-covered stones below.

A great wordless scream of animal rage erupted from him. Aurelia, trapped by the boxes she had hoped would protect her, scrambled frantically, futilely to scuttle out of his reach.

And then another sound, louder, stronger, rose above Joshua's scream. Even in his rage, he turned to it, and the rage became horror. His face white in the morning light, he backed away from the relentless advance of his attacker until there was nowhere to go.

Had the brittle glass of another age not been broken by the pistol, he might have reached for and found the support he needed to see the truth. But the glass was gone, and his balance, already precarious, gave way.

He must have been so stunned by the emptiness that he did not even cry out as he, like the pistol, fell to the courtyard below.

23

Not even the nausea that assaulted Aurelia when she saw the man she had known as Joshua MacKinnon fall through the broken window could stop her from clasping an ecstatic Galahad to her bosom and burying her face in his coarse, dusty fur. He tried to wriggle free, with excited yips and playful swipes of his tongue that indicated he thought the whole thing a delightful game, but she held on until the shock gave way to relief.

She became aware of someone holding her as tightly as she held Galahad, and then of that someone helping her to her feet. The dog squirmed out from between them, but though Aurelia kept her eyes closed and wrapped herself in the silence, she felt the constant brush and bump of Galahad as he danced around her and the man who held her.

She felt the wind and knew it rushed in a broken window, but she clung to the warmth with which Kit surrounded her. She smelled the dust that swirled around them, but she tasted only his desperate, devouring kisses.

She heard and saw nothing. Until the images and echoes faded, she wanted nothing else connected with them, tainted by them.

But slowly, reality reasserted itself. Kit's kisses became words, pleas for reassurance penetrating the silence.

He kissed her ear, her cheek, her nose, brushing his lips across her closed eyes. "Did he hurt you? My God, Aurelia, speak to me!"

She had to answer, but she had to have her own reassurance, too.

She opened her eyes and raised her hands to his face. The sight of him, cobwebs in his hair, a streak of dust across his unshaven cheek, was not enough. She traced cold, trembling fingers across his furrowed brow and pushed back a lock of dark hair.

Knowing that he had not been harmed, she breathed, "Yes, I'm all right." She could look at him, but not at the window, nor at the painting propped crookedly against the wall beneath it.

There was more she had to tell him, but before she could find the words, another voice intruded.

"What is going on here?" the duke of Winterburn asked. "No one is supposed to be here. Joshua, is that you? I heard glass breaking and someone screamed."

Aurelia looked from Kit to face the two old men who stood in the doorway. Charles MacKinnon leaned on his cane and shook off Morton Sullivan's assistance. The faded eyes squinted against the light, but there was an expression almost of fear on the ancient features.

He could not see the broken window, only the glare of sunshine streaming across the room, but Aurelia knew the stiff breeze that blew through the Winterburn ruins would soon reveal the truth to him.

She separated herself from Kit, letting her grandfather's imperfect vision register a second silhouette against the window.

"I ordered you not to set foot in here, Aurelia," he snarled. "Joshua, why have you let her in? Never mind. Both of you leave at once. I have business to take care of."

He hobbled forward with the single-minded determination of one who expected his orders to be obeyed.

Tears welled in her eyes as she watched him approach. Whatever selfish use he had made of her these past few days to try to keep his illusion alive, Charles MacKinnon had treated her with kindness for twenty years. She would not let anyone else break the news to him. Truth, in its innocence and ugliness, was her responsibility. He would expect no less from her, and she expected no less from herself.

She heard voices outside, the cries of a woman and the shouts of several men. Someone called for a doctor, and Aurelia thought she detected the words "alive" and "neck," but she had no time or attention to spare for what was left of the false Joshua MacKinnon now.

Despite the cold, Kit obeyed Aurelia's silent summons and left her alone with the man who for over half a century had called himself the duke of Winterburn. She was in no danger now, and Kit knew this was a place he did not belong. What remained to be said was between her and her grandfather.

He did not even wait for Morton Sullivan to accompany him, though the secretary appeared confused as to his own duties for the moment. He had lost some of his officiousness—or, Kit thought as he made his way down the worn stone steps, maybe Morton Sullivan was merely transferring his allegiance.

The lower level of Winterburn looked far different with sufficient daylight to illuminate it, so much so that Kit had a moment's confusion of his own trying to find the passage to the courtyard. But find it he did, and with no need for stealth, he quickly made his way to the oak-sheltered corner behind the chapel.

He paused long enough to survey the scene laid out before him. There would be questions, and he needed to assure himself he knew the answers.

He skirted around the chapel and came up from behind, rather than draw unnecessary attention to the still secret entrance to the castle. Most of the onlookers gathered in the early morning quiet were stable hands and other servants, the guests not having risen at this hour. Their voices were low, as soft as the steamy clouds of their breath in the frosty air. Here, more sheltered by the walls, the wind did not blow as briskly as it had gusted through the broken window two stories above the courtyard, but the air was cold, and made colder by the presence of death.

Dr. Ward, lacking his usual elegance, knelt in the snow beside the nameless stranger who would have been Joshua MacKinnon. Kit made his way through the crowd until he stood behind the physician and peered emotionlessly over the man's shoulder.

The snow had cushioned Joshua's fall, but it had not saved his life. The twisted angle of his head and the odd repose of his limbs were all Kit needed to recognize a broken neck and paralysis. The gray eyes held no pain, only a slight bemusement.

"Serena told me greed would be the death of me," Joshua said, each word coming with effort. If he knew he was dying he gave no sign. "I had to kill her, you understand. It were her idea to start with, but she'd have settled for too little, and there was so much more to be had. We started wi' nothing; we had nothing to lose." He tried to clear his throat, but the muscles did not cooperate.

Kit could not hold back bitter triumph. "And now you've lost everything."

The doctor looked up at him, a disapproving scowl on the features that had not shaken off sleep.

"For God's sake, Mr. Ballantyne, the man is dying!"

"He killed three others; I've no pity for him."

A low gasp rose from the crowd, which had grown steadily. Kit heard Adam Braisthwaite's belligerent voice asking for explanations; the viscount's son apparently did not want a closer look for himself. Everyone hushed, however, when Joshua spoke again.

"I'd've had it all if you hadn't come along, Ballantyne." The claim was little more than a croak. "The title, the money, the score settled between me and the MacKinnons. Henry said I couldn't act, called me a puppet wi'out strings. Proved 'im wrong, and his boy-lover, too, di'n't I? Proved 'em all wrong, I did, Serena. All of 'em."

He took another breath, and another, but his eyes never blinked again, until Dr. Ward reached out and closed them for the last time. Kit, too, closed his eyes, and murmured a quiet, "Thank God."

A fire crackled merrily in the grate, warming the cottage bedroom comfortably. Kit, his shirtsleeves pushed up to his elbows, brought the lamp closer to the sheet of yellowed parchment spread out on the dressing table. Only a few words were easily decipherable from the faded script of half a millennium ago. Kit struggled to recall his schoolboy Latin and made out what he thought were *Scots, castle,* and a few others, including one that might have been *wolf.*

The bold *E* of the signature remained regally clear, and the date written in the same hand beneath it.

"You can't abandon a five-hundred-year-old title," Aurelia admonished as she turned down the bed. "Edward the First signed that writ in 1295, summoning Richard MacKinnon, first duke of Winterburn, to Parliament."

"Richard and his daughter, it appears. Either his daughter Ann or his 'year'; my Latin's a bit rusty."

With a puzzled frown, Aurelia left the bed and walked to the dressing table to peer over Kit's shoulder at the document her grandfather had told them they would find behind David MacKinnon's portrait. She had stayed in that cold, windswept room with Charles MacKinnon for hours after Joshua's death and listened to the old man's tale of anger and hurt over what he saw as his beloved brother's betrayal, and his own shame for then betraying David. After so many years torn between the two and then being confronted by Christopher Ballantyne and the proof of his claim, Charles's hold on reality had snapped. He had resorted to lies in an attempt to cover other lies, only to fail as, deep down, he had known he must. By the time he had finished telling her everything, from the scene with David and the young Jeremiah MacKinnon to his almost daily visits to the damaged portrait and his penitent communion with the brother he had denied, she knew he had at last found peace.

"Turn up the light, Kit," she ordered in a soft voice while continuing to read the royal writ, albeit with some difficulty and even more surprise. "It appears the MacKinnons, father and daughter, were renegade Scots who didn't want to see their country ravaged in a long war with the more powerful English. Ann was Richard's only child, and a widow; he intended his estate to go to her and then her sons, who fought with him. He extracted the promise from his king."

She looked up and rubbed her eyes, then chuckled. "It's not so different from reading Morton Sullivan's scribbling!" Her laughter faded as quickly as it rose. "He will never forgive himself, you know. He thought he was doing the right thing, protecting the man he had worked for all his life."

"Like Henry the Second's knights, who did away with Becket because they thought their lord wanted him dead?" Kit sighed. "I suppose we should have thought of the loyal Mr. Sullivan sooner. He alone knew that I'd told His Grace who I was that night, and Joshua was too terrified of horses to venture close enough to put that burr under my saddle."

Kit reached for the open ebony box beside the parchment. The pearls were gone, returned to Ruth, so that the wolf's head ring lay alone on its velvet. He lifted the onyx fragment and in the brighter light studied the shank and the single *A* engraved inside it.

The explanation was fantastic, beyond anything they had ever dared imagine, but at the same time the evidence would not be ignored.

He turned the ring to the light to catch the wolf's snarl, and said, "Dare we speculate that Ann, whose finger might have fit through this ring, who fought beside her father and for her sons, was the she-wolf of Winterburn?"

An eerie shiver slithered down Aurelia's spine as she met Kit's gaze in the mirror.

"If she was, and if in her own way your mother did the same, then that's all the more reason you can't walk away from Winterburn."

"My countrymen walked away from all titles, and the form of government that went with them. Even David MacKinnon. Can you imagine me, in wig and scarlet robe, in the House of Lords?"

"Better you than Freddie Denholm, or, I hate to think of it, Adam Braisthwaite."

Again Kit chuckled. "Exactly the point, my dear. Freddie and Adam have no more business conducting the business of government than Galahad."

At the sound of his name, the deerhound looked up from his comfortable sprawl in front of the fire and thumped his tail on the hearth rug.

"On the other hand," Kit added slowly, as though contemplating changing his mind, "I could never walk away from you."

Aurelia unwound the twist of her hair and reached over Kit's shoulder for her brush. Staring at their joint reflection in the mirror, she did not try to hide a smile. She in her nightgown, warm, serviceable flannel as always, he with his sleeves pushed up and his shirt open at the throat—they were a far cry from the stiff formality of the dukes and duchesses whose portraits filled the gallery walls in

Nethergate. Perhaps Kit was right. And perhaps his judgment about her own place, her future, in America was also right.

"Besides, it's not mine to walk away from," he continued. "Not yet, at any rate. My uncle is still alive, and so is my mother." He groaned and finally looked up from his intense study of the faded writing. "She will be impossible to live with. Mathilda Ballantyne, Duchess of Winterburn. Charleston will never hear the end of it."

As Aurelia began to draw the brush through her hair, Kit swiveled on the dressing table stool and pulled her down onto his lap.

"You are much too hard on your mother," she scolded. "I am quite certain she is not half the monster you pretend she is. She sent you here, didn't she? For that I, at least, shall always be grateful."

She let him kiss her briefly, though it was clear he would have gone on if allowed.

"My mother is a tyrant who loves nothing better than to say, 'I told you so.' It will be the first thing she says to me."

"And rightly so. She told you the truth and you did not believe her."

As if to keep her from taking his mother's side any further in this argument, he kissed her more fully this time, sliding his fingers into the loosened mass of her hair. Coyness, like a lie, was beyond her capacity; she eagerly welcomed the sleek insinuation of his tongue. He did not, however, press his advantage.

"Ah, God, Aurelia, if you weren't already in your nightgown and I too eager to get you out of it, I'd suggest we ride to Scotland tonight and forget this Church of England nonsense of banns and licenses. I want you mine, irrevocably, forever."

She felt the blatant truth of his arousal beneath her bottom and squirmed against it, eliciting a groan from him.

"Dukes are not married by Scottish blacksmiths and two handy witnesses," she scolded. "Besides, this is hardly the time of year to be sailing across the Atlantic, so you might as well enjoy your stay in England. And perhaps," she added, plying her brush once more, "before the banns are read and we can be legally wed, you'll have changed your mind. We have, after all, only known each other a few days."

A few days, a lifetime. For all her flippancy, Aurelia's heart skipped a beat as she offered Kit an escape from the promise he had extracted from her.

"I'll not change my mind," he vowed and took the brush from her to put it back on the dressing table. "Do you know how many deaths I died, watching him hold that gun to your head? And to hear you lie, though it saved our lives, was like having the heart cut out of me. Worst of all was knowing that it was all my fault."

He pulled her close, and she felt the shudder slice through him.

They had hardly spoken of the events that brought them to this moment, not only because there was still a rawness to the pain and shock, but also because there had been no time. Aurelia had stayed with her grandfather while Kit saw to the impostor Joshua MacKinnon, and by then the entire household was in an uproar. Now, alone, just the two of them with no one to interrupt or intrude, the words and the feelings could be—indeed needed to be—explored.

"It was not your fault. We had no way to know he would be there, waiting for us."

"I should have looked, made sure it was safe, before we went into that room."

She shook her head, then kissed the worried crease between his brows.

"We don't even know now where he hid. You might not have found him. Or, worse, he might have killed you first. Then where would I be?" She rested her cheek against his shoulder, satisfying herself that she was here, with him. "Let us not speculate on what might have happened."

"You're absolutely right." He kissed the top of her head,

and beneath their combined weight the little stool creaked in protest. With a mild chuckle, Kit stood, cradled Aurelia in his arms, and nudged the seat under the dressing table. "The great colonial brute, smashing the furniture to smithereens."

"You are not a brute, Kit. A colonial, yes, but not a brute."

"You certainly thought I was the night I arrived. You treated the horses better than you did Emil and me."

"And you treated me like a trollop."

He laughed. "Because I kissed you? No, Aurelia, I treated you like the beautiful, passionate woman I saw beneath the prim and proud lies." He kissed her again, quickly, to silence her, then set her down upon the open bed with a heap of pillows behind her back. "I had only to touch you to know the truth."

She watched as he walked to the dressing table and blew out the lamp. Only the light from the fire remained, but that was enough even after Kit carefully banked the coals. Then he pulled off his shirt and tossed it carelessly toward the stool. When he grinned back at her, Aurelia realized with a blush that she had already begun to untie the ribbons on her nightgown.

"Do you suppose we shall ever know the truth about Serena and Joshua?" she asked, stilling her fingers for a moment.

"If you mean was she really his mother's sister, as Dr. Ward claimed she told him, it could be true." He shrugged. "He admitted he blackmailed Serena into bringing him to Nethergate, so he undoubtedly knew something about her. I suspect he had secrets of his own. He did well enough on Emil's injuries, but I don't think he practiced that kind of medicine on the streets of London. If he knew Serena from her days in the Haymarket, he probably provided the women of her profession with services that could take him straight to the hangman.

"But did Henry steal Joshua's lover and patron? I suppose that's possible, too. If Serena felt responsible for her nephew, she might have concocted such a scheme for revenge, but she did not strike me as the type to care as much about someone else as she did herself. Or even to have the patience to carry out such a plan. I doubt we'll ever know, any more than we'll know if the story you made up about the wolf of Winterburn is true. You lied to Joshua about the tree branches, and I must admit that was a shock to me. But the wolf of Winterburn?"

He cocked an eyebrow at the patent outrageousness of her tale before he unbuttoned and stepped out of his trousers. If he had granted Aurelia the modesty of a nightgown, he seemed unconcerned with his own nudity and, after a final grateful pat to Galahad's head, came to the bed and settled himself between the sheets.

"Is something wrong, my love?" he asked when Aurelia sat silent for a long minute.

She toyed with a half-untied ribbon and answered slowly, unable to look at him even when he sneaked his foot under the covers to stroke his toes along her calf.

"I'm not sure the story is entirely a lie," she said. "Have you ever said something or done something and afterward you don't have the faintest idea how you knew it? And then you think about it, and even when you know you must have learned it somewhere, somehow, you still don't know where or how?"

"You lived here for twenty years, Aurelia, surrounded by nothing but Nethergate and its atmosphere. Perhaps it was a story you heard as a child, a local legend told as a tale in the village."

She shook her head.

"No, it was something I *knew* the minute I saw the slash on the painting. It was as if I heard the argument between Grandfather and his brother all those years ago. When I asked him today, he would only tell me he had taken the ring from David and thrown it into the fire. David pulled it out with the poker and tried to destroy the portrait with it. When Grandfather called in servants to drag the 'impostor' out of Nethergate, the ring broke in the struggle that followed, but Grandfather thought David had dropped it. By the time he found the broken piece and realized the rest—the proof—was in David's possession, David was gone, the portrait ruined."

"But the writ was safely concealed behind the canvas. Do you think that's what David was trying to do, reach the document that would prove his identity?"

"I don't know, and this is, of course, more of that idle speculation we said we were not going to indulge in. All I do know is that when I mentioned the wolf of Winterburn to Grandfather, he accused Morton Sullivan of betraying him."

Kit reached up to finish untying the ribbons on Aurelia's nightgown.

"And what did the inestimable Mr. Sullivan have to say about that?"

Aurelia tried only halfheartedly to push his insistent hand away.

"He swore, repeatedly, with his usual stammer when he's excited, that he had never mentioned the wolf of Winterburn to anyone, except for the day he told my grandfather the seal on your letter matched the scar on the portrait. I overheard part of that conversation, the part where Grandfather told Sullivan I had my 'uses.' But I never heard that phrase. And of course Grandfather never told Henry or even Robert about it, and certainly not Joshua."

"Henry explored Winterburn and even brought you with him. No doubt he knew about the portrait, which had to be hanging in the gallery until David ruined it. Henry would have noticed when Charles replaced it, and accepted his father's explanation, whatever that might have been, until he found the original tucked away in the castle ruins. If he was as honorable as you say, then he might very well have figured out the truth—or even confronted his father with it."

"All the more reason for Charles to accept the blame for Henry's death and compound his own guilt. There was no need to tell Michael, and he dared not tell Robert."

The ribbon and the two more left holding her gown closed surrendered to Kit's attentions. With a shivery sigh of delight, Aurelia, too, surrendered and slid down under the blankets into his embrace.

"He told only his loyal secretary," Kit said, with a trace of mockery, "who alone knew the secret of the portrait in the castle. And of the obsessive guilt and devotion that drove Charles MacKinnon to steal his brother's title and yet honor the promise he had made to that brother to watch after Nethergate. The loyal secretary who, to protect his master's secret, tried to kill me and then tried to shut you in the ruins."

"You make it sound so . . . melodramatic. Mr. Sullivan admitted he did it only as a warning, to make sure you stayed away. And he never thought the outside stairs from Winterburn would prove so dangerous an exit."

"He was wrong. It was dangerous *and* melodramatic," he argued, slipping his hands under the edge of her nightgown to raise it up and over her head. The ribbons became tangled in her hair and she dissolved in giggles, which prompted a growl of frustration from Kit before she finally pulled free. "And it is pure speculation, all of it. I prefer the truth, the naked truth. Or perhaps I prefer only you, my love, my touchstone, naked in my arms."

She giggled again as he curled one hand around her breast, but the giggle subsided into a soft moan of pleasure. Her nipple hardened and sensitized against his palm, and when he leaned over her to take her mouth in a warm, possessive kiss, she hungrily pulled him closer.

Had it been only four days since an icy storm blew Christopher Ballantyne into her life? So much had happened that she felt as if he had been part of her forever—or that her life had only begun the moment she opened the door of Nethergate and admitted him. The only truth that mattered now was that she wanted to spend the rest of her life—the rest of forever—with him.

"Oh, Kit, you are *my* touchstone," she breathed.